# THE MAYOR OF LEXINGTON AVENUE

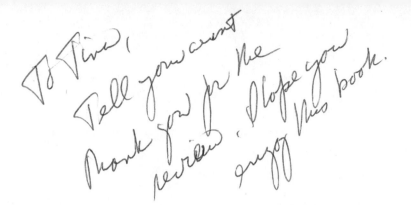

To Tina,
Tell your aunt
Thank you for the
review. I hope you
enjoy this book.

# THE MAYOR OF LEXINGTON AVENUE

## [A NOVEL]

*James Sheehan*

**YORKVILLE PRESS**
NEW YORK, NEW YORK

**YORKVILLE PRESS**
NEW YORK, NEW YORK

**www.yorkvillepress.com**

LIBRARY OF CONGRESS CATALOGING-IN-PUBLICATION DATA

The mayor of Lexington Avenue / by James Sheehan.

p. cm.

ISBN 0-9767442-1-X (alk. paper)

1. Attorney and client—Fiction.  2. Judicial error—Fiction.
3. New York (N.Y.)—Fiction.  4. Florida—Fiction.  I. Title.

PS3619.H438M39 2005

813'.54—dc22

2005013171

DESIGN BY
Tina Taylor, T2 Design

ISBN: 0-9767442-1-X
Printed in the USA by Quebecor World
jms 10 9 8 7 6 5 4 3 2 1

## A NOTE TO READERS

*The Mayor of Lexington Avenue* is a work of fiction. Names, characters, places, and incidents either are the product of the author's imagination or are used fictitiously. Any resemblance to actual persons, living or dead, events, or locales is entirely coincidental.

## DEDICATION

*In memory of my parents,*
*Jack Sheehan and Mary Tobin Sheehan,*
*who gave me everything in my life*
*that I needed to succeed — unconditional love.*

*You are always in my heart.*

∼

PART

# [ O N E ]

[ O N E ]

January 1986, Bass Creek, Florida

Lucy liked to fish in the daylight. She enjoyed seeing her prey, but it was even more important that they see her. Focus their eyes on the feast while she set the hook ever so gently. She hooked Rudy the first time she walked into his store in her dungaree short-shorts and tight tank top.

"Hypnotize 'em and hook 'em," she would have told her class if she had taught the sport. Rudy could have been exhibit number one. He couldn't keep his eyes off her and he couldn't hide it either. Luckily there was only one other customer in the store, an old man Rudy rang up without so much as a glance. Lucy could tell she had him without even looking.

"Weight on the line. That's how you do it, ladies. It's all feel. And be patient. Don't yank too quickly or he'll get away. Let him run a little till he's out of breath. Then you've got him. Catch him first — you can always throw him back."

Rudy could have done some fishing of his own if he'd known how. Unlike Lucy, who packed it all into a small, tight body, Rudy was tall, the olive skin of his chiseled face punctuated with fierce brown eyes and framed by thick, coal black hair that shone like silk — hair that women dreamed about for themselves. Lucy wasn't the

3

first woman who had tried to hook young Rudy. They came in every night to the convenience store where he worked, every shape and size and age, but Rudy had been oblivious until now.

Lucy did that to the men from the barrios wherever she went. This one was on the outskirts of Bass Creek, a small town in the central portion of Florida just north of Lake Okeechobee. It was populated by Mexicans, Colombians, Indians, Puerto Ricans — mostly pickers, mostly seasonal. They lived in single-wides or housing provided by the growers — cinder block shacks with running water.

But Rudy didn't live in the barrio, he wasn't seasonal and he wasn't a picker. He had come to Bass Creek with his mother, Elena Kelly, when he was a boy. They had lived in a run-down motel for a while until Elena got a job as a maid at the Bass Creek Hotel, the largest hotel in town, located just under the new bridge over the Okalatchee River.

Everybody liked the idea of the new bridge when word got around that they were going to build it. The old drawbridge was ugly, slow and cumbersome and it caused backups every fifteen minutes as it raised and lowered for the steady flow of river traffic. The new bridge would be modern and sleek and high enough so even the largest sailboats could cruise by unimpeded. The new bridge was supposed to provide local jobs and money. Unfortunately, it didn't work out that way. Outside contractors were hired for the construction and brought their own people. Those workers stayed during the week and filled up the hotels but they were a vile lot, drinking and fighting and abusing the town. Elena, who was probably the prettiest woman in Bass Creek, had to stay hidden behind a locked door after dark. Rudy saw the change in her but never really understood it.

When the bridge was finally completed, the workers left and the cars flew by in one continuous stream. No need to stop anymore to let the highway of sailboats pass. No need to pull into this little town to browse, or eat, or perhaps spend the night. Bass Creek had been a rest stop on a friendly stream for tourists on their way to Miami or Fort Lauderdale. The old bridge had been the comma that caused those tourists to pause. Now the pause was gone, and the folks of Bass Creek who didn't own orange groves, who survived in the service industries, took the brunt of the loss.

Sure, they still had the fishermen, but the fishing on Lake Okeechobee was a far cry from what it had been fifteen, twenty years ago. Overfishing and pollution had taken their toll on the old lake. Elena had worked hard those first few years before the new bridge and she'd made good money. And Bass Creek had been a good town to live in. Now it had lost its vitality. Stores on Main Street had been forced to close. McDonalds and Burger King had built out by the highway and lured back some, but few of them were trickling into town.

The Bass Creek Hotel stood a full three stories high, the largest building in town. Before the new bridge was built, its coat of bright yellow paint had shone like the sun itself in the afternoon light. Part of Elena's compensation had been a room to live in and meals in the hotel dining room for her and young Rudy. After she had inherited the manager's position when the old manager deserted the place, Elena took over the large apartment in the back, which had two bedrooms and a full kitchen, and both she and Rudy had loved it. But now the hotel lay hidden from the sun, separated from the rest of the town, a gloomy, desolate place.

~

"How much is this?" Lucy was leaning on the counter holding a liter of Diet Coke with the price tag clearly visible. Rudy tried to concentrate on her bright white teeth, which were wrestling with a wad of gum, but in her low-cut, body-tight top, Lucy was providing him with a glimpse of something much more exotic. He couldn't help but steal a glance. The store was now empty.

"How much?" Lucy broke the spell momentarily.

"Oh. Sorry. Ninety-nine cents. It's on special."

"You're sure? You're not just giving me a special deal, are you?" Lucy leaned all the way over, and Rudy could see the full contour of her breasts. He was thankful the counter shielded him from the waist down, but Lucy knew anyway. The hook was in.

"No. No. That's the price," he answered, his voice cracking.

"Well, I don't believe you." She crossed her arms tight against her breasts as she leaned. Rudy thought they were going to pop out right there on the counter. His mouth hung open in anticipation. "I don't take a favor without returning one," Lucy continued. "You come to my trailer tonight. Forty-four Mercer Street. It don't matter what time, I'll be there." Rudy just nodded. He was too far gone to speak.

As soon as she left he grabbed a pencil and wrote down the address. Rudy was handsome and his smile could light up a room, but he was slow. "Not retarded, just slow," the doctor had told Elena when she took him to be tested at age four when he hadn't spoken one word. There was some technical jargon about a lack of oxygen when he was coming down the birth canal but Elena had been too shell-shocked to take in the details. Eventually, she had learned to cope and taught young Rudy to do the same. Writing things down right away was one of his methods. Staying out of dangerous situations was another. Something inside him warned that Lucy was danger but the urgings from another part of his body were all that Rudy heard.

He closed up at eleven and practically ran over to Mercer Street. There were no street lamps and at first he couldn't find Forty-four but then he saw it, set back from the street in the darker shadows.

As he stood outside her door and got ready to knock, Rudy was as excited as a kid on his first date, which wasn't too far off. Sure, he'd been out with girls during high school, but there hadn't been many. He knew why, too. He'd heard the all-too-loud whispers behind his back. Nobody really messed with him because he'd quieted the first couple of kids who called him "Dumbo" or "Dunce" or "Shithead" to his face, but the whispers had never stopped. In fact, Rudy had never even made it to the proverbial second base. It was a part of his life that he tried not to think about, that he kept sealed behind a locked door, a lock that Lucy had picked in a matter of seconds.

She was waiting for him but she didn't answer right away. "Let the anticipation build," she would have told her class. Lucy had a doctorate in the subject of men, or so she thought.

She'd put on her ruby red lipstick. She always saved it for nights like this. Rudy hardly noticed. When she opened the door, all he saw was a sheer white teddy barely concealing those wondrous breasts he hadn't stopped thinking about since she'd first teased him with them in the convenience store. He steadied himself from shaking. Lucy moved closer so he could catch the scent of her perfume.

"Are those for me?" she asked surprised, as she looked down at the bouquet of cheap flowers Rudy had grabbed off the counter as he charged out of the store. For just a moment she was touched: Not too many men brought her flowers. Rudy was so enraptured he'd forgotten he was even holding them.

"Oh, these? Yeah, I brought them for you."

"Why, thank you!" Lucy took his hand, led him through to the living room and sat him down on the couch. "Now you relax. I'll put these in some water and I'll be right back."

She threw the flowers on the counter in the kitchen and was back in an instant, carrying two frosty mugs. She was eager to land this fresh young catch and alcohol always helped.

"I only have beer," she lied as she handed him the mug. A red flag went up in Rudy's head. Alcohol was another one of those dangers his mother had warned him about. But somehow he couldn't say no, couldn't bring himself to disrupt the mood. He took the beer and gulped down a quick mouthful.

Lucy slithered up next to him and tucked her feet underneath her. Rudy was afraid to look down, afraid to discover if she was really wearing panties. They sat there like that making small talk for a half hour or so, Rudy sipping nervously at his beer and Lucy becoming increasingly impatient. Finally, she took his mug and headed to the kitchen for a refill.

She had no formal education but Lucy was wise in the ways of the world. His first few words had told her he was just a boy in a man's body, and she had pretty much decided she was going to call it a night. But she couldn't stop thinking about the excitement in his eyes. She hadn't seen that kind of anticipation in a long time. *Maybe it will be fun,* she thought. *And he is so beautiful....* She poured a shot of Jack Daniels into his second beer.

The Jack Daniels did it. Rudy began to relax, touching her face gently with the palm of his hand, massaging her neck, all the while responding to her passionate kisses. He moved his hand slowly to the edge of her teddy, and then, at last, he was caressing those warm, perfect breasts. Waves of delirious pleasure washed over him, and he could feel the blood rushing from his head.

Suddenly it was all too much. He was dizzy, his head was reeling and his stomach was churning. He knew he was about to be sick. He made a mad dash for the front door and the outside air but his knee hit the coffee table as he started to rise, tipping his beer mug over. Already off balance, he tried to grab the mug and caught it just as he hit the floor, smashing it to pieces. The mood was permanently and irrevocably broken.

"I'm sorry," he spluttered as he gazed at his hand, which was bleeding profusely from a nasty gash and dripping blood onto the carpet. I'll clean everything up." He still felt sick but the accident had erased the sudden urge to puke, at least momentarily. Lucy stared at the broken glass and the blood on the carpet. She stifled the urge to scream.

"That's okay, I'll get it. But I think you should go now." Without waiting for a reply she helped him up and ushered him to the front door, grabbing some paper towels on the way and stuffing them into his still-bleeding hand. "I'll call you," she told him as she not-so-politely pushed him out and closed the door behind him.

Rudy staggered down the street a few doors until he could no longer hold it, then puked on a patch of grass that masqueraded as the front lawn of Carlos and Pilar Rodriguez.

~

Farther south on Mercer Street, Geronimo Cruz was drinking

beer with two of his "friends," Raymond Castro and José Guerrero. Geronimo was from Texas, and he always carried a knife. Ray and José hung around with him only because Geronimo had chosen them and they were afraid to turn down the invitation.

Ray and José had been sitting on the stoop of Ray's apartment one night about a month before when Geronimo showed up.

"Got an extra cerveza?" he inquired.

"Sure," Ray responded. That was all it took. They couldn't get rid of him after that. Every night he stopped by, and every night he was empty-handed. He told them about men he had stabbed, women he had raped, always brandishing his knife with the serrated edge. Both men wished they had never met him.

They knew he was seeing Lucy because he bragged about her. Two or three nights a week, they watched him stroll over towards her trailer after a few beers. They knew Lucy, knew of her affinity for men like Geronimo. They figured she could handle herself.

They were on their third beer the night Rudy came stumbling down the street and started puking on the Rodriguez lawn. Geronimo's eyes narrowed.

"Who the fuck is that?"

"I don't know," Ray responded. "I saw him go in Lucy's just before you showed up." The words came out without thinking. Ray wanted to slap himself when he realized what he had done. Geronimo immediately put down his beer and drifted into the shadows, walking towards Lucy's trailer.

"I'll see you guys later," he said without looking back. Moments later he was at Lucy's door.

"What are you doing here?" she asked when she answered his knock.

"Who was that that just left?"

"None of your business. I don't answer to you." He was itching to smack her with the back of his hand but that was too easy. He decided to play her game for a while.

"I just was curious, that's all." He wasn't all that convincing but she didn't want to piss him off too much. Like Ray and José, she had a healthy fear of Geronimo.

"It was the kid from the convenience store. He was drunk. He just stopped over." She had just finished picking up the broken glass.

"How long was he here?"

"Just a couple of minutes. I sent him home." Geronimo knew she was lying. She'd worn the same skimpy little teddy the first time she had him over. He didn't expect the bitch to be faithful, but lying he couldn't tolerate. Lucy could tell that he was on to her. "Well, I'm glad you showed up," she said as she kissed him on the lips and pressed up against him. When he put his arms around her and returned her kiss, she hopped up and wrapped her legs around his waist and gave a breathy sigh. He carried her into the bedroom, dropped her on the bed and roughly pulled the teddy up over her head.

Moments later they were naked and at each other. Lucy was on the bottom, on her knees, face down, moaning into the sheets. It was violent, even brutal, but she loved it.

As she was about to climax, the thought hit Lucy that she belonged with a man like Geronimo. At that same moment, Geronimo reached down and slipped the serrated knife out of his pants. As Lucy raised her head for one final scream of ecstasy, Geronimo grabbed her hair with his left hand, yanked her head back, and cleanly slit her throat with one smooth slash of the knife. The force of the slicing knife and Lucy's instinctive reaction caused her upper torso to twist around to such a degree that she fell back on the bed face up, blood spewing everywhere.

No bitch is going to lie to me," he told her already dead ears.

[ **T W O** ]

"Get all those people back. Send them home if you can. And I don't want anyone in here except who I tell to come in." The barking voice belonged to Sergeant Wesley Brume of the Bass Creek police. He was standing at the door of Lucy Ochoa's trailer. The place was alive with cops and people from the neighborhood. Murders didn't happen every day in Bass Creek.

They had gotten the call at six that evening. One of Lucy's co-workers, Brenda Carrero, had stopped by on her way home to check on Lucy because she hadn't shown up for work that day. That was highly unusual for Lucy. Her job was to keep track of the pickers' attendance and their count, so she was pretty fastidious herself about calling in if she was sick or had to miss work. Brenda had knocked for several minutes but there was no answer. She shouted Lucy's name. Still nothing. Maybe it was the neighborhood dogs sniffing around the trailer or maybe it was the flies, she really couldn't explain it, but for some strange reason she tried the door. It was open. A whiff of something putrid hit her as she stepped inside, like maybe a rodent had crawled under the trailer and died.

"Lucy?" Brenda called in a quiet, worried voice as she peered into the kitchen, then walked hesitantly through the living room and back towards the bedroom. What she saw next burned into her brain forever, an image that would haunt her nightmare-plagued sleep for months.

Lucy's bed was crimson. And propped in the middle, lying on her back as if on display, was Lucy. Mechanically, Brenda focused first on the source of the blood, the gaping hole across the throat where flesh and tissue had been sliced clean through. Her eyes moved next to Lucy's face. The poor girl appeared to have died screaming.

When her mind registered what her eyes had taken in, Brenda Carrero started screaming herself. She ran out of the trailer as if death itself were chasing her, stumbling down the street until a neighbor, Hector Aviles, stopped her.

"What, what? What are you yelling for? Calm down!" Brenda tried to pull away but she couldn't, so she tried to get it out of her — away from her.

"She's dead! She's dead! Blood everywhere. Oh my God! Lucy!" She was screaming and flailing her arms against Hector's efforts to hold her and calm her down. Then she sank to the ground, whimpering and muttering Lucy's name over and over again. Hector's wife had rushed out of their trailer when she heard the commotion and now bent down to Brenda, whispering to her softly, "It's all right, it's all right." She looked up with worried eyes at her husband, who set off at a trot down the street towards Lucy's trailer. His jog slowed to a walk and then he stopped, staring blankly at the trailer's open door, and the dogs sniffing at the entrance.

~

The police force of Bass Creek numbered seven officers in total, including the chief. There was no homicide division, just two detectives: Del Shorter, who was assigned to collect forensic evidence, and Sergeant Wesley Brume, who was assigned to direct him in that endeavor. Brume ran the show at every crime scene.

There were several constants in Wesley Brume's life. He had always been short and fat, and he had lived his whole life in Bass Creek. The only time he had ever left the town for an extended period was when he joined the Marines for four years after high school. In high school, Wes never conformed to the limitations nature had imposed on him. He tried out for the football, basketball and baseball teams, never getting past the first cut. But his determination was monumental. Whether attempting to throw a block, make a layup, or hit a curveball, Wes gave it his all, heaving and grunting as he missed each time. His classmates were so amused by the noise he made in his efforts to become an athlete that they called him "the Grunt." It was meant to be derisive and funny, but Wes wore it as a badge of honor and aspired to be just what he was labeled, a "grunt" in the marines.

He served two years in Vietnam, receiving a Purple Heart and a Bronze Star for bravery. When he came home, the police department was the perfect fit for him. Wes had learned that if you carried a gun and were not afraid to shoot or be shot at, you could command respect even if you were short and fat.

Although many of the citizens of Bass Creek were poor and there was a large transient population, there wasn't a great deal of crime — a smattering of robberies, burglaries, drugs and domestic stuff. Most of the department's time was spent catching speeders racing for the new bridge and the big cities beyond. In his twenty-two years on the force, Wes had only investigated seven murders, and in five of those cases, the identity and whereabouts of the murdering husband were hardly a mystery.

Nonetheless, Wes and Del were well versed in forensic techniques, having been all too eager to spend the taxpayers' money on any and every seminar addressing the subject, whether it was in San Francisco or Scotland Yard. Unfortunately, book training was no substitute for experience.

When the two men walked into Lucy's trailer and saw her corpse immersed in her own blood, Del's first reaction was to follow Brenda Carrero down the street. The throng of locals outside nixed that option, so his second choice was to head for the john and puke his guts out. The Grunt held his ground. He'd seen worse in 'Nam.

After Del emerged chalk-faced, they started their investigation, donning their plastic gloves. Contamination had been drilled into their heads by the experts. Wes sent two uniforms to canvass the neighborhood and find out if any of the neighbors had seen or heard anything unusual in the last few days. At that point, they had no idea when the death had occurred.

"Write down everything they tell you verbatim," Wes told them, mimicking the words of one of his seminar teachers. "You never know what might be important."

Next, Del took pictures — pictures of the body, the bedroom, every inch of the trailer. They searched for evidence of a break-in or robbery but found nothing. The house was in perfect order except for the body and the blood on and around the bed, and a bloodstain on the living room carpet. Wes walked around the body looking for obvious clues like a knife or footprints or handprints in the blood, but there was nothing he could see with the naked eye. He didn't want to touch the corpse. *Let the coroner handle that,* he told himself. It was Del who searched the garbage and found the broken mug with bloodstains on the glass. It was the only clue they had besides the bloodstain on the carpet and, of course, the blood on and around Lucy's corpse.

Harry Tuthill, the coroner, arrived a half hour later. Harry had been the medical examiner of Cobb County for twenty-five years, but even he was overcome at the sight of Lucy's body.

"Holy Jesus!" he exclaimed to Wes. "Who the hell would do something like this?"

"I don't know, Doc. We've got nothing." Harry had relaxed by then — it never took him long — and he considered it time to break the tension with a little humor.

"Let me see, I'd say death was caused by a knife wound to the throat."

"No shit, Doc. Tell me something I don't know."

Harry gave up. He hated working with dumb cops.

[ T H R E E ]

*1957, New York City*

*Summer in the city was hot and muggy and sometimes downright intol-*
*erable, but not for a seven-year-old kid with places to go. Johnny was up*
*and out of the house every morning at nine on his way to summer school at*
*P.S. 6 with his buddy Mikey, who lived upstairs in the same tenement*
*building off Third Avenue. Patty, another neighbor, sometimes went with*
*them but only when Johnny's mother gave him strict instructions to call on*
*her and walk with her over to school. He and Mikey didn't like girls, period,*
*although if he was pushed he'd have had to admit that Patty was different*
*than most. She didn't wear dresses and walk slow and whine to them to*
*wait for her. She was right there with them stride for stride in blue jeans or*
*shorts, and she had her own Spalding that she bounced and caught as she*
*walked. Mikey liked her more than he did, always picked her on his teams*
*and with good reason — she was a better athlete than most of the boys.*

*They usually started the day inside with a game of Ping-Pong, knock-*
*hockey or checkers before the big kids came. The big kids never came early*
*but when they arrived they took over everything, pushing the younger kids*
*out of the way. They didn't push Mikey, though. Paulie Cane tried it*
*once. Mikey pushed him right back. When Paulie went to push him again,*
*Mikey punched him in the face and jumped on him, knocking him to the*
*ground before a counselor broke it up. Paulie was twelve at the time,*

Mikey just eight.

"I'm going to get you for this, Kelly," Paulie yelled.

"Anytime," Mikey responded, not an ounce of fear in his voice. Johnny, who was standing next to him in shock, truly believed that Mikey meant it.

"Come on. Let's go home," Johnny pleaded after the counselor took Paulie away. "Those guys aren't playing around."

"Neither am I, Johnny. Neither am I."

He didn't leave and Paulie never came after him. Somehow Paulie knew that Mikey was not a person to mess with no matter how old he was.

～

The afternoon was spent outside playing punchball or on the third floor playing dodgeball. The younger kids had their own punchball court. Mikey was always a captain and Johnny was his first pick even though he wasn't the best athlete available. Patty was much better but Mikey could get her with his second or even third pick because she was a girl. Mikey counted on that. He made Johnny feel good and he didn't lose anything in the process. Johnny suspected as much. It was part of the reason he wasn't crazy about Patty always tagging along.

Sometimes Johnny skipped their own game to watch the older guys play on the big court. He loved watching Joey Maier snare a ball hit down the line with his right hand and flip it over to "Spider" at first. There was no hitting above the fielders' heads on this court. You had to "punch" it through, and the shortest distance and the best place to try for a hit was down the third base line, which Joey patrolled and protected. Rarely did a ball get by him. He'd flip it underhand to first where Spider was a vacuum cleaner, always catching the ball with one hand, his left. Never missing.

They were his idols in those days. He spent hours emulating them, throwing the rubber ball against the concrete wall across the street from his house, picking up the return grounder with his right hand, flicking it back against the wall and snaring it on the fly with his left. In those moments, he was Joey and Spider all wrapped in one.

Saturday mornings they huddled in front of the television at Mikey's house. It was a black and white, maybe fourteen inches, with a lot of fuzzy white lines. The Kellys were a brood, six kids in all, and they were scattered over the couch, chairs and floor, transfixed for hours on the Saturday morning lineup: "Fury," "My Friend Flicka," "Mighty Mouse," "The Lone Ranger," "Tales of the Texas Rangers," "Roy Rogers" and "Sky King."

Johnny always found a spot on the floor. Mrs. Kelly would walk among them silently handing out bowls of cereal. Johnny got Raisin Bran because Mrs. Kelly knew that was his favorite.

On Sunday after church, the teenagers played stickball right on his block, hitting towering shots sometimes two, three sewer covers long with that little rubber ball, the Spalding, and somebody's mother's broomstick. Only two guys in the neighborhood could hit it over three sewers, big Joe Coyle, who lived across the street, and Jimmy Hayes, who lived next door. People hung out of their windows just to watch those guys play. Years later, Boyle became a college football halfback and Hayes a basketball star, but to Johnny their best days were out there on the street.

~

Those were the only days of his life that were magical as he lived them. No worries, no cares. A life that was full. Things would change soon enough.

[ **F O U R** ]

Word of the murder of Lucy Ochoa spread through Bass Creek like wildfire. At first Rudy didn't know who it was because Lucy had never told him her name. But as customers filtered in and out over the next week talking about the young woman and describing her, Rudy started to wonder. He only knew for sure when the *Bass Creek Gazette* finally obtained a picture of Lucy and published it on the front page a week after her body was discovered. Rudy was shocked. He went to the *Gazette* building, which was a block away from the hotel on Oak Street, and bought every paper for the last week. Then he carefully read everything about the murder of Lucy Ochoa.

According to the coroner, the murder had happened on Wednesday, January 16th, or early in the morning of the 17th. Rudy retraced the days in his mind. *That was the same night I was there!* The time of death freaked him out even more. The coroner had estimated the time of death to have been somewhere between 10 p.m. and 2 a.m. Rudy knew he had locked up the convenience store at eleven and gone directly to Lucy's trailer, but he wasn't sure what time he'd left. He read further: Her throat had been cut, probably with a knife. There were no signs of a break-in or a robbery.

After he'd read everything, Rudy sat and thought about it for a long time. He'd been at the murder scene during the time the murder was supposed to have happened. But Lucy was fine the last time he saw her. She didn't seem to have any problems pushing him out the door. Should he go to the police with what he knew? That idea scared him. They were nice enough when they came in the store but he'd seen them beating up a guy on the street one night, a guy he knew to be a harmless old drunk, and they did it to other innocent people, too — he'd seen it on TV.

At that moment, it hit Rudy like a bullet to the brain that he might actually be a suspect and that the police might try to make him confess, just like they did to people on TV. *I'm not confessing to nothing,* he told himself. *What should I do? Should I tell Mom?* He'd have to tell her about why he was at Lucy's house — and about the drinking. That just wasn't going to work. In the end, he decided to do nothing. *Nobody knows I was in her house,* he concluded, and promptly tried not to think about it again.

By the end of the week, the police had analyzed all the blood samples: from Lucy's body, the bed, the carpet and the pieces of glass. The neighborhood had been canvassed but most of the neighbors hadn't seen or heard anything unusual that night. Pilar Rodriguez remembered someone with dark hair throwing up on her lawn somewhere around midnight, but she hadn't gotten a good look at his face. Maybe it was that kid from the convenience store — Rudy was his name — but she really couldn't be sure. Farther down the block, a young man named Ray Castro said that he'd seen someone, a tall, dark-haired man, go in Lucy's trailer sometime after eleven and then come stumbling down the street from that direction less than an hour later and puke in the Rodriguezes' front yard. His friend José Guerrero had seen the same thing. There had been a third person with them that night, a guy named Geronimo, but neither knew his last name and he couldn't be located. And neither of them mentioned his relationship with Lucy or that he'd headed that way after they'd all seen the dark-haired guy.

The only bombshell — and it really wasn't a bombshell yet because the only person Harry Tuthill told was Wesley Brume — was the coroner's aside to Brume that Lucy had had sexual intercourse that evening. He had managed to extract a semen sample and had checked for signs of rape. There were none.

On Thursday morning, January 24th, Wes Brume was summoned to the office of Clay Evans IV, the Cobb County state attorney, to discuss the evidence in the Lucy Ochoa murder. The state attorney's office was just down the block from the police department, so it was a short trip for Brume. The woman's murder had already been headlines across the state and Clay wanted it solved and the perpetrator brought to trial while interest was still at least lukewarm. Too often the press reported the murder but not the aftermath. If a suspect was discovered early on, the story might continue for a while. But the only surefire way to keep the press on the story was with a trial. They loved trials the way normal people loved sex and they were teaching the public to love them too. Clay desperately wanted that publicity.

Clay Evans IV was a WASP — a fifth generation, blue-blooded Florida WASP. Great granddaddy had once been the governor. His own father had been a state senator from Cobb County and eventually secretary of state for Florida. There had been money once too — citrus groves as far as the eye could see. But granddaddy, the weak link in the family line, had sold all the land at a bad time and squandered most of the money, leaving behind just the blue blood and the arrogance. Clay's poor father, the Third, had been forced by circumstance to go to work for a living.

The Fourth followed daddy's footsteps to the University of Florida and eventually to law school. He wasn't a good student, spending most of his time golfing and partying, and would never have made it into the law school on his own merits, but there were qualifications and there were qualifications: Great granddaddy, the governor, had been a three-sport man at Florida and had attended the law school. So had daddy and he was personal friends with the president of the university and the present governor.

Clay attacked law school with the same laissez-faire attitude he had displayed as an undergraduate. When he had occupied his seat for three years he was given a law degree and finally, after three failed attempts, he managed to pass the bar.

Despite his loathsome resumé, Clay still had assets that attracted many of the big firms in Florida. He had his father's height and thick brown hair and an easy manner about him and, most important, he had a pedigree that granted him access to the halls of power in Tallahassee. When the offers came in, Clay weighed them carefully, reassured that life was going to continue to be good.

He chose the Miami firm of Eppley, Marsch & Maloney simply because he knew that Miami was a fun place to live and play. Unfortunately, reality was about to set in for the Fourth. Everyone at Eppley, Marsch was required to put in seventy- to eighty-hour work weeks and the competition among the associates was fierce. It didn't take the Fourth long to realize that life in the big firm was not for him. So he called dad.

"Can't you get me an appointment to something?" he whined to the Third. "I can't do this anymore."

"I'll see what I can do," the Third replied. Two weeks later, he called back.

"The Cobb County state attorney is retiring. I think I can secure the appointment for you."

"What do they have, five attorneys over there? I'd be lost in oblivion. Can't you get me something a little bit better than that?" At that moment, the Third wished that he had taken the time and the effort years before to throttle his son. He thought to remind the boy that he was being offered a state attorney's position having never tried a case, but he knew that logic would never work with the Fourth. So he stuck with manipulation.

"It's a stepping-stone, son. You probably don't remember, but I was once the Cobb County state attorney. Stay in the job a couple of years — fill in your resumé, so to speak — and I'll find something for you after that. The governor's a good friend of mine and if he's reelected, which is likely, he'll be in office for six more years."

It was a winning argument. Clay took the appointment and was soon running an office that specialized in speeding tickets, petty theft and every so often a grand larceny or two. Something happened, however, that neither the Third nor the Fourth had planned on. Governor Hal Bishop was caught cheating on his wife and was voted out of office after his first term. He was replaced by a Republican who couldn't stand the Third.

The Fourth was stuck and he'd been stuck for almost ten years when Wesley Brume walked into his office to discuss the investigation of Lucy Ochoa's murder. This case might be the opportunity he'd been looking for to jettison himself out of Cobb County once and for all. He had to control it, publicize it, and most important, make sure he won it.

Neither man liked the other. Wes saw Clay as a pompous ass and Clay saw Wes as a dumb cop, but a dumb cop who could be manipulated under the right circumstances.

"What have you got so far?" Clay asked after the formalities of shaking hands and making very small talk were over. He'd already read the investigative file but he wanted the latest and he wanted it firsthand.

"Well, we've had the blood analyzed and we've canvassed the neighborhood. We've got a suspect, a kid who works at the convenience store around the block from the murder. One of the neighbors identified him and two others described him pretty close."

It was an overly optimistic description of the evidence, but Wes could always be overly optimistic if the circumstances called for it.

"We've done a profile on him — no priors. Everybody we talked to seems to like him. He lives with his mother. He's a little slow. I went over and talked to his high school principal and looked at his school records. The principal confirmed the kid had a low IQ but he worked hard and his mother was very involved both in his education and with the school. The last two years he couldn't do the work so they put him on a vocational track and gave him an attendance certificate after four years."

The Fourth was anxious for the bottom line. He didn't want a biography.

"Did you pick him up?"

"No. I was waiting to talk to you. We don't want any screwups."

"You've certainly got grounds to pick him up for questioning. Take his blood, see if it matches. Put him in a lineup and let the neighbors pick him out."

Clay started to walk out of his office. It was his signal to Wes that the meeting was over, but the portly detective didn't move.

"There is one problem," he added before the Fourth could sweep out of the room to go God knew where. Clay stopped in his tracks and wheeled around.

"A problem? What problem?" He was in his superior role now, glaring down at the pudgy little detective. Wes wanted to drop the bastard right there but this was important business.

"You know about the semen?" Wes asked.

"Of course." Harry Tuthill had filled him in that very morning.

"We were able to get a blood type from it. The blood type in the living room and on the glass is O positive but the blood type in the semen is AB."

Clay turned this new information around in his brain. *Two people did this murder? Not likely. A robbery or a burglary maybe, but not this. This could be a problem.* A thought rolled around in the Fourth's devious skull but he needed more information to pursue it.

"Bring the kid in right away for questioning. If he's as dumb as you say he is, maybe he'll confess. Do your first interview without a video or a tape recorder. If he gives you something, you can always redo it on tape. If he's wishy-washy, it's your word against his."

Wes knew exactly what Clay was talking about. He'd used the same tactic many times in the past. It was strange, he had never seen this side of Clay before. Usually Clay didn't give a shit one way or the other. He headed for the door but the Fourth called him back.

"Who else knows about the blood samples?" he asked.

"Just me and Harry."

"Don't tell a soul about it. I'll talk to Harry."

"Will do," Wes replied. He knew the Fourth was up to something, but he couldn't tell what.

[ **F I V E** ]

Rudy had a morning ritual before going to work. After breakfast he would take his boat and go fishing down the Okalatchee. "Boat" was stretching it — it was actually an old dinghy he'd bought from one of the sailboat owners who docked on the river at night. The owner had hung a "Dinghy For Sale" sign on his mast and was asking a hundred and twenty five dollars for it.

"I've got thirty-five cash in my pocket," Rudy told him. He had his mother's directness and some of her bargaining skills, which he'd picked up by watching her over the years.

The boat owner, a retired IBM executive, was amused by Rudy's attempt to tantalize him with the cash. He had no need for the money or the sale but he saw an opportunity to let this kid win for once in his life. He crossed his arms and rubbed his chin with his right hand. They were standing on the dock and Rudy kept stealing glances at the dinghy, *his boat*. Finally, when the older man figured he'd built up enough anticipation, he relented.

"You drive a hard bargain, son, but if you've got the cash right now, I've got to sell this boat to you." Rudy practically hugged him. He helped him take the dinghy off the sailboat and in five minutes it was in the water and he was heading down the river. That was three years ago, and since then Rudy had learned to take the little engine on his boat apart and put it back together again with his eyes closed.

It was something he could get his hands on and his mind around.

The Okalatchee was Rudy's daily escape from the world. The birds didn't look at him like he was stupid. Nobody yelled at him for making the wrong change. Out on the river, he fit in. The fishing pole was his prop. Although he threw it in the water once in a while and even caught a fish or two from time to time, mostly he drove around exploring. When he found his perfect place for the day, he turned the motor off and drifted, watching and listening. He didn't stick to the main waterways either. The river had a thousand winding little fingers that led to nowhere, and Rudy was determined to explore them all. When he turned off the river, he was immediately lost in a world bordered by thick mangroves and tall pines that shot up from roots deep under the water's surface — a world where the gator ruled the water and the osprey ruled the trees.

The osprey wasn't like the gator. He allowed the herons and the egrets to poach in his waters and the other birds to sing and fly. His was a benevolent kingdom. But when he took to flight, his white chest protruding, his massive brown wings extended, there was no doubt who ruled. Rudy sometimes imagined himself to be an osprey, perched high above the madness, proud and brave. As an osprey, he had no fear.

In Rudy's mind, this was the real world, a world that had not changed since God first created it. The other world was temporary, unreal, out of harmony with the universe.

~

While Rudy was getting ready for work after spending Thursday morning on the river, Wesley Brume was at the convenience store talking to his boss.

"I want to take your boy in for questioning when he comes in for work this afternoon," he told the owner, Benny Dragone.

"What for?" Benny asked. He hated cops, especially the fat little bastard standing in front of him. He'd seen Wes in action before.

"I'm not at liberty to say. It's police business."

"You're not at liberty to say. Does his mother know about it?"

"What are you, his fucking father or something? Is there something going on here I don't know about?" Wes was getting his dander up a bit.

"No, I just watch out for the kid. I don't want you guys fucking with him. You know he's not all there. I'm not going to let you talk to him without his mother's permission."

"You're not, eh? How about if we fuck with you instead? How about I get the health department over here right now? Check out your bathrooms, check out your walk-in."

"Wait a minute. Wait a minute. Hold on here. We don't have to get drastic about this. I was just asking a question, that's all." Benny was from Chicago. He knew how bad things could get if the cops got city hall on your ass.

Wes knew from Benny's demeanor he had the upper hand.

"No offense taken, Benny. I just want to talk to the kid for a while. If you can stay here for a bit I'd appreciate it. I'll have him back as soon as I can."

Benny thought about it for a minute. It stunk. He'd heard the rumors about Rudy being at Lucy's house the night of the murder. It was all over the neighborhood. He was sure the cops had leaked the story and now they wanted to talk to Rudy. He also knew that Rudy was too stupid to defend himself. But what could he do? He didn't like it but he had a business to run.

"All right," he responded weakly. "But take it easy on the kid, will ya? He ain't all there upstairs."

"I know. I talked to his principal. You can count on me, Benny." *Sure,* Benny thought, *I can count on you to bend me over a sink somewhere in the middle of the night.*

Wes was there when Rudy showed up for work. Benny introduced him.

"He wants to take you down to the station to talk to you. It won't take long. I'll cover you here and you won't lose any money, I promise."

Benny felt like the gatekeeper at the Coliseum feeding one more Christian to the lions. He saw Wes standing there licking his chops. Rudy could see Benny's fear, but he had just come from the river and he had seen an osprey. He had seen him float down from his perch high in the sky and scoop up a fish in his talons. Rudy felt like an osprey, strong and fearless. Nobody was going to get the best of him today.

"It's okay, Benny. I'll go, no problem." Benny watched as the kid led the fat little grunt out of his store.

As soon as Wes's unmarked Ford left the parking lot, Benny picked up the phone and called Elena. He had always liked Elena. Ever since his wife Maria had died, he had fantasized about being with Elena. It was one of the reasons he hired young Rudy. *Why else would I hire a kid who has trouble making change for a dollar?* But Elena had no time for him or any other man.

"Elena," he said when she picked up the phone in the hotel lobby. "It's me, Benny. The police just picked Rudy up for questioning. They're taking him down to the station."

Elena was alarmed but not overly so. Working at the hotel, she had not heard the scuttlebutt about Rudy and Lucy that was spreading through the barrio like so much cow manure.

"Now Benny, what would the police want with my Rudy?" she asked lightly, almost as if she was trying to calm Benny down instead of it being the other way round.

"They're questioning him about the murder over here in the barrio." That made some sense to Elena. Rudy worked nights at the convenience store. He might have heard something. But why the station?

"Is there something you're not telling me?" she asked, a little more worry in her voice. Benny hesitated. He just couldn't bring himself to tell her that her son was suspected of killing Lucy Ochoa.

"No. I'm just concerned, that's all. I don't trust those damn cops. And Rudy, sometimes he's his own worst enemy."

It wasn't his words but the hesitation in his voice that made her suspect this might be a little more serious than Benny was letting on. *But how serious? Was Rudy a witness of some sort? Perhaps the killer had stopped in the convenience store before the murder? Maybe Rudy could identify him? Yes, that was probably it.* She hated Rudy working at that store at night. It was too dangerous. But he needed a job for his own self-esteem, and that was the only one he could find. To be safe, she decided to put her head waitress, Teresa, in charge and head down to the station to find out firsthand what was going on. She thanked Benny for his concern and hung up the phone.

Five minutes later, after she had given Teresa explicit instructions, Elena stepped into her beat-up old Camry and headed for the police station a few short blocks away. It was a beautiful afternoon, a little nippy with a slight breeze blowing. She would have preferred to walk but there was no time to waste.

The receptionist politely assured Elena that someone would be with her in a minute and asked her to take a seat. It was a small room with only a few chairs and a door that presumably led to the inner offices of the police department. Rudy was in there somewhere, but the door was closed. The sign on the wall next to it said it was locked and could be used only by police personnel. *Big Deal,* Elena thought. *They make it sound like people actually want to go in there.* But at that moment there was nothing she wanted more. The only possibility was to get the young woman at the receptionist window to buzz her in. She decided to sit and wait, at least for a few minutes. She looked at the clock above the receptionist's desk. It was 3:16 p.m.

After a few minutes she walked up to the window. "Please, Miss, could you please call back there and let them know I'm here? I really don't want anyone talking to my son outside of my presence." The receptionist gave her a look but picked up the phone and delivered the message to someone on the other end of the line.

"And can you please write down that I arrived here at 3:16?" Elena didn't know why she did that. *It might be important later on,* she told herself.

Inside the station, Wes Brume was about to start questioning Rudy. He led him to the interrogation "facility," an eight by ten foot bare room with olive walls and a concrete floor. The furniture consisted of a nondescript metal table in the middle surrounded by four metal chairs. There was no two-way mirror for other cops to observe the festivities, but there was a tape recorder on the table and a video recorder had been permanently installed to record a suspect's every facial expression during an interview. The Grunt did as he'd been told and left both devices off. He motioned Rudy to sit in one chair and he sat directly across from him with a new yellow pad and pen in front of him. He handed Rudy a document spelling out his Miranda rights and told him to sign it. "Just a formality," he assured him. Rudy pretended to read through it but barely did so, then signed his name at the bottom.

Wes had played this interview over in his mind several times before he'd picked Rudy up. He decided to start by handing Rudy the rope and seeing if he could fit it around his own neck. He leaned over and spoke softly, almost in a whisper.

"Do you know why you're here, Rudy?"

"No, sir."

"I want to ask you some questions about the Lucy Ochoa murder. Did you know Lucy?" Rudy hesitated for a moment. He knew he couldn't lie.

"Yes, sir."

"Tell me everything you know about her murder." Rudy was relieved the question wasn't directed towards him personally. This was a question he could answer without hesitation. As he began to speak, the Grunt started writing on his yellow pad. Rudy looked at the ceiling as he tried to recall everything he had read in the newspaper.

"I know the murder occurred between 10 p.m. and 2 a.m. on the night of January 16th." His eyes were almost closed as he strained to remember. "I know her body was found in the bedroom and she was naked. I know her throat had been cut with a knife. I know she was lying on the bed." Rudy hesitated; his eyes were completely closed now as he searched his brain for any other facts he might have read. Wes waited patiently. He noted in his pad that Rudy had closed his eyes when he spoke, "as if he was recalling a past event in his mind."

"That's it," Rudy concluded with a smile of satisfaction. "That's all I know."

"That's good. Very good." Wes had picked up on the play, realizing his was the role of the satisfied schoolteacher. Manipulation was the name of the game. No open-minded reasonable observer of this conversation would ever have suspected Rudy of being the murderer. The Grunt didn't fall into that category, however. His mind was already made up. What he was doing now was window dressing — filling in the necessary blanks to feed a hungry jury.

"Now Rudy," Wes continued, "I have to ask you some personal questions about that night. It's important for me to know everybody who was in the vicinity of the murder so I can eliminate them as suspects. You understand, don't you?" Rudy nodded his head. He was starting to feel comfortable with Officer Brume. "Some of the neighbors indicated that you were on Mercer Street a little after eleven o'clock on the night of the murder, is that true?"

"Yessir." Rudy was a little afraid, even embarrassed about the admission, but he was glad too. Glad to get it off his chest, especially in a nice conversation like this.

～

Elena had been sitting in the waiting room for twenty minutes. She had grown more and more impatient, and now was starting to suspect that something really wasn't right. She walked up to the window again.

"I've been waiting twenty minutes. I want to know where my son is," she said in a firm but steady voice.

"I'm sorry ma'am," the woman replied. "I'll call back there again." Elena stayed at the window, watching as the woman called.

After a moment she hung up and said, "Someone's coming out to talk to you." Elena stayed where she was. If someone didn't walk through that door immediately, she was going to do something — she didn't know what. All she knew was that the time for being polite was over. Almost immediately, a man walked through the door from the inner sanctum. He was dressed in black pants, a short-sleeve white shirt and a plain black tie, open at the collar. Elena guessed he was in his mid-thirties. He was as nondescript as his attire, neither short nor tall, fat nor skinny, handsome nor ugly — the perfect face in the crowd.

"Ma'am, I'm Del Shorter." He stuck his hand out, which Elena stiffly accepted. Del motioned to the waiting room chairs. Elena noticed that he had closed the door to the inner sanctum behind him. She reluctantly sat down. "Ma'am," Del began, "my partner, Detective Brume, is talking to your son as we speak. We're investigating the Lucy Ochoa murder and your son may be able to help us. He works at the convenience store nearby. He may know the girl, know who she was coming in the store with. Maybe even saw her that night. These are things we need to know. We need descriptions. We're showing him photographs. He could be a big help to us."

It was a lie but a plausible lie, something that played into Elena's own thoughts about the matter. Still, she wasn't ready to sit calmly and wait. Rudy was too vulnerable.

"I accept what you're saying but I'd like to see Rudy. I'd like to be there when you're questioning him."

"I'm sorry, ma'am, but that's against department procedure." Del knew he was treading on thin ice so he supplemented his response. "Technically, since this is an investigative stop, we've advised Rudy of his rights, so I'll advise you as well. He does have the right to remain silent, he does have the right to an attorney —" Elena interrupted him.

"Mr. Shorter, you don't understand. Rudy's a little slow. If someone asks him a question, he's going to answer it whether you advise him of his rights or not. I'm his mother, and I don't want him answering questions."

"I'm sorry, ma'am. He's an adult and he must make those decisions himself. But you can hire an attorney for him and if his attorney advises us that we cannot talk to him, we'll certainly stop." Elena finally got it. This was a stonewall. And why would they be stonewalling her if her son was not a suspect? She glared at Del Shorter.

"You're not going to let me see him?"

"No, ma'am."

"And you're going to continue to talk to him?"

"Yes, ma'am."

Elena turned to leave. She had to get a lawyer over there immediately. *But who do I know?* And then she had a thought. "Is there a public phone here?" she asked the receptionist.

"Yes, ma'am, right outside the front doors."

In the other room, Wes's chat with Rudy was moving along quite well.

"Rudy, were you in Lucy Ochoa's house that night?"

"Yessir."

"What time?"

"I'm not sure but I close the store at eleven and I walked right over." Rudy knew the next question would be about what he did at Lucy's house and when he left. This was nothing like he imagined. He felt comfortable, relieved. He would tell Wes what happened and then he would go home. Unfortunately, his new best buddy, Wesley Brume, did not ask the logical next question.

"You killed her, didn't you, Rudy." It wasn't a question: It was a demand.

Something kick-started in Rudy's brain when he heard the question, like he was on a treadmill walking slowly and all of a sudden somebody hit a button and everything went into warp speed.

"No, no, no, I didn't," Rudy replied in a fractured voice that continued racing along. "She invited me in. We had a couple of beers. I started to get sick — tried to get out of the house but I fell over the coffee table. Broke the glass, cut my hand. Then she kicked me out."

The Grunt kept the pace moving.

"You wanted her, didn't you? You went over there to screw her, didn't you?"

"No, no, no, it wasn't like that. I mean in a way, yes, but I was hoping she wanted me."

"And when she didn't, you got angry. You took her in the bedroom. You slit her throat. You laid her on that bed and you watched her die."

"No, no, no!" Rudy started to cry, the tears flowing down his cheeks. "I couldn't do that, not to Lucy, not to anybody." He was crying hard now. The Grunt decided to cut it back a bit. He handed Rudy his handkerchief. Rudy took it and wiped his tears.

Del came in at that moment and whispered something in the Grunt's ear. Wes seemed a little perturbed.

"I'll be done by the time she gets someone," he told his partner. He turned his attention back to Rudy as Del walked out.

"Sorry, Rudy, but I had to do that. I had to test you." Rudy nodded as if he understood, but he didn't. Wes waited a few more moments to make sure Rudy had calmed down before he went at him again.

"What did you go over there for, Rudy?"

"Lucy invited me over."

"At eleven at night?"

"She told me to come over when I got off no matter what time it was."

"You weren't going over there to make small talk — did you think you were gonna get you some?" It was an accusation already made but this time Wes smiled as he asked it, as if they were old high school buddies conspiring over a little sex. Rudy again took the bait.

"Yeah, I did." He had a sheepish, embarrassed smile on his face but he was relaxing again.

"What was she wearing at her house?"

"A little white nighty."

"See-through?" Wes had his smile on again.

"Pretty much," Rudy smiled back. He was one of the boys, finally.

Wes took a few moments to write the conversation down. He put a star next to the "little white nighty." He remembered seeing it at the side of Lucy Ochoa's bed the night of the murder.

"Were you mad at her, Rudy, when she turned you down?"

"No. I was out of the house before I knew what was going on."

"Were you frustrated that you didn't get laid?"

"A little."

"But not angry?"

"No, sir."

"What would make you angry — angry enough to kill somebody?"

"Nothing. I don't think."

"What if somebody killed your mother?"

Rudy stiffened. "Yes, that would make me angry enough to kill somebody."

"What if somebody raped your mother?"

"Yes." Rudy was getting angry just thinking about it.

"Let's say you were married to Lucy and somebody raped Lucy, your wife."

"Yeah, I could kill them." Rudy thought of some of the guys at school who had taunted him. Sometimes, he felt that he could have killed them too. Suddenly it dawned on him that he could kill someone. That's when the Grunt started building up to his sliest hypothetical.

"Rudy, is it possible that Lucy said or did something to you that night that made you so angry you could have killed her and you just don't remember?"

"I already told you, I didn't kill her." Wes could hear the anger now.

"I know you didn't kill her but is it possible that she could have said something to you that night that made you so angry you could have killed her?"

Rudy could feel the pressure — it was causing his chest to burn.

"I don't know what you're asking me, Mr. Brume. Woulda, coulda, shoulda — I didn't get angry at Lucy that night." Rudy was shouting now.

"I know you didn't, Rudy. And you didn't kill Lucy either. I know that. But you could get angry enough to kill somebody who killed or raped your mother and you could get angry enough to kill somebody who killed Lucy if she was your wife. What I want to know is, could Lucy or anyone say something that would make you so angry you could kill them?"

Rudy immediately returned in his mind to his classmates taunting him. He closed his eyes thinking back, picturing them. He stayed there for more than a minute.

"I guess so," he said without opening his eyes. His voice was again calm.

"So Lucy theoretically could have said something that night that could have made you so angry you could have killed her?"

"I guess so." The eyes were still closed. He was tired now, confused. He just wanted to go home.

"Do you forget things sometimes when you're angry?"

"I guess so." The eyes were still closed. Rudy had a headache now. He wanted it to stop.

"If theoretically you got angry at Lucy that night and did something, you might not remember it?"

"I don't know, I guess so. I don't even know what you're talking about anymore."

The Grunt took a moment to write in his pad. "She might have made him angry enough to kill her. He could have killed her. He doesn't remember." It was time to wrap it up.

"All right, Rudy, you can go now. Someone's going to come in and take some blood from you. It will only take a second. Do you need a ride home?"

"No, I'll walk." He needed the fresh air.

Rudy was glad it was over. He had no idea his nightmare was just about to begin.

The Grunt stepped towards the door but then turned back. "One more question, Rudy. Do you own any knives?"

"Sure."

"How about a serrated knife — do you own a serrated knife?"

"I don't know what you mean."

"You know, the kind with the little grooves along the blade."

"I might have one. One of the guests in the hotel gave me an old tackle box once and it had a few knives in it. I think one of them had that kind of blade." The one question had become several.

"Where do you keep that tackle box?"

"In my room, under my bed. Why?"

"No reason." Wes walked out of the room.

[ **S I X** ]

Austin Reaves was a rakish old coot. He was a transplanted Yankee whose parents had moved to Fort Lauderdale many years ago when he was only sixteen, but forty years later he was still considered a Yankee in Bass Creek. Those who knew him well called him something far worse — a carpetbagger. He was an attorney specializing in wills and trusts, hardly a lucrative practice in Cobb County, but the work was fairly easy, it paid the bills, and it left Austin free to pursue his true vocations — fishing and drinking good booze. He was a big, wide man with thick reddish brown hair that didn't have a hint of gray. No worries, he would reply when people would remark about the robust color of his hair. The rest of him fit well with his age.

Every weekend and every Wednesday, Austin was on his boat out on the lake. Every afternoon promptly at the stroke of three, he could be found placing his generous rump on his favorite barstool at the Bass Creek Hotel. Drinks at the Bass Creek were a little more expensive than at the local dives around town, but Austin wouldn't go anywhere else. He loved the old bar: the thick Southern atmosphere that hung from the old oak walls like Spanish moss, that called to him and cradled and comforted him in his time of need — which was every day at three. He was not unique in that regard. Many well-to-do inebriates called the Bass Creek home. It was, after all, the best place in town to get a steak after a few highballs.

Austin was in residence at his usual spot, taking a long, satisfactory pull on an authentic Cuban cigar, when the call came in from Elena.

"Now hold on, Elena. Slow down a bit. I can't understand a word you're saying, girl. Start slowly and for God's sake, speak English." As she often did when she was upset, Elena had slipped into her own brand of Spanglish. She forced herself to calm down.

"It's Rudy. They have him at the station and they're questioning him about the murder of that girl in the barrio. I told them to stop but they told me only Rudy or his attorney can stop him from talking. I want you to be his attorney and call them and tell them to stop talking to him. I'll come and get you and we'll go to the station together."

"I'd love to help, Elena, but I don't know the first thing about that kind of law. I do wills, wills and trusts."

Elena had no time for niceties. "Austin, I don't care what you do. I want you to call the police station now and tell them to stop talking to my son. I'll pick you up in five minutes." She hung up the receiver before he could lodge any further protest.

Austin was in a pickle and he hadn't even been drinking that long. He knew Elena and Rudy well enough from the bar but not well enough to stick his neck out for them. He didn't know anybody that well. On the other hand, he didn't want Elena as an enemy. Making a phone call, driving to the station — that would be easy and it might make him a real hero at his favorite watering hole. Besides, it might prove to be a profitable venture down the road. He picked up the phone and made the call.

Austin could sound very authoritative when necessary. In just a few seconds he was talking to Del Shorter and then Wesley Brume. Wes's conversation with Rudy had just ended but Rudy hadn't had his blood taken yet when Austin emphatically demanded that Wes cease and desist.

Austin was standing outside the hotel when Elena pulled up just a few minutes later. Having had a quick shot of Lord Calvert before exiting the bar, he was more than comfortable in his new role as defender of the innocent.

"I've already shut them down," he told Elena. "We'll have Rudy out of there in no time." Elena could tell from his words that Austin had stepped over the line separating mere tipsiness from outright intoxication, and her shoulders sagged as he dropped into the passenger seat.

But Rudy was already walking down the street from the police station when they pulled up. Elena now had to restrain Austin from going into the station and giving the police "a piece of my mind." She convinced him to come back to the hotel with her and Rudy instead. While Austin dined on a complimentary porterhouse, Rudy told them everything.

Elena felt like she had spent her whole life anticipating the pitfalls that would confront her son as he grew. She had known, for instance, that he would face ridicule at school because he was "different," so she had enrolled him in a karate class when he was six years old. By the time he was fourteen, he was a brown belt, which eliminated much of the direct heckling from his male peers. She immersed him in structure and routine: Always come home right after school, she said; always leave messages where you're going to be, who you're going to be with; call if you're going to be late; avoid strangers, unfamiliar situations. She took him into the hotel bar when he was twelve, told him about what alcohol did to people's lives, how it was an addictive drug. Told him to look at the faces at the bar and to check every day to see if they changed. The message stuck with young Rudy as he witnessed the same soap opera day after day. The star of the show happened to be sitting next to him eating a steak at that very moment.

Elena had done her job well. Still, after all the training and preparation, Rudy had fallen headfirst into the maelstrom. But this was no time for second-guessing. The only important question now was, *Where do we go from here?*

Surprisingly, it was Austin who got them headed in the right direction.

"You're going to need a top-notch lawyer right away. Somebody who's not from here and specializes in this stuff." The steak was sobering him up somewhat. "I know the perfect person. Tracey James. Her main office is in Vero Beach but she has several branch offices inland, including one in Bass Creek. She's an expert in criminal law and I could call her if you like."

Elena had heard of Tracey James. Who hadn't? She was the most famous lawyer in the area, perhaps in the whole state. Elena had seen her billboards on the highway and her name and picture in big ads in the phone book.

"Would you, Austin?"

"Why certainly, first thing in the morning. But I must caution you, Elena, she is very expensive."

"We'll cross that bridge when we come to it," she said. At the moment, money was the last thing on her mind.

## [ S E V E N ]

*Summer 1960*

"We're going to boy scout camp in July. Why don't you sign up?"

"Who's we?" Johnny asked.

"My brothers and me," Mikey replied. Mikey had two older brothers, Danny and Eddie. Eddie was eighteen months older than Mikey, and Danny was sixteen months older than Eddie. Irish triplets.

"I can't. You know my parents. They'd have to look into it for a year. My father's just not a spontaneous guy." Johnny's father was a bank clerk. Mr. Kelly, on the other hand, was a fireman, a big burly fellow, afraid of nothing. He gave that same confidence to his sons.

"I'll tell you what." Mikey had his thinking cap on. "I'll ask my mother to talk to your mother. She'll think of something. She'll be sure to tell her that my brothers will look after you and all that shit."

"Will she do it?"

"Sure. My mom loves you. Sometimes more than me, I think." Johnny looked at him to see if he was serious. Mikey flashed him that million-dollar smile. Mikey's smile. It was like a magic wand. He always looked like a saint when he was smiling.

～

Two days later, Johnny was having the conversation with his parents in the living room of their tiny four-room apartment. He could not believe they were actually considering letting him go. Of course, his father had to place a few obstacles in his path.

"You have to keep up your summer reading."

"I'll bring the books with me, Dad."

"And you've got to get somebody to serve Mass for you at the convent." There was a convent on the corner of his block, and he and Mikey alternated serving Mass there every morning.

"I know. I'll take care of it." He was wearing them down. He could feel the decision coming his way. His mom was already won over.

"I trust the Kelly boys, dear. They'll look out for him."

"The older two are a little rowdy for me," his dad replied and just stood there for a minute, his hands on his hips. Johnny could feel the pendulum swinging back again — but there was nothing he could do.

"All right," his father finally said as if he were making the decision to start World War III. "You can go, but if you don't get your reading done and if you have any problems, this will never happen again. You understand me?"

"Yessir." He was so excited he could barely contain himself. Two weeks away from home — two weeks! He just kept saying it over and over.

&sim;

Ondawa Lake scout camp was in a lovely wooded section of upstate New York, a four-hour bus trip from the city. There were as many as two or three hundred boys there at any one time, mostly troops from the city. About fourteen kids from Johnny and Mikey's scout troop made the bus trip from Manhattan. They were led by John Miller, the scoutmaster, and Tom Daly, his assistant.

The troop had their own little campsite, a half-acre clearing with a large campfire planted in the middle. There were two wooden lean-tos on one side of the campfire and two rows of white canvas tents on the other. An outhouse was set at the edge of the clearing, fifty yards or so from the nearest tent.

"Pair up. Find yourselves a tent," scoutmaster John Miller shouted.

The boys raced for the tents, Johnny following closely behind Mikey. They picked one in the middle of the row. Eddie and Danny picked one across from them about thirty yards away.

Each tent sat on a wooden platform and had two cots. There was a large burlap and a small burlap sack on each cot. The boys were told to stash their gear under the beds and bring their sacks. They walked, tripped and ran down a long, narrow trail to another clearing with a haystack in the middle.

"The big sack is your mattress, the small sack your pillow," Mr. Miller told them. "Fill 'em up." The boys attacked the haystack with a vengeance.

It was an inauspicious start for young Johnny, who suffered from hay fever. He didn't sleep well that first night. His nose was stuffed, his mouth dry, his face swollen, and the crickets droned incessantly. On the other side of the tent, less than three feet away, Mikey was sound asleep, as if he had grown up in the woods.

Sometime in the middle of that first night, Johnny had the urge to pee. He opened the tent flap and peered out into a darkness he had never known. The outhouse looked a hundred miles away. Who knew what creatures were lurking in the woods? As he stood there, scared and exhausted, wiping the drip at his nose with his hand, Johnny wished his father had said no. But it was too late for wishes. The cool night air hit his half-naked body and nature took it from there. He flipped down his fruit-of-the-looms and pissed off the platform of his tent, trying not to make a puddle at the entrance.

Maybe a half hour later, in a dream state, he heard Mikey doing the same thing.

Things picked up after that first night. The camp had everything: baseball fields, basketball courts, woods to explore — in the daylight, of course — and the largest lake they had ever seen. Being city kids, they spent as much time on the lake as possible, swimming and boating. It was amazing to them that they could go down to the lake and sign a rowboat or a canoe out at any time.

There was ritual, too: Every morning before breakfast the entire camp gathered at the parade field for the Pledge of Allegiance and reveille, and every night after dinner for God Bless America and taps. All scouts had to be in uniform for these events: collarless, short-sleeve scout shirt with kerchief, short scout pants, and knee-length scout socks with tassels. They hated the uniforms, especially the shorts, but they weren't alone. The other city boys, like the troop from Harlem, didn't take to the short pants either.

By the end of the first week, Johnny had adjusted to country life, even his bedding full of hay. He slept with his mouth open and a canteen full of water at his bedside. When his dry mouth woke him, he took a sip of water and went back to sleep. When he was full to the brim, he stood at the front of his tent and relieved himself. Sometimes he and Mikey stumbled out of their cots at the same time. On those occasions, they had a contest to see who could pee the farthest and the longest. They didn't know they were being watched.

On Saturday night, there was a bonfire at the parade grounds. All the troops attended. The scouts roasted marshmallows and drank sodas. When darkness fell, the scoutmasters took turns telling scary stories. One of the stories was about a ferocious wildcat that roamed those very woods. It even scared Mikey, who clung to Johnny on the trail back to their campsite. That night the sodas caused them to wake several times to pee.

After their second contest, they had a visitor. Johnny was lying on his side facing the tent wall when assistant scoutmaster Tom Daly came in and lay beside him in his cot. Johnny was half asleep. After a few seconds, Daly took Johnny's arm and pulled it towards him. Johnny jumped up, almost knocking the bed and the whole tent over. Mikey woke up instantly.

"What are you doing?" Johnny shouted.

"You know what I'm doing," Daly replied, standing up. He was a big man, heavily muscled from weightlifting, an imposing figure now standing at the entrance to the tent. Johnny's reaction had startled him a bit.

"No, I don't," Johnny replied. Daly turned to Mikey.

"You tell him what I'm doing here. I'll be back in fifteen minutes and you'd better be ready."

"What'd he do?" Mikey asked as soon as Daly left.

"He pulled my arm back until my hand touched his dick."

"Nooo. That is so gross."

"What are we gonna do, Mikey? I'm scared. He's coming back."

Mikey thought for a moment. "Grab your pillow and cover," he told Johnny. "We're getting out of here."

They ran over to Eddie and Danny's tent and told them the story. Mikey's brothers, although they were only thirteen and fourteen at the time, were tough boys.

"Stay here," Eddie told them. "Get under our beds. Hide behind the knapsacks and duffel bags. He won't be able to see you."

"What if he wants to search the room?" Johnny asked, trying to plan for every contingency. He was still in shock.

"We'll tell him to go fuck himself," Danny replied. That was the last word on the matter and it made Johnny feel secure. He wasn't in this alone.

~

A half hour later, assistant scoutmaster Daly showed up at the tent.

"Have you guys seen Johnny and Mikey?" he asked. Eddie sat up.

"Nope. Did you check their tent?" he asked nonchalantly.

"Yeah. They're not there."

Danny sat up too. "Can't help you," he said, looking Daly right in the eye. Danny's right eye wandered a bit, earning him the nickname "Dizzy" in the neighborhood. When he stared at you with that wandering eye, it was disconcerting no matter how muscular you were.

Daly knew they were lying. If their brother was truly missing, those boys would have been out of their beds in a flash. But he also knew from Danny's look that they weren't bluffing. If he made a move into that tent, he was going to have to fight those boys. He wasn't afraid — after all, they were just kids — but he was already drawing too much attention. He closed the flap of the tent and walked away.

Nobody said anything for about a minute.

"Do you think he'll come back?" Johnny finally asked.

"Nah," Danny replied. "He's done for the night."

"What about tomorrow?" Johnny pressed.

"Relax, Johnny," Eddie told him. "We'll think of something tomorrow. We ain't gonna leave you hangin' out there by yourself." It was the answer Johnny needed. He was silent again, but only for a few minutes.

"Why me?" he finally asked. "Why'd he pick me?"

Danny felt it was time for a little levity. "Maybe he thinks you're better-looking than Mikey."

"I think he saw us peeing together," Mikey replied. "Figured we were a couple of homos."

"Go to sleep, you two. We'll talk about it in the morning," Eddie told them.

"This is what short pants breeds," Danny added. The rest of them had a solitary chuckle over that one. They knew Danny was serious.

They fell asleep after that, except for Johnny. Lying on the floor under Eddie's bed, he wondered why assistant scoutmaster Daly thought he was a homo. What had he done?

~

At the mess hall the next morning, Johnny stayed close to Danny and Eddie. Assistant scoutmaster Daly was at his usual spot next to the scoutmaster, talking and laughing as if nothing had happened. He didn't even steal a glance at them when they walked in.

"Look at him over there," Danny said when they had been through the cafeteria line and were sitting at their table. "I'd like to cut his fuckin' tongue out."

It was Eddie who was the more practical one. "We're gonna have to get rid of this guy," he said to nobody in particular.

Vinny Schaeffer, another kid from the neighborhood, was sitting with them. "What are you guys talkin' about? What's goin' on?" Eddie and Danny ignored the question while Mikey filled Vinny in on the events of the previous evening.

"Whoa!" Vinny exclaimed. "This guy's gotta go."

Johnny couldn't believe they were actually talking about getting rid of an assistant scoutmaster. He was scared all over again.

"After breakfast when he takes that little walk of his into the woods,

47

we'll follow him," Danny said in a low tone as they all bent their heads in together. "We'll jump him before he starts jerkin' off or whatever he does out there by himself." Johnny wondered what they were going to do after they jumped him, but nobody said a word about that.

Sure enough, after breakfast Daly headed into the woods, the boys following a safe distance behind. Danny had his hunting knife with him. About a quarter of a mile in, Daly stopped and sat on a fresh stump. Danny motioned with his hand for the others to creep forward. They spread out and moved silently towards the assistant scoutmaster, who seemed deep in thought. At Danny's signal, they all ran at the same time and jumped on him. He was so surprised he didn't make any move to defend himself. They had him on the ground in a second and Danny had his knife out, the flat pressed hard against the assistant scoutmaster's throat with the sharp edge up.

"Don't move or I'll cut ya," he said in a voice that was almost gleeful. He was daring him to move.

Daly looked into those malevolent eyes, saw the devil's own smile on Dizzy's face and felt the cold steel against his throat. He didn't move a muscle.

Danny could see the fear in his eyes — felt it in his sweating pores.

"Me and the boys been wonderin' what to do with you," Danny continued. "They wanna report you. Me? I just wanna cut your fuckin' dick off and stick it in your mouth." He pressed the blade even harder into the assistant scoutmaster's throat. "But we reached a compromise, so to speak. You're gonna leave here today. Make up some fuckin' excuse. You homos are good at that. And we ain't never gonna see you again. Got that?"

Johnny was holding Daly's right leg, which wasn't moving at all. There was no struggle in the man. Johnny was wondering when and where this plan had been hatched. He'd been with Danny, Eddie and Mikey every minute since the previous evening and there had been no discussion. He looked at Mikey, who was holding the other leg, intently watching the proceedings. There didn't appear to be any confusion in Mikey's mind. Assistant scoutmaster Daly, his well-muscled body lying limply on the ground, slowly nodded his head up and down.

"That's a good boy," Danny told him, his left forearm pushing down on the man's head. "Now we're gonna walk away from here and you're gonna stay right where you are for a few minutes. Got it?" Daly slowly nodded as best he could. "And then you're gonna disappear." Danny got up but kept the knife pointed at his prostrate victim. The other boys released his arms and legs and started to back away. Johnny expected Daly to jump up and overpower them with his massive frame but he just lay there passively until they were out of sight.

They laughed all the way back to the campsite.

"I can't believe he just lay there and took it, " Eddie said.

"He was shittin' his pants," Danny chuckled. "You shoulda seen his eyes."

"We shoulda checked his underwear for brown spots." Vinny was laughing so hard he could hardly get the words out. "You scared me, Danny. I thought you were gonna cut him."

"Were you?" Johnny asked.

"Hell no!" Dizzy replied. "Do you know what my old man would do to me if I cut that guy?"

"Maybe he'd understand 'cause of what happened?" Johnny said with questioning eyes.

"Nah," Eddie cut in. "Danny's right. Dad's old school. Military. You report it up the chain. He'd beat Danny and then me and Mikey because we were the half-wits that followed him." Danny, Eddie and Mikey started laughing again. Half-wit was their father's favorite word.

⁓

Daly wasn't at dinner that night but Danny still wasn't through with it. He boldly walked up to the scoutmaster after they'd eaten.

"Where's Mr. Daly?" he asked innocently.

"He had to leave. Some kind of family emergency," the scoutmaster replied without looking up.

Danny turned towards the other boys back at the table and gave them the high sign. It was over.

They went out on the water the next day, Danny and Eddie in a canoe and Vinny, Mikey and Johnny in a rowboat.

"I'll row," Vinny told the two younger boys. "You guys really don't know how to do it." Johnny and Mikey looked at each other and shrugged.

"All right," they said in unison. If Vinny wanted to row, they'd just sit in the back of the boat and relax.

The lake was fairly large, more than a mile wide and at least two miles long. When they got out to the middle, they pulled their boats close and proceeded to light up the cigarettes they'd brought along. They could sneak a drag or two in the woods now and then but out here they could smoke in peace. It was a beautiful day, only a few clouds in the sky — a little nicer surroundings than the street corner. They smoked, sunned and talked — about baseball, boxing, who the toughest guys in the neighborhood were (besides Dizzy) — and generally drifted away from the events of the previous day.

Johnny had just lit his second cigarette when he saw Vinny's eyes grow wide. He looked at Mikey and they both started to smile. Vinny was a little crazy, always pulling stunts for a few laughs. But this wasn't one of those times.

"Look!" Vinny shouted. He pointed behind the boat. The boys turned and saw a fin slicing through the water a hundred yards away, headed right for them. "Shark!" Vinny yelled and then started pulling on the oars like a madman.

"Hurry!" Johnny screamed. "He's gaining on us." Johnny looked at Mikey and for the first time in his life, he saw the look of fear on Mikey's face.

"Ohhhh shit!" Mikey yelled as he hugged Johnny.

Vinny was rowing as hard as he could but the fin was still gaining on them. From the side, Johnny could see Eddie and Danny paddling straight at it. Crazy sons of bitches! Just before they reached it, Eddie, who was in front, picked up his paddle and started beating the water. The fin immediately went under. Vinny kept rowing for a few more seconds but finally stopped when he saw Danny and Eddie sitting still in the water. The shark was gone.

Vinny started in on his passengers as soon as he knew the crisis was over.

"The two of you were shittin' your pants just like Daly."

"We were not," Johnny replied.

"Oh yeah? What the hell were you huggin' each other for?" The two boys looked at each other and burst out laughing. Vinny joined them.

Suddenly, Vinny saw the fin again between them and the canoe. He started to shout but it was too late. The shark slammed into the canoe.

Everything slowed down for Johnny as he watched the attack unfold. The canoe was wobbling from side to side. Danny and Eddie stood up and started beating the water with their paddles. In no time, they were both in the water. Johnny and Mikey, at the same time, without so much as a glance at each other, dove in after them.

"What are you doin' here?" Danny asked Johnny when he swam up to him.

"I dunno. I guess I was going to save you or something."

"Do I look like I need saving? Where's my paddle? Where's the fuckin' shark?" For a brief moment, Johnny was actually concerned about the shark's safety.

Thank God Vinny kept his head. He pulled the rowboat alongside of them.

"You'd better all get in here," he said. "You're never gonna turn that canoe back over. Two guys on each side. Keep the boat steady. And hurry up. I don't know where the hell that shark went." Vinny helped them in the boat one at a time. The shark was nowhere to be seen.

They probably could have righted the canoe but nobody wanted to try. As they started to shore, they let the tension out the only way they knew how.

"That fuckin' shark is lucky I didn't catch him," Danny said, which caused them all to crack up.

"Dizzy would have given him the evil eye," Eddie continued. Only the brothers had the nerve to joke about Danny's wandering eye.

"What the hell did you guys jump in for?" Danny asked. "You wanted to make sure the shark had a full course meal?" Johnny and

Mikey just shrugged again. They didn't have an answer but they felt good about themselves and they knew Eddie and Danny appreciated what they'd done, even though they'd never admit it.

"I thought sharks were only in the ocean," Eddie remarked.

Vinny was ready for him. He'd been thinking about this one. "That's what most people think," he said. "But I read that they can show up in lakes. They come in through underground caverns." That was Vinny, always telling stories. But he told them with such authority, he almost made you believe they were true.

One of the counselors gave him up when they arrived on shore.

"That was no shark," he laughed. "It was a snapper turtle. Some of them get to be three hundred pounds. They live in caverns way below the surface. Sometimes when they swim on their sides they can resemble a shark. You boys must have made this one awful mad. They usually don't attack people."

They had a field day with Vinny on the way back to the campsite.

"At least I knew about the underground caverns" was all Vinny could say.

## [ E I G H T ]

The next morning, Friday, Wes and Del were in Clay Evans's office to update him on the investigation. Clay looked at the two of them in their black-and-white getups and wondered what planet they came from. *Maybe I should have stuck it out in Miami. I could be a partner by now instead of being stuck in this backwoods dive, conspiring with a pair of lunatics.* Just then, adding an exclamation point to Clay's inner rumblings, Wes put his thumb to one nostril and honked out the other. He wiped off the snot that was hanging from his face with the back of his hand. Del didn't even notice. A few minutes before, Clay had been at that point in his daily musings when he almost had himself convinced this career move could still work out. When Wes ended his performance by putting his hands in his pockets, Clay gave up.

"How'd the interview go?" he asked halfheartedly.

"Great!" Wes replied. "The kid admitted he was there. Had a couple of beers with her. He said he got up to go outside because he was sick and fell over the coffee table and cut himself on the broken mug, which makes the blood and the fingerprints his. He says she kicked him out after he fell but he also says he could have killed her and just not remembered it." That last part grabbed Clay's attention. Wes wasn't looking like an alien anymore.

"He actually said he could have killed her and not remembered it?"

"Yup."

"Did you arrest him?"

"No. I let him go home."

"You what?"

"His mother came to the station during the interview," Del cut in. "She demanded that she be allowed into the interview and then demanded that we stop. I told her that wasn't going to happen but that she could get a lawyer. A few minutes later Austin Reaves called demanding that we stop the interview."

"Austin Reaves? Doesn't he do wills?"

"Yeah," Wes chimed in. "But he drinks at the Bass Creek Hotel. We figured the mother was in a pinch and this was the only guy she knew."

Clay thought about that for a moment. Austin Reaves was probably just a band-aid. These people were dirt poor. They probably couldn't afford a criminal lawyer for the trial, which meant they'd be stuck with old Charley Peterson, the public defender. Having Charley for a lawyer in a case like this was like playing Russian roulette with a fully loaded gun. Clay smiled for the first time that day.

"Did you take blood?"

"Yeah. It'll take a few days to get the results. Maybe Monday or Tuesday. He owns a serrated knife, too."

"I'm not following you."

"The coroner told us the knife wounds were made by a serrated knife, you know, the ones with the grooves in them. Well, the kid told me he owns one. Told me where he kept it too," Clay laughed.

"He really is stupid, isn't he?"

"Yup." All three of them chuckled.

"Wait for the results of the blood test, then pick him up. And call that reporter that you know, Wes. What's her name?"

"Pam Brady?"

"Yeah, that's the one. I want her to get a picture of this kid for the front of the paper to kind of remind our witnesses who they're supposed to pick out in the lineup." They all laughed again. It was an uneasy laugh, however, since one big problem was sitting in the middle of this case like an invisible white rabbit. Clay knew it was time to address that problem.

"Del, could you leave us alone for a moment?" Clay walked to the door with Del and closed it behind him. When they were alone, he pulled a chair close to Wes's.

"How sure are you that this kid did it?" he asked.

"Dead sure," Wes replied. "He was there. Puked outside after it was over. He did it. I don't think it was premeditated but he did it. He was probably mad because she turned him down." It was Clay who was now eager for background.

"Tell me about this Lucy Ochoa."

"She's seasonal, been coming here for years. Married once. Divorced. Very loose. Neighbors say she's always had a lot of guys come and go. Hard to keep track of her. But nobody saw this kid from the convenience store over there before."

"You're sure it's him?"

"Positive." Clay needed that commitment before he went any further. Clay was a master manipulator, probably the only thing he did very well. It was in the blood. Although he had no use for the fat little bastard sitting in front of him, after ten years he could read Wes like a book. There were no nuances in Wes Blume's life. Everything was as black and white as the pants and shirt he wore every day. When his wife decided to go back to work after their second child started school, Wes left her because he believed a woman's place was in the home. It was that simple.

"There were no signs of rape?" Clay inquired, although he already knew the answer.

"Nope."

"You know what a defense attorney is going to do with these two blood types." It was like waving a red flag in front of a bull. Wes hated defense attorneys. They manipulated facts, evidence, coached their clients to lie — anything to win, even if winning meant putting a criminal back on the streets. He could hear the son-of-a-bitch now, claiming some "phantom fucker" was responsible for the murder while his client, who just stopped in for a cup of tea, was totally innocent. Wes's face was turning red. He just didn't understand how the Constitution guaranteed a scum-sucking parasite the right to be represented by a scum-sucking lawyer.

"Yeah, I know," was all he said to Clay, but Clay had caught it all. It was time to make his pitch. Slowly.

"Let's assume this kid's blood matches the blood on the carpet and the blood on the mug, which is a pretty good assumption based on what he told you. Are you with me?" Wes nodded.

"And let's assume that we conclude from the physical evidence that there was no rape. She must have had sex earlier that evening, don't you think, Wes?" Clay could tell Wes hadn't really thought that part through. With Clay's help he would get it... eventually.

Wes nodded his head again, but a little uncertainly this time. "I believe under those circumstances we could exclude the semen as evidence in the murder investigation completely. Do you agree?" Wes had it now. It was brilliant. There was no rape so don't give them that evidence. Don't let them confuse the jury with that "reasonable doubt" voodoo bullshit. And it made perfect sense that somebody else had fucked her earlier, a slut like that.

"I agree."

"Good. But we've got to keep this close to the vest. Can you swear Del to secrecy?"

"No problem. But what about the coroner?"

"Harry Tuthill? Don't worry about Harry, I'll handle him."

Since they were officially co-conspirators now, Clay had a few other housekeeping matters to discuss.

"Start a separate rape file."

"Why don't we just ditch the semen?"

"No, too dangerous." He knew Harry would never go along with eliminating the evidence but he didn't tell that to the Grunt. "If it ever comes out we can explain our position, but if we destroy the evidence, it will look very bad."

"But why start a rape investigation if our position is there was no rape?"

"We have no probable cause to believe there was a rape but we're continuing that investigation. That keeps the evidence from becoming part of the public record. If it was in the public record, any newspaper idiot could request all evidence that we found at the trailer and we'd have to give it to them. Hell, they'd get more than we gave the defense in discovery. We'd look very bad. We need to hide that information for now and this is the best way. Down the road when the hubbub dies down, we'll declassify it, so to speak. The Feds do this all the time."

Once again Wes was impressed with the way Clay was thinking everything through. He obviously had a talent for this kind of thing. He left Clay's office shaking his head. He still couldn't believe how great the meeting went. He'd been looking for a prosecutor like this all his life.

[ **N I N E** ]

While Clay Evans IV was plotting to parlay her son's life into new career choices for himself, Elena was making arrangements to visit the law offices of Tracey James for her initial consultation. Austin had made the call for her and scheduled the meeting for the following Tuesday. Elena was amazed that he'd managed to get her in so quickly. Austin conveniently neglected to tell her that he was an interested party.

"Her main office is in Vero Beach," Austin told her. "You have to go there if you want to see her on Tuesday."

"That will work out fine, Austin. Thank you so much for setting this up."

"No problem, Elena. I was happy to do it for you." *And for myself, of course.*

Elena didn't mind the drive at all. Rudy was under investigation for murder. If she had been asked to walk to Vero Beach to clear his name, she would gladly have done it.

Tracey James's headquarters was an ostentatious three-story building northwest of Vero. It originally had been built as a nursing home, but when the financing for the project fell through, the building lay empty until Tracey discovered it and purchased it for a song. There had been relatively little needed in the way of renovation. The second and third floors were all patient rooms except for the cafeteria, and Tracey filled those rooms with her adjusters. It was the downstairs and the outside that needed to be fixed. Outside, she had installed a circular driveway with a fountain in the middle. On both sides of the entrance to the grounds she had placed huge identical stones with the words "The James Law Firm" and "*Let the James gang fight for you!*" carved in the center. Columns were placed at the grandiose entrance. Inside, she had built a marvelous marble-floored foyer and waiting room. The receptionist's desk, an antique mahogany table with a phone, anchored the middle of the waiting room, which was always empty.

Tracey scheduled her clients hours apart, a technique designed to make each one feel special. At the appointed hour, the chosen one was brought through a narrow hallway to Tracey's office, which took up a full third of the downstairs and was bordered on the entire west side by a picture window that looked out on a magnificent multi-flowered garden, a garden that Tracey had never set foot in. Nor could she name one flower that sprung from its rich soil. The garden was designed to soothe the client. The magnificent Persian rug, the plaques, the white mahogany desk, the soft blue leather couch and matching chairs — all of it was there to impress on each of them that they were in the presence of a great lawyer.

Elena was born in Puerto Rico in a run-down shack on a farm where her father was a sharecropper. When she was five, her family moved to New York City and she grew up on the tough streets of Spanish Harlem. At twenty-two, when she realized her husband was a hopeless alcoholic, she took her son and two hundred dollars and moved to Florida to start a new life. She had lived in squalor without heat and running water. She had worked for the worst people imaginable. She was a hard person to impress and, as she sat in the soft leather chair looking out at the garden waiting for the queen to make her grand entrance, she had this uneasy feeling, like she was on the subway at rush hour and somebody was about to grab her purse. At that moment, Tracey entered the room from a door located behind her desk, a too-sweet smile pasted on her face. Elena instinctively pulled her handbag close to her body.

Tracey rarely noticed her clients. Of course, she looked directly into their eyes when the time came to be sincere, but it was all part of an elaborate dog and pony show. She schmoozed them and after they hired her and left, she couldn't remember the first thing about them until the next time she needed to see them. For some reason, Elena was different. Tracey swept in the room with her usual smile, prepared to spit out the same old spiel, but Elena stopped her dead in her tracks. Tracey wasn't quite sure why. Maybe it was her natural beauty and the stark contrast between them: Elena was dark, her skin creamy caramel, her silky hair jet-black. Even sitting, Tracey could tell that she was long and lean but with the ample curves of a woman. It was more than that, however. Perhaps it was the way Elena looked at her, like she was looking right into her soul.

Tracey didn't realize that Elena and her son were about to become the greatest challenge of her career and that how she handled this woman and this case would become one of the defining moments of her life.

Tracey Goldberg had been a marketing major in college, following in her father's footsteps. Her mother had died giving birth to her and it had been she and her father ever since. Dad had been a businessman and Tracey had planned to be one too.

"Go to work for yourself," Dad had advised. "You'll never get rich working for somebody else."

Tracey took the old man's advice to heart. She decided to make the law her business. She could start her own firm, be her own boss. Before she ever set foot in her first law school class, she had a preliminary marketing plan in place, identifying and anticipating the pitfalls of the practice.

She traversed the state checking out the small, very successful firms. Personal injury was where the big money was for the small practitioner, and advertising was the means to getting the best personal injury cases.

"Experience is the only teacher," Daddy had told her, over and over again. The last conversation on that subject was just a month before his death. "Don't set your feet in stone until you know the lay of the land. Look into each nook and cranny. You never eliminate the risks but you can minimize them."

Again Tracey followed the sage advice of her father. After graduation, she started slow, spending two years at the state attorney's office in Fort Lauderdale, doing misdemeanors and minor felonies. That experience made her somewhat comfortable in a courtroom, although she didn't intend to be there too often in private practice. It also taught her there were too many attorneys in the big cities, all gnawing on the same bone. The path to success had to be outside the major metropolitan areas, but that was the enigma: How do you make money outside the centers of money?

There were many small towns in the interior of the state in need of good legal services. It was an untapped market but a risky one. You couldn't just pick one town and try to make it there. You'd starve. You had to have a base of operations large enough to sustain yourself while at the same time reaching out to the small towns.

That became Tracey's plan. She chose Vero Beach as her headquarters, a sleepy town on the east coast populated by retirees but large enough to sustain a practice on its own. She took out a substantial bank loan and started advertising in the yellow pages, then radio, then billboards. Television was too expensive at first. Although personal injury clients were her target, she threw in criminal law as well. It was all part of the plan.

There were other parts of the package that had to be massaged. Tracey was fairly attractive but she needed work if she was going to stand out. It was her own assessment, an honest marketing evaluation not based on any insecurity — at least that's what she told herself. She was tall and she stayed in shape through daily workouts and a stingy diet, but her nose was too big and her breasts were minimal. So part of the loan money was spent on a nose job and implants, her dingy brown hair went platinum, and Tracey Goldberg became Tracey James — *Let the James gang fight for you!* Now wherever

Tracey's ads appeared, her full-length picture accompanied them. She definitely had separated herself from the boys in the blue suits.

Immediately, the calls started coming in. Tracey instructed the two girls who answered the phones to screen each potential client using a detailed questionnaire that she had "borrowed" from another firm. Later, she reviewed every answer to determine who was worth seeing and who wasn't. Her research after law school had told her to aim for the middle: not the small soft-tissue cases or the high-end million-dollar cases, but the fifty to a hundred thousand dollar cases that proliferated between them. If liability was clear (that could be established through the questionnaire) and insurance coverage was good, those cases could be settled without ever stepping into the courtroom or filing suit. They might be settled for less than they were worth, but the focus was volume not people.

Based on the number of calls she was getting, Tracey hired two retired insurance adjusters to interview the selected clients, obtain medical records and insurance information and, eventually, make a settlement demand. She allotted herself ten minutes with each person. Within a month, she had twenty-five good cases. Within a year, it was three hundred and there were six adjusters handling the claims.

The adjusters were an idea she had also "borrowed," from an attorney in Tampa she'd never met. When she toured the offices of Mr. Dale Willingworth, she spoke only with the office manager. There wasn't an attorney in sight but the place was teeming with insurance adjusters. She learned that adjusters knew the claims process inside and out; knew what a case was worth; knew how to work it up; and knew how to get the most money. Theoretically, if the selection process was good enough and the case was in the target range, a lawyer was superfluous.

As she drove out of Tampa that day marveling at the huge billboards on the highway advertising the Willingworth law firm (*"Need a Lawyer?"*), Tracey wondered if Mr. Willingworth even existed. She laughed out loud to herself, almost veering into the outer lane of traffic, imagining a law firm without any lawyers.

Two years after law school, she was the most successful personal injury lawyer in Vero Beach even though she had never filed a civil complaint, never argued a motion, and never appeared before a judge. What she did do to maintain her credibility was take some criminal cases. Criminal cases, unlike civil cases, needed to be handled at all stages by an attorney because there was so much courtroom involvement. Like she did with the civil cases, however, Tracey cherry-picked her criminal clientele. She only did felonies unless the client was wealthy and willing to pay. The retainer was fifteen thousand dollars, payable up front, and twenty-five thousand for a capital case. When the balance in the account hit five thousand, the retainer had to be replenished. If it wasn't, when the money was gone so was the James gang. There were no exceptions, no lost causes. She had every client sign a document saying they understood the rules. Tracey's motto was the same as Abraham Lincoln's: "A lawyer's time is his stock in trade." Unlike Honest Abe, however, she intended to be paid for every second.

Daddy would have been proud.

The James Law Firm had been in operation for five years when Elena made her first visit. Things had changed dramatically since the not-so-humble beginnings. The firm had expanded into the small communities in the interior of the state. Tracey had offices in ten cities from Arcadia to Okeechobee. Offices without lawyers — at least without lawyers paid by her. She negotiated with a local lawyer in each community to provide office space for her when she needed it; established a local telephone line and an 800 number. Her picture went on the back of the local telephone book and on several full pages throughout and she was on billboards heading into and out of town: a full body shot, artfully done. Tracey was standing in a tight navy blue business suit, her silky blond hair resting on her shoulders, a smile breaking from her ruby red lips. The caption was always the same — *Let the James gang fight for you!* — in large, bold print always level with Tracey's breasts. You had to read the small print at the bottom of the ad to know that Tracey was advertising her legal services.

If somebody called the local office, the local attorney's secretary would use the same questionnaire that the receptionists used in Vero. The questionnaire would then be faxed to the main office. If the James firm decided to take the case, the local attorney would receive twenty-five percent of the settlement as a referral fee in a personal injury case and twenty-five percent of the retainer in a criminal case. Of course, to satisfy any bar inquiry, local counsel would have his or her own file complete with copies of everything that ever happened in the case.

Tracey's local attorney in Bass Creek was none other than Austin Reaves.

The established practice at headquarters was to try and get criminal clients in right away because of speedy trial considerations and also because they paid cash — the more severe and expensive the case, the quicker the appointment. Even a lawyer as successful as Tracey James was concerned about cash flow.

"Elena, is that correct?" Tracey held out her hand. Elena hesitated for a second but finally extended her own.

"Yes, that's correct." Tracey sat in the soft leather chair facing Elena rather than behind her desk. It was the intimate touch.

"I've read your file, Elena. Has your son been arrested yet?"

"Yes. They arrested him yesterday."

"And the charge?" It wasn't the question so much as the fact that she had to answer that caused Elena so much turmoil. She almost couldn't bring herself to say the words.

"First-degree murder," she said, fighting back the tears.

Tracey almost licked her chops like a lioness about to feast on a helpless gazelle. Murder was the big one, the twenty-five thousand dollar retainer. She rarely got the big ones and she didn't know why. Perhaps the money cases were all in Miami. Perhaps the people in the small cities who were charged with murder couldn't afford to pay for their own attorney. Not once did Tracey consider the possibility that she didn't get the capital cases because she had never tried one in her life. She wasn't thinking about that now. Now she was focused on sliding that money out of Elena's purse. She didn't notice how tightly Elena was holding on.

Tracey stood up and walked around the room pretending to be deep in thought.

For her part, Elena was not impressed at all. The nose job was too obvious and the tits too big, although the sight of them made her remember the lump she'd found in her own breast a few weeks earlier. It seemed like so long ago, but she couldn't do anything about that now. Her focus now was this plastic personality prancing around the room. Elena wasn't trusting Rudy's life to this woman!

Tracey knew it wasn't working, that her rhythm was off. She changed tactics, something she *never* did, sitting down and for a moment just shutting up. She picked up Rudy's file, which had been placed on the desk by her secretary. She'd already read it. Suddenly, from the recesses of her brain, a small picture of a dark-haired woman popped up. It was the only picture of her mother she'd ever seen; it had sat on top of her father's dresser. From that picture, as a little girl, she had created her mother in her dreams: beautiful, with long flowing black hair and the brightest smile. Elena had a striking resemblance to that woman. For the first time, she saw one of her clients in a different light. This was a mother trying to save her son from a lifetime of prison, possibly death.

"I have no idea what kind of a case they have, Elena. Can you tell me a little about it?"

It was hard but Elena took her through everything she knew: from the first day when the front page screamed that a young woman's throat had been cut to her conversation with Rudy when he told her of being there and drinking and falling down and cutting himself. Tracey listened carefully, asking questions from time to time. She could now see where the state was coming from.

She could also see that it was going to be a difficult case to win. Her first inclination was to bail out. Difficult cases ruined her unblemished record of success. Hers was not a reputation built on brilliant courtroom tactics. But she could *see* Elena — so strong, so focused — a beautiful, powerful mother. Tracey just couldn't walk away from her. Not yet.

"Somebody had to be in that house after Rudy left, Elena. If we can find that person, Rudy will walk. My investigative team is the best. My chief investigator, Dick Radek, was a detective for twenty years at the Miami police department, ten of those in homicide. We will leave no stone unturned. Before we're through, we'll know everybody in that neighborhood by their first name."

She was so sincere when she said it, Elena started to believe her and with good reason: It was the truth. Tracey had the best investigative team north of Miami and south of Jacksonville. Almost all of her cases were won at the investigative level, by turning over stones the police just tripped on. But Elena still wasn't convinced.

"The police have already done an investigation —"

"I'm sure they have," Tracey cut her off. "But the police in these small towns are notoriously lazy. Once they found your son's blood in the trailer, their investigation stopped. They only need one suspect to look good."

That made sense to Elena. She was sure it was true. Those words and something else, something that had changed in Tracey since she initially sauntered into the room, convinced her that Tracey was the right person for the job. Elena *felt* her sincerity. She also felt something else, something that Tracey was so successful at hiding from the world — vulnerability. Not necessarily what she was looking for from the lawyer representing her son, but maybe from the person.

Now that she was sold, it was Elena's turn to press her case.

"I don't have much money." It was a line Tracey had heard a thousand times before and usually, based upon their appearance, the car they were driving, what they did for a living, it was Tracey's cue to walk them to the door, apologetically telling them that she couldn't help them. She couldn't do that to Elena.

"Listen," Tracey cut in again. "I usually require a twenty-five thousand dollar retainer for capital cases like your son's. I've never reduced that retainer before," another absolute truth, "but I believe in your son's innocence. I believe we can find the evidence to exonerate him. I'll agree to reduce my retainer to fifteen thousand dollars, but when that money is gone you *must* replenish it. I can't make any exceptions to that rule."

"I have five with me," Elena answered.

"I can't accept that. Go home. Talk to your relatives, your friends. See if you can raise the money. But do it quickly. Time is your enemy."

Sentiment only went so far with Tracey James.

[ **T E N** ]

Rudy had spent the whole weekend on the river — fishing, lying around, thinking. There was an old two-story houseboat down one of his narrow trails that had sunk but was still lingering half out of the water like an old ship before it turns keel up for the final dive. Rudy loved to anchor his boat there and make up stories about how it had got that way. One time it was a brothel. Two men fighting over the same woman pulled out their guns and started shooting. One of the bullets put a hole in the side of the boat that nobody noticed until the next morning when it was too late. Another time it was a hideout for members of the Dillinger gang who shot it out with the FBI. Some of the dead bodies might still be inside. That's why the gator was always hanging around. It was trying to figure out a way to get at those bodies without getting trapped inside.

This Saturday morning, however, Rudy's thoughts weren't on the houseboat. He was thinking about Lucy. Why would anybody want to kill Lucy? It didn't make sense. He just couldn't get his brain around it. And now Momma and Austin were saying he would probably be arrested for the murder. What were the police going to say? *She kicked him out of the house so he got mad and killed her?* Were people going to actually believe that? Just then he saw an osprey gliding over the water. It veered sharply and crashed into the murky waters, emerging seconds later with a fish clutched in its talons. It was a marvelous sight, one Rudy had seen many times before. It was murder of a sort but it was murder with a reason. The dumb animals of the world didn't kill without a reason. Maybe people could do that, kill for no good reason. But Rudy wasn't like that. He was more like the osprey, or the gator. And he just didn't have a reason to kill Lucy — couldn't they see that?

For a brief moment, Rudy toyed with the idea of ending it all in this place that he loved so much. He wouldn't last in prison, he knew that. They would see that he was *different* and he would have to be on guard at all times. Thank God he had stayed with the karate. He was sure there weren't too many black belts in prison. In the end, his mother was the reason he didn't go swimming with the gators. She was fighting so hard for him —he just couldn't do that to her.

They came for him on Monday morning about eleven, after the blood test results came in. Two uniforms were with the two detectives, and somehow a reporter had received a tip to be there with a photographer. Rudy was usually on the river at that hour but he didn't go out that morning. Elena had suggested he stay in. They both knew why but neither spoke of it — they had already talked it to death. Elena didn't want him out on the river when they came. Those idiots would make a circus out of it with police boats and helicopters. Rudy would go quietly *for now*. The battle would be in the courtroom.

They handcuffed him right at the front door of the hotel so the photographer could get a good shot for the morning paper. Read him his rights while they were doing so, a useless exercise at that point since the Grunt had already taken his statement and had him sign a written waiver at the time. Then they put him in the back seat of the squad car. They had a search warrant too but they didn't search the whole apartment. They went right to the tackle box under the bed, opened it to make sure the contents were as advertised, and took it with them. They were gone in a matter of minutes, just long enough for a small crowd to gather. The reporter, Pam Brady, started to approach Elena to get her thoughts and feelings about what had just happened, but she thought better of it after she caught a glimpse of the fire in Elena's eyes. Those eyes told her all she needed to know. Elena wanted to spit on all of them: the police, the press, the gawkers — her neighbors. Couldn't they see this was a family tragedy? Didn't they know what she and Rudy were going through?

The next day, when she returned from her meeting with Tracey James, Elena called her sister in New York. She had to start raising the money and her sister was the only person she could turn to.

"Marguerite, I need ten thousand dollars," she told her after a brief exchange of pleasantries.

"For what?" Marguerite asked as she started searching for the right words to turn her sister down. Elena told her the whole story.

"My God, Elena, what are we going to do?"

"I've got a lawyer, a good one, but she wants a fifteen thousand dollar retainer."

"That's just the start with those thieves. They'll run that dry and they'll want more."

"Maybe, but I think I can work with this woman."

"Woman? You got a woman to handle a case like this? Baby, you need a man."

It was starting all over. Big sister telling her what to do, criticizing the choices she had already made. *Baby* wasn't just a word she used in conversation. It had a definite meaning in their relationship. This was one of the reasons she had left New York. Elena bit her tongue.

"She's the top criminal lawyer in this area. Besides, that's not part of this discussion. I've already hired her. Can you help me or not? I've got nobody else to turn to." She tried to be matter-of-fact about it, not wanting to beg, but Marguerite was her older sister, and she sensed her sibling's desperation no matter how hard Elena tried to hide it.

Marguerite had a good job. She had worked for UPS for fifteen years, was one of their first delivery women. Unfortunately, she lived the high life.

"Elena, I could probably scrape up five thousand dollars but that's it." There was a pause on the line. Marguerite could hear the tears. "Let's think about this for a minute. There's got to be somebody. What about a bank?"

"Marguerite, I need this money tomorrow."

"What about Mike?"

"What about him?"

"He's doing well now. He's been off the sauce for years, has a fairly decent job."

"Marguerite, he hasn't seen or heard from me or Rudy in sixteen years."

"So? He's still the boy's father. Mike knows why you left. He knows it was his fault, he's told me as much."

"Listen, can we not talk about my ex-husband right now? I need help."

"Why don't you take a day to think about it, Elena, and I will too. If we can't come up with anybody else, I'll call Mike. There won't be any strings attached. I'll just tell him the boy got into a little trouble and you called asking for five thousand dollars and I didn't have it. He can make the decision from there." Elena thought about it for a moment. She was so desperate anything sounded good, even contacting the man she had avoided for the last sixteen years.

"All right," she told her sister. "I'll call you tomorrow."

Marguerite took Elena's "All right" as a tacit consent to call Mike, which she did as soon as she hung up. She and Mike still lived in the same neighborhood. She had been an observer through the rough years as he drank his way to oblivion. She had also watched him pick himself out of the gutter and slowly crawl back, inch by inch. He'd been in AA nine years now and had a good job with the telephone company. They met sometimes in the morning for coffee.

Marguerite considered Mike a friend, but her loyalty was to Elena. Elena didn't want Mike to know where she and Rudy were, and Marguerite honored her wishes. That didn't mean from time to time during their morning conversations she couldn't let Mike know that his son was doing well.

Mike answered the phone on the second ring.

"Mike, this is Marguerite." He recognized her voice even though she rarely called him on the telephone.

"What's up, Marguerite?"

"Nothing much." She was trying to play the whole thing down. She knew that if Mike knew the real truth, he would stop at nothing to find out where his son was. But that decision was Elena's, not hers. "I just talked to Elena. She told me that Rudy was in a little trouble and she asked to borrow five thousand dollars. Mike, I don't have that kind of money."

"What kind of trouble?"

"I don't know and I didn't ask. She said it was minor." She was pretty sure she was pulling off the nonchalant act. Lying over the telephone was a lot easier than lying in person.

Mike could tell that she knew more, but Marguerite was his only connection to his son — he couldn't alienate her. This was an opportunity and he had to play according to her rules.

When Elena had first left, he was furious. Angry enough to have done something he would have regretted for the rest of his life. *How could she do this to me?* But he didn't try to find her or his son. He didn't have time. Another paramour had entered his life, one he had known for years, a lover who dominated his every breath.

It wasn't until he sobered up years later that he had put the pieces of the puzzle in their proper place. Elena hadn't done anything to him. *He* had done it to her and his son: staying away from home for days on a bender; coming home drunk, yelling and screaming; lying passed out on the front stoop for all the neighbors to see; spending the grocery money on booze. It was a wonder she'd stayed as long as she did, pleading and begging him to stop. Telling him she loved him, that she'd help him. He had tossed her aside like a toy he had outgrown. He didn't need her: He didn't need anybody — until the chickens came home to roost....

Oh, it was difficult down there in that cesspool, seeing his reflection for the first time in a long time in its fetid waters — more difficult than the slow climb back up. But he knew if he didn't take the time to see himself in all his grotesqueness, he would never make it all the way back. He also knew that if Elena hadn't left him, if she had continued to provide the crutch for him to cling to, he would never have looked in that mirror.

Now he lived in the hope of somehow making it up to them. This was the first time he had ever been contacted. This was the first time they needed him. He had to respond without reservations or conditions.

"I can have the money for you tomorrow," he told Marguerite.

"You can? Oh Mike, that's great."

"I'll go to the bank first thing in the morning and I'll meet you at the coffee shop at, say, nine or nine-fifteen."

"That's good. Mike, I know both Elena and Rudy will appreciate this." She wanted to say more, to tell him that she would encourage Elena to call him, to let him know where she was. So at least he could visit his son. But that was not her decision and she didn't want to raise any expectations in Mike's mind.

She called Elena right away — no sense letting her worry all night about the money.

"Why did you do that?" Elena demanded.

"Because I knew it was the only way. I didn't tell him where you were and he didn't say anything about wanting to see Rudy. I told him you had asked me for the money and I didn't have it. That was it. I'm meeting him at nine o'clock in the morning. Give me your bank information and I'll wire-transfer the funds right after that."

Elena paused for a long half minute, and then with a deep breath said, "Thanks, Marguerite, you're right. I guess I have no other choice."

[ E L E V E N ]

As soon as she received the fifteen thousand dollar retainer, which Elena personally delivered to her office, Tracey James went to work. Her first call was to Dr. Harold Victor Fischer, a forensic psychiatrist in Vero Beach, whom she had worked closely with in the past. H.V. had impeccable credentials and always seemed to find a way to provide Tracey with just the right professional opinion she needed. She then walked up to the second floor to visit with Dick Radek, her investigator. After that, she prepared a Notice of Appearance, a pleading she filed with the court saying she was representing Rudy, and a Demand for Discovery, calling for the state to turn over every shred of evidence it had in the case against Rudy.

Her plan was simple but shrewd: Dr. Fischer, after meeting with Rudy and performing an "independent" psychiatric evaluation, would provide an opinion that Rudy, because of his limited intellectual ability and his nature, did not have the capacity to refuse to engage in conversation when the police began questioning him. Because the police knew of his limited intellectual ability, they should not have begun the interrogation in the first place. At the very least, when his mother arrived before the questioning began and demanded that it be stopped, they should have acceded to her wishes. Armed with this opinion, Tracey was going to file a Motion to Suppress Rudy's statement to the police. She wasn't sure what evidence they had yet but she knew from Elena that Rudy's blood type was O positive, something he shared with millions of other people. If the confession and the blood were it, he'd be walking if she won the motion. If some of the neighbors had seen him, she'd have Dick talk to them and find out exactly what they were going to say. It was a tentative plan based on assumptions, but it was the best she could do until she knew more.

Tracey had told Dick Radek to send someone to Bass Creek for two weeks to hang around the barrio and find out as much as possible about the murder, the neighbors, and Lucy herself. When Tracey received Wes Brume's file, Dick's people would re-interview each and every witness. Perhaps the police had missed something. Perhaps she could put someone else in that house at the time of the murder.

~

Elena had a new problem to deal with when she got home from her second trip to Vero. Her boss, Philip Randle, was waiting in her office. She knew it meant trouble as soon as she saw him. Phil was the managing partner of a syndicate that owned the hotel and several other commercial properties throughout the state. He showed up on a Monday once every six weeks to go over the books with her and discuss any problems. From the day he gave her the job, Phil had had the utmost faith in Elena's ability. His stay usually lasted less than three hours. Then he was off over the big bridge, heading back to his home in Miami.

Today, however, Phil had a sour look on his face, a look that spoke volumes.

"We have to let you go," he told her abruptly after the usual pleasantries. Elena wanted to demand a reason but she already knew. She wanted to ask for another chance but she was too proud to beg. She just sat there in the office chair staring at Phil, who felt an obligation to explain.

"It wasn't me, Elena. I argued against it. You've done a great job here from day one and I will give you a letter of recommendation wherever you go. Somebody sent a copy of the newspaper to me and my partners. You know, the one with the front page picture of Rudy getting arrested in front of the hotel. Every one of my partners called me. They don't know you, Elena. To them it's just business, and the picture was extremely bad publicity for the hotel. I tried to talk them out of it but it was no use."

Elena didn't say anything. She continued to stare at Phil, who felt compelled to fill the silence with words. "They want you to leave right away but I'm going to give you a week's severance pay along with my letter of recommendation." He handed her an envelope and made a move toward her to hug her goodbye. Elena stiffened, took a step back and glared at him. Phil got the message. He headed for the door but stopped before leaving.

"We're sending someone over tomorrow as a temporary replacement. Her name's Alice Stevenson. Please give her the keys and show her around." He didn't wait for an answer.

[ **T W E L V E** ]

When Clay Evans received the Notice of Appearance from Tracey James, he almost shit his pants on the spot. He'd never tried a case against her, nor had any of his staff, but he'd seen her billboards all over the state. There was no doubt she was big time. He'd been wheeling and dealing to make this case a slam dunk for himself on the assumption that good old Charley Peterson would be defending the kid. Having Charley as your attorney was like being represented by a dead man, which seemed most appropriate in a murder case: the dead representing the about-to-be-dead. Clay really got a chuckle out of that line the first time he thought of it. Now it didn't seem so funny. He'd hidden evidence. He'd had a knock-down-drag-out fight with the coroner, Harry Tuthill, to convince him to alter his report — all based on the assumption that he could pull the wool over Charley Peterson's lazy old dead eyes. And now he had Tracey James on the case. *There's still time. I could go back and fix things. I could drop the charges. Or... Tracey James is big time — lots of publicity. If I really want to get out of here, I've got to take certain risks....*

His session with Harry Tuthill hadn't gone as smoothly as he would have liked, either. Harry was like him, an old blue blood in a dead-end job. They often had a few drinks on Friday afternoon and bemoaned their present status in the world, which usually meant slamming Bass Creek and most of the sorry souls who resided there.

Clay thought he could count on Harry but Harry balked. He was in his sixties, on the verge of retirement. Harry's window of opportunity had closed a long time ago.

"You want me to leave information out of my report? That's illegal."

"Look, Harry, you know what they're going to do with that information once they get it. This kid is going to sail out of here." This time, however, Clay wasn't preaching to the choir.

"I don't care, Clay, I'm just the medical examiner. I report the findings and let the chips fall where they may. The fact is this woman had semen in her body — I can't leave that out of my report."

"You do agree, don't you, that there were no signs of rape?"

"Yes."

"And you know that the blood type on the floor and the blood type in the semen were different."

"Yes."

"What do you conclude from that?" Clay was practicing his direct examination.

"Either she had sex with someone she knew before she was killed or her lover killed her right after sex."

"What about the other blood? How do you account for that?"

"I don't. That's not my job."

"Think about it for a minute, Harry. Have you ever seen or read about a lover killing another lover right after sex without some evidence of a battle: the room's a mess, bite marks, scratch marks?"

"Of course I have, Clay. You're reaching for straws now. Besides, we haven't seen the lover. He might have bite marks or scratch marks on him."

"But there's no evidence of an argument in that bedroom."

"Look, she was killed in the bedroom. She had sex that night. She could have had sex with somebody who left the scene and then Rudy could have come over and killed her, or Rudy could have come and left and someone else could have arrived and had sex with her and killed her. Those are the two possibilities, one equally as plausible as the other. In either scenario, she didn't fight with the person who killed her and there is no evidence of a break-in. "

"You're wrong, Harry. We've got the broken glass in the garbage, blood on the carpet — different type from the semen. We do have evidence of a struggle *with a different person than her lover.*" It was an accurate analysis and Harry mulled it over.

"I guess you're right. We have evidence that she might have struggled with Rudy, which would make him the more likely suspect — assuming that a struggle occurred."

"You know as well as I do that it was Rudy, Harry. As the evidence stands now, we both know I won't even be able to get an indictment. This kid is going to walk unless you help me, Harry. " Harry hesitated for a minute before declining Clay's invitation to become a co-conspirator for the second time.

"No. No. I can't do it, Clay."

"Wait a minute, Harry. You were thinking about something. You were thinking about a way to do it, weren't you?" Harry didn't answer right away. He was still thinking. Finally, he started thinking out loud.

"Are you certain Charley Peterson is going to handle this case?"

"Yes, I am," Clay lied. It was a reasonable lie. He was pretty sure the mother couldn't afford a private attorney, which only left Charley. He knew where Harry was going. If Charley Peterson was on the case maybe he could fudge things a little.

"The report isn't complete yet. Toxicology tests are still being performed. We could issue a preliminary report. I could inadvertently not mention the presence of semen in the original preliminary report but include it in the supplemental report. There's no problem in doing that. I could delay the supplemental report for a couple of months, but after that you're on your own. Anyone who asks for the supplement gets it. And if Charley Peterson is not the lawyer on this case, all bets are off."

Clay was ecstatic. Harry had given him more than he had asked for, a legitimate way to hide the evidence. Charley Peterson in his normal state of inebriation couldn't even spell supplement. He'd never ask for it in a million years, especially since the toxicology tests had nothing to do with the cause of death.

Clay's initial ecstasy at Harry Tuthill's compromise was all in the past now. Everything had changed dramatically with the appearance of the famous — more like infamous as far as he was concerned — Tracey James. There was no way he could hide the supplement from her.

[ T H I R T E E N ]

Harold Victor Fischer had purchased an old two-story Victorian house on the outskirts of Vero Beach to serve as his professional office. Vero was for the most part a typical example of modern urban sprawl, Florida style, littered with high-rises, mobile home parks, and characterless, vanilla homes, block after block, one after the other like a monopoly board gone haywire. U.S. 1, which ran through the middle of town, was bordered on both sides by every restaurant chain in existence, their multicolored signs poking up at different heights like wild, psychedelic weeds on an ill-kept lawn. H.V.'s place stood out like a cultured, well-heeled thumb, which is exactly the way he wanted it — to stick out, that is. Culture wasn't really his game, although H.V. was a most pretentious son of a bitch.

He'd originally set up his practice in Miami but the competition had been fierce. All his money had gone into advertising. He wasn't bilingual and besides, everything in Miami was turned upside down. The vast majority of the people were absolutely certifiable, so H.V. typically found himself helping the marginally sane cope with the wholesale insanity of the world around them. It was a unique perspective, one that he never forgot, but as a daily diet he found it terribly unsatisfying — and it was beginning to tear at the borders of his own psyche. So he moved up the road to Vero, which was like taking a trip from Mars back to Earth.

H.V.'s reasons for choosing Vero were similar to Tracey's. He wouldn't have the competition of Miami but he'd be in an area large enough to attract a lucrative clientele. With H.V., the emphasis was on *lucrative*. He was definitely in it for the money.

He became a forensic psychiatrist, which meant that he didn't treat people or "cure" them anymore — he sold his services to the highest bidder as an expert witness on cause and effect and everything else in between. He found Tracey, or she found him, soon after his move to Vero. It was a marriage made in heaven. Tracey moved clients through her office like logs through a paper mill, and a good percentage of them saw H.V. during the trip. Tracey and H.V. shared the opinion that everyone who was injured through the negligence of another had a psychiatric problem as a result.

Because Tracey usually settled cases at an early stage, H.V. was rarely deposed, so the public record of his opinions on behalf of her clients was scant. If the entire record were available, it would have revealed hundreds of opinions suggesting Tracey's clients had psychiatric conditions ranging from mere depression to the more exotic, like post traumatic stress disorder, all caused by whatever trauma had befallen them. Those opinions translated into hundreds of thousands of dollars in settlements for the James gang and some tidy fees for H.V. as well — not that he didn't deserve them. On the rare occasions when he did have to testify, H.V. was always well prepared, well spoken, concise and impossible to cross-examine. His credentials were more than solid: He had received his undergraduate degree from Cornell and his medical degree from Penn. When asked about having worked with Ms. James in the past, the doctor's pat answer was: "I seem to recall that I have but I'm not sure of the name of the client, or clients, or the date. I am called by a great number of attorneys."

In the modern world of relativism it was known as selective recall.

Rudy was a little different from H.V.'s run-of-the-mill clients. H.V.'s testimony in criminal cases had usually related to insanity or competency to stand trial. But in Rudy's case Tracey wanted to test a unique legal theory: that because of his limited intelligence Rudy was unable to comprehend *and* waive his Miranda rights. It was about more than competency, an argument Tracey knew she might lose. It was about competency combined with naiveté. Tracey wanted to be able to argue to the judge that, because of his diminished mental capacity, Rudy simply could not refuse to talk to Wesley Brume when Wesley asked him a question, regardless of the fact that Wesley had advised him of his right to remain silent. Because it was a tricky point, H.V. had been given carte blanche in the spending department, an opportunity he did not fail to exploit. The first order of business was a trip to Bass Creek to visit his patient.

⌒

Rudy had been in the Cobb County jail for about three weeks when H.V. showed up. Like everyone, Rudy had heard horror stories about jail and was expecting the worst. But it was all quite calm — boring, actually. There were very few prisoners in the county jail and Rudy settled into a routine early on: breakfast in the morning at seven, karate exercises after that, then pushups and situps. The guard had told him he'd literally have to fight for his ass when he hit the state prison system and Rudy wanted to be ready. In the afternoon he did some cardiovascular work, playing basketball or running around the exercise area.

Elena came in the afternoon. She was allowed to come every day because it was county jail, but her visits were hard on Rudy. He was used to hugging and kissing his mother. Seeing her every day but not being able to touch her was like torture. It might have been better if her visits had been less frequent, but nobody could convince either of them of that fact. Elena had never been overprotective of Rudy. She knew it was going to take longer for her son than most young men, but she had always wanted him to stand on his own two feet. Now he was in prison and it was, at least in part, her fault. This was new territory. She didn't know if Rudy was strong enough to handle such an ordeal. She just wanted him to know she was there for him — every day.

At night, he had books and magazines to read that Elena had brought. Sometimes, though, in the middle of the night he'd dream about state prison and being attacked by gangs of men. They'd call him "stupid" and "dummy" as they held him down for the final act of humiliation. Rudy always woke up before it happened. Shaking and sweaty, he'd lie there for hours, afraid to close his eyes.

*I'll never let it happen,* he told himself. *They'll have to kill me first.* Then he'd think of the osprey. Flying above it all, swooping down at the perfect moment for the kill. Or the gator, biding his time, always staying cool. *I'll be like them. Fearless, ready to kill.* Only then could he fall back to sleep.

His first visitor, besides his mother, was Tracey James herself. Tracey came the second week. She really didn't need to see Rudy, didn't need to hear his story at this point. She just wanted to eyeball him, get a feel for the extent of his intellectual deficit, so she could provide a firsthand observation to the judge when the time came. Unlike regular visitors who talked to the prisoners through a screen, Tracey actually met Rudy in a room where they could face each other and talk.

"I'm your lawyer," she told him after she introduced herself. Rudy smiled.

"I know. My mother told me all about you. She said you're the best." It was Tracey's turn to smile, even blush a little.

"I don't know about that, but we are going to do our best to get you out of here."

"I know." Rudy repeated the words with such confidence that even Tracey was taken aback. Most of her clients were a little less confident and a little more demanding and colorful in their choice of words. Tracey felt the need to file a disclaimer.

"I can't guarantee anything. There's a possibility we'll lose."

"I know," he repeated again, still smiling at her. "But you'll do your best."

Tracey didn't know how to respond to such a pleasant, reasonable observation. "Yes, well, I have a few questions to ask you and I want you to respond to just those questions and nothing more. We'll talk more after I get a copy of your statement to the police, but for now let's stick to the questions I ask. Okay?"

"Sure," Rudy replied, the same smile on his face. *Doesn't he know where he is?* Tracey wondered.

⁓

Later that day, Tracey filed her motion to have bond set. Rudy was now being held without bond and she debated whether to file the motion at all. Elena could barely raise the reduced retainer and she had no property that could serve as collateral. Bond in a capital case was going to be over a hundred thousand dollars, at the very least. Elena could neither post bond nor convince a bondsman to post it on her behalf. As a practical matter, the motion was a waste of time. However, it was a billable waste of time and Tracey's specialty was churning hours.

⁓

When they first met, H.V. had not been surprised by Rudy's upbeat nature even though he was in jail. H.V. had worked with retarded children in Connecticut for a year during his residency and had noticed that they were consistently cheerful. He remembered one of his colleague's remarks as they were observing a classroom of children laughing and having fun:

"And they're the retarded ones. I don't think so."

H.V. recalled those words the moment Tracey told him about Rudy and his inability to say no to Detective Brume. None of those kids he remembered would have or could have refused. The hard part would be explaining this to a judge.

H.V. tried to be as upbeat as Rudy during that first meeting, pasting a smile on his face and extending his hand.

"Hi Rudy, I'm Harry Fischer." He never, ever referred to himself as Harry. It had taken him years to cultivate the moniker H.V.

among colleagues and patients and the few friends that he had. But this was a rare event — fieldwork — and a unique assignment that called for a different, more flexible approach. He needed Rudy to feel totally relaxed in his presence.

"Hi, Harry," Rudy replied, shaking Harry's hand. Harry seemed like a nice guy but he looked a little out of sorts dressed in blue jeans, tee shirt and running shoes. "Can I get you something, Harry? Coffee? Tea?"

H.V. looked around somewhat bewildered. They were in a small room with a table, the same room where Rudy met Tracey James the week before. H.V. wondered how the kid could order up drinks. Rudy watched him looking around but didn't say anything.

"They let you do that?" H.V. finally asked. He saw the smile start to form on Rudy's face and he knew he'd been had. Nothing left to do but laugh at himself.

They laughed a lot that day. Harry really enjoyed himself. It brought him back to a time in his career when he was working with kids and having fun, even making a difference. He came away from the meeting convinced that Rudy was a lot smarter than his IQ suggested, but he did have that simple, wonderful naïveté of the retarded. He had convinced himself. Now he had to convince the court that Rudy could no more have refused to talk to Wesley Brume than a dog could refuse to chase a cat that ran across its path.

Before that day in court, however, H.V. had a lot of work to do: gathering school and medical records and poring over them for hours; a few more visits to Rudy; psychological tests; intelligence tests. Most of it was fluff, window dressing for his underlying opinion. But it would serve its purpose in one important regard — as justification for his exorbitant fee.

## [ F O U R T E E N ]

1966

*It had been a sweltering summer in the city and this night in late August was no different. Johnny was in the back room of his parents' four-room railroad flat, his room, lying in his bed by the open window trying to drift off to sleep.*

*"You're not sleeping, are you?" He recognized Mikey's voice coming from the fire escape.*

*"No. But not tonight, Mikey. I can't. I'm too tired." All summer long the boys had been saying goodnight to their parents, going to bed, and then sneaking out the back window, down the fire escape, and up the alley to the street and freedom. They didn't do it every night, usually just Friday and Saturday, but this week had been unusual and Johnny was exhausted.*

*"I don't want to go out either. Just wanted you to know I lined up a job for us when school starts." It was the "us" that caused Johnny to sit up and take notice. Mikey was always lining up jobs for "us" — like the job at Jimmy the Shoemaker's. Johnny loved the job but Mikey made most of the money.*

*"I make thirty dollars a day, sometimes forty on a Saturday," he had told Johnny when he was recruiting him to be his understudy. Johnny had forgotten to ask how much he was going to make. And that wasn't Mikey's only job. In the wintertime, he worked at Schuler's cleaners on Lex, just a*

*few stores up from Jimmy's, delivering dry-cleaning.*

Johnny started to protest but gave up. When Mikey had an idea, he was so positive and enthusiastic there was no talking him out of it, so why try?

"So what's the new job?" Johnny asked, his eyes still half closed. Mikey leaned against the fire escape and folded his legs up so that his knees were at the same height as his shoulders. He was dressed in nothing but his fruit-of-the-looms. He never wore an undershirt.

"We're gonna be ushers at church."

"What? Us? Ushers? That's a job for rich old men. They'd never hire us. Besides, I've had enough of church to last me a lifetime."

His response didn't even cause Mikey to pause. "We're all set. I've already talked to Tom. We've got the job." That was Mikey. Tom Roney was a funeral director who had buried almost every prominent New Yorker who'd ever lived. He supervised the ushers as a public service. Somehow he was "Tom" to Mikey. "Pays eight bucks a Mass. Four Masses a week. And we don't have to hang around for the whole show. We just have to seat people, take their money halfway through and usher 'em out at the end. You get it? That's why they call us ushers."

"How'd you line this up?"

"I ran into Tom last week after church. He told me he was looking for a couple of ushers. Asked me if I knew anybody. I scoped it out a little more as to time and money, then I told him you and I would take the job.

"Why'd ya do that without talkin' to me?"

"Hey, it might not be there tomorrow. Ya gotta strike while the iron is hot. You can always back out." He paused for a moment like Johnny knew he would. "But you won't wanna. This is easy work. Easy money." Johnny just nodded. Like it was going to be real easy staying out all Saturday night and getting up at the crack of dawn on Sunday. He didn't say anything, just smiled to himself. He knew it would be fun. Everything he did with Mikey was fun.

They started the next week, eight o'clock Mass, and they actually made it on time: black suits, black ties, black shoes, white shirts. Very white faces, at least for Johnny. He'd puked before leaving the house that morning. He was sixteen now, Mikey was seventeen, and they'd started drinking — courage for the Saturday night dance. Maybe they could meet a girl. Maybe they could "make out," although Johnny would have been happy just to get to the meeting stage. You needed courage to do that. At least he did. Mikey just liked to drink. "Courage" was a couple of half quarts of Colt-45 malt liquor. Malt liquor got you buzzed quicker than the regular stuff but it also made you a whole lot sicker. Johnny spent his first day on the job seating people, puking; taking the collection, puking; ushering people out at the end of Mass, puking. So far this job was working out as expected.

Father Charles Burke was the pastor of St. Francis parish, a big Irishman with a warm heart and a predisposition for good scotch. He too was one of Mikey's fans. In fact, he gave Mikey his nickname after nine o'clock Mass one Sunday. Johnny had just finished escorting Mikey's mother down the church steps because Mikey was incapacitated at the time. It was his turn to "hug the bowl," as they endearingly called it.

"Good morning, Mary," Father Burke sang in his best Irish brogue. (He was born on Jerome Avenue in the Bronx.) "And where's the Mayor of Lexington Avenue?" He looked at Johnny, who didn't have a clue what he was talking about.

"Who?" Mary Kelly asked.

"Young Michael. The Mayor of Lexington Avenue." He repeated the title as if they both should have recognized it as a matter of course.

"And why do you call him that, Father?" she asked. They were standing on the sidewalk in front of the church. It was a beautiful, sunny Sunday morning but Mary Kelly, the mother of three boys, was sure a very dark rain cloud was about to pass over her head. "The Mayor of Lexington Avenue" was a prelude to something bad, she was sure.

"Well, Mary," Father Burke replied, "the boy serves Mass for these people. He ushers them in and out of church on Sunday. He delivers their dry-cleaning and shines their shoes — all with that smile of his. He knows everybody and everybody knows him. He's more popular than me and I've got God and the pulpit on my side."

"Why thank you, Father," Mary replied, wondering where this was going. She found out soon enough.

"He's seventeen now, Mary. Has he ever thought of the priesthood? He'd make an excellent priest. Perhaps you should mention it to him." Johnny wanted to crawl under the car that he was leaning on at the time. He had no idea why Father Burke broached the subject while he was there. He just hoped he wasn't next. His mother was already thinking that way. Just one word from Father Burke and they'd be packing him up and shipping him off to the seminary. He hadn't even gotten laid yet. He stared straight down at the sidewalk and waited for Mrs. Kelly to give up her youngest son, his best friend. "Better him than me" was the thought that whizzed through his brain.

Mary Kelly was not about to deliver Mikey to the priesthood, that morning or ever. She understood how people could see Mikey as some sort of angelic person: the red hair, the freckles, the smile — that smile. He had a little space between his two front teeth that made it even more enchanting. Not to say it wasn't genuine. Mikey had a zest for life and an affection for people that was unique. But he was no angel. Neither was this tall, pimple-faced sixteen-year-old next to her — his partner in crime. They were all boy and they were heading in many directions at once but none of those roads led to the priesthood — Mary Kelly was sure of that!

"Thank you for suggesting that, Father. I'll certainly talk to Michael and my husband about it." Father Burke smiled back but he could tell far better than Johnny that she was not interested.

Johnny couldn't wait to tell Mikey about the conversation. He found him in the bathroom, the one on the second floor that nobody else used.

"You can't have anybody come in while you're puking," Mikey had told him that very first morning when they were searching for a place for Johnny to spill his guts.

Mikey was leaning over the bowl but he appeared to be done. He might have had a few more dry heaves in him but nothing more of substance was coming out.

"Something real bad just happened," Johnny said. Mikey was in no mood for games. The headache was on him now and he was hanging on for dear life.

"Whaat?"

"*Father Burke just told your mother you'd make a good priest. He asked her to talk to you and she said she would — with your dad.*" Mikey, in all his pain, ventured a weak laugh, although he didn't move from the bowl. He wasn't laughing so much at what Johnny said but the way he said it. As if his parents were going to stuff him in a bag and deliver him to Father Burke.

"*What's so funny?*" Johnny asked, a little angry that Mikey wasn't as upset as himself.

"*My mother was just being polite to Father Burke. She's not going to talk to me and neither is my father. It's nothin'.*" Johnny was a little disappointed at Mikey's reaction, so he gave him the other piece of news.

"*He called you the Mayor of Lexington Avenue.*"

"*Who?*"

"*Father Burke. He said you knew more people than he did and he had the pulpit.*" Mikey just smiled.

"*I like it,*" Mikey said. "*It's a perfect nickname for you.*"

"*Me? He didn't say it about me, he said it about you.*"

"*Who cares what he said. You're the Mayor of Lexington Avenue. You know as many people as me. Besides, a mayor's got to be smart and he's got to know how to run things. That's you, Johnny, not me. People look up to you. They know you got something that the rest of us don't have.*"

"*Really?*" Johnny asked. "*Me?*"

"*Yup. That's why the Mayor of Lexington Avenue is so perfect for you. I'm going to make a prediction, Johnny. Someday, you're going to do something great — like the things a mayor does. I'm not sure what it is or even if it's one thing but it'll be about me and you. And when it's over — because you'll finish it, whatever it is, you finish everything you start — I want you to remember this day and what I told you.*"

"*Come on, Mikey. You're scaring me with this vision voodoo shit. Why don't we just forget about what Father Burke said.*"

"*No. Now tell me you'll remember.*"

"*C'mon, cut it out.*"

"*Tell me, Johnny.*"

"*All right, I'll remember. I promise.*"

"Good. Now, if Father Burke knew the other half of the people we know, he'd have another name for the both of us."

~

The "other half" were the people in the neighborhood Father Burke would never meet. Jimmy the Shoemaker's was a great place to meet those people. So were the streets between two and six in the morning when your parents thought you were sleeping.

Jimmy the Shoemaker was actually a shoe repairman. The neighborhood bestowed the title of "Shoemaker" on him because he was so adept at his craft. Nicknames — they were everywhere. On Saturdays, however, Jimmy did double duty, plying another trade at which he would never excel. Jimmy Donatello liked to gamble about as much as he liked to breathe and, although he worked hard and was an excellent shoe repairman, he tried not to let work interfere with his gambling, especially on Saturday.

The front part of the store, although it contained the one big noisy machine Jimmy needed to do his repairs, was rather small. Mikey worked the shoeshine booth, which was elevated and had two chairs each equipped with "golden stirrups" where customers set their feet for the shine. Mikey always positioned their feet just right before he began his work.

"The worst thing that can happen," he told his young protégé Johnny, "is one of their feet fall off the stirrup. So set it in there good. Lock the heel in place."

All the action happened in the back room, which was larger than the front. It started at eight in the morning when Jimmy opened up. Artie was the first to arrive. Artie was like clockwork. He was usually there before the boys and sometimes before Jimmy. Being the low man on the totem pole, Johnny's first job on Saturday morning was to go up the block to Pete's restaurant for coffee and cigarettes. He loved those early weekend mornings when the city was just waking up and the streets were empty except for the shopkeepers working like busy little ants, setting up for the day. There was something so clean and crisp and serene about it all. Pete would start to prepare the containers of coffee as soon as he walked in the door. There was no need to speak. The orders were the same every Saturday — Jimmy was milk and one sugar, Artie was black, no sugar and the boys were regular (milk and two sugars).

By the time he returned to the store, the first game of blackjack had already begun. The front door had a little bell so Jimmy in the back room could hear a customer entering. He had a great knack for leaving a game, waiting on a customer, and jumping right in where he left off. On Saturdays, however, he had the added luxury of Mikey, who had worked at the store for years. He not only knew how to use the machines and repair shoes, he knew the customers. Jimmy took great pride in knowing a customer's shoes without ever looking at a ticket. By watching closely, Mikey had acquired the same talent. He practically ran the store on Saturdays and while he was busy taking care of customers, Johnny would shine shoes. The boys lived for Saturdays.

Vito showed up with Carmine at ten and the craps game began. The back room was full by then, which meant there were ten guys back there at most. Smoke so thick you couldn't see yourself, and dark except for a few lights in the corners where the games were being played — a real den of iniquity. Everybody talked at once and money passed from one hand to the next with words like, "I got twenty on this one" or "I got you covered." On the rare occasions they were allowed to go in the back, the boys were mesmerized by the show.

Vito was their favorite. Vito was cool. He was always impeccably dressed and he always stopped for a shine before going in the back. It wasn't just that he gave a big tip, although that helped. Vito actually noticed them, spent some time with them, showed an interest in their lives. To everybody else they were just kids, although that changed when Mikey spread the word that Johnny was the "Mayor of Lexington Avenue." After that, everybody wanted to get a shine from "Hizzoner." Johnny didn't like it at first. He felt like a fraud since Father Burke had pinned the name on Mikey, but he started feeling better about it when his pockets were bulging with dollar bills.

"You boys pokin' any of them high school girls yet?" Vito would ask every week.

"Yeah. Three this week," Mikey would reply. Sometimes he'd change the number. It didn't matter. Vito knew he was lying.

"Listen to old Vito," he would say —he was about thirty-five at the time. "You gotta treat them nice. Treat them with respect and they'll be all over you. You gotta dress nice too. They don't wanna go out with no bums." Then he'd laugh and the boys would laugh with him and he'd prance into the back room. Vito was a dandy in his silk shirts and shark-skin pants but the boys knew he was not a person to mess with.

At one or thereabouts, Frank would arrive. He never came alone and he never entered the store until Jimmy came out and invited him in. Guys were running out of money by one o'clock, and Frank was there to replenish their pockets.

Frank was a loan shark and his arrival always caused a stir. When Jimmy went out to get him, some guys would disappear, quickly walking out the front door, their shoulders hunched, their hats down over their foreheads. They never acknowledged Frank and he never acknowledged them.

"Frank's a gentleman," Jimmy told the boys one day after everyone had left. "He never tries to collect when he's at my store." Apparently the guys who disappeared every week when Frank arrived didn't know about that part of the arrangement.

Gambling was only part of the program at the shoe store. Jimmy's nephew Tony worked around the block at Doc Feeney's animal hospital. Doc was a regular shine but only on weekday afternoons, never weekends. He always sat in the same chair, put his already-shined-the-day-before loafers on the golden stirrups and philosophized about life. Two things were constant with Doc: He was always drunk, although most folks couldn't tell, and he included everyone in the conversation.

"What are you kids smoking for?" he challenged Mikey and Johnny one afternoon, a cigarette dangling from his jaundiced fingers. Doc had the knack of hanging an ash on his cigarette forever. He wouldn't flick the ash off and he wouldn't allow it to drop of its own accord.

"'Cause we like it," Mikey replied. Mikey was respectful but never deferential to adults.

"Yeah. But it'll kill you. If I knew then what I know now, I never woulda started."

"Why don't you quit?" Mikey asked.

"Can't. Besides, I like it too much. If I'm gonna go, why not go from something I like?"

Jimmy piped in then. "Hey, ya go when your time's up. There was a guy in this neighborhood, you know, a rich guy from Park Avenue, rich like you, Doc." They all laughed at Doc, who was from Westchester. "I used to do his shoes. This guy ran every day — over to the park, around the reservoir. Never smoked, never drank. Every time he came in here he was drinking orange juice. Dropped dead on the street at thirty-five years old. When your time comes, it comes."

"When my time comes, I want to be pickled," Doc replied. Johnny and Mikey looked at each other. That was one wish they knew was going to come true.

Carl worked for Doc. He'd been at the animal hospital for twenty years and like Doc, Carl was always drunk. The difference was that Carl actually looked drunk. He was black and Doc made him wear a blue uniform, probably so people would think he was the janitor or something. His pants were always hanging down below the crack, which you couldn't see because his shirt was always hanging out over his pants. Carl only had a few teeth and they were a cross between yellow-green and dark brown. His cigarette, a Lucky Strike, was always dangling from his lips about to fall every time he opened his mouth, which was constantly. For the first year they knew him, the boys never understood a word Carl said, partly because of the way he talked and partly because of his constant state of inebriation. Eventually, they picked up the language, just like people living in a foreign country start understanding what people around them are saying. Osmosis maybe. Whatever. When they finally started to understand, the boys found Carl to be quite funny.

Doc was funny too in his own sardonic way, but Doc was an aristocrat — perfectly manicured, perfect white teeth, richly dressed. The thought that the two worked closely together was hysterical.

It wasn't until Jimmy's nephew Tony started working at the animal hospital that the boys — and Jimmy — learned just how close Carl and the Doc were.

"Carl does everything, including the surgeries," Tony told them. "The Doc and Carl make the diagnosis together, then Doc goes and meets the people in his office. They never see Carl. He comes to work through the back door."

"No kiddin'?" Jimmy asked. He was as surprised as the boys.

"Yeah," Tony replied. "I'm his assistant and I don't know nothin'. Carl gives 'em the anesthesia and cuts 'em open, jawin' all the time about who knows what. If those people from Park Avenue ever found out about who was operating on their animals, we'd all be in jail."

"Well, I'll be," Jimmy murmured. "Old Doc's got more balls than I thought. I don't think Carl ever got past the third grade."

～

Mikey was right, Father Burke didn't know the half of it.

[ F I F T E E N ]

Joaquin Sanchez bought a boat with a trailer the day he retired from the Miami police department. It was a used twenty-six-foot outboard whaler with one seat and a small canvas canopy. Joaquin didn't want or need any company. Like Rudy, Joaquin enjoyed nothing better in life than to be on the water by himself — observing, feeling, being a part of nature. Catching fish was secondary. Joaquin had a fish camp just outside of Indiantown on a small tributary that fed into Lake Okeechobee. When he wanted to fish for grouper or mahi, he trailered his boat from his home in Homestead to the Keys. It was a solitary life but one he enjoyed totally.

"After twenty-five years being a Mexican cop in a Cuban town, I deserve to do nothing," he told his friend and former partner Dick Radek over the phone one day. He was kidding but he meant it, too. Only Dick, who had served beside him for twenty years in patrol and as a detective, understood both the humor and the serious side of the statement. Discrimination had many layers. Cubans, who were often snubbed by whites, rarely missed the opportunity to harass the Mexican cop for nothing more than doing his job.

Dick was a private investigator now, making big money with some hotshot lawyer in Vero Beach. They usually talked once a week. They had watched each other's backs and saved each other's lives too many times to lose track at this point.

"I'm going to be like your ex-wife," Dick told Joaquin when he retired. "You're never going to be able to get rid of me."

Joaquin laughed. "Don't sell yourself short, my friend. You're much better-looking than she was."

From time to time, when Dick needed help on a job, he called Joaquin. He called him ten minutes after Tracey gave him the Bass Creek assignment.

"Hey partner, wanna make some extra change?"

"Not really. Working as an executive for Exxon for all those years, retiring with that multimillion-dollar severance, I don't need the money. But humor me — do I get to spy on the wife this time? Is she decent-looking? Does she have bamboo curtains?"

Dick started howling at that one. He'd hired Joaquin to work a domestic case years before when Tracey had experimented for a time representing the rich and famous in their marriage dissolutions. Joaquin's assignment was to follow the stunningly beautiful wife, who the husband believed was cheating on him. For some unknown reason she had decorated her bathroom with bamboo curtains. They looked nice but at night when the lights were turned on, they were, well, pretty much transparent. Joaquin called Dick first thing the next morning.

"I'm in love," he crooned.

"What happened?"

"You mean after she did a striptease in front of the bathroom window?"

"You're shittin' me."

"I shit you not. Come by yourself tonight. I'll buy the popcorn."

That night Dick and Joaquin took turns sharing binoculars in the bushes watching Mrs. Jane Ashland prance around her bathroom buck-naked. They felt like teenagers seeing a naked woman for the first time.

～

"This assignment isn't so rosy," Dick remarked, bringing them both back to the present.

"Don't be cagey with me, Dick. What is it?"

"Have you read anything about a murder a month ago in a little town called Bass Creek?" Dick already knew the answer. Being a former homicide detective, Joaquin read about every murder that hit the papers and he was undoubtedly familiar with the details.

"The woman whose throat was slit in her bed? Didn't they just arrest the kid who worked at the convenience store?"

"You mean our client."

"Our client. I see. Okay, you got me —what do you need me to do?"

"The murder was in the barrio. Tracey wants me to go over there and hang out and find out everything I can, basically redo and expand the police investigation. I just got their report. As you can imagine, it's pretty flimsy. Those yahoos couldn't find a hippopotamus in an ant farm." Joaquin couldn't help but laugh.

"Anyway, I figured I would stick out like a sore thumb but you wouldn't."

"You mean there's a difference between me and you other than the fact that I'm much better-looking?"

"Yeah, you've been out in the sun a lot more than me. Whaddya think? It'll probably take a couple of weeks."

"I'm *not* working in the fields." It was Dick's turn to laugh. Talking to Joaquin was good for him, the only time he laughed anymore.

"You *can't* work in the fields, Joaquin. You're too old. Nobody would hire you. Just find the local hooch joint and hang around. Get to know the people in the neighborhood. We need to find more witnesses."

"Are you telling me how to be a detective?"

"Nothing more than I did for the last twenty years."

Four days later, a Monday, Joaquin and his boat arrived in Bass Creek. He rented an efficiency at the Skyline Motel for two weeks. If anybody inquired, Joaquin was a retired truck driver in town for a couple of weeks of fishing. And he intended to fish. He hadn't been on this side of the big lake in a long time.

Joaquin spent his first evening hanging out in the barrio, getting the vibe. He'd already studied the police report and written down the names of streets and witnesses. His first stop was the convenience store where Rudy worked. Benny Dragone was behind the counter. Joaquin picked up some Red Man chewing tobacco, some Cokes and a bag of chips.

"What's biting these days?" he asked Benny.

"Not much of a fisherman myself, sorry," Benny said as he rang up the items.

Joaquin plowed ahead. "Any decent place around here I can park my butt for a couple of drinks?"

Benny didn't even look up. "Rosa's is two blocks down. It ain't much, a beer and wine joint."

"That'll do. Ain't lookin' for nothin' fancy. Much obliged." Joaquin walked out, intending to head next for Mercer Street and the scene of the crime. He'd wanted to pick the grocer's brain a little more, but Benny hadn't exactly been a scintillating conversationalist and had even seemed a little wary of Joaquin. He decided to play it safe and turned instead for the motel — just in case Benny was watching.

Benny was. He followed Joaquin's progress from the window, saw him walk the two blocks to the Skyline. Saw the boat outside on the trailer. Only then did he relax. He didn't know why, but he was distrustful of just about everybody these days.

That night Joaquin took a short walk that ended at Rosa's. Benny wasn't lying; it wasn't much — a hole in the wall with a few stools at the bar, a dartboard and some tables in the back. Bob Marley was playing on the jukebox. Joaquin pulled up one of the stools and ordered a cerveza from the middle-aged woman behind the bar, who seemed about as chatty as Benny. He drank quietly for a half hour or so until the bar started to fill up. Rosa seemed to pick up when the crowd did.

"Another cerveza?" she asked him.

"Sure." Some of the patrons who had just come in eyed him suspiciously. Joaquin knew it was time to get his story out. He struck up a conversation with the man sitting next to him, a fisherman himself of sorts.

"I catch frogs," Geraldo Martine told him after a couple of beers. "Sell them to the big restaurants. They're what you call a delicacy." *Some way to make a living,* Joaquin was about to say, but he knew Geraldo would take it as an insult so he kept it to himself.

"So how do you catch them?"

"Gotta go out in the dark, along shore. You can hear 'em and even see their eyes. They glow, you know." Joaquin didn't know. He also didn't know if Geraldo was making it up as he went or not. He just nodded, trying to appear as interested as possible. "Then you shine your flashlight right into their eyes. It freezes 'em. And you stab 'em with a long pole. You gotta be quick and you gotta be fast."

Joaquin nodded again. "I'd love to see you do that sometime."

"Be at the boat dock at four in the mornin', any mornin', and I'll take you out."

"I just might take you up on that," Joaquin assured him, then he nonchalantly unloaded his story about being retired and coming to Bass Creek to fish. After that, he paid for his two beers and left. He knew Geraldo would tell the others.

It seemed safe now, so Joaquin took a detour down Mercer Street on his way home. He walked by Pilar Rodriguez's house — whose lawn Rudy had fertilized with the contents of his stomach a few weeks before. The house was dark. He proceeded farther down the street to Lucy Ochoa's trailer, which was also dark and looked abandoned. Joaquin knew it was going to stay that way for a long time. He walked on to Ray Castro's place, hoping he might find him and José Guerrero sitting on the stoop drinking a beer. There were lights on inside but nobody outside he could casually chat with. He stood there for a moment, looking back in the direction of the abandoned trailer. He couldn't actually see it because it was set back, but the path to it was less than a hundred yards away. After reading the police investigation, Joaquin had become convinced that the key to breaking this case was somewhere in the mix between Ray Castro, José Guerrero and the mysterious Geronimo guy the two of them had mentioned. He could smell it from the report itself: These guys weren't telling the truth. And why did this Geronimo suddenly disappear? If he could find a connection between Lucy Ochoa and Ray, José or Geronimo, that would be a good start. He then had to make up those hundred yards and put one of them in the trailer the night of Lucy's murder.

He decided to fish only in the morning. In the late afternoon he'd take a walk, maybe meet some of the neighbors, strike up a chat about Lucy — who her friends were, that sort of thing. He didn't plan on re-interviewing Ray or José or Pilar until he had picked up as much information as he could. Of course, if he ran into them during his sauntering, he'd try to steer the conversation in the right direction.

At four o'clock the next morning he was standing at the boat ramp waiting for Geraldo, who didn't show up until almost five. He'd taken Geraldo for a talker. Maybe, just maybe, out on the lake in the early morning hours, he might learn something about the characters he was pursuing. Geraldo didn't notice him at first; he was busy setting his small boat in the water. Joaquin came up behind him.

"Told you I'd take you up on your invitation," he said almost in a whisper. Geraldo, who was in his own little world, almost jumped out of his shoes.

"Jesus, you scared me," he said with no look of recognition in his eyes. Joaquin picked up on it right away.

"I'm Joaquin. We met at Rosa's last night. You invited me to come out on the boat with you."

Geraldo hesitated for a moment, wondering if he was going to end up as a distant memory washed up on shore if he took this guy out with him. Then a very dim light went off in his brain and his suspicions ebbed.

"Oh yeah, I remember now," he replied. "Let me just get my pole and my flashlight and we'll head out. Sorry I'm late."

"No problem."

They set out on Geraldo's rowboat, which was fitted with a fifteen-horsepower motor. It took about twenty minutes to reach the lake. Geraldo made a quick left turn and cut the motor, pulling it out of the water. He then set his oars and began to row in towards shore.

"The motor scares 'em," he whispered. "Gotta be real quiet." They were the first words he'd spoken since they left the dock. Close to shore, Geraldo pulled in the oars and let the boat drift. His left hand grabbed his flashlight, his right a long pole with a pointed end like a spear. He looked in at the shoreline with an intensity that surprised Joaquin.

Joaquin was used to being out on the water before dawn, just drifting, listening, hearing nothing but the occasional splash of a wave or a fish jumping — but this experience was quite different. There was no moon. The lake behind them was a vast black canvas of nothingness, the shore like a jungle. A cool breeze was blowing across the water, making it much chillier than the sixty-degree temperature. Joaquin, in a short-sleeve tee shirt, was hugging himself. The shore was alive with the sound of scurrying creatures. Frogs were burping and crickets were droning. It made the experienced old detective a little jumpy. He half expected the Swamp Thing to rise out of the murky water at any moment and devour the two of them. Just then, Geraldo snapped his flashlight on and lunged with the long pole at something on the shore.

"Got 'im," he whispered. "First of the day." He pulled a fairly large frog into the boat and slid it off the pole into what appeared to be a shoebox. He repeated this procedure about twenty more times before light started to break on the horizon. Then, without a word, he moved the motor back in position in the water, started it and headed for home. At no time during the entire trip did Joaquin see any frog's eyes — or any frog, for that matter, before Geraldo had it skewered. And at no time, including the ride back, did Geraldo utter a thing other than "Got 'im." Apparently, the man saved his conversation for Rosa's.

At the dock, Geraldo packed up quickly. "Gotta sell these babies to the restaurants so I can get to Rosa's at a decent hour." And then he was off, leaving Joaquin standing there trying to figure out how much Geraldo could possibly make from this business.

By the third night of his trip, the suspicious stares had disappeared and Joaquin started to settle in at Rosa's. Geraldo was now his best friend. Apparently somewhere out there in the chilly darkness they had bonded. Geraldo had no useful information for Joaquin but he introduced him to everybody. Joaquin now had a routine: In the late afternoon he would walk the streets near Mercer making idle talk with the neighbors and hoping to pick up some useful tidbits. At night, he was a fixture at Rosa's. He'd seen Pilar a few times during the first week but never had an opportunity to speak to her. Ray and José were nowhere to be found. It wasn't until Wednesday of the following week that Joaquin's routine produced anything worthwhile.

His name was Pablo Gonzalez. He was one of Rosa's regulars, a tall, heavyset man with a wide face, thick lips and a flat nose. He usually sat at the opposite end of the bar from where Joaquin made his nest. Joaquin had caught Pablo staring at him from time to time. It wasn't a pleasant look, either: Joaquin was an interloper in Pablo's lair. But on this Wednesday night, Pablo came in and sat right next to Joaquin, who was already nursing his first of the day. Pablo didn't say anything at first but after a couple, his tongue started rolling. He was from Cuba, a baseball player in his youth but now a Dolphin fan.

"That Billy Purcell, man what a pitcher he would have made," Pablo said with a slight shake of his head. Joaquin nodded. He was a fan of the Dolphin quarterback himself. "One of these days he's going to win the big one," Pablo continued. Joaquin agreed again. Eventually, after a few more beers and shared sports stories, when the alcohol had taken hold enough to make them believe they were friends, Pablo told Joaquin about his trip across the ocean to

America. It had been the man's defining moment.

"We left just after dark, a moonless night," Pablo began. "Those bastards always lie to you when they're taking your money. You'd a thought we were taking an excursion on a damn yacht, not forty of us on a boat that fit ten. It was cold and the waves were high. The boat was a piece of shit and the motor kept quitting. I knew we were never going to make it. Just before dawn, a storm hit and the boat capsized. We were miles offshore, how many I couldn't tell. I grabbed one of the tires that had been lashed to the side of the boat and so did four others. We just started to kick in the direction the boat had been heading. And we prayed. At least, I did." At that moment Pablo put his hand on Joaquin's arm. "My friend, I tell you I was sure I was going to die that night. I was waiting for a shark to rip my legs off. But we made it through the night and the blistering hot sun the next day and the next night. By that second night I didn't care anymore. The sea, the sharks — whoever wanted to could have me. We hit shore at dawn the next day. Dehydrated. Exhausted. Only three of us were left. The other two simply drifted off into the night. I didn't know them at all but I think about them every night. I see them in my dreams. I know every detail of their faces although I didn't when they were alive. I still keep in touch with the others." He was silent after that, as if the story had drained the life out of him all over again. Joaquin was silent for a time, too. He knew about these things. Now it was his turn.

"We didn't have an ocean to cross, just a little river that could be treacherous in parts. I'd heard of people stepping in a hole and never being seen again, taken under by the current. We had woods and open fields to cross and border guards who would pick you off like a wooden duck in a sharpshooting contest. I made it okay. Some of my friends didn't." Pablo squeezed his arm when he was finished. They were both silent for a long time after that, praying to their beers.

"Now we live like kings, eh?" Pablo laughed. "More like paupers."

"You're right," Joaquin replied. "But what's the alternative?

Cuba? Mexico?" Pablo just nodded, his head low. He loved his country but he knew he could never go back.

"Yep. I guess that's the best we can say about America: What's the alternative? But it's getting worse — crime and drugs everywhere, even a small town like this." There it was, hanging out there — an opportunity. Joaquin took it slow.

"I heard about the murder here a few weeks ago."

"Right around the block," Pablo said, nodding toward the door. "A young gal — they slit her throat. You want to catch the bastard who did that and strangle him with your bare hands, know what I mean?" Joaquin nodded.

"Thank God they did catch the guy," he prompted Pablo, who didn't need much prompting.

"They caught shit. Those idiots couldn't catch the right guy if he bit 'em in the ass. They locked up this kid because he's stupid."

"What?" Joaquin asked, trying to look surprised. He hated playing this game with Pablo but he convinced himself they were both after the same thing.

"Yeah." Pablo was excited now. "They locked up this retarded kid — I guess he's not retarded all the way but he's slow. Nice kid — wouldn't, couldn't, hurt a fly. He works at the convenience store right down the block. They go in — Frick and Frack, Bass Creek's finest — and browbeat this kid until he supposedly confesses. Meanwhile, the real killer is miles away."

"Who's the real killer?" Joaquin asked. It was the logical next question. Pablo looked at him. Looked around. He realized he'd started this story and he had an obligation to finish. He leaned closer to Joaquin and out of the side of his mouth said, "A guy named Geronimo — you know, like the Indian chief."

"No last name?" Joaquin asked.

"Not that I know of."

"How do you know this guy did it?" Joaquin was trying not to sound like a cop but he didn't want to lose his best — perhaps his only — lead. He ordered two more beers and took a small stainless steel flask out of his back pocket. "Join me in a little kicker?"

Pablo smiled. This Joaquin was all right. He took a long pull, followed it with a swig of beer, wiped his mouth with his arm and resumed his story.

"There's a guy I knew named Ray who lived on Mercer Street — hung out on his stoop most nights with a buddy drinking beers. He said this Geronimo used to stop by all the time and bum a beer." Pablo leaned closer and continued in his conspiratorial tone. "He was there the night of the murder."

Joaquin handed the flask to his new best friend, who might just need some help getting the rest of this out. Pablo took another long drink. "Apparently Geronimo was having a thing with this woman who was killed. Her name was Lucy. She was a little loose, to be honest with you. Anyway, the kid from the store was at her trailer that night — Ray and his friend saw him go in and they all saw him later coming from that direction, stumbling down the street, then throwing up on somebody's lawn. Ray said Geronimo got pissed when he found out the kid had been at Lucy's and headed for the trailer. He went behind some other house or something because they didn't actually see him go in. But they know he did it. He disappeared right after that. Both of them said he was a badass dude. Always carried a knife."

Joaquin himself took a hit from the flask. "Did they tell the police?"

"Not really. They mentioned that he was there but that's it."

"Why?"

"You know. In this community you don't ever tell the police more than you have to. And they were afraid Geronimo might kill them. They didn't know those idiots were going to charge the kid."

"Well, what about now? Geronimo's gone. An innocent man's in jail."

"Now would be a good time but those boys were spooked. They could finger Geronimo and he knew it. They're long gone — out of the country. Ray was from Guatemala; he went back there. The other guy, I don't know, Nicaragua maybe. I don't think anyone will ever find them, though." He motioned to Joaquin for the flask, poured some of the whiskey into his beer and drained the mug. He looked relieved.

But Joaquin wasn't finished.

"Why don't you tell the police what you know?"

"Me, an old drunken Cuban? Amigo, do you honestly believe they would listen to anything I have to say?"

"Why did this guy Ray tell you?" He was really sounding like a cop now but Pablo was drunk enough not to notice.

"I knew his father years ago. We were close. He had to tell somebody. It burns inside your stomach like hot tar. You have to tell someone. I had to tell you. Now it's done. I just hope that boy gets off."

The conversation ended after that. Joaquin ordered another round and they just sat drinking the last beer in silence. Joaquin knew his undercover work was done for the night.

He decided to stay in town one more day. He wanted to talk to Pilar and comb the neighborhood one last time.

He was at Pilar Rodriguez's house at eight the next morning.

"Ma'am, my name is Joaquin Sanchez. I'm a private investigator." He showed her his investigator's license. "I'm investigating the murder of Lucy Ochoa."

"Are you working for Elena?" she asked eagerly. She was about sixty, with a weathered face but a strong, thick body.

"Yes, ma'am, for her lawyer."

"You tell Elena or her lawyer that I can't identify Rudy. I already told the police that. Tell Elena I *won't* identify him. I misspoke that night, that's all. I plan on telling her myself, just haven't gotten around to it."

Joaquin chatted with her a while longer before trying to politely exit. But Pilar was like a battery-operated, nonstop talking machine and it was impossible to turn her off once she got started. "They fired her, you know. Poor thing. Threw her out of the hotel and everything. No respect. They treat you like a dog even though you work your fingers to the bone for them. I know. She got another job waitressing over in Silver Creek, about five miles away. She lives in a broken-down old trailer two streets over. I should have been by to visit already."

Joaquin didn't know if she was ever going to take a breath. He waited patiently, his left foot behind his right, ready to run when the occasion presented itself. "It's a crying shame what they did to her," Pilar continued. Then, as if on cue, she started to cry.

Joaquin felt terrible but he knew this was his chance. He patted Pilar on the shoulder, then bolted for his pickup.

"I'm sorry for your troubles," he shouted over his shoulder as he scurried down the driveway.

On Friday morning, he hitched his boat trailer early and headed straight for Vero. Dick Radek was waiting for him when he arrived.

"Catch any fish?"

"Plenty, but not the kind you're looking for." Joaquin told him about Pablo, Ray Castro, José Guerrero, and Geronimo. "This guy Geronimo did it but nobody's around who can finger him. I spent my last day interviewing everybody in the neighborhood who would talk to me. Nobody knew his last name and nobody ever saw him with Lucy. At least that's what they told me."

"We can't even tie him to the girl?"

"Nope. Apparently they never went out. He just showed up at the trailer."

Dick banged the desk in disgust.

"This really sucks. We know who the killer is but we have no proof. You got any ideas about how to find this Geronimo guy?"

"Not without a last name. We could check payroll records for the pickers. Maybe find out where he lived and see if we can get the rent receipts. But these guys are illegals. You're almost certainly not going to find anything in writing. Everything is under the table."

"Yeah, but we need to try anyway. Anything else?" Joaquin told him about his conversation with Pilar and his struggle to get away.

"Don't get me wrong, Dick. She was a very nice lady and she cares about this boy and his mother, but I felt like I was back home in the kitchen and my ex was screaming about something and I couldn't get out." Dick just laughed.

"Good job, Joaquin. You turned over the only stones that could be found."

"I'll send you a written report. Keep me posted," he said as headed for the door.

"Sure will," Dick replied. "I'll call you next week." As soon as Joaquin left, Dick headed downstairs to talk to the boss.

Tracey was not as upset as Dick thought she would be. "Every cloud has a silver lining — even this one, Dick."

"How do you figure?"

"Well, we didn't find the killer and we probably won't be able to find the two guys who could finger him." Dick nodded. He was with her so far. "But Clay Evans has no witnesses to place Rudy at the scene, either. Two are gone and, if Pilar Rodriguez is true to her word and I believe she will be, the third won't be able to make the identification. Which means, if we can suppress Rudy's confession, he walks."

"What about the blood?" It was a question he could have answered for himself if he had taken any time to think, but Tracey was moving a little too fast for him.

"Oh yeah, the blood," Tracey said with a smirk. "That'll help them. Rudy's got the most common blood type in the world. The blood is meaningless. The confession is everything."

The conversation bothered Tracey for another reason, however, which she didn't share with Dick. If Elena had lost her job and her home and was living in a trailer in the barrio as Pilar had reported, she was destitute. There would be no more money forthcoming and the retainer was almost gone. *She got the money the last time*, Tracey told herself. *Maybe she can do it again.*

[ S I X T E E N ]

Despite his initial trepidation (to put it mildly) when he first learned that Tracey James was going to represent Rudy, the Fourth had started to feel more confident each day as the proceedings moved along. He would still have to convince Harry Tuthill to stay on board but was confident he could. After all, Harry had come this far with him.

Tracey had filed a Motion to Set Bail that was a joke. Bail was set at $150,000 and Rudy remained in jail. She had also called him about having her psychiatrist see Rudy in jail.

"I could file a motion," she'd told him. "But I'm hoping we can avoid that."

"What are your grounds for the psychiatric evaluation?" Clay asked, knowing he had no basis to refuse. She was either trying to set up an insanity defense or a fitness to stand trial defense.

"I want to try to show that Rudy did not have the capacity to refuse to talk to Detective Brume."

Clay almost started laughing into the phone. "I'm not sure I'm familiar with that motion."

"I don't know if it has ever been argued before."

"Well, you certainly have the right to make the argument. Why don't you send me a stipulation and I'll forward it to the judge."

"Fine."

There was only one circuit judge in Cobb County, Gabriel Wentwell, and Clay had appeared before him enough times to know that the motion Tracey planned to file wasn't going to fly anyplace but straight into the trash can. Judge Wentwell was a fine man in many ways: distinguished military career, church deacon, good family, and a good lawyer. His tenure as a judge had been marked with the same colorless consistency as the rest of his life. There were no surprises with Judge Wentwell — no politics, no favoritism. He was not the kind of man who was going to go out on a limb for some novel theory of law. He'd listen politely and he would pause appropriately to think about it, but ultimately he would just brush it aside in favor of the known, traditional rule of law.

Clay didn't know — or care — what sort of evidence his opponent might present to try to make her point. His confidence was brimming again, and all he could think about was what a cakewalk this was turning out to be after all. But there were other things he didn't know that might have given him more pause. He didn't know that Ray Castro and José Guerrero had left town, because Wes had never told him. He also didn't know that Pilar Rodriguez had come in for a lineup and failed to identify Rudy. As far as he knew, he had three witnesses ready and waiting.

Elena didn't tell Rudy that she had lost her job and had to move out of the hotel. She thought it would upset him too much, but she underestimated her son. Rudy was doing well in the county jail sticking with his routine. He had made friends with the guards and some of the other prisoners, one of whom, Juan Morales, was a prison veteran. Juan, like Rudy, was Puerto Rican, a skinny little fast-talking, chain-smoking con man who had all the answers. He took Rudy under his wing and gave him some expert advice about how to handle himself if he ended up in the general prison population.

"In the beginning, you wanna act a little crazy. Most of 'em are afraid of kooks. All you wanna do is be left alone. I don't wanna tell you this but you're young and handsome, they'll be on you like shit on flypaper." Rudy tried to picture shit on flypaper but he couldn't. He had no idea what Juan meant but Juan was on a roll — he didn't have time to stop and explain things. "You're gonna be tested early. You can wait or you can make the first move."

"The first move?"

"Yeah. You know, kick somebody's ass. Pick a white guy. The blacks and Latinos will like that. Beat him good but not too bad. You don't wanna create a vendetta or anything."

"How do I start a fight with somebody I don't know?"

"You catch his eye, then you say, 'Are you lookin' at me? Are you lookin' at me?' Say it louder the second time so everybody will hear you. The shower's a perfect place because it gets the point across. Then you hit him and you don't stop hittin' him till he's down. Pick a big guy. The biggest, toughest-lookin' white guy you can find."

Rudy certainly appreciated Juan taking the time to tutor him on prison life. One thing puzzled him, though: Juan was about five foot two and a hundred and thirty pounds soaking wet and he didn't know karate like Rudy did. How did he get by? Something inside told him not to ask the question.

So Rudy was doing just fine, but he could tell from his mother's face during her most recent visits that something was wrong and it wasn't what was happening to him. At first she had handled his situation with a fighter's disposition and had actually been upbeat when Tracey took the case. Now she was sad all the time, her shoulders slumped. When he asked about the hotel and all the regulars, her answers were short and didn't really tell him anything. Usually she loved talking about the colorful cast of characters who breathed life into the old place on a daily basis. Rudy's first inclination was to ask a direct question, but once again something inside told him to let it go.

[ **S E V E N T E E N** ]

As soon as H.V. gave Tracey the word that he was ready, she filed her Motion to Suppress and set it for hearing on the judge's calendar. She made sure she reserved enough time to present all her witnesses. The motion itself was nondescript, reciting only the basic theory that she had already related to Clay. She didn't want to give him any more notice than she had to, afraid that he might wake up to what was coming. The Fourth should have caught on, however, when she set a simple motion for an all-day evidentiary hearing. Tracey was coming loaded for bear. It was up to Judge Wentwell to determine if she had brought the right ammunition.

The Fourth was desperately trying to stir up some publicity for the case at the early stages. He called a *very* good friend of his from one of the Miami television stations, but he couldn't convince her that it was worthwhile to send a news team up for a motion hearing.

"Don't worry, Clay, I'll send somebody up for the trial," Stacey Wilson assured him. "Better yet, I'll come myself. I haven't done a field assignment in a while. Do you think you can find a little time for me if I make the trip?"

"You bet, honey, especially if you come for this motion hearing." Clay wasn't giving up so easily.

"Clay honey, I can't do it. Listen, I'll call a friend of mine at our affiliate in Vero. Since it's Tracey James, she'll be interested. I'll get her to send somebody over. You convince the judge to let her in the courtroom."

"Will do. Thanks, Stacey. I'll see you in a couple of months at the trial." Clay knew there was no way Judge Wentwell was letting cameras into his courtroom. He had commented to Clay on many occasions that he would never let the media turn his courtroom into a circus. Clay wasn't even going to make the request — might piss the old man off. But there was no need to tell Stacey that. All he wanted was to get a news crew to show up; he'd get the publicity he was after from interviews on the courthouse steps.

It took three weeks to get an all-day hearing set before Judge Wentwell. Tracey used the time to prepare. This motion was going to be a mini-trial. It had been three years since her last trial, a misdemeanor case that lasted half a day. She needed this hearing and she needed to win it, although she wasn't quite sure why. The uncertainty bothered her. Confusion was not her forte. She always knew what she wanted and she made a plan to get it. Maybe it was Elena and that faded connection to her mother. Maybe it was Rudy himself, or perhaps her desire to be a lawyer for once rather than a businesswoman. She just didn't know. All she knew was that something else was driving her this time besides the money, and it was driving her hard. She hoped the feeling didn't last long.

There were no crowds outside the courthouse on the day of the hearing or inside the courtroom either. It wasn't that nobody cared. The people of the barrio were behind Rudy one hundred percent, but they had to go to work. Kelly McDowell from the local affiliate in Vero Beach was standing on the courthouse steps with her camera crew wondering why in God's name she had agreed to drive over from Vero for this. Tracey James was the only reason it was even remotely worthwhile. If she could get an interview with Tracey, maybe she could salvage something from the trip.

As for Tracey, Kelly McDowell was the last person she wanted to see. She never liked media attention when she faced the possibility of losing. But she knew she couldn't duck Kelly so she planned on making the best of it.

Clay reached the courthouse before Tracey arrived. Kelly didn't have to hunt him down for an interview. He practically grabbed the microphone from her. He was all smiles, tall and elegant in his charcoal gray suit — cocky and confident like a quarterback before the big game. Kelly smiled right along with him.

Not long after Clay went inside, Tracey arrived with Elena. Tracey's gray suit over a light blue blouse was stunning and the picture of professionalism, but Elena actually outdid her in a conservative but tight-fitting navy blue dress she had purchased only the day before from the local thrift shop.

Despite her concerns, Tracey struck the perfect note when Kelly got to them. "How important is this hearing today?" Kelly asked, trying to lob the softball in a perfect arc so Tracey could smash it.

"It's very important. We believe Detective Brume violated Rudy's constitutional rights when he interrogated him. Rudy is a fine young man, but he has a mental incapacity. He's slow. Not retarded, but slow. He was at a distinct disadvantage in this interrogation, which, by the way, was neither recorded nor videotaped. His mother, Elena, who is here with me had asked to be with her son during the interview to protect him, but her request was denied." She hadn't wanted the interview, but she had enough self-awareness to realize it was turning out to be a good one — like a dress rehearsal for how she wanted to present Rudy to the court. When she finished her statement, she didn't wait for another question but took Elena by the arm and ushered her up the steps and into the courthouse.

Since witnesses were going to be providing sworn testimony and it was going to be more like a bench trial than a hearing, Judge Wentwell decided to hold the proceedings in the courtroom rather than chambers. He had another reason as well. This case was about a murder that had been reported extensively throughout the state. Even though public interest seemed to have waned in the time since the event, the judge felt that any hearing to suppress evidence in a case such as this should be held in open court with all its formalities.

Clay Evans noticed Elena as soon as she walked into the court-room. She looked exquisite in that blue dress. *Maybe I could agree to life imprisonment for a little action.* The thought had barely flickered into consciousness before he reminded himself that his career was at stake in this case. Lust would definitely have to take a back seat for the time being. Tracey wasn't looking too shabby herself, although he sensed the woman had a hard edge to her. Maybe he could impress her with his courtroom skills. God, he was feeling good today.

Once the lawyers were seated, the bailiff let the judge know everything was ready. At the appropriate moment, the judge knocked on the door three times, signaling the bailiff that he was ready. The bailiff then told everyone to rise and the judge entered the courtroom.

Judge Wentwell was a tall man, almost as tall as Clay, and ram-rod straight, with a full head of white hair. Elena, who was seated in the spectators' seats directly behind Tracey, felt for a moment like she was in church and the bishop had just come out to the altar. Rudy was not there. Tracey had told Elena it would be best if he were not in the courtroom. He didn't need to hear what H.V. was going to say about him and Judge Wentwell didn't need to see how handsome he was and how bright he appeared to be.

The Cobb County courthouse had only two courtrooms: the small one for county court cases, misdemeanors and arraignments; and the large one, Judge Wentwell's court, which handled all the major civil trials and felony cases. It was a cavernous old room with rows of oak benches for the spectators, even a balcony. The judge ruled from an elevated mahogany dais. The witness chair was to his right and below him. The jurors' chairs, which were empty on this day, were to the right of the witness. The lawyers' tables were front and center where the judge could look down on them without turning a lick.

"Counsel, are we ready to proceed?" Judge Wentwell asked after everybody had been seated. Clay popped up.

"The state is ready, Your Honor," he said briskly.

Tracey was a little more deliberate. "The defense is ready, Your Honor."

"Ms. James, since it is your motion, you may proceed."

"Thank you, Your Honor. The defense calls Detective Wesley Brume to the stand." The bailiff left to retrieve Wes from the witness room.

Calling Wes was no surprise to Clay. Tracey had to lay the facts of the interview out and Wes was the only person to do it since Rudy would not be testifying. What Clay didn't know was that Tracey would be playing a little Ping-Pong that morning using Wesley Brume as the ball.

She started politely asking him to tell the judge his name and how long he'd been a police officer and the different positions he had held in the police department. She had no idea the judge already knew Wes quite well. Many years before, Wes had pulled the judge over for speeding, something Judge Wentwell never did.

"Going to a fire or something?" Wes had asked the distinguished jurist as he walked up to the driver's side window. "Whaddya think, the law doesn't apply to you? A few days in the slammer will straighten you out. Come on, let's see your license and registration." It was the usual banter he delivered to everyone — it made him feel good and made the routine of chasing speeders more enjoyable. The judge handed Wes his license without looking up. People had been coming into his courtroom for years claiming that they hadn't been speeding and that they had been treated quite rudely by Officer Wesley Brume, exactly what he had just experienced and exactly what Wesley Brume had denied every time. Wes read the name on the license and knew he was in deep shit. He thought about backtracking, pretending he knew it was the judge all along, but the look of guilt on his pudgy face had already betrayed him.

"Hi, Judge, how are you?" was all he could muster.

"Fine, Officer Brume. Finish with your ticket."

"On second thought, Judge, I think I stopped the wrong car. It was the one in front of you." There had been no car in front of Judge

Wentwell and they both knew it. The old man glared at Wes and drove off.

The next day, the police chief received a hand-delivered letter from the judge detailing the whole incident and demanding that Wesley Brume be stripped of all authority to issue speeding tickets and that all his officers have explained to them the importance of ticketing people who actually were speeding. Needless to say the incident did not go over well with the chief.

The whole affair was also unknown to Clay, who sat supremely confident as he watched Tracey ask Wes one warm and fuzzy question after another. All that was about to change.

"Officer Brume, why did you pick up my client for questioning?"

That was an easy one for Wes. "He was identified by three people as a suspect."

"Would those three people be Pilar Rodriguez, Ray Castro and José Guerrero?"

"Yes."

"Is it accurate that you did not interview those three people?"

"Yes, that's accurate. Officer Barbas interviewed them." Everything seemed to be moving along quite well to Clay. The pace had a nice rhythm to it. Wes was answering the questions quickly and directly.

"I have Officer Barbas's interview of the two men in my hands here. It says they described a tall man with black hair, is that accurate?"

"Yes."

"So they didn't identify my client?" Tracey said, staring intensely at Wes.

"No, but their identification was consistent with what he looked like and Ms. Rodriguez said the man who puked on her lawn looked like the boy who worked at the convenience store. She even said his name, Rudy."

"But she didn't see this person who looked like Rudy come from Lucy Ochoa's trailer?"

"No."

"And isn't it true that she could not identify Rudy in a lineup?"

"That's correct." It was Clay who was glaring at Wes now. *How could you not tell me something like that, you idiot.*

Wes needed to redeem himself. "If I could explain." Tracey knew what was coming. She had tried to use the fact that *ultimately* nobody identified Rudy without placing those facts in a time sequence. Wes was about to call her on it. "At the time we picked your client up for questioning, Ms. Rodriguez had said the man who puked on her lawn looked like Rudy and he also fit the description the other two men gave us. I believe that gave us enough reasonable suspicion to question him."

"Did you read him his rights?"

"Of course. I had him sign a document explaining his rights."

That was important to the judge. "Did you bring that document with you?" he asked.

"Yes, sir."

"Let's see it." Wes showed the original to the judge.

"Is this your client's signature?" he asked Tracey.

"Yes, Your Honor."

"Then what are we doing here, Ms. James?"

"I want to show you how it was obtained and why it should be stricken."

"Then get on with it, Ms. James. Stop wasting our time with these unnecessary questions that are meaningless." It was a definite *slap*, one Tracey was not used to receiving.

"Before you picked my client up, you talked to his high school principal, Mr. Bill Yates, is that correct?"

"Yes."

"And Mr. Yates told you that Rudy had an intellectual deficit, that he couldn't keep up with the other students academically, correct?"

"Yes."

"They passed him academically to the tenth grade, although

they shouldn't have, but after that he just received an attendance certificate, correct?"

"Pretty much." That answer wasn't good enough for Tracey. Too much wiggle room.

"Pretty much? Is there anything in my question you want to qualify?"

"No, it's correct."

"You're sure?"

"Yes."

"Did Mr. Yates tell you anything else about Rudy?"

"No."

"You're sure?"

"Yes."

"He didn't tell you that Rudy was very affable, that he'd agree to everything you'd say; that in all fairness you shouldn't question him without either his mother or a lawyer present — the principal didn't say those things to you?" Tracey was starting to squeeze. The Grunt resisted, just as she had hoped.

"No. I don't remember him saying anything like that."

"You don't remember him saying anything like that or he didn't say anything like that: Which is it, Officer Brume?"

"Detective Brume."

"Okay. Which is it, *Detective Brume?*" She was getting under his skin already.

"He didn't say anything like that," the Grunt replied defiantly. This bitch wasn't going to push him around. At counsel table, Clay put his left hand on his forehead. He knew now what was coming.

Tracey moved on.

"You picked Rudy up at the convenience store where he worked, correct?"

"Yes."

"Did you speak to his boss?"

"Yes."

"Was he reluctant to let Rudy go with you?"

"Somewhat."

Tracey bit his head off again. "What does 'Somewhat' mean, Mr. Brume? Does it mean he was reluctant or he was not reluctant?"

"It means he didn't want me to take Rudy at first but after we talked and I told him the importance of the investigation, he agreed that Rudy should go with me."

"You mean he agreed after you threatened him with the health department?"

"That's not true. I would never do that." Wes didn't dare look up at the judge. He had used those exact words before in a speeding hearing.

"Did Mr. Dragone want to call Rudy's mother to let her know what was happening?"

"I don't recall that."

"Did you discourage him from doing that?"

"I don't recall that." Wes had hit on a new answer. He remembered a former president had used it very effectively.

Tracey kept the pace moving, mindful that the judge might wonder where all this was going. She picked up the police report from her desk, held it in her hand.

"So you took Rudy to the police department?"

"Yes."

"And you began questioning him, correct?"

"Yes."

"And according to your report, you began questioning him at 3:18 p.m., correct?" She showed him the report. Wes glanced at it.

"Yes, that's correct."

"And isn't it true, *Officer* Brume, that before you started your interrogation of Rudy, his mother arrived at the station and demanded to see her son and that you not question her son without her being present?" The Fourth jumped to his feet. It was his first opportunity to stop Tracey's rhythm.

"Objection, Your Honor. Compound question." It was a valid objection but meaningless under the circumstances. There was no jury and Judge Wentwell certainly knew it was a compound question.

"Overruled. Proceed, Ms. James."

"Do you need me to repeat the question, *Officer* Brume?" Tracey asked.

"*Detective* Brume. No, I recall the question. To my knowledge the mother didn't arrive at the station until I was almost finished with the interview."

"When she did arrive, did she request that you stop the interview?"

"Yes."

"But you didn't?"

"No."

"Why?"

"He'd agreed to talk to me. He's an adult and she's not a lawyer."

"Did you tell him his mother was outside and she wanted to see him before he answered any more questions?"

"No."

"Is that because you knew that he wouldn't talk to you anymore if he knew his mother was outside?"

"No. I was almost finished anyway. At that point it wouldn't have made a difference."

"You hadn't taken his blood yet, had you?"

"No."

Tracey changed subjects again. "Where did this interrogation take place?"

"In the interrogation room at the police department."

"I've heard about that room. It's equipped with a television camera, is that correct?"

"Yes."

"And you have audio recording equipment in there as well, correct?"

"Yes."

"But you didn't use either?"

"No, I didn't."

"Was there a reason why you didn't, *Officer* Brume?" The Fourth was on his feet again.

"Objection, Your Honor. She's harassing the witness. He's already told her several times that he's a detective." Unfortunately for Clay, Judge Wentwell was enjoying the harassment.

"He may be a detective, Mr. Clay, but he's also a sworn police officer. I don't see how addressing a police officer as 'Officer' can constitute harassment. Objection overruled. You may proceed, Ms. James."

"Thank you, Your Honor. Do you need me to repeat the question, Officer Brume?" Tracey asked politely as she turned her focus back to the fat little cop.

"No. There was no reason in particular. We rarely use the video camera. And I didn't have a tape available."

"What would you have had to do to use the camera, just get a videotape?"

"Pretty much."

"Is that a 'yes,' Officer Brume?"

"Yes."

"Where was the videotape?"

"In the equipment room." He was being evasive but Tracey didn't mind. His evasiveness would have been obvious to a two-year-old.

"And where is the equipment room?"

"Down the hall."

"And the recording equipment, would you have found a tape for that in the equipment room as well?"

"Yes."

"Can you be more specific, Officer Brume? How long would it have taken you to walk down the hall, fetch the video or recording equipment, or both, and install them before beginning your interview?"

"Three to five minutes," the Grunt replied nonchalantly. It was that cavalier attitude that made Clay Evans want to strangle him.

*Does this idiot have any idea where she's taking him?*

"Is it accurate that this recording equipment was in the interrogation room to be used for interrogations?"

"Of course." *What a stupid question,* Wes thought.

"Is it accurate that when you brought my client in for questioning he was already a suspect in this murder?"

"Yes."

"And he was your only suspect at the time?"

"Yes."

"And is it accurate, Detective Brume, that in your twenty-plus years as a police officer in this department this is the most heinous crime you have ever investigated?" She had deliberately called him detective. She was starting to give him the respect he deserved, or so it seemed.

"No question about that," he responded. Tracey had him cornered. It was time to drop the bomb.

"So you bought this hi-tech equipment for the specific purpose of interrogation, you're investigating the most heinous crime ever, and you make a conscious decision not to video or even audio record it, correct?"

"No, that's not correct," Wes replied, realizing too late the crater that he was sitting in. Tracey was not about to let him squirm his way out by asking him to explain his answer. She switched gears.

"Did you have Rudy make a written statement?"

"No, but I had him read my notes and sign them."

"Did you tell him to sign them?"

"Yes, of course."

"Was he allowed to make changes?"

"I don't understand."

"It's very simple, *Officer* Brume, did you let him edit your notes?"

"Of course not."

"You just had him sign them."

"Yes."

"No further questions, Your Honor." The abrupt termination of the examination surprised the Fourth. He had expected Tracey to grill the Grunt on the questions and answers he'd written down, but Tracey was only interested in the procedure, not the substance.

Now it was Clay's turn. His immediate task was to cauterize Wes's wounds to prevent further bleeding. Wes hadn't really suffered a direct hit but he was bleeding profusely from several minor wounds. The Fourth could choose either to cut his losses and get the poor man off the stand, something that required great restraint, or to ask more questions and open the Grunt up for even heavier artillery. He chose the latter course, rising slowly and calculating his questions as he walked to the podium. He had to rehabilitate the fat little toad.

"Detective Brume, in your twenty-plus years with the police department has your credibility ever been questioned?" Tracey was on her feet in a heartbeat.

"Objection, Your Honor. The character of Officer Brume is not an issue in this case, although his credibility in this particular case is." It was classic litigator-speak, something the public probably wouldn't understand. But Tracey didn't care about the small group of regular folks observing the proceedings from the gallery. The only person in the room who mattered to her at that moment was Judge Wentwell, and he was sure to get it.

"This court is in recess for the next twenty minutes. I want to see the lawyers in my chambers with the court reporter." The judge stood and left the courtroom. Clay and Tracey followed him to his chambers. When everyone was seated and the court reporter was set up, the judge began.

"I did not believe it was necessary to disclose this information at the beginning of this hearing, but the testimony has brought me to a place where I must disclose some pertinent information to you that I'm certain you're not aware of." Tracey and Clay looked at each other quizzically then turned back to the judge, who proceeded to tell them about the little "speeding" incident he'd had with Wes.

"I agree with Ms. James," the judge went on, "that Officer

Brume's credibility is at issue here, not his character. However, Mr. Evans, since I will be deciding what evidence the jury hears, it is my duty to disclose to you that my opinion is somewhat tainted regarding Officer Brume's credibility *and* character. I do not believe that will affect my decision on the legal issues in this hearing or at trial. However, if you wish, I will step down from this case."

Clay was almost shaking by the time Judge Wentwell finished. He wanted to take a bazooka back into the courtroom and blow Wesley Brume to kingdom come. *How could he do this to me? How could he not tell me about his encounter with the judge?* But that was old news. Now Clay had to make a very important decision, a decision that would definitely affect the outcome of this case.

Seated next to him, Tracey was trying desperately not to smile. Things had definitely just taken a sharp turn for the better. And her best witnesses were yet to come. On the other hand, Clay had no choice but to ask the judge to recuse himself, and she wasn't so sure she wanted to lose Judge Wentwell.

Seconds passed. The judge waited patiently while Clay thought it through. Judge Wentwell was a law-and-order guy. He would follow the law strictly. He wasn't about to buy into a new theory of evidence even if he didn't believe one word that came out of the fat little toad's mouth. And a new judge might not be so conservative in his or her thinking.

"Judge, I believe this court will be able to separate any personal views in deciding issues of law. I will not ask you to recuse yourself." Tracey was nonplussed. The judge turned to her.

"Ms. James, do you have anything to say?"

"No, Your Honor. I believe your full disclosure has said it all. Like the prosecutor, I do not believe your personal experience with Officer Brume will affect your decisions in this case."

*I'll bet you don't!* the Fourth said to himself, hoping he had made the right decision.

Minutes later they were back in the courtroom, Clay standing at the podium.

Judge Wentwell spoke first.

"Mr. Evans, you may proceed."

"No further questions, Your Honor." Since the judge knew the Grunt was a big fat liar, there was no point in trying to rehabilitate him. Wes stepped down, not sure where things stood but pretty sure from the look on Clay's face that he was annoyed about something.

"Call your next witness, Ms. James."

Tracey had set up the state's case with the Grunt's testimony. Now she was going to rip it to shreds.

She started by calling Rudy's high school principal, Bill Yates, to the stand. After he introduced himself and explained that he'd been Rudy's principal for all four years, Tracey got right to it.

"Mr. Yates, did Detective Wesley Brume visit you a couple of months ago?"

"Yes."

"And could you tell the court the reason for the visit?"

"He wanted to find out about Rudy, how he had been as a student."

"And what did you tell him?"

"I told him that Rudy was a very nice, motivated young man but that he was a little slow. I think his IQ was somewhere around eighty or a little below. We're a small school. We don't have special programs for children like that so we did the best we could. After two years we put Rudy in a vocational program. He never received a high school diploma, just an attendance certificate."

"Did Detective Brume tell you why he was inquiring about Rudy?"

"Yes. He said Rudy might be a suspect in the murder of the young woman in the barrio."

"And what was your response to that?"

"I told him he must be mistaken. I knew Rudy very well and I did not believe he was capable of anything like that."

"Did Detective Brume tell you that he was going to bring Rudy in for questioning?"

"Yes."

"How did you respond to that?"

"I suggested that if he did anything like that he should contact Rudy's mother or at least make sure he had a lawyer. I told him that Rudy was a very affable person and very naive. He would not know how to protect himself. He would respond to every question the officer asked even if it was not in his best interests to do so."

"Is there a reason why you told the detective that?"

"Yes. I figured that he wanted to conduct a fair investigation and I thought it was something he needed to know."

"Thank you, Mr. Yates. I have no further questions."

Judge Wentwell looked at Clay. "Cross-examination, Mr. Evans?"

"Yes, Your Honor." Clay was certain this was a witness he could score some points with. He stood up but stayed at the counsel table.

"Mr. Yates, could Rudy read and write?"

"Yes."

Clay approached the bench and retrieved the consent form Rudy had signed. He handed the document to the principal.

"And in your opinion could he have read this document and understood it?" Principal Yates put his glasses on and read the document.

"Yes, I believe he could."

"And, even though he was a very affable person, if Detective Brume had presented this document to him before he began his questioning and Rudy had read this document, in your opinion he would have *understood* that he had the right not to speak to Detective Brume?"

Bill Yates hesitated for a moment. He could see that Clay Evans had backed him into a corner. He didn't want to hurt Rudy but he had to answer the question honestly.

"Yes. I believe that he would have understood that he had the right to refuse to speak to Officer Brume but —" Clay cut him off before he could go any further.

"Thank you, Mr. Yates. I believe you have answered my question.

One other thing: Does Rudy in your opinion know the difference between right and wrong?"

"Yes, I believe he does."

"Thank you. No further questions, Your Honor."

Tracey had no re-direct. Clay had scored his points but she wasn't arguing that Rudy did not have the capacity to understand what he was signing.

"Call your next witness, Ms. James."

Tracey followed Bill Yates with Benny Dragone.

"Detective Brume wanted to take Rudy off the job and over to the station for questioning," he told Tracey in response to a question. "I told him that I wouldn't let him speak to Rudy until I talked with his mother."

"Why did you tell him that?"

"I knew he was looking at Rudy as a suspect in that girl's murder and I didn't trust him. I knew Rudy just couldn't handle himself with a snake like that."

"Objection." Clay tried to sound outraged but his opinion of Wes actually coincided with Benny's.

"Sustained," Judge Wentwell replied, not waiting for argument. He looked down at Benny. "Mr. Dragone, stick to the facts. We don't need the derogatory comments."

"Yes, Your Honor. Sorry."

But Tracey wasn't letting it go just yet. "The person you referred to as a snake, Mr. Dragone, who was that?"

"Objection."

"Overruled. The record needs to be clarified. You may continue with this one question, Ms. James."

"Thank you, Your Honor. Do you need me to repeat the question, Mr. Dragone?"

"No. The snake I was referring to was Wesley Brume."

"Thank you, Mr. Dragone. Now, what was Detective Brume's response when you told him you wouldn't let him speak to Rudy until you called Rudy's mother?"

"He threatened me."

"He threatened you? How did he do that?" Tracey did her best to sound surprised, as if she didn't know what was coming next.

"He told me he'd get the health department over to my store for an inspection. I knew what he meant."

Tracey decided to end her questioning there. Leave it up in the air a little. See if Clay had the guts to jump in. "No further questions, Your Honor."

"Your witness, Mr. Evans."

"Thank you, Your Honor. Mr. Dragone, to your knowledge did Detective Brume need to ask you for permission to take Rudy in for questioning?"

"No, of course not."

"So he could have just come into the store, asked Rudy to come with him and left without even saying hello?"

"I guess so."

"But he was polite enough to talk to you and explain to you what he was about to do?"

"I wouldn't exactly call it being polite."

"Whatever, he did explain to you what he was about to do?" The Fourth snapped the question out.

"Yeah, I guess so," Benny replied, almost reluctantly. It was that noncommittal answer that angered Clay, causing him to go a little too far.

"And you also 'guessed' that because Officer Brume mentioned the health department after looking around at your premises that he was somehow making a threat?"

"No, that wasn't a guess. That was a fact." Clay had pressed Benny's button. "I come from Chicago. I know a threat when I hear one. Any fool knows when a cop tells you he wants somethin' and you refuse, and then he says he's gonna call the health department — that's a threat."

"In your opinion?" It was all Clay could come back with although he bathed the question in sarcasm.

"Yeah," Benny replied. "In my opinion and a thousand other people if they were asked the same question." Clay had no place else to go so he just stood there looking at Benny with disdain, hoping he could convince the judge that Benny was an uncooperative piece of shit who insulted lawyers.

"I have no further questions of this witness, Your Honor."

Tracey called her next witness, another surprise for the Fourth, who was starting to feel like a punch-drunk fighter.

"The defense calls Maria Lopez." The name did not ring a bell with the Fourth.

"I'm the receptionist at the police department," Maria told Tracey. She went on to tell the judge that Elena had arrived at the police station at 3:16 p.m. on January 24th. She knew the exact time because Elena had asked her to write it down.

"What happened when Elena —Ms. Kelly — arrived at the station?"

"Nothing. I was told to have her sit and wait."

"For how long?"

"Maybe twenty minutes. Then Detective Shorter came out to talk to her."

"Did he come out on his own or did you have to call him?"

"I had to call him. Ms. Kelly insisted that I call again to let them know she was there."

"Was she allowed to see her son after that?"

"No."

"No further questions."

Clay had no cross.

Tracey kept the pressure on, following Maria Lopez with Elena, who repeated Maria Lopez's testimony almost verbatim, adding only the substance of her conversation with Del Shorter.

"He told me that my son could be a very valuable witness to them since he worked at the convenience store. I almost believed him but when he continued to talk and finally admitted that he wasn't going to let me see my son, I knew it had been a stall all along. Detective

Shorter flat out lied to me about what was going on."

Clay couldn't let that last statement stand. "I move to strike the last sentence, Your Honor. It is opinion testimony."

"I believe a witness can give an opinion about whether she believes somebody is lying to her or not," Tracey said.

"I'll allow it," the judge ruled. "Motion denied. Any further questions, Ms. James?"

"No, Your Honor."

"Cross-examination, Mr. Evans?"

Clay wanted to take a shot at Elena, wanted to establish through Rudy's own mother that he had the capacity to read and write and make decisions. But he already had that testimony from the principal, and it was always dangerous to keep a sympathetic witness on the stand.

"No questions, Your Honor."

The stage was now set for Harold Victor Fischer. He strode confidently into the courtroom dressed in a dark blue suit, white shirt, red tie — his power outfit. Actually, H.V. didn't fit the mold very well. He was tall enough but slumped over like a sack of potatoes, soft in the middle and around the shoulders — more like the Marshmallow Man than Superman.

Tracey started building him up right away, having him recite his credentials: Cornell, Penn medical school, and so on. When she was finished, she simply turned H.V. loose. It was on the stand, lending his expertise to the process, that H.V. transformed into a formidable figure.

"Doctor, have you had occasion to visit Rudy?"

"Yes, I met with him for approximately two and a half hours."

"And have you formed any opinions in this case?"

"Yes." And off he went. "I not only met with Rudy, I performed a battery of tests including the Wechsler Aptitude Test. I have reviewed his entire medical chart and his school records.

"Rudy's IQ is seventy-five, which means he is not retarded but is what we call borderline. He has many characteristics of the retarded, including his affect. What do I mean by affect?" Posing his own questions was classic H.V. "I mean that Rudy always had a smile on his face, always greeted — no, greets, even in his present circumstances — the world with open arms. He's a happy person, very gullible, very naive.

"There have been case studies about retarded children and their inability to make the right decision under similar circumstances — mostly teenagers exposed to the general population of other teenagers. I remember one case in particular. A group of teenagers in Ohio had convinced a retarded student in their class that they were his friends. They took him out to a high bridge and convinced him to jump into the river below. They assured him they were all going to follow. The jump didn't kill him. He drowned because he couldn't swim, a fact he hadn't thought to tell his newfound friends.

"I mention this case study in particular because it is an appropriate analogy. Young Rudy told me during our interview that he liked Detective Brume, that he thought Detective Brume was his friend. A normal person in his circumstances would definitely not share those sentiments. When you befriend an individual like Rudy, he does not have the capacity to refuse to do what you ask. He could not refuse to talk to Detective Brume once Detective Brume became his friend. I think Detective Brume knew this instinctively. From my conversation with Rudy, it became clear that Detective Brume tried to establish a friendship before ever discussing the murder.

"Under those circumstances, Rudy could not refuse to answer his questions."

～

H.V. was a veteran of the game. He knew the more he said, the more ammunition he gave to opposing counsel on cross. When he had completed his expert opinion on *the* issue, H.V. simply shut up and waited for the onslaught.

It never came. Clay Evans had no desire to engage in a game of wits with Harold Victor Fischer — one he'd probably lose anyway.

He fell back on drilling home a few fundamentals for the judge's benefit.

"Doctor, can Rudy read and write?"

"Yes."

"Can he distinguish right from wrong?"

"Yes."

Clay retrieved the written confession from the clerk who was now holding the evidence. He handed it to H.V.

"Could he read and understand this document?" H.V. glanced at the confession. He had seen a copy of it in the documents Tracey had sent him.

"Read it, yes. Understand it, yes. But you're not getting my point —" Clay cut him off in mid-sentence.

"You've answered my question, Doctor. Thank you."

Tracey couldn't let it end there. She accepted a redirect.

"What is the point that Mr. Evans is not getting, Doctor?"

"The point is that reading and understanding are not the only questions you have to ask when you consider the issue of 'consent' with a person like Rudy." This was a statement Tracey hadn't heard from H.V. during their two-hour preparatory meeting the day before. It was new even to H.V., who had just arrived at the thought on the stand. Up to now, Tracey and H.V. had conceded that Rudy had the capacity to understand *and* consent, but they had planned to contend that his affable nature wouldn't allow him to refuse to talk to someone he considered a friend. Now H.V. was about to change the issue to one of *capacity* itself, and Tracey could see that this would turn out to be a much better argument for the defendant. Apparently Clay Evans could bring a person to new heights even on cross-examination, she thought, trying to conceal a smile.

H.V. continued. "With a retarded person or a borderline retarded person, you must also consider the circumstances under which the confession was made. If a relationship of trust was established between the questioner and the defendant, then in my opinion the defendant would not have the *capacity* to refuse to speak. Therefore, he would not have the *capacity* to consent."

H.V.'s intellect was in free flow now. He was having a break-through right on the stand. Not only was he testifying for money, he was testifying for truth. He truly believed what he was saying and he truly believed he was about to save Rudy's life. He turned toward the judge and started speaking directly to him.

"Your Honor, if I may be permitted to make an analogy. It's similar to a will contest where the issue is undue influence. The question is not necessarily whether the elderly person has the ability to make decisions regarding his or her property, it is whether that person has a *diminished capacity* because of his or her age and that fact, combined with the beneficiary being in a position of trust, a *fiduciary* capacity, has robbed the person of the ability to make a *voluntary* decision concerning his or her property." It was a highly intellectual legal argument made very simple. Tracey was blown away. It was a perfect analogy and she had never thought of it. *What was the logical argument to counter it?*

One thing was for certain: The logical counterargument was not floating around in Clay Evans's brain. He was having a hard enough time just trying to figure out what H.V. was talking about. But Judge Wentwell was going to give him a chance to dive in if he wanted to take it.

"Mr. Evans, since this issue of lack of capacity was more or less raised on redirect, I'm going to give you an opportunity to recross." *Don't take it! Don't take it!* somebody was screaming in Clay's brain. But Clay had been making terrible decisions his whole life — he wasn't about to stop now. He decided to counter intelligent discussion with sarcasm and derision.

"Is this a will contest, Doctor?"

"Of course not."

"Is Rudy an elderly person?"

"No." It was ugly, almost stupid, but like a blind man walking in a minefield, the Fourth finally stepped on something that made a little noise.

"Is there something here I'm missing? How long did this kid Rudy know Detective Brume?"

"I don't think they knew each other before the interview."

"And how long did the interview last?"

"Thirty-eight minutes, according to the reports I've seen."

"And in that thirty-eight minutes, you're saying they developed a *fiduciary relationship?*"

"In a way, yes."

"What does that mean, 'In a way, yes'?" It was an open-ended question, and H.V. didn't miss the invitation.

"It means that the detective, who clearly had the superior intellect, established a position of trust with Rudy in that interview room. He pretended to be Rudy's friend. Rudy still believes Detective Brume is his friend. He still believes the detective is trying to help him."

"Are you saying that Detective Brume lied to Rudy?" The Fourth asked the question with such surprise in his voice Tracey almost started to laugh out loud. H.V. was possibly the only witness who had not attested to the Grunt's lies.

"Not at all," H.V. responded. "He just used the situation to his advantage." Clay took the answer as a concession. He was done but he took a moment to stare at H.V. as he had done with Benny Dragone.

"I have no further questions of this witness," he finally told the judge, acting as if he had beaten H.V. to within an inch of his life.

"I have nothing further," Tracey told the judge when Clay sat down. The judge looked at the courtroom clock. It was ten after two. Everybody was hungry and tired.

"Mr. Evans, do you plan on having any rebuttal?" Clay thought about it only for a second. *Who would I call? The Grunt again? Del Shorter?*

"No, Your Honor."

"Why don't we take a lunch break. Come back at three. When you return, I want to see the lawyers and the court reporter in my chambers. Ms. James, the boy's mother can come if she wants. Court is adjourned until 3 p.m." The judge stood and walked out of the courtroom.

~

Tracey and Elena ate lunch at one of the two little restaurants across the street that specialized in quick sandwiches for the courthouse crowd. Elena was very nervous and had questions she was dying to ask, but she waited patiently until Tracey had given the waitress her order and had her first sip of coffee.

"I thought you were magnificent today."

"Thank you, Elena."

"Dr. Fischer was great too. I think he had the whole situation pegged."

"He did. And his analogy was unique. I'll have to do the research but I don't think anyone's ever made that argument before."

"Do you think the judge will accept it?" Elena asked.

"I don't know."

"Why did the judge say he wanted to see us in chambers?" Tracey did have an idea about that and it wasn't good. She decided against speculating and upsetting Elena unnecessarily.

"I don't know, Elena. We'll just have to see." The waitress arrived with their sandwiches at that moment. They ate in silence.

~

Judge Wentwell still had his robes on when he entered the hearing room, which was surprising to both Clay and Tracey. Usually chambers meetings were more informal. Perhaps he wanted to maintain the formality because Elena was present. Perhaps he had other reasons.

The hearing room was a rectangular room adjacent to the judge's private office, with a long table that extended from the front of a desk. It was similar to a hundred other hearing rooms that Tracey had been in during her career. The judge sat behind the desk, the lawyers on each side of the table. Elena sat next to Tracey. The court reporter had her own chair slightly to the right of the judge but in front of him. The trick for her was to see the judge's lips as he spoke, as well as the lawyers'.

Elena was fascinated by the court reporter. She had this little machine and when people spoke in the courtroom she typed into the machine. But it wasn't a typewriter. Nobody could type that fast. She typed symbols. Elena could see the symbols on the paper that came out of the top of the machine as she typed.

"It's a unique kind of shorthand," Tracey had explained. "Just one of the special talents necessary to be a court reporter. She also has to watch everybody's lips so she catches every word. Later on she translates the shorthand into English. It's called a transcript of the proceedings."

The court reporter was dutifully watching Judge Wentwell's lips, waiting for him to begin.

"I've asked you to come to my chambers this afternoon because I am prepared to rule." He looked at the two lawyers. "I know that you both have prepared closing statements to assist me in my deliberations but I don't need them. I've heard the evidence." The judge paused for a moment to gather his thoughts. Elena was so nervous she was digging a hole in the seat with her nails.

"I'm ruling in chambers because I want most of this record sealed." That statement confirmed Tracey's speculation. "I'm going to make factual findings for the purposes of this hearing and any appeal that ensues. If this case proceeds to trial, the jury will not be bound by my findings. They will not even know of them. However, I am ruling that the jury may hear the same evidence as I have heard.

"I find that Principal Yates, Mr. Dragone, and Ms. Lopez were all credible witnesses. They had absolutely no incentive to mislead this court. On the other hand, I find that Officer Brume had a total lack of credibility. Specifically, I find that Principal Yates advised Officer Brume to make sure that Rudy had either a lawyer or his mother with him when he was questioned for the boy's own protection. I find that Mr. Dragone was threatened by Officer Brume." The judge glared at Clay Evans. "I also can recognize a threat when I hear one." He paused to let that sink in before continuing. "I find that Rudy's mother, Elena, arrived at the police station before questioning began. I have no doubt, based on what I have heard, that Detective Shorter lied to her about why they were questioning Rudy.

"Most troubling for this court was Detective Brume's own admission that he chose not to use the readily available video or audio equipment, which were purchased by the department for this very purpose. If he had done so, I could have either watched or listened to the actual questions and answers. This is especially troubling because of the total lack of candor displayed by Officer Brume in his testimony here today.

"Having made the above findings, however, I still cannot suppress the confession. The only issue in a suppression hearing is whether the defendant was advised of his rights, which include his right to counsel, and voluntarily waived them. It is clear that Rudy was advised of his rights in writing, understood them, and waived them. His mother is not a lawyer. She did not have the right to be present during questioning. The way she was treated, however, is relevant to assess the credibility and intent of the police officers involved. The testimony of Dr. Fischer intrigues me and I am not ruling on the issue of Rudy's *competency* to consent to be interviewed by Officer Brume at this time. I think both sides need to do comprehensive briefs on that issue and present them before trial to your new judge."

Both lawyers looked at him somewhat surprised. The judge returned their questioning stares.

"Yes, I'm going to recuse myself on my own motion. I will not be able to sit as a fair and impartial arbiter in this case. My own experience with Detective Brume prevents that. Another judge, probably a retired judge, will be appointed to take over the trial. I don't think there will be any appreciable delay.

"Once again, the only evidence of this hearing will be a written order denying the Motion to Suppress. You are all bound to silence about my factual findings. I will not tolerate a discussion of these findings in the press." He glared at the two lawyers, who nodded their assent. "I am ruling, however, that all the evidence presented today, including the testimony of Dr. Fischer, may be presented to the jury at trial. It is my belief that twelve reasonable men and women could find that the *substance* of the confession as transcribed by Officer Brume, based on all these facts and circumstances, is untrue. This hearing is adjourned."

It was unlike Judge Wentwell not to solicit questions or clarifications after a ruling, but the old man had had it. He was so disgusted by the Grunt's testimony. He looked at Elena for a brief moment before he stood up and left the room. The look was different from the lustful glances she'd been getting all day from the Fourth. It was a look of compassion, as if to say, *This is all I can do. It's out of my hands now.*

Elena learned at a young age to hide her emotions from the outside world. Where she came from, the vultures could smell vulnerability. But as she walked out of the courthouse that day, she was visibly shaking. Tracey put her arm around her and pulled her close, something she had never done with a client before. She felt so much for this woman and her son. That corset of business at all costs that she wore so tightly was starting to loosen.

"Elena, I know you're disappointed but this is good news really. We still have a chance if we can convince the new judge to listen to Dr. Fischer's opinion. And even if we go to trial, we have all this evidence." Her arguments were falling on deaf ears. Elena had always believed in America, the Constitution, and the jury system. She even believed in the death penalty because if a jury convicted you beyond a reasonable doubt, you had to be guilty. Now for the first time, as if in a vision, she saw how illusory it all was. None of the people from the barrio were going to make it on the jury. They weren't registered voters. Rudy was going to be judged by people who knew nothing about who he was or how he lived. They were going to hear that he was in Lucy's house, that his blood was found there, that he puked outside — and that was going to be it for them. This other stuff about Detective Brume's credibility and Rudy's rights wasn't going to mean a damn thing.

"I believe we can win this case even with the confession," Tracey continued, still trying to sound convincing. "Look, I'm going to stay in town overnight. Let's meet first thing tomorrow morning and discuss where we go from here, okay?"

Elena just nodded. She knew what tomorrow's discussion was going to be about. Tracey was part of her vision now.

## [ EIGHTEEN ]

They were to meet at nine the next morning at Austin Reaves's office. Both women wanted to be prepared for the negotiation they knew was about to transpire.

A fire was burning in Tracey, a passion to help Elena and save Rudy from the electric chair. But she was also afraid. Rather than embrace the flame, she let the fear consume her. Today had been one of her finest days in the courtroom, but she had since convinced herself that her business was about money and winning, not lost causes. Late in the evening when she was nursing her third scotch, something she rarely did, the realization came to her that this case was a lost cause. She had to get out. She disguised it a little for herself: *I have bills to pay and a staff with families who rely on me for support. I have a moral duty to them.* If Elena could come up with just ten thousand dollars more, she would stay on. That amount was still a discount for a case like this, but she could live with the compromise. It was the right thing to do, she assured herself. Still, she needed that fourth scotch.

Elena knew that Tracey was staying over until the next morning to talk about money. She remembered the original retainer amount. It was going to take at least ten thousand dollars, maybe more. *Where can I get the money?* Her first thought was her sister, Marguerite. But Marguerite had been tapped out by the first retainer. *Who else? Mike.*

Mike had provided five thousand dollars the last time. He might have more. *But I can't ask a man whose child I kept from him for seventeen years for money,* she told herself. *What would I tell him? "Leaving you was the right thing to do, but now your son's in jail for murder"? What kind of a mother have I been?* She dismissed the thought of calling him but as she became more desperate, Mike kept popping up. *I can't call him,* she told herself. *I can't talk to him.* Her fear kept colliding with what she knew she had to do for Rudy. She decided instead to call Marguerite. Put the idea in Marguerite's head. Marguerite would make the call.

"Just don't tell him what it's for," she said after asking her sister to call Mike. Marguerite's first inclination was to argue with her. *You have to tell the man something!* But she realized it would be no use. When the time came she'd tell Mike what he needed to know. She couldn't tell him everything, though. He'd be on a plane that night and Elena was clearly in no shape to see him.

"All right," she told Elena. "I'll call you later." Fifteen minutes later she was on the phone with Mike.

"Elena needs more money."

"What for?" Mike asked. He needed more information this time.

"I can't tell you." Mike was furious. He wanted to scream into the phone but he kept his voice calm.

"That's not fair, Marguerite. If Rudy's in trouble and Elena needs my help, I'm entitled to know what this is about."

"I know, I know, Mike, but I just can't. It's serious, though, and Elena is desperate. I'm sure that if you can come through this time, you'll be able to see Rudy eventually."

"That's not good enough," he said, his voice getting angrier. "I feel like I'm being blackmailed to see my son."

"It's not like that, Mike. I'd tell you myself if I thought it was best. Elena is overloaded right now. She can't handle this situation with Rudy *and* you. Trust me on this. Right now we just need the money."

Mike didn't know what to do. He trusted Marguerite to a certain extent but this was getting ridiculous. On the other hand, it was now pretty clear that Rudy was in some deep trouble and it did make sense that Elena couldn't deal with him and Rudy's trouble at the same time. He decided to bide his time. Eventually, he'd demand to be involved. He was aching to know what was happening to his son.

"There's not much I can do anyway. The last five thousand is all I had in savings, and my credit's been bad for years. I don't own a credit card."

"I know what you mean," Marguerite replied. "I'm maxed out on all of mine." They were both silent for a moment.

"I assume she needs the money right away?" he asked.

"Yeah."

"Give me a few hours. I'll call you back later tonight."

Nick Mangione had dinner at Julio's five nights a week. It was a small Italian restaurant, maybe twenty tables, on the corner of Ninety-third and Second. The word on the street was that Nick owned the building and maybe a piece of the restaurant but nobody knew for sure. From seven to nine, Monday through Friday, Nick occupied the back table at Julio's and met with whoever came to see him. He was hard to miss. The joke about Nick, told in a whisper, of course, was that he was six feet tall and six feet wide. Anybody caught telling that joke, however, would find themselves six feet under.

Mike was a full two inches taller than Nick but hardly as thick. His had once been an athletic body, now ravaged by years of alcohol abuse and little exercise. He never ate at Julio's. The food was good and the prices were moderate but he just didn't eat out. This night he headed straight for the back table. Nick was alone.

"Mike, *paisan*, long time no see! Sit down. Angie, get Mike a plate of spaghetti." Nick certainly gave directions like it was his place. But he was genuinely glad to see Mike. They'd known each other a long time. As Mike pulled in his chair, Nick poured him a glass of red wine.

"No thanks," Mike said, looking at the wine like it was poison.

"How you doin', Mike? Tell me this is a purely social visit." He'd seen Mike at his worst in the old days, bailed him out a few times. They still weren't totally even.

"It's not."

"No, Mike — you're not back on the sauce, are you?"

"Nothin' like that, Nick. My kid's in trouble. He needs money."

"What kinda trouble?"

"I don't know." Mike took out a cigarette and lit up.

"You don't know? He won't tell you?" Mike wanted to kick himself. He should have known Nick would ask questions and he should have had a story ready. Now he was stuck with the truth.

"I haven't talked to him. His mother called Marguerite."

"That Puerto Rican bitch. You remember the gutter she put you in last time, don't you?" Mike wouldn't let anybody else get away with that kind of talk, but there were no percentages in having words with Nick.

"Look, Nick, this isn't about her, it's about my kid."

"How old is he now?"

"Nineteen." Just then, Angie set a large plate of spaghetti and meatballs in front of Mike.

"*Mange, mange,*" Nick told him, gesturing with his hands like a benevolent despot. Mike dug in while he waited for the next question. He knew what it was going to be.

"How much?" Nick finally asked.

"Ten thousand dollars."

"Michael, Michael." The hands were flying again. "Ten thousand dollars! I remember when I used to lend you a couple of hundred to get through the month and you couldn't pay that. Anybody else woulda had their legs broken. Mike, this is a business. What kind of collateral you got?"

"Me. I'm a hard worker. I've got a decent job — " Nick cut him off.

"You know how much you gotta pay for ten thousand dollars?"

"How much?"

"Two hundred forty dollars a week. You probably don't make much more than that. It's a death sentence, Mike. I'd have to kill you for that kind of money."

"I need it," Mike told him. "I don't know what the trouble is but it's serious." Nick just looked at him. He felt sorry for the poor slob. Pulling himself out of the gutter, then jumping right back in. He wasn't going to have that on his conscience. Still, they went back a long way.

"I'll tell you what, Mike. I'll lend you twenty-five hundred and you pay me back a hundred twenty-five a week for twenty-five weeks. But if you tell a soul, I'll have to cut your tongue out." Nick smiled as he said it — the kind of smile that let you know he might be joking, but then again he might not.

Mike knew it was over. He wasn't getting the money, at least not all of it. He took a drag off his cigarette.

"How about five, Nick?" Nick didn't answer right away. He just looked at Mike. Took a sip of his wine.

"You know you're one crazy son-of-a-bitch. All right, five. You pay me the same amount for sixty weeks, but if you miss a payment, I'm gonna treat you like everybody else." Mike nodded. He'd lived in the neighborhood long enough to get the picture. "When do you need it?"

"Tonight."

"All right. Be here at ten. Now finish your spaghetti and tell me what's been goin' on with you these last few years."

∽

Mike called Marguerite at 9:30 and gave her the bad news.

"It'll just have to do," Marguerite told him. "I know where you're getting it from too, Mike. Nobody expects you to get your brains beat out." Mike didn't respond. He had a picture of little Rudy in his mind. He wondered what he looked like all grown up. *Will I ever see him?*

Marguerite called Elena right away and gave her the scoop. "I'll just have to talk her into taking five thousand," Elena told her sister.

Marguerite paused before responding. She didn't know if this was the appropriate time, but it needed to be said.

"You know he went to a loan shark to get this money."

"Why are you telling me this?"

"I just think you should know, that's all."

Elena had arrived at Austin Reaves's office a few minutes early so she could get the lie of the land before Tracey showed up. She was dressed in black, another purchase from the local thrift store. She'd read in a women's magazine that it was a power color, and she wanted all the help she could get for the upcoming negotiation.

Tracey swept in promptly at nine. She also wore black, a suit. She invited Elena into the spare office and sat behind the desk, a definite power move. Elena could tell from the dark spots under her eyes that Tracey hadn't slept well. That was a good sign. Maybe Rudy's case was getting under that thick skin.

Tracey wanted to avoid Elena's eyes as much as possible. She didn't want to think of her mother and that one little picture on her father's dresser. She didn't want to recall the beautiful dark-haired woman of her childhood dreams. This was business. This was the essence of who she was. Or was it? Perhaps today would be the day she would find out. She took her father with her for insurance — perched him on her right shoulder. She needed his voice of reason in the event Elena's eyes caught her off guard.

She began by reiterating how well the hearing had gone the day before. It was a move Elena had expected. She then talked about the additional evidence they could put on at trial.

"I think we can focus on this Geronimo guy. I believe he is the murderer. We can tie the police department's failure to find Geronimo in with their desire to frame Rudy. I think the jury will pick up on that fat little detective's lazy-ass methods. I don't think it'll be hard for them at all."

It was a good speech and it had the desired effect. Once again, Tracey had raised Elena's hopes. What she failed to mention was the fact that the only *admissible* evidence had Geronimo down the street drinking a beer. Joaquin Sanchez's conversation with Pablo at Rosa's bar was all hearsay and totally inadmissible.

Elena didn't respond and they were both silent for a moment. The subject of money was floating around the room like a hawk hovering over a crafty prey. Finally, Tracey had to move in for the kill.

"Elena, we need to talk about the retainer. The money's all used up and then some. You remember our agreement. The retainer has to be replenished." Tracey was prepared to accept ten thousand but not right away.

Elena was ready with a rapid-fire response. "I've lost my job, had to move out of my home. I've got a lump in my breast and I can't even afford to go to the doctor, for Christ's sake." She wasn't putting her five on the table either. Tracey sighed. This wasn't going to be easy.

"Elena, I know this has been hard on you." *You don't know shit!* Elena wanted to scream, but she kept her composure. "But I'm running a business. I've got an office full of people and their families that I have to support. I can't work without getting paid." Tracey could hear the words coming out of her mouth. She knew how hollow they sounded. Knew this shouldn't be about money for her either. But daddy was whispering in her ear now, telling her she was doing the right thing. She had no choice. "A case like this, Elena, would normally cost at least fifty thousand dollars from start to finish. That's why I normally require a twenty-five thousand dollar retainer up front. You've paid me fifteen thousand dollars. Pay me another ten and that's all you'll have to pay. You're basically getting my services for half price. That's the best I can do."

Elena just sat there. Now was the time.

"I may be able to get five from my son's father. He hasn't seen his son in seventeen years but I think I could convince him to give me the money under these circumstances. He doesn't have much, though."

Tracey could see the play. She knew Elena already had the five but no more than that. *She probably worked the phones last night. She's a smart woman. She knew what was coming this morning.* Deep in her heart, Tracey wanted to make it right for Elena. What was an extra five thousand dollars anyway? All she had to do was say yes. It was a win-win situation for both of them. But then there was daddy. She could hear him sitting there on her right shoulder. *Don't take the bait, honey. Don't let her get away with this!* Another sigh.

"I'm sorry, Elena. Five thousand won't do." Tracey hoped that Elena had a few thousand more in her repertoire. If she did, Tracey would take it. Anything! Daddy be damned. But Elena just sat there silent. A moment later she stood up and walked out the door, leaving Tracey alone with her ghost.

[ N I N E T E E N ]

As he watched his mother walk into the visitors' room, Rudy knew the news wasn't good. And now she had to break it to him. Her shoulders were slumped, her lips pursed in a frown. She didn't appear able to even hold her own head up. For a moment, Rudy had a glimpse of his mother as an old woman. Her beauty for him had always been in the sparkle and dance of those large, bright brown eyes. When she finally raised her head and looked at him, Rudy saw nothing but darkness and gloom. It was his job to start the music again.

"Momma?" he asked when she was seated.

"Yes, Rudy."

"Momma, do you remember when I was very young and I used to stay in my room all the time? And you were worried that there was something wrong with me and you took me to the doctor?" Elena just nodded. "And he asked if I was smiling when I was in the room by myself?" Elena nodded again, wondering where this was going. "And then he told you I was all right, I just liked to be alone?"

"Yes, Rudy, I remember."

"Well, that's the way it is for me now, Momma. I have a lot of time to think and talk to God and listen when he talks to me. I miss the river, for sure, but nothing else. And if God takes me, I'm ready to go. Ready for the next adventure." Rudy smiled at her, that wonderful, innocent smile that she had loved for so many years. *And they call him slow!* She forced herself to smile back and as she reached across and took his hands, the music in her heart began to play. It would be a long time, however, before her eyes danced again.

## [ TWENTY ]

*July 1967*

"*Johnny, wake up!*" *Mikey whispered from his crouched position on the fire escape next to Johnny's bed. It was 11:30 on Saturday night.*

"*Shhh. I'm awake,*" *Johnny replied.* "*My mom just went to bed about a half hour ago and my dad's still watching TV.*"

"*C'mon, he ain't gonna check on you before he goes to sleep. You're fine.*" *Mikey could sound so convincing when he wanted to. But he was right. Johnny's dad never came in to check on him before he went to bed.*

"*All right, gimme a second.*" *Two minutes later he was crawling out the window onto the fire escape. Then the two of them lit out down the stairs and up the alley to Lexington Avenue like tomcats on a midnight prowl. Ten minutes later, they were on Eighty-sixth Street.*

*The alley was often the boys' method of travel in the neighborhood. It was the space between the backyards of the buildings on one street and those of the buildings on the next street over. Both backyards had fences that abutted each other. The fences were all different types and sizes. Travel in the alley consisted of negotiating the various fences while moving along. Both boys were expert alley climbers.*

*Earlier that evening on Eighty-sixth Street, they had helped fold the different sections of the Sunday paper into one giant sandwich. It was a ritual every Saturday night. Wooden tables were set up and the folding* began. The boys weren't paid and they didn't even know who they worked for. It was just something to do.

There was a payoff of sorts. After the papers had been arranged in bundles and tied off with copper wiring — and after the boys had gone home and returned — they had the privilege of taking a ride with "Cuz." Sometimes it was just the two of them. Some nights Eddie and Danny came along or the Curtins, two brothers who were friends from the neighborhood.

Cuz was a smallish man, always on the move, always talking, always smiling. He acquired his nickname simply because he called everybody Cuz. It was only natural that the boys responded in kind. Nobody knew his real name.

When Cuz was ready, they loaded the papers in the back of his truck, a smallish box truck with no back door, and hopped in. Cuz's route was a rambling, no-holds-barred race from Eighty-sixth through the streets of Harlem. At every small candy store or newspaper stand, Cuz would stop and yell back to the boys how many bundles to unload. They'd throw the bundles onto the sidewalk and off they'd go again. It was the middle of the night, it was dangerous, and it was the ride of their lives. Cuz sped through the streets and the boys either sat on the bundles and smoked cigarettes or hung onto the handles on the back and played "bustin' bronco" as Cuz hit every pothole on the route. They didn't appreciate that one slip and their lives might come to a tragic end. Neither did Cuz.

This Saturday night it was just Johnny and Mikey on board and they spent the entire trip riding the handles. Johnny's foot slipped several times but he hung on. It was a rush. Afterwards, the boys were walking home still pumped up, still ready for some action. It was three o'clock in the morning.

"Hey, look at this!" Mikey called Johnny over to a little red Mustang convertible that was parked on the avenue. "The keys are in there." He waited for Johnny to come over to look, waited for Johnny to make the suggestion. Johnny hesitated. It was a wild idea, but he was afraid. Mikey was still waiting. What the hell, Johnny thought.

"Whaddya say, Mikey, let's go for a spin." Mikey didn't hear the commitment he was looking for. He decided to stall until he got it.

"I don't know. It's dangerous."

"We'll bring it back. Park it right back here. Nobody's around. Nobody'll ever know it was gone."

"Are you gonna drive?" Mikey goaded him.

"Sure, I'll drive." Johnny had never driven a car before in his life.

The first few blocks were the roughest as the Mustang lurched forward and stopped, lurched forward and stopped. Finally, when he realized there was a very real possibility that he might go flying through the windshield, Mikey took over.

"Pull over here slowly. Put it in park. Easy." Johnny took one last shot at killing them both before slamming on the brakes and easing the car into park.

"I'll drive," Mikey told him as he opened the passenger side door and got out. Mikey had driven a car many times on his uncle's farm in Patchogue.

Pretty soon they were gliding down Lexington Avenue with the convertible top down and the stereo blaring. There were no other cars on the road at that hour, so the boys had the limelight to themselves.

The patrolman spotted them at the corner of Forty-fifth and Lex as they flew by. The speed wouldn't have woken him but the music sure did. He also noticed that one of the headlights was out.

In the Mustang, the Stones were singing "Satisfaction" as loud as the radio could play it when Mikey just happened to glance in the mirror and saw the flashing lights — no way could he hear the siren. He wondered for a moment what he was doing wrong. He wasn't speeding — maybe a few miles over the limit but that was supposed to be okay. Then reality set in: He was in a stolen car! There was probably an APB out! No time for rational thinking. Mikey gunned the engine.

Johnny was sitting in the passenger seat playing his imaginary drums as Mick wailed, oblivious to the crisis, until he was almost propelled into the back seat.

"What's goin' on?" he yelled at Mikey. The speedometer was rising: seventy, eighty. Suddenly Mikey lurched the car to the right and sped up

Thirty-first Street to Park Avenue, where he made another right on two wheels and headed uptown. Johnny was in shock! What the hell was going on? Mikey hadn't answered him. He was too intent on his driving. After a few seconds, Johnny looked behind. He counted four sets of flashing lights about three blocks back.

"Holy shit, Mikey!"

"How far back?" Mikey shouted.

"Three blocks but they're gaining."

"We gotta do something." That sounded like a good idea to Johnny. They were doing ninety and the terror that eluded them on the back of Cuz's truck had finally caught up with Johnny. "Get ready," Mikey yelled over the still-blaring radio. "I'm gonna slam on the brakes. Then get out and run. Find an alley."

As soon as he touched the brakes the back end started to fishtail. Mikey let up and stayed off the gas. When the car slowed up some he hit the brakes again and threw the shift into park. The car actually started to hop onto the sidewalk, sounding as if it was choking to death.

Johnny jumped out while the car was still in its death throes. He ran as fast as he could, heading east on Thirty-fifth, flew down some cellar stairs and then was out in the alley, with no sign of anyone behind him. He'd made it.

Mikey was not so lucky. He tried to jump out as the car was lurching but slipped and fell, slamming his shoulder into the pavement. The pain was almost unbearable. He struggled to get up, but the cops were already on him, guns drawn.

"Up against the wall, punk, hands over your head."

"I can't. I think my shoulder's dislocated."

"Don't give me that shit," one cop snarled as he grabbed Mikey's left arm and yanked it over his head. Mikey let out a scream and passed out on the spot.

"Weren't there two of them?" another officer asked as they waited for the ambulance.

"Not likely. We'd at least have seen the other one running away."

Mikey was eighteen at the time, an adult legally, and was charged with the crime of grand theft auto. His lawyer convinced him and his parents to accept a plea of three to five years in prison. "He'll be out in one, two at the max," the lawyer told them.

Johnny's name was never mentioned. He talked to Mikey a few times before the plea bargain but the conversation was always strained and awkward. Mikey was taking the rap for both of them — what else was there to say?

## [ T W E N T Y - O N E ]

Tracey had one more card to play before she filed her Motion to Withdraw. She sent Clay Evans a letter, attaching Joaquin Sanchez's report on his conversation with Pablo Gonzalez.

> *You can see from this interview that the real killer is this Geronimo person. Find out who he is, check out his record — maybe he's in prison somewhere right now — and you will find your killer. The boy you are holding right now is innocent and we both know it.*
>
> *Release the boy or at least delay the trial until we can jointly investigate who and where this Geronimo person is. Let us work together to see that justice is accomplished.*
>
> *Sincerely,*
> *Tracey James*

Tracey waited two weeks after that, hoping that Clay or Elena would call her. If Elena hadn't just gotten up and walked out of their meeting, she might have relented and taken the five thousand, or at least that's what she told herself. She might still take the five, she didn't know, but Elena needed to call.

Elena had no intention of calling Tracey James. And Clay Evans

— he had a good laugh over her letter. He was about to toss it but decided to take a walk over to Wesley Brume's office first. He wanted to make sure that Brume didn't have any information about this Geronimo character that he had conveniently forgotten to mention. Clay was still bristling from Brume's lapses of memory at the suppression hearing. When Brume scoffed at the letter, Clay felt comfortable shredding it.

Tracey attached her written agreement with Elena, which spelled out the terms of her representation, to her Motion to Withdraw. The motion was granted by Judge Richardson, the new judge on the case, after a short hearing that Elena chose not to attend. Rudy's life was now in the hands of Charley Peterson, the public defender.

~

Charley Peterson had been the public defender for the last ten years. He was a bright fellow, an honors graduate of Georgetown, but Charley had developed a void in his life over the years, a dry spot that constantly needed to be refreshed — with vodka. It was his drink of choice simply because he believed the myth that vodka didn't smell. He kept a bottle in his desk and when he needed or wanted a drink, he locked his door and had one. He was fooling nobody but himself. His penchant for vodka was well known throughout the office and the courthouse. Word around the office was to catch Charley in the morning if you wanted to have a serious discussion about a case. In the afternoon, he was practically incoherent. Oh, he could talk without slurring his words and he could carry on a conversation that seemed to make sense. But if you wanted legitimate answers to questions, see him in the morning.

Perhaps Charley was miscast: Perhaps he should have been a tax lawyer. He certainly looked like one. A short, slightly built man with thinning blond hair, he certainly didn't inspire confidence at first glance, although Charley had been a pretty good trial lawyer in his early years. Good enough, at least, to secure the appointment as public defender without any political affiliations to speak of. But something happened along the way that caused Charley to fizzle and finally burn out. What it was, nobody knew.

Charley had been following Rudy's case in the newspaper simply because it was there, usually on the front page. It held no particular interest for him and he had no feeling about Rudy's guilt or innocence. The last thing he wanted was to be Rudy's lawyer, but when Tracey James was removed from the case, it was transferred to the public defender's office.

He could have assigned it to one of his four underlings, but only two of them had any felony experience and neither had ever tried a capital case. Try as he might, Charley couldn't duck this one. People were watching. People who didn't want to believe the courthouse scuttlebutt.

It took him two weeks to review the file, including the transcript of the suppression hearing. His first order of business as Rudy's new attorney was to attend a status conference, at which he told Judge Richardson he would be ready to try the case in a month. Charley's belief was that he could plea-bargain down to manslaughter or perhaps second-degree murder. After all, it was a circumstantial evidence case and a fairly weak one, although Charley had no idea how weak it really was. He never requested Tracey James's file, never reviewed her investigative notes, and never saw her last letter to the Fourth. Still, he was confident something could be arranged. He had worked well with Clay Evans in the past, mainly because Clay was as lazy as Charley and they were both partial to working things out rather than having to undergo the ordeal of a trial. Charley didn't realize until after the status conference that this case was different for Clay. Clay wanted the trial and the publicity.

"I won't even accept a plea of second-degree murder," Clay told Charley when they finally had their discussion.

Charley took Clay at his word. In fact, if Charley had offered to plead to second-degree murder, Clay would have had to accept it. Tracey James had pointed out all too well the weaknesses in his case. The possibility of losing was simply too great to turn down such a plea. But the plea never came. Instead, Charley began his preparation for trial. He locked his office door, opened his bottom desk drawer, and took out a bottle and a glass.

PART

# [ TWO ]

[ **T W E N T Y - T W O** ]

August 1996

Her heart was racing — she was ten minutes late, the coffee wasn't done, the newspapers weren't delivered and she wasn't sitting at her desk with a big smile on her face like a good cocker spaniel waiting for its master. She was moving in overdrive now, trying to get it done. Not that he would ever acknowledge the work. The son-of-a-bitch barely acknowledged that she was there. But if it wasn't done, if everything wasn't perfect, she'd hear about it. Not from him. God knows he never spoke to the help. No, he'd tell his executive secretary, Ms. Corinne Singleton, and she, in turn, would tell Rick Woods, the office manager who supervised the lowlifes below the rank of executive secretary, and Rick would call her into his office for a little talk. She wasn't a virgin. She knew his spiel verbatim.

"Nancy, could you come to my office for a chat," he'd say sometime in midmorning after the complaint had been lodged. It was always a casual pass-by of her station. The first time she didn't know whether to be alarmed or excited. Maybe they wanted to give her a raise or something. But the looks from the other girls quickly dispelled that notion.

"Corinne has informed me that Mr. Tobin's coffee was not ready when he arrived this morning. And while the *Miami Herald* and the

*New York Times* were on his desk, the *Cobb County Press* was missing." Nancy would just look at him like a defiant teenager in the principal's office. *You can skip the facts, pal. And there ain't gonna be any mea culpas, so let's get to the penalty phase.* Rick hated that about her. He wanted some genuine remorse. The others always bowed their head and at least pretended to feel guilty.

This morning was a tad better than her past performances when she had arrived late. She'd almost gotten it done. The coffee was made; a fresh cup was on his desk. And the papers were there — all except for the damned *Cobb County Press.* They didn't deliver that rinky-dink little rag; she had to go downstairs to a special store two blocks away and buy it every morning. She could have picked it up on the way in but she was already in a panic by then. Now it was too late.

At nine sharp, she planted herself at her desk, pasted her best fake smile on her face and waited for Old Sourpuss to pass by.

"Good morning, Mr. Tobin," she chirped at the appointed moment, as she always did. He didn't look her way — he never did. The only acknowledgment was an ever so slight tip of his head. She hadn't noticed the head tip her first two months of employment. She was sure he was ignoring her altogether. She only found out after whining to Corinne one morning.

"Oh, he wouldn't ignore you, dear," Corinne, the dutiful servant, told her. "He nods. You have to watch closely, but he nods." As if the nod made any difference.

It wasn't any easier for Corinne. She would have to take his briefcase and greet him in that sweet, syrupy professional voice she had mastered over the years. *An office mommy,* Nancy decided, *treats him like his mother did when he was two. Only she wears prim and proper dresses and she never scolds. Office mommies don't have that kind of power.*

And every morning he would simply ask, "Do I have any calls?" And Corinne would give him his messages and he'd disappear into his office for the day, never getting anywhere close to cracking a smile or dropping a pleasantry. But Corinne didn't seem to mind.

She had that loyalty thing going.

Jack Tobin was one of the three senior partners ("The Big Three") at Tobin, Gleason and Gardner, a one-hundred-man Miami firm. The other two, Tom Gleason and Jim Gardner, were dead. *Maybe that's why he walks around so morose all the time,* Nancy thought. *He knows his turn's coming.* But Nancy knew that couldn't be true. At twenty-four, she had a fixation for hard bodies and she couldn't help noticing — although she tried like hell not to — that Jack Tobin, who had to be pushing fifty, was a hard body. The man stood ramrod straight, not an ounce of fat on him. Although his short, almost punk-style gray hair was thinning on top and non-existent in some places, his skin was taut, slightly tanned and glowing with health. He looked good — ruggedly handsome, like a tough old marine. His eyes were an attractive blue, but they were eyes that had no sparkle.

*With his money,* she mused, *if he could ever force a smile, he'd be dating those Vogue models half his age who hang out on South Beach. Maybe he is, maybe the sardonic look is just a front for the office staff.* God, she hated the bastard.

⁓

As he passed her desk that morning, Jack Tobin saw the smile, heard the greeting, and knew, instantly, that she'd been late. It was the eyes. You could always tell from the eyes. Most men never looked but he'd been a trial lawyer for over twenty years; it was his job to look — at the eyes, the hands, the posture. And listen — to the words *and* the inflection of the voice. Truth was never discerned from the words alone.

It didn't really bother him. It was an annoyance that Corinne would handle. He didn't even have to mention it anymore. Corinne knew to check for the *Cobb County Press*. If it wasn't there, Nancy'd been late. That was her name, Nancy, he was almost sure of it. She'd been with the firm for almost a year, a cute young girl from what he could tell. He usually only saw her from the waist up, sitting at her desk. She had auburn hair. He liked that. There was some depth there. He hated blondes, at least in theory. At the right time and the right place he could love anyone — and had. He hadn't always been miserable, only for the last five years or so, but all that was going to change.

He'd been getting the *Cobb County Press* for about a year now. Change was something that happened slowly for him. It had started as an idea, actually someone else's idea. Then it churned into a dream and coalesced into plans. Now it was about to become a reality. He loved the law, really did. Loved to try a good case. But he despised the big firm, the rich clients — the high-profile crap. It had never been him. He was a good lawyer but success had brought him to a place he didn't belong. It had taken him twenty years to make the decision to go, but he was about to do it.

Cobb County was located at the northwest corner of Lake Okeechobee in the south central part of the state, where the word "cracker" didn't refer to something you ate. It was the smallest county in Florida, with a population under 15,000, the majority of whom lived in the small town of Bass Creek. Although it was infinitesimal in size compared to Miami, Bass Creek had its own McDonalds and Burger King, and rumor had it the Colonel was opening a franchise in the near future. In the winter, transients piled in from who knows where, old and young, rich and poor — but mostly poor. Citrus was the crop and pickers, many illegals, from Mexico, Colombia, Guatemala and other points south of the border always arrived for the harvest.

Jack had grown up in New York City but he was a Florida cracker at heart. For the last ten years, he'd spent his weekends and vacations out on the lake boating and fishing. He'd been alone for the last five, since Reneé, his third wife, left him. She'd told him she didn't marry a successful Miami lawyer to spend her weekends in a seedy, backwoods town while he went fishing. The woman had a point, but Jack wasn't going to give up the one thing in life he truly enjoyed. So they parted ways. It hadn't been a conscious decision, but he'd shut himself off after that.

The plan was to open a small office in "downtown" Bass Creek. He was going to represent anybody who walked through the door, the only contingency being that he would have to believe in their case. He was going to be the proverbial country lawyer and he was sure it was going to be a hoot. He didn't need the money anymore but he did need something. What did Bob Marley call it — "Redemption"? But from what he wasn't sure. Maybe it was from all those people whose legitimate claims he had defeated in court over the years on behalf of those bloodsucking insurance companies he represented. He'd always told himself it was just business but he knew. Hell, everybody knew. He was just a high-paid prostitute who sold his soul instead of his body. You can only live with that so long, and he had lasted longer than most.

Jack had given the firm notice last year, and they had negotiated for more than six months before arriving at a buyout figure of twenty million dollars, enough for a thousand people or more to live their lives out comfortably in Cobb County. But there was a snag. There was always a snag. As a trial lawyer he knew that intuitively. Never saw a perfect case.

This snag had been his own fault. He'd been at one of those fundraisers he hated, stepped outside for a minute to talk to his old friend Bob Richards, who happened to be the governor of the state — and blew it. There was no other way to put it. He blew it. Bob Richards was a friend the way wealthy people and politicians are friends — they drank together, socialized some and generally networked with others of their ilk. It didn't go any deeper than that. But there he was at a fundraiser, the master of playing his cards close to his vest — Old Sourpuss himself — spilling his guts about his future to the governor.

"There's a rumor going around that you're leaving the firm," Bob casually mentioned when they were out on the terrace alone. It was fall in Miami and this night was the first break from the tropical summer heat. It was about seventy-five, a slight breeze blowing, clear skies — the kind of night that people in Buffalo would soon be having wet dreams about.

"Yeah, it's time to go. Make way for the young turks."

"What are you going to do? I never took you for the retirement type." There it was. He could have shrugged. He could have made some innocuous comment like "I'll get used to it." But no, he had to be honest.

"I'm not going to retire. I'm going to open a little office in Cobb County. Be a country lawyer."

"Cobb County," the governor mused. "I seem to recall old Harry Parker is about to retire from the circuit bench over there." That was Bob, a politician's politician. He couldn't find his way through a spreadsheet, couldn't recognize an environmental issue if it reached up and bit him in the ass, but he knew every open political appointment in the state.

"I don't want to be a judge," Jack told him flat out.

"No, I know that." Bob replied, looking up at the stars and rubbing his chin.

"Besides, I've already committed that position to Bill Sampson, the state attorney, but Bill's position is open. Jack, you'd love it! It's a small office — only four other lawyers, no pressure. You'd be doing trial work. Whaddya say?"

That was Bob, the ultimate salesman. What could he say? A flat no would have been appropriate. But he was never one to turn down opportunity. It was trial work and he wouldn't have to set up an office and hire staff. And he would have a few months off before he started. So he said yes. Not that night. He fumbled and fidgeted a bit and it took several phone calls from ol' Bob, but eventually Jack relented. And that was it. The dream that he had planned for so long was gone — replaced by somebody else's dream. Why he let it happen, he didn't know. Perhaps it was fate.

~

After he passed Nancy on the way to his office, Jack instinctively felt something was wrong. He hated to admit it but he was a man of habit and somebody had thrown a wrench into his ritual. He recognized the problem soon enough. Corinne was not there to take his briefcase and give him his messages. For a moment he thought to ask Nancy where she was but decided against it. He walked into his office and called Rick Woods instead. He was a little on edge, a little concerned. Corinne had never been absent or late for work before.

"Rick, where's Corinne? She's not here," he demanded when Rick picked up the phone.

"Relax, Jack. She called in sick. Apparently, for the first time in her life Corinne has the flu. You're going to have to struggle through the day with Nancy." Rick was being a little testy. The deal had already been made with Jack. He was leaving the firm soon — the sooner the better, from Rick's perspective — and there was no longer any incentive to appease his every wish. Jack hung up the phone. He thought of calling Nancy in but he knew she was already on her way to get the *Cobb County Press*. Even Nancy's screwups were part of his ritual. Something was still bothering him, though, and he wasn't sure what it was. *I can't be this upset simply because my secretary is out sick. It has to be something else. I can feel it.*

He walked to the closet, took off his blue suit jacket, meticulously placed it on a wooden hanger and hung it up. He walked back to his desk, picked up the *New York Times* — he always read the *Times* first — sat down in his comfortable burgundy leather chair and began to read: world news first, then the local section, then the obituaries, then... his intuition was right. Something else definitely was wrong.

⁓

Nancy didn't exactly run the two blocks to the newspaper stand. She'd already learned from Rick Woods that Corinne was sick and that she was going to be Jack's secretary for the day. No reason to hurry back to the office.

"Think of it as an opportunity," Rick had replied when she

unthinkingly cursed into the phone after he gave her the news. She dreaded the thought. *If they didn't pay so well, I'd just keep walking.* But that wasn't an option. She needed the job.

~

His chair was facing away from the door and towards the window when she quietly stepped into his office. She walked right up to the desk with the paper and the messages. No sense being shy. They both knew she was late and had forgotten the paper. If he wanted to be a jerk about it, she was ready for him. She didn't hear the sobs until she was right at the desk. Big sobs. His shoulders were heaving. She saw the paper on his lap. *The obituaries. Somebody died, and he's actually crying. Maybe he did have a mother after all. Maybe blood does run through his veins.* The thought of him having a heart was almost too much for her. But there was a much more immediate problem — she was standing in his office, intruding on a very personal moment. What should she do? She couldn't tiptoe out, although that was the most enticing option. And she didn't want him to know that she had actually witnessed him in his moment of being human. Having no real choice, she finally decided to just drop the paper on his desk, making as much noise as she possibly could while at the same time pretending she'd seen and heard nothing.

He turned suddenly at the noise — so quickly, he startled Nancy. His red, swollen eyes confronted her.

"I have your messages but I can come back." It was the best she could come up with. He didn't say a word. He was still so overcome with emotion, he couldn't speak. He motioned her to sit. *Oh my God, he wants me to stay! I need a drink.* As if he'd read her mind, he opened a drawer in his desk and pulled out a bottle of Jack Daniels and two glasses. It wasn't her drink of choice, especially at 9:30 in the morning, but she graciously accepted the glass and took a long sip simultaneously with him. Then he poured them both another. After the second shot, she started to relax.

"Nancy — it is Nancy, isn't it?"

"Yes sir."

"Nancy, have you ever lost anyone close? I mean very close?"

"I lost my mother when I was fifteen." That made him pause a moment. She knew it would. It always shocked everyone.

"I'm sorry to hear that."

"It's okay. That was nine years ago. I'm over it now."

"You never get over it, Nancy. My father died ten years ago and I'm still not over it. He's still with me, my harshest critic."

Nancy couldn't believe she was having this conversation with Old Sourpuss. She felt like asking for another shot to get her through when he suddenly stood up.

"Nancy, you and I are going to have to go to a meeting outside the office." He walked over to the closet to retrieve his blue suit coat, still clutching the bottle of Jack Daniels. Nancy was bewildered. Corinne never left the office for meetings with him — let alone with a bottle.

"Should I call Rick and let him know?" she asked.

"No. I'll straighten him out when we get back." She grabbed her purse and practically ran to catch him as he walked out the front door. The other office personnel who saw them leave just looked at each other.

He had her drive his black Coupe de Ville, which made her even more nervous. It was a lot bigger than her Honda and with two shots of Jack on an empty stomach she wasn't exactly sure of her instincts.

"Where to?" she asked when she had successfully maneuvered the monster out of the parking garage.

"Do you have a neighborhood bar?"

"My father does, but it's twenty minutes away over towards Homestead."

"That sounds lovely. Let's go there." They drove in silence, Nancy concentrating on the road, trying to get used to the big car and Jack deep inside himself, sipping absentmindedly from the bottle of Jack. She stole a glance at him from time to time and saw him looking out into space, his eyes teary. She didn't dare interrupt him. *It must be his mother,* she thought.

Twenty minutes later they pulled up in front of a dingy-looking place that appeared deserted from the outside. The sign out front simply read Fitzpatrick's. The word "Bar" would have been superfluous from the looks of the place. Nancy got out first and led the way. Following her, Jack couldn't help but notice, perhaps for the first time, that she had a striking figure — a compact torso, well-toned muscles, very attractive. *Where the hell have I been for the last year?* he asked himself. Five years was more like it.

"Hi, Nance!" the bartender, a strapping young Irishman, greeted her as they entered the front door.

"Hey Tommy," she replied, a little embarrassed. It wasn't necessarily a good thing to walk in a bar in the middle of the day with your boss in tow and have the bartender address you by your first name.

Jack didn't seem to notice. He was looking around, checking the place out. Nancy led them to a booth in the back. He would have preferred the bar but this was her place, her terms. It was a great place, though, very dark, with dark mahogany paneling throughout, black ceiling, dark green linoleum floors. The only light stole through the few clear spots in the dirt-stained windows. The joint certainly had character. Once they were seated in the old wooden booth, Nancy stood to get the drinks.

"Jack on the rocks?" she asked. He nodded. A minute later she was back with two of the same. "I ordered a pastrami sandwich because I have to have something to eat and they don't serve breakfast here. Do you want something?"

"No thanks."

"By the way, just so you know, Tommy and I went to high school together." Jack smiled. *He actually smiled,* she told herself.

"I'm glad you told me that because I was starting to suspect that you were a rummy." A joke! *He actually made a joke.* And it was an Irish joke of sorts. "Rummy" wasn't a word used in too many circles. She laughed. She couldn't help it. She was starting to warm up to Old Sourpuss. *Maybe he's human after all.*

They drank in silence for a while after that — he with that far-off, teary-eyed look. Nancy waited what she considered to be an appropriate period of time, but after three shots of Jack, her fear of her boss had worn off almost completely, and she wanted some conversation.

"So who died?" she asked. He just looked at her for a moment, a little surprised at her directness.

"An old friend," he finally answered. He was slurring his words now. "A dear, dear old friend who I lost touch with many years ago." He drifted away again for a few minutes. Then he began to talk.

"We grew up together in New York, lived in the same apartment building. He was my best friend," he laughed, his watery blue eyes shining. Nancy could see him drifting back in time with that laugh. "New York was a very aggressive place back in those days. It's probably worse now. It was like a small town every few blocks. Each neighborhood had its own crowd. They weren't gangs really but guys and gals who hung out together on street corners, strutting their stuff. There were always fights, sometimes between crowds, sometimes within the crowd. And there was a hierarchy — the strong picked on the weak. Not Mikey, he was different. He always looked after me. If he didn't, I think the neighborhood would have chewed me up and spit me out.

"You know, an old parish priest gave him a nickname that he loved and that fit him to a tee, but he pinned it on me because he knew I needed it and that it would give me confidence. He made up this story about how I was going to do something someday for the both of us —just to make me feel better about myself.

"For the rest of my life, whenever I was in a tough situation, whenever I doubted myself, his faith in me always helped me get through. I wish I could have had one minute with him — just one minute — to tell him how much of an influence he had on my life — to tell him I remembered."

The tears were running down his cheeks as the memories poured out. He was no longer looking at Nancy but straight ahead as if into another dimension. Then he suddenly looked directly at her.

"I've never told anyone that story."

"I won't tell anybody," Nancy replied. "I swear."

Jack smiled. "I didn't mean it that way. It's just that I keep things to myself — too much maybe."

Tommy arrived just then with Nancy's pastrami on rye. He looked at the table and noticed the glasses were empty.

"Can I get anybody anything else?" Tommy asked. He could afford to be polite: Jilly Newton was the only one at the bar and he had already started talking to himself.

"I'd like a glass of water," Nancy replied. Jack just nodded and pointed to the empty glass to let Tommy know he'd continue with the same poison.

"Sure," Tommy replied to both of them and walked back towards the bar. Nancy followed him with her eyes, wondering if there was something about Tommy that she'd missed. Watching his lumbering frame shuffle across the linoleum floor, she quickly concluded that she hadn't missed a thing. Tommy was Tommy — not the best conversationalist but a good listener and therefore a good bartender.

Her thoughts turned back to her boss. She wondered what had happened between Jack Tobin and his friend Mikey so many years ago. He'd said they had lost touch, but the way he said it made her believe there was more to the story. Perhaps whatever happened had something to do with the sadness this man dragged around with him every day. But she wasn't going to get an answer to that question anytime soon. Jack had just closed his eyes, rested his head against the dark mahogany paneling, and gone to sleep.

[ **T W E N T Y - T H R E E** ]

Johnny Tobin met Patricia Morgan in a sandbox when he was three years old. They lived in the same apartment building and their mothers were friends. The moms took the kids to Central Park most summer days and let them play in the sandbox while they sat and talked.

Johnny was at the school playground the day Billy Maloney punched Pat's older brother Jimmy in the eye during recess. Jimmy and Billy Maloney were in the third grade, two grades ahead of Johnny and Pat. Billy stood there laughing over Jimmy, who was on the ground crying. Pat walked up to Billy and punched him right in the nose, and when he fell to the ground, she jumped on top of him and kept punching until a teacher pulled her off kicking and screaming. The girl had a temper.

Pat played all the street sports. Nobody ever thought of excluding her because she was a girl. She was as good or better than everybody else and besides, nobody had the balls to tell her she couldn't play, except maybe Mikey — and Mikey always picked her to be on his team. The three of them were great friends until high school, when Pat all of a sudden developed "curves" and "bumps" and started to wear dresses. The boys felt uncomfortable hanging out with her after that, although they didn't totally dislike the change.

"Don't get me wrong," Mikey told Johnny one day when they saw Pat walking demurely down the street. "I like girls and especially girls who wear nice dresses and have big tits. I just never thought Patty was going to *be one of them." That was probably the best explanation why they drifted apart in their teenage years. The boys liked girls and fooled around with girls, but they weren't going to fool around with their own Patty.*

∽

Jack had a strange affinity for wakes and funerals. His paternal grandmother came from a family of thirteen and it seemed that when he was a kid he was attending a wake and a funeral every other weekend. Irish wakes were a gathering of the clan, and while there was a good deal of weeping for the dead, there was also a lot of hugging and kissing and laughing, usually around an open coffin, and after the funeral they always had a party. Of course, they weren't as lighthearted as the other parties his parents threw. There were tears interspersed with the laughter and the drinking, but those funeral parties had something different, something special — the warmth and familiarity of family and close friends. He was a nephew or cousin or great nephew to almost everyone in the room, some of whom he hardly knew, and that made it all the more special.

Mike Kelly's funeral was going to be different, he knew. Mike's relatives weren't his, and after twenty-five years whatever close relationship he had with them was long gone. He expected a cold reception. *What kind of friend would never contact someone in twenty-five years?* He knew the answer Mike's family had probably arrived at if they thought about it at all: *The rich, big-shot lawyer.* And for that the big-shot lawyer had no counterargument.

He saw her as soon as he walked in the room at John Mahoney's funeral home. After all those years, he picked her right out of the crowd. She was talking to two people, a smile on her face, her lips doing double time. Like radar, just as he recognized her, her eyes looked up and caught his. She excused herself and walked towards him. He tried not to but he couldn't help surveying her as she approached. She still looked good from a distance — that tall, athletic body, thin legs, nice *bumps.*

Her arms opened.

"Johnny!" she exclaimed as she enveloped him. Jack felt her warmth smother him. For that moment, it felt good to be home. Finally, Pat released him. "I knew you'd come," she said. "How long has it been — fifteen years?" At that moment, Jack looked around and saw others from the crowd looking at them and listening. The cool, smooth Miami lawyer still could feel embarrassed among the people he grew up with.

"No, it's been about ten — my dad's funeral."

"That's right. Well, no matter how long it's been, you look great." She sensed his unease and took his hand. "C'mon, let's go say hello to Mrs. Kelly and the boys."

Before he could voice a protest, or tell Pat how good she looked — and she did look good, even on closer inspection — they were standing before Mrs. Kelly, Mike's eighty-year-old mother.

"Mrs. Kelly, you remember Johnny Tobin," Pat said as she introduced him to the old woman. Jack didn't know what to expect. Mary Kelly's wrinkled face broke into a big grin.

"Of course I do. I'll never forget your face, Johnny, the day Father Burke offered to recruit my Mike into the priesthood. I thought *you* were going to have a heart attack." Everyone around them laughed. Mrs. Kelly squeezed his hand. "What was that he always called you — the Mayor?"

"The Mayor of Lexington Avenue." It was just like Mikey to convince his own mother, who'd been a witness to Father Burke's words, that the moniker belonged to Jack.

"Yes, that's it. Thank you for coming," she said, her gentle eyes focusing directly on his. "Mike would be happy to know you are here."

Mike's brothers, Danny and Eddie, were there as well, next to their mother. Danny hugged Jack, which again surprised him. This was not the reception he'd expected.

"Thanks for coming, Johnny. Mike was always so proud of you — the big-shot lawyer." Jack didn't know what to say.

Eddie was in a wheelchair. He tried to talk but just mumbled. He grabbed Jack's arm with his left hand and smiled. There were tears in his eyes. Jack put his free hand on top of Eddie's and smiled back.

"He had a stroke three years ago," Pat whispered in Jack's ear. "Never recovered."

After he said hello to everyone else in the family, Jack approached the coffin to pay his respects to his childhood friend. He had thought about this moment on the trip up. He didn't know how he was going to feel. Would he even recognize Mikey after all these years? But his emotions started to surface before he even looked into the half-open casket. This was his first friend — *my best friend* — and that was something the years could never erase. He knelt down to say a prayer, looked into the coffin and saw Mikey. The red hair was gone, as were the freckles and the smile — that joyful smile, the forerunner of many an adventure for the two of them. Jack began to cry. It was the last thing he wanted to do and he tried to keep it to himself but he was visibly shaking.

Pat knelt next to him, a comforting arm around his shoulders. He initially was too upset to speak but after a few moments he started to regain some of his composure.

"I don't want to make a scene," he whispered to her.

"You're not. And even if you were — we're Irish. It's expected."

"I just never had a friend like Mikey."

"I know," she said softly. "Me neither, except you." Jack looked at her.

"Yeah, you're right. Except you."

They met later on at McGlade's, although the name had been changed to Pat Herrity's Irish Bar. "Have a Jar at Herrity's Bar" was the new slogan that adorned the outside of the place. The interior had been substantially upgraded as well. They sat in a back booth. Jack ordered a Guinness, Pat a chablis. The conversation started light.

"I've been wanting to tell you this all day, Pat — you look great."

"Why thanks, Jack."

"So what are you doing these days?"

"I'm a CPA with Harrel and Jackson. Been with them for twenty-five years now."

"Very impressive," Jack crooned. "That's a high-powered firm."

"Yeah, well don't get too impressed because I'm retiring in two weeks. I've had enough. How about you? We've all heard you're with this big, successful law firm in Miami."

"Not anymore. I'm about to retire myself — any day now, actually. I haven't decided when. I'm moving to a small town. I'm still going to work but only while I'm enjoying it." Jack decided not to get into the sordid details of how he'd accepted the state attorney's job in Cobb County.

"Really?" Pat replied. "That sounds nice. Are you married? Any kids? I know you were married ten years ago but I can't remember the kids part."

Jack laughed. "I can't remember anything either anymore but the answers to your questions are — 'Nope' and 'Nope.' I've been married a few times but it never worked out for me. How about you?" They were friends who hadn't seen each other in years, but Jack was more comfortable at that moment than at any time he could remember.

"I never did get married," Pat replied. "I had a few relationships over the years but, like yours I guess, they just didn't work out. Frankly, I think I'm a little hard to take on a daily basis."

"Me too," Jack said, and they both laughed. The small talk was over.

"I read it was cancer?"

"Yeah, lung cancer to be exact. Mike was never able to kick the habit and I tell you, Johnny, if I had lived his life, I'd still be smoking myself."

"You know, I left home after college and I didn't see Mikey on my trips home after that like I saw you. I don't know much about his life after I left."

"How much time do you have?" Pat asked. "Because it's a long story."

"I've got all night — and tomorrow if need be."

Pat laughed. "We have a funeral to attend tomorrow, but I'll give you the short version."

"Hang on a second." Jack caught the waiter's attention and ordered a second round. "Never thought I'd see a waiter in McGlade's."

"Bernie's probably rolling around in his grave at the thought," Pat laughed. Bernie McGlade had run the place by himself when they were kids. There were tables even back then, but if you wanted something to drink you had to go to the bar to get it.

They were always in there as youngsters, usually because their fathers were in there. But there was another reason. Depending on the season, Bernie always had a supply of footballs, basketballs, or baseballs and bats on hand that the neighborhood kids could take to Central Park. It was a small part of the neighborhood that no longer existed.

"When he got out of jail," Pat began, "Mike kinda slipped back into the old neighborhood routine. His uncle got him a job with the steel workers and he made good money. We'd all get together right here on Friday and Saturday nights. There was a hard edge to his personality after prison, something that most people wouldn't notice, but I did. He spent two years upstate, you know." Jack just nodded, his head down. That was the part he felt responsible for. Right there in the beginning — the first pebble in the landslide.

"He started drinking a lot — too much. He was drunk all the time. He almost lost his job a couple of times but his uncle saved him. Apparently, his uncle was a bigwig in the union. Anyway, he met this Puerto Rican woman, Elena — lovely girl — and they started dating and he straightened up. They eventually married and had a little boy. I thought he had gotten over the hump, but he hadn't. Six months after his son was born, he started back again, worse than before. I don't know if it was the added pressure or what. He lost his job. She finally fled — and I mean *fled*. She didn't even tell him where she was going. She just vanished.

"He didn't stop even then. He just kept drinking until he was living on the street — a total bum. After doing that for years, one day he just stopped. It was a long process back, as you can imagine, but eventually he got a job and an apartment and started to settle in again. We'd meet for coffee once in a while, had dinner once a month. He was fine, but the thing with his wife and kid was always eating away at him."

"He never heard from the kid?" Jack asked.

"Let me finish, I'm getting there." Pat said, motioning at him with her hand. "You can't rush a storyteller." Jack sat back, feigning a chastened look.

"About ten years ago — and I don't know the particular facts very well, Mike just gave me snippets from time to time — he got a call from Marguerite, his wife's sister. The boy was in trouble and they needed money."

"He hadn't seen or heard from the wife or child since they left?" Jack asked his question again. He couldn't help himself.

"Not for seventeen years."

"That's pretty ballsy."

"Or desperate — and it turned out to be desperate. Mike gave what he could. The sister, Marguerite, gave money too but apparently it wasn't enough. The kid was charged with murder. The private attorney quit because she — I think it was a woman — wasn't getting paid. The public defender handled the case and, I guess, screwed it up because the kid got convicted of first-degree murder. He's on death row right now."

"Death row? Holy shit!"

"Yeah, holy shit is right. You don't hear from your wife and kid for seventeen years — and don't get me wrong, I think she should have left him and started a new life, I'm not blaming her—but after all that time, you finally hear from them and your son is on trial for his life and eventually gets convicted. It's enough to start a man drinking again."

"Did he?" Jack asked.

"No. He probably would have but it's kind of amazing what happened next — one of those things that happens only in real life. Even though he had been contacted and sent money, Mike still didn't know where his wife and kid were — everything was through Marguerite. It wasn't till the boy was convicted that Elena called him personally. Mike told me she was at the end of her rope. She apologized for leaving him, she apologized for being such a bad mother — she thanked him for sending the money and told him where they were living."

"What did he do?" Jack asked.

"He flew down there a few days later — visited his son in jail. Spent a few days with Elena talking things out. He explained to her that she had every right to leave him and that he should be the one apologizing. When he came back, he told me that the boy was a sweetheart. He was certain after talking to him for two minutes that Rudy — his name's Rudy — never could have committed the crime he was accused of. Well, he and Elena spent the rest of their lives working on proving Rudy's innocence. There were two appeals that I know of before Elena died. She died about two years ago of breast cancer.

"You know, in the midst of all this really, really bad stuff, I'd never seen Mike happier. He and Elena were together again. He was in Florida twice a month. She even came here sometimes. He visited the boy a lot and he told me the boy — I shouldn't say boy. Hell, Rudy was almost a man. Anyway, he said the kid really lifted his spirits. He said Rudy was always happy, never afraid. And he was overjoyed that Mike and his mother had rekindled their relationship, regardless of the circumstances."

"I wonder why he never called me," Jack pondered out loud. "Did he know I was in Miami? I could have helped."

"He knew you were there. He was always so proud of the fact that you were a big-time attorney. But once Rudy was convicted, they had one of those death penalty centers working with them at no cost."

"That's such bullshit and you know it," Jack replied. "We both know why he didn't call me." He stared at her. Pat stared back, not saying anything. Finally she spoke. She was ready for him.

"Let me see if I can guess what's in your head and what's been in your head for all these years. If *you* didn't get the bright idea to steal that car, Mike wouldn't have gone to jail. And now you can add to that — he wouldn't have become a drunk and Elena wouldn't have left him and Rudy would never have been in Florida and charged with murder. How am I doing? Oh, I left out the most important part. It's all *your* fault. Everything."

He almost smiled. How could she smoke him out and be so dead on point?

"This is really weird. You and I haven't spoken in years and I feel like I'm talking to my sister about something that happened yesterday."

"Well, get over it, Johnny, because the important things in your life did happen yesterday, no matter how long ago they occurred. Same with the people you grew up with — we could go a hell of a lot more years without seeing each other and I could still read your mind."

"What made you so smart?" Jack felt like he was a kid again, fighting back.

"For one, I never left this neighborhood. I've been living with these issues through Mike. I can't tell you how many times he talked about calling you and I know you felt the same way. It's not hard really and it's nobody's fault."

"That's where you're wrong," Jack said. "I didn't go to prison, Mikey did. I was the successful one. It was my obligation to call — my duty to make everything okay between us. I didn't do that."

"Let me just tell you what Mike said about that whole incident. He said it was his idea to take the car for a joyride. He only made it seem like it was your idea. He set you up and he never felt you were responsible for him going to prison."

"Then why didn't he call me?"

"I tried to get him to, but he was as stubborn as you. He figured you got on with your life and you didn't need to be reminded of this stuff. I think he knew he was kidding himself, though. Two days before he died — he was in the hospital in very bad shape — I was sitting by his bed. He opened his eyes and looked at me and said, 'When Johnny comes, tell him about Rudy.' Then he closed his eyes and never opened them again."

The tears started to well again in Jack's eyes. He waited a moment before he spoke. *His last words were about me. How did he know I would come? Why couldn't I have called him when he was alive*, he asked himself, but there was no answer. There would never be an answer.

"Why didn't you tell me that before? Why'd you give me that shit about them having one of those law centers handling the case?" he asked Pat.

"I wasn't sure you cared. I wasn't sure you wanted — needed to know."

"And now you are?"

Pat just nodded.

"Two more questions and then I'll drop the subject. It's too much for one night. If it's been ten years since Rudy's conviction, his execution must be scheduled."

"Eight weeks from now — to be exact, October 22nd. Apparently they like to schedule these things just before the holidays. You know, give the families a little something extra for the season."

"Whoa. That's right around the corner."

"Yeah. And it was weighing on Mike."

"Last question: Where did this murder take place?"

Pat put her hand on her forehead. "I can't remember the name of the town where they lived. It was a small town in the middle of nowhere, I remember Mike telling me that. *Something* Creek, I think."

"Bass Creek?"

Pat pointed at him. "That's it!"

Jack knew right then what he was going to be doing for the next eight weeks.

[ **T W E N T Y - F O U R** ]

One week later Jack was in Bass Creek doing a little real estate shopping. He bought a building on Broad Street two blocks west of the Bass Creek Hotel, right on the Okalatchee River. He'd spotted the place years before when his dream about being a country lawyer was still fresh. Now that dream was over — almost. He still had a few months of freedom before he became the state attorney, and he planned to put that freedom to good use for the next seven weeks. The office was the first step.

The next day, back at his plush digs in Miami, Jack called Nancy in. His relationship with her had changed considerably since Corinne had taken her first and only sick day less than two weeks before. He stopped and talked to her every morning. Some days he invited her into his office and they sat and chatted about anything and everything — sports, the news, her love life or lack of it, even his love life or lack of it. Nancy was totally relaxed with Jack now, as he was with her. That one morning they'd shared had broken down the culture of formality and separation that Tobin, Gleason and Gardner had always demanded from its partners and employees — at least for the two of them.

Elsewhere within the firm, though, their relationship was causing an uproar. Corinne was dumbfounded by the lack of protocol and she had taken her concerns directly to Rick Woods, who had spoken to Jack about it just that morning.

"You know, Nancy," Jack said when she'd sat down, "Rick came in earlier to talk about our relationship." He was leaning back in his chair with his feet up on the desk, his usual posture these days.

"Which means he's probably going to fire me," she said, not really meaning it.

"You're probably right."

Nancy was shocked. She'd thought as they'd grown closer that he would protect her. But Jack had another plan.

"Listen," he continued, seeing the look of consternation on her face, "I'm leaving here, probably in the next few days. It all depends on how soon I can get my affairs in order."

"Where are you going?"

"To a little town called Bass Creek — ever hear of it?"

"Sure. My father's taken me there a few times when he's gone fishing," she replied. Jack knew there was yet another reason he liked this girl: *She goes fishing.*

"Why are you going there?" she asked.

"Well, it has always been my dream to open a little country office."

"You? A country lawyer?" The incongruity overcame her concern for a moment and she started laughing.

"Why not?" he asked, a smile breaking across his face.

"Jack, those are real people over there. They've got mud on their boots. They spill coffee on your carpet. There's no Momma Corinnes over there." Jack was laughing wildly now. Corinne could hear him from the outer office. She wondered what the two of them were doing in there this time. It was awful and she was so embarrassed.

"Stop, you're killing me," Jack said, and then he was serious again. "I've been planning this for a long time but some pieces are missing."

Nancy got it all at once. "Oh no, not me. I'm not going to be your Momma Corinne. You need to find somebody else," she protested.

"Think about it for a minute or two, Miss Impulsive. I'll give you a twenty percent raise, same benefits. Do you know what you can do with that kind of money in Bass Creek? Hell, you can buy the best house in town with an apartment for your father if he wants to visit or even stay. I'll tell you what, I'll *buy* you a house. I'll give you a mortgage and you can pay me." Jack had done his homework. He knew the points to hit and to hit quickly. He could see Nancy turning the offer over in her mind, picturing her own house and her dad fishing every day.

"Why are you doing this? Why me?"

"Because I like you and I want to be comfortable in my new digs — none of this formal crap. We'll work hard and we'll have fun and you'll learn a lot, I promise you. Maybe you'll be a lawyer someday."

Nancy blushed at the thought. "Can I think about it? I want to talk to my dad."

"Sure. Take your time. I can probably take Rick for another two days or so." They both laughed again. It was good, comfortable. Nancy stood up.

"I'll let you know in two days."

⁓

Two weeks later, Nancy started her new job in Bass Creek. Jack had already been there for a week. Before she made her final decision, he'd let her know what his plans were both for Rudy's case and for the aftermath.

"I may burn a few bridges before this is over, in which case I'll go back to my original plan, being the country lawyer. Either way — at the state attorney's office or in private practice — you'll be with me and you'll have the same salary and benefits we agreed on."

He'd lived up to his other promises as well. A week after she agreed to take the job, she'd found a place in Bass Creek for her and her dad, a two-story clapboard house with hardwood floors and a huge front porch shaded by two giant oaks — a house she could only have dreamed about in Miami — and Jack had bought it for her. It had a garage apartment but she had already decided that dad was going to live in the house with her. If she ever met somebody and they decided to roll around in the sack, *they* could use the garage apartment. The house was unoccupied and Jack paid cash, so the closing was a few days later. The mortgage he drew up for her was a sweetheart deal as well — thirty years with an interest rate well under prime.

"What if I quit tomorrow?" she asked him just before signing the note.

"Nothing," Jack replied. "No strings attached."

"All right," she said as she put pen to paper. She knew she was in for the long haul anyway.

He'd also advanced her five thousand dollars to buy furniture and had given her that first week to shop for whatever she needed. When she started her new career with Jack, Nancy and her dad were already living in their house. She and Jack had five weeks left to try and save Rudy.

~

That Monday morning, as Jack and Nancy sat down in his office to discuss their plans for the next five weeks — he behind his desk in his new burgundy leather swivel, she in one of the two equally impressive burgundy leather early American client chairs — there was a knock on his door. Before he or Nancy could get up to answer it, Pat Morgan walked in.

"Am I late for the meeting?" she asked, a smile spreading across her face. Jack was totally perplexed.

"What meeting?" he stammered.

"The first meeting with your investigative team on the Rudy Kelly case, what else?" she replied.

"How did you know we were having a meeting on Rudy's case?"

"Let's just say a little birdie told me." Pat looked at Nancy and they both laughed. Jack was still completely puzzled so Pat filled in the blanks.

"You told me to ask for Nancy when I called you at work if you weren't there, so I did. And Nancy and I started talking and she told me what your plans were and I decided to come down and help." Jack started to break in, but Pat went right on.

"Look, I'm retired like you. I don't know what to do with myself, so I decided you needed my services. I'm organized; I'm good with figures; I know computers; and I can cook and even wash dishes."

She sat down in the vacant client chair. Jack looked at Nancy, who just shrugged her shoulders and then broke into a big beaming smile. This was a deal that had already been made.

"I guess it's settled then. We now have a chief cook and bottle washer. Welcome aboard, Pat," he said as he stood up and came around the desk to give her a hug. "And may I introduce my executive secretary, Ms. Nancy Shea?" and they all started laughing.

"All right, let's get started," he said, once they'd all taken their places again. "Let me tell you what we're up against. Two appeals have already been filed and denied in this case. The only way we will have even a remote chance of success is if we come up with some new evidence — something that was missed, something that creates a reasonable doubt about Rudy's guilt.

"My initial plan is to gather all the documentation that exists on this case. I've already made a public records request with the state and the public defender's office for a copy of their files — they should be here soon. I need to read and reread that information until I'm thoroughly familiar with everything that has been done in the past. Then we need to look for the holes. What evidence was missed? What lead wasn't followed up on? If there are holes in this case we have to find them. That's our only chance on appeal."

"What about solving the murder?" Nancy asked. "Isn't that better than an appeal?"

"Absolutely!" Jack replied. "But we're ten years down the road. Solving the murder is the remotest of possibilities. Finding a winning issue for an appeal is still possible. Let me give you the timetable: Two weeks from now I have to file my brief with the

Florida Supreme Court. Because this is a death case the court will immediately set a schedule, probably giving the state five or six days to file a response and setting oral argument five or six days after that. They'll have a decision a couple of days before the execution date because, if they rule against us, we'll have one last shot with the United States Supreme Court.

"Any investigation — any new information — has to be uncovered in the next two weeks.

"Pat, you and Nancy start setting up to receive all this information," Jack continued. "Make sure we have all the equipment we need so this operation is completely computerized and that we have a system in place where we can retrieve information instantly. You know what I mean."

Pat nodded. "I know exactly what you mean. But it's going to be expensive."

"That's not important. Let's just do what we have to and give it everything we've got. Any other questions?"

"Yes," said Pat, with a twinkle. "What are you going to do before these documents arrive while we're working our tails off?" It was a question Jack had never been asked at Tobin, Gleason and Gardner. He looked at Nancy, who had that big smile again. She obviously liked Pat's style.

"I'm going to do something I've never done before," Jack replied. "I'm going to go solicit a client. I have an appointment to see Rudy tomorrow morning at Raiford Prison."

Before he left that afternoon on his trip to the Florida State Prison, commonly known as Raiford, which was just outside the town of Starke, in the northeast section of the state, Jack called Pat into his office.

"How long are you staying?"

"For the duration, Jack. I decided that I need a worthwhile cause to complete my resumé."

"Where are you staying?"

"At the Bass Creek Hotel."

"Why don't you stay with me? I've got a big house right on the river five minutes from here. There's plenty of room."

"You sure I won't cramp your style?"

"Pat, I don't have a style to cramp." They both laughed.

"Are you sure this isn't too much?"

"Positive. Besides, you've already offered that you could cook and wash dishes," he smiled at her. Pat smiled back.

"All right," she said with a little nod. "I accept the invitation."

"Good. Here's a set of keys. Nancy will show you where the house is and help you move your bags. We'll get to know each other again. It'll be fun."

[ **T W E N T Y - F I V E** ]

Jack was a little apprehensive about his meeting with Rudy and he rolled the reasons over in his mind during the long trip to the prison. Perhaps it was because Rudy was Mikey's son and seeing him might stir up all those conflicted emotions again. Maybe he was afraid Rudy was guilty and he would sense it right away. Or worst of all, maybe he would just know Rudy was innocent but wouldn't be able to help him. Whatever the cause, Jack was nervous and he dealt with it by arriving early at the motel in Starke and spending the rest of the evening meticulously making notes in preparation for the interview. The nervousness was new. The note-taking was a habit he had formed many years ago to make sure he covered all the bases when meeting with a client or a witness.

He also spent some time thinking over the call he'd received just before leaving the office from his old friend the governor. It was a call he had expected, though not quite this soon.

"Jack, Jack, good to hear your voice," Bob Richards said after Jack answered the phone. "Congratulations on your retirement. Already set up shop in Bass Creek, I hear. Don't you believe in vacations?"

"This is a vacation, Bob. It truly is. I'm sitting at my desk in a pair of jeans thinking about the one case I have." He knew that would get the ball rolling.

"That's what I want to talk to you about, Jack, the one case you have. I just received a call from Bill Sampson, the state attorney — the guy you're replacing. Bill says you're looking into the Rudy Kelly case. Says you made a public records request for the case file. Says you asked for the public defender's file as well." *That's a little unusual,* Jack thought. *The public defender informed the state attorney of my request to him?*

Bob finally got to the point. "Bill is a little concerned that the man I'm appointing as the next state attorney is asking questions about a convicted felon on death row."

The call presented another opportunity for Jack to tell the governor to find somebody else to fill the position. But it was an opportunity Jack did not take. Again, he wasn't sure why.

"Rudy Kelly is the son of an old friend of mine, Bob. I'm just doing him a favor, making sure all the i's were dotted and the t's were crossed in his son's prosecution — you know, making sure *justice* was done. You and Bill don't have any problem with me making sure *justice* was done, do you Bob? I mean, isn't that a state attorney's job?"

"Sure, sure — that's exactly what it is. I think Bill is just a little mistrustful of defense lawyers. It comes with the territory. I'll call him and tell him that you're just making sure things were done properly — kind of keeping yourself busy until you take over. He'll be okay with that."

"Thanks, Bob. Tell Bill it's an exercise for me. I need to learn criminal law and this is as good a way as any." Old Bob laughed on the other end of the line.

"That's a good one, Jack. I'll tell Bill that one. He'll get a kick out of it. Listen, sorry I bothered you. I'll talk to you soon. So long."

"So long, Bob."

Jack had sugarcoated it a little bit but what he had said was essentially true. He simply didn't tell Bob what was going to happen if he found out justice had not been served.

~

Raiford was nine miles outside Starke, an isolated complex of rectangular concrete buildings, some white, some blue, some shaped like airplane hangars. There were parking lots, recreational areas and some open fields, all enclosed behind shiny steel chain-link fences topped with razor wire. Guard towers with spotlights were strategically placed along the fence line. If some ambitious prisoner somehow made it over the fence, he would find himself in an open meadow where the spotlight could easily pick him up and the guards could just as quickly mow him down.

Jack was there early the next morning and stopped at the front gate, where the guard gave him directions to the main building. From there another guard, this one with an automatic rifle, escorted him to one of the three-story concrete buildings. Jack signed in and was handed off to yet a third guard, who escorted him through a gate of thick yellow steel bars that led to a second gate of thick gray steel bars. When the first gate closed, the second gate opened.

From the moment he walked through the first gate and it clanged shut behind him, Jack was in an alien world, surrounded by concrete and steel, where every sound reverberated. As he followed the guard down a long corridor, he was overwhelmed by the chaos of noise — shouting, screaming, even crying, and the clanging of prison bars opening and closing — the background music of Raiford.

He was taken to a small room equipped with a gray table and four gray chairs, all bolted to the ground. He was told to wait there and sat down in one of the chairs.

Rudy was escorted into the room by two prison guards. His ankles and wrists were cuffed and chained. It was a major project to shuffle him into the room and get him seated. The noise of the chains clinking against the metal chair was unnerving even to an old pro like Jack. He'd been to prisons before to interview witnesses but he'd never been to a maximum-security facility like Raiford and he'd never interviewed someone on death row.

One of the security guards remained in the room standing at the door. Jack's first inclination was to protest the lack of privacy but he decided against it. He knew the only other choice would put a barrier between him and Rudy and he didn't want that. They could whisper if necessary.

Rudy looked across the table directly into Jack's eyes, smiled and extended his cuffed hands as far as they could go.

"Hi, Mr. Tobin." Jack saw the resemblance right away. Rudy certainly didn't look Irish with his shiny, thick black hair and olive skin. It was the smile and the eyes — not the color but the way they lit up when he smiled. There was no doubt this was Mikey's son.

"Hi, Rudy. Please call me Jack." Jack had to extend his hand almost across the full length of the table.

"Okay, Jack, thanks. You know, when they first told me a Jack Tobin was coming to visit me, I had no idea who you were. Then I remembered my dad's stories about being a kid in New York and hanging out with his best friend Johnny — Johnny Tobin."

"He actually talked about me?"

"Oh yeah. He told me the 'shark' story. How you guys climbed through the alleys, hitchhiked on the back of buses, snuck out down the fire escape — you guys had some life. And I feel honored to finally meet the Mayor of Lexington Avenue."

Jack smiled. "He told you about that?"

"Oh yeah."

"Did he tell you that it was actually his nickname?"

"He told me that Father Burke came up with the name but it fit you better. He told me the whole story." He said it in a way that told Jack Rudy knew about his father's prediction.

They were nice memories and it was even nicer that Mikey had told them to his son. They were five minutes into the interview and Rudy had already won him over with his charm and his warmth. He knew instinctively that he was not talking to a murderer. He would have enjoyed reminiscing more with Rudy — but there was so little time.

"Rudy, do you know why I'm here?"

"Yeah. I figure you want to help me in some way. Maybe file

another appeal or something."

"How do you feel about that?"

"Well, I'll tell you, Mr. Tobin — I mean, Jack. One of those groups that are against the death penalty tried to help a couple of times, but, um, I guess you can tell, it didn't work. When you're in here, you don't get your hopes up."

"Well, I'd like to try, Rudy. It certainly can't hurt."

"I don't know about that, Jack."

Rudy's answer surprised Jack. He had expected a little ambivalence at first, but this was more than that, more definite sounding. Jack didn't get it — where was the harm? Hell, he was so sure Rudy would say yes to his representation that he'd opened his office, hired Nancy and started discovery. Who wouldn't want another chance?

"I don't understand, Rudy."

Rudy smiled. "I didn't think you would. But here's the thing, Jack. A lot of good came out of all this bad that happened to me. My mom and dad got together again. I know seeing me in prison and all was hard on them, don't get me wrong. But I also know I saw something in my mom's eyes that I hadn't ever seen before, when I saw them together. They were truly in love, you know.

"And I got to meet my dad. We didn't spend a lot of time together. I mean we only met here in prison. But almost every time was a real good time, and over ten years it can add up. And I learned all about you."

Jack started to speak but Rudy held his hand up.

"Let me finish. Maybe those things would have happened anyway, I can't say. The other thing is — I never really had any friends other than my mother. You probably read all about me being slow and everything. If there's anything I miss it's her and being out on my boat riding up and down the canals. The way I figure it, Jack, when this is all over that's where I'm gonna be. I don't understand it all — but I'm happy to think I'm gonna be a part of nature and I'm going where my mother and father are. I'm not praying for any delays.

"So you can do this thing and if it works, I guess there's a reason for me to be part of the world again. But if it doesn't, I don't want you to feel bad about it. Okay?"

Jack didn't say anything for a moment. He just drank in Rudy's words. Maybe Rudy lacked book-learning smarts and a respectable IQ, but he had a deeper understanding of his place in the world than most people would ever have. He had no fear about taking the next step. At that moment, Jack took his own next step.

"Rudy, I don't know for sure why I'm doing this myself. All I know is that your father and I loved each other and we let things get between us. I've been planning on retiring in Bass Creek for about five years. When I went to your dad's funeral and found out about your situation and where it all happened, I just knew I was supposed to do something."

Rudy nodded but didn't say anything for a long while.

"Then let's do it, Jack." And then Rudy took a breath, like he was really thinking hard about what he was about to say, trying to find the right words. "Jack, maybe you have to do this just to do it, I guess I understand that. But where it leads you may not be what you want or what you expect. Okay?"

Jack wasn't quite sure what Rudy meant but the guard signaled that time was up. He just nodded to Rudy and stood to leave.

"One other thing, Jack. Do you think people can see the future when they're about to die?" Jack figured Rudy was talking about himself, and he didn't know how to respond.

"I don't know, Rudy."

"See, the thing is, the last time my dad came to see me, he knew he was dying and he said the strangest thing to me just before he left. I didn't understand it at all until now. He said, 'When Johnny comes to see you, tell him from now on when he's talking to you, he's talking to me.'"

Jack left quickly, ran to his car, drove out of the main gate as fast as he could — and when the razor-wire fences and the towers were safely out of sight, he pulled the car to the side of the road, turned the ignition off and wept.

[ T W E N T Y - S I X ]

"How did it go with Rudy?" Pat asked as soon as he was settled at his desk the next morning.

"Good. He has Mikey's smile," Jack said, and then started shuffling some papers. Pat wasn't letting him get off the hook so easily.

"That's it? He has Mike's smile? By the way, we stopped calling him Mikey about thirty-five years ago."

"Yeah, I know, but the reference in my memory bank is Mikey. And that's not *it* by a long shot. Rudy was amazing. He was warm. He was friendly. He was intuitive. And he *is* innocent."

Pat noticed how Jack clenched his jaw when he said those words. "Wow! Sounds like quite an interview. I thought he was slow — easily led — and that's how he got convicted."

"He may be slow in the way we measure intelligence. And he may be too trusting — too believing in people — something we commonly consider a character flaw. But he is wise beyond his years in other ways. Pat, I want you to meet him. I'm going back next week. Why don't you come?"

"I'd love to. I mean, I don't relish the idea of visiting death row. But I'd like to meet Mike's son, especially after what you've just told me about him."

"Great," Jack replied. "You'll see, he's got a lot of his father in him — and something more."

Pat knew from that moment forward that Rudy was going to have the best representation possible — someone who believed in him with his mind *and heart*. It really must have been quite an interview.

~

Two days later, the voluminous files from the state and public defender's office arrived — in a truck. Jack had the movers load them all against one wall in his office. He planned on taking the next few days to immerse himself in those documents.

He started that first morning with the initial police reports after the murder. He immediately began to see why the police had focused on Rudy. He had been at the victim's house on the night of the murder. Pilar Rodriguez had given the police a pretty accurate description although she hadn't picked Rudy out of a lineup. Raymond Castro and José Guerrero had also been positive in their description to the police — before they disappeared. The blood on the carpet and the broken glass matched Rudy's — but hell, that was the most common blood type around, so all that did was not rule him out. But then there was Rudy's confession, or to put it more precisely, Wesley Brume's notes of Rudy's confession. *Is there a recording of the interview? And if not, why not?* So far, that was the only red flag he'd found.

He next read the coroner's report — nothing he didn't already know in there. Her throat had been severely cut by a blade with a jagged edge.

When he'd read all the investigative material twice — the second time in greater detail — he felt satisfied that he had an overview of the prosecution's case. Something was gnawing at him, though. *There's something I'm missing in this evidence, something I'm not seeing,* he told himself. *Maybe that's it. Maybe what's bothering me is what's not there?*

He left the office about three and took some of the files home with him. Pat arrived a little after five with bags of groceries. Jack was sitting on the living room floor, leaning on the sofa. Papers were strewn everywhere. He looked like a college student, albeit an old one, pulling an all-nighter to write a term paper on a subject he knew nothing about.

"How's it going? Have you solved the puzzle yet?" she asked.

"Not hardly. I've just jumped into the swamp with the alligators."

"Well, I'll make you a nice meal tonight — fatten you up good — so when they eat you, at least they'll be satisfied."

"Thanks. Seriously, I thought we'd eat out tonight."

Pat dropped the grocery bags on the table. "That's fine with me."

"There's a little Mexican place in town. It's my favorite place to eat. Do you like Mexican?"

"I love it, but I can't go right away. I've got to run first and then do my exercises."

"I didn't know you were a runner."

"There's a lot you don't know about me, Jackie boy."

"Why don't I run with you? While you do your exercises I'll do my swim. Then we can go eat."

"That's what I like — a planner," she said as she finished putting the groceries away.

Five minutes later, they were both in their running outfits and heading out the door. Jack couldn't help but notice how fit Pat was. Her long legs were toned, her midriff was tight, and so was the sports bra she was wearing, compressing those "bumps" he and Mikey first noticed years ago.

*I have to check that out,* Jack found himself thinking. But then he caught himself. *Whoa, boy! That's Patty you're talking about!*

"How far do you want to run?" he asked after they'd both spent a few minutes stretching. "I've got a three-mile course, a five-mile course, eight miles, ten — you name it."

"Well, since I just arrived in town and haven't run in a few days, why don't we start off with three?"

"Okay."

Jack didn't have to slow too much to stay with Pat. She held a good pace. *Probably eight and a half minute miles,* he thought. He was usually under eight minutes but this was fine. He'd work up a sweat and it was fun to have somebody to talk to while he ran.

Pat knew he'd want to talk about the case. He'd lived with those files all day — he'd have to spill some of it out. She decided to be proactive.

"So what did you find today?"

Jack shrugged his shoulders as he jogged. They were running along the river. It was a typical fall evening in Florida — clear skies, cool, crisp air. The river was calm. A few small motorboats, a cabin cruiser and a sailboat puttered by in the "No Wake" zone, but for the most part it was peaceful and quiet.

"Well," Jack began, "Rudy was definitely at the victim's house on the night of the murder *around the time of the murder*. He admits that himself. But he says he got sick and tried to get out of the house to puke and he tripped and broke his beer mug and cut his hand. Then Lucy, the victim, kicked him out of the house."

"So his blood was found in the house?"

"Yeah."

"And the only other blood found was the victim's?"

"Yup."

"Sounds like you've got real problems."

"That's not the half of it. The only way that it could have happened the way Rudy says it happened is if somebody else came to the house *after* he left. Now there were three guys down the block, two of whom saw Rudy going to Lucy's and coming from the direction of her trailer later — but those two up and disappeared, and the police never even got a chance to talk to the third guy, he was gone so fast."

"Sounds fishy."

"Yeah, but sounding fishy gets you nowhere. If there was some evidence that put somebody else inside that house that night, then we might have something. Then the disappearance of these guys might sound *and smell* fishy."

"And there's nothing like that?"

"No. These local cops are yokels. Mind you, I'm not very

experienced at crime scenes myself, having been a civil lawyer all my life, and this was ten years ago. But when somebody is murdered, especially a brutal murder like this, there's usually some clues left behind — fingerprints, footprints, hair follicles—something! These guys found nothing. It's almost as if they found traces of Rudy's blood and stopped looking."

"It could be that Rudy was the only one there," Pat offered. "You can't discount that possibility."

"I can if I believe Rudy, and I believe Rudy."

Pat didn't respond. They were already back at the house and she couldn't even remember the run. It was amazing how fast time passed when you were engaged in a good conversation. But that good conversation worried her. *Jack's taken the plunge, but what if Rudy is really guilty or there's no way to prove him innocent? How will Jack deal with all of that now that he's met Rudy and apparently is taken with him?* From the little she'd heard, it sounded like a strong circumstantial evidence case against Rudy. *And didn't they have a confession as well?* Pat suddenly was rethinking her decision to visit the prison. *Do I want to get to know somebody — especially Mike's son — just before he's about to die?*

The Taqueria was on the edge of the barrio but it was a notch or two above the dives that functioned as restaurants within the barrio itself. There was a dining room and a separate barroom for the "just drinkers." The décor was haphazard, overdone, and decidedly un-Mexican: A stuffed gator hung from the ceiling, and Florida, Florida State and Miami pennants adorned the walls nestled between deer heads, stuffed jackrabbits and other assorted paraphernalia — including a rectangular sign that read, "Tips up, Aspen, Colorado". A large poster of El Cordobes, the famous matador, hung on one wall but he was of course Spanish, not Mexican.

Jack and Pat found a place in the corner to the left of El Cordobes and seated themselves. Pat kept looking around, fascinated by the décor.

"I think I finally found the Redneck Riviera," she said with a chuckle. They were both freshly showered and dressed in jeans and tee shirts.

Jack laughed. "Wait until you taste the food."

"Is it that bad?"

"No, I'm just kidding. It's *really* good."

When the waiter came they both ordered chicken burritos and bottles of Dos Equis beer. The beer came right away and Pat took a healthy sip.

"It doesn't make a whole lot of sense to run three miles and then start drinking beer, huh?" she said, smacking her lips.

"Sure it does," he said, clinking her bottle. "The beer makes you feel good, the running makes you look good — *and you look good.*"

She raised her eyebrows and then smiled. "Why, thank you, Jack. And you look pretty good yourself, especially in that Speedo." She was referring to the very skimpy bathing suit he'd worn to swim his laps in the pool at his house. "It doesn't leave much to the imagination."

Jack's face reddened. Suddenly he was seeing his old pal Pat.

"I didn't know you noticed."

"Well, I did." She looked directly into his baby blue eyes.

Jack returned her gaze, and the new Pat came to the fore again. "Me too," he said.

The mood was momentarily interrupted by the waiter who brought the burritos.

They ate in silence, each contemplating what had just happened. Pat certainly hadn't planned to make a remark loaded with sexual connotation. She hadn't ever thought that way about Jack — at least, not until she'd opened her mouth. *I just told him he looked good,* she reassured herself. *You can't read too much into that.* Jack was telling himself the same thing. Pat decided to change the subject.

"So Jack, how are you adjusting to this new life? I mean, this is a far cry from Miami and the big firm."

"Actually it hasn't been an adjustment at all. I've spent my weekends here for years. The adjustment was always going back to Miami. The big firm was never me. I was successful but I was miserable. When I left it was like walking out of a role I'd been playing for twenty years. This is the real me. I guess I'm really a Florida redneck."

"'Cracker' is the appropriate term," Pat replied. "I've been reading up on old Florida. This is cracker country. But you're not a cracker either, Jack. You're just a kid from the neighborhood who made it big and you've never felt comfortable in that role."

"You're right. I've certainly wasted a lot of time."

"Well, you've got the rest of your life to make up for it. Do you think your professional life had something to do with your marriages failing?" It was a question she hadn't thought about asking. Once again, she heard the words as they left her mouth as if she was a bystander to her own thoughts.

"I'm sure that was part of it. I've thought about that a lot. The world of status has its own pressures. But I just don't think I was husband material anyway. All my wives told me the same thing: 'You're not here for me. It's like you're always somewhere else. You don't talk to me.' All three of them said the same thing at one time or another. I never knew what they were talking about. I thought I was a good husband, a good provider. I talked. We talked every night. I guess I never talked about my feelings but that's just not the way I am. I don't like to argue. If I'm mad at you I'll process it myself. I don't need to tell you I'm mad at you and what you did wrong and how you hurt my feelings and blah, blah, blah. I don't need to process the shit that happens at work. I'll be over it tomorrow.

"I was accused of being insensitive, distant, sweeping things under the rug — you name it. I thought I was being an adult, getting on with life. But eventually, I decided I just wasn't husband material."

Pat nodded knowingly and smiled. "I can't tell you how many times I've heard my girlfriends say the same things about their husbands and my guy friends say the same things about their wives. You're not any different, Jack. This problem has existed since time began. Women want to talk about their feelings, men don't. Women feel closer when they're sharing emotions. I'm not sure exactly what men feel but they don't like to do it. Men are more action-oriented. They assume their wives love them because of their actions, not their words, while their wives are simply waiting for them to say 'I love you.' I guess we want strong men who are sensitive, too, but if they're too sensitive, we think they're wimps. It certainly can get complicated."

"Yeah, well my job was complicated enough. I needed simplicity at home. But I'll say this — and I'm sure you've heard this before — none of them had a problem spending the fruits of my labor."

"Sounds like you still have some issues there."

"Probably so. That's why I'm alone. What about you? What's your story?"

"There is none, really. I had a few long-term relationships but they kind of just fizzled out. I don't know why for sure. I think maybe I was a little too strong and independent for the men I was with. I made more money than they did too, which may have been a factor."

Jack was watching her intently as she spoke. He noticed how smooth and soft her skin was. She had few wrinkles and almost none around those large green eyes — *beautiful green eyes*, he thought. "Well, it's their loss," he heard himself saying, feeling the necessity to take a swig of beer right after the words left his mouth.

"Why, thank you again, Jack. Two compliments in one night — my my," she said, fanning herself with her hand.

"It's true," he mumbled, feeling as awkward as a teenager on his first date. *What the hell is going on here?* he wondered.

Pat just smiled. She knew what was going on. A small fire had been lit — unexpectedly. But this was a fire that needed to burn slowly, if at all. After all, there was a friendship at stake.

[ **T W E N T Y - S E V E N** ]

It took another two days and nights but Jack finally got through almost every file. There were a few very thin ones in the last box that he didn't get to but he was sure he had read all the important stuff. And on their evening runs he took Pat through what he had learned that day. It was good for both of them: Pat was learning about the case in depth, knowledge that she shared with Nancy the next morning at work; and Jack was organizing and summarizing his thoughts as he spoke.

"You were right that Rudy's private attorney was a woman. Her name was Tracey James, apparently a real hotshot, based in Vero Beach." They were on the stretch by the river. There were no boats around, just two pelicans swimming along together. A third dive-bombed into the water not far from them, scooped up a fish and flew away, ignored by the two swimmers. *They must have already eaten,* Jack thought, knowing how pelicans would fight over the tiniest of morsels. *Or maybe they're in love....*

Pat interrupted his daydream. "And she really did quit because they weren't paying her enough?"

"Who?"

"Who do you think? This Tracey James woman you just told me about."

"Oh yeah. I don't know exactly. The files only say she dropped off the case before it went to trial, but if Mike told you that, I'd believe it. It's not like I never heard of a lawyer only being in it for the money. Anyway, that's how Rudy got stuck with the public defender. She did a good job, though, before she withdrew from the case. She took the investigating officer apart on the stand at a preliminary hearing. If that had happened at trial, I suspect Rudy would be walking the streets today."

"Why didn't it happen at trial?"

"Because the public defender was either a drunk or an idiot."

"Isn't that a basis for an appeal?"

"Yeah, but they already tried it and got nowhere. Anyway, at the preliminary hearing Ms. James raised a very interesting issue — whether Rudy, because of his intelligence deficit and his personality, could actually refuse to talk to the police. She also raised the issue of whether the police should have stopped interrogating him when his mother arrived at the police station."

"I guess the judge didn't buy it, huh?" It was getting a little deep and Pat was struggling to follow. Luckily, they were running five miles that night.

"Actually, he did. He didn't grant the Motion to Suppress the evidence but he allowed them to bring up all the circumstances of the confession — how they kept Elena in the other room, how they had video and audio equipment available and never used it. And the confession itself wasn't really a confession. This detective simply got Rudy to admit that if he was mad enough, he could kill somebody."

"And you're saying the public defender didn't use any of that evidence?"

"None."

The next night they did a seven-miler. Jack explained to her how the legal advocacy group handled the appeals. The first appeal was based on the denial of the Motion to Suppress. The Supreme Court of Florida denied that appeal, finding that Judge Wentwell's solution — to allow the circumstances of the interrogation to be presented to the jury — was a proper legal ruling. The second appeal was based on the ineffectiveness of counsel, the public defender, who failed to put into evidence the circumstances of the interrogation.

"I think it was a pretty good appellate strategy," Jack continued. "Let the court rule that the evidence could have and should have been presented, then follow it with a second appeal based on the fact that the public defender failed to present this crucial exculpatory evidence."

"Well, how the hell did they lose the second appeal then?" The more she understood the details, the more outraged Pat became.

"You have to understand something: There's more at stake here than meets the eye. First, appellate courts are reluctant to overturn trial courts — only about fifteen percent of cases are overturned on appeal. Second, the public defender is the trial lawyer in this case. He is a state employee just like the prosecutor. The court is going to be very reluctant to find the public defender ineffective in the performance of his duties. And third, the public likes the death penalty — they don't like *activist* judges who interfere with a jury's decision. The court is not immune to public opinion."

Pat was livid at what Jack was telling her. They were running through the woods now in a totally secluded area. She started screaming. "This is about somebody's life! Who cares about public opinion or politics or public defenders or any of that shit. *This is about somebody's life!*"

The more excited Pat became, the calmer Jack got. "Do you remember that old psychology question? 'If a tree falls in the woods and nobody is around, does it make a sound?'"

Pat had no idea where he was going. She was emotional and upset and Jack was going off on some stupid tangent. "Yeah. So what?" she replied tersely.

"Well, in this context the answer to that question is no. We know that murder trials, especially those based on circumstantial evidence — eyewitness accounts with no physical evidence, or some physical evidence but little else, as in this case — are fundamentally flawed. As high as thirty or forty percent of the defendants are *innocent.* Yet people are still being sentenced to death *because nobody is listening. Nobody cares.* Don't take this personally, Pat, but you didn't care until it was Rudy. Neither did I. *Nobody cares.* They're putting children to death, retarded people. The state of Texas has executed one hundred and forty people in the last eight years — and they don't even have a public defender system, which means people are being represented by court-appointed lawyers, some of whom are drunk or sleeping during trial, or whatever. You're seeing firsthand how a case can get fucked up, but it happens every day in courtrooms all over this country. And it will continue to happen until people start listening *and hearing.*"

When their run was over, Pat went straight to her room. The thought of eating after that conversation made her want to puke.

## [ TWENTY-EIGHT ]

Jack tried several times to get Tracey James's number from information so he could call her office and make an appointment to see her. Strangely, she was not listed.

*Why would a lawyer not be listed in the phone book?* It just didn't make sense. Maybe she'd relocated. Vero Beach was just an hour's drive east, so early on Monday morning he decided to drive over and make some inquiries. *She can't hide from me,* he thought, half joking. *And why would she?*

His questions were answered soon after he arrived in town. Jack's professional investigative procedure was to stop at every law office he saw and ask where Tracey James's offices were located. The receptionists in the first three places had never heard of her, making him begin to wonder if she even existed. He hit pay dirt, however, on the fourth stop. *Perseverance pays off,* he told himself. He'd been at it for about half an hour.

"I think someone here used to work for her," the receptionist at Blaine & Dewey told him. She gave him a look before she went to find her co-worker — a look that said there was something she knew and he didn't but should have.

*Maybe I'm reading too much into people's expressions,* he thought, forgetting that this was the first meaningful expression he'd seen that morning.

Five minutes later, a short, overweight woman who appeared to be in her mid-fifties stepped into the waiting room with a grim expression on her face.

"Are you the person who asked about Tracey James?"

"Yes. I understand you worked for her?"

"Right up to the end," the woman replied, her head downcast. "She was a good boss. Paid well." *Everybody who pays well is a good boss*, Jack thought.

"Right up to the end — what do you mean?"

"You don't know?"

"Know what?" He hated the twenty questions game.

"Ms. James was killed in a traffic accident a year ago."

Jack felt compelled to express some sympathy although he didn't know Tracey James. "I'm sorry to hear that," he said. The woman appeared ready to burst into tears at any moment.

*Maybe Tracey James really was a good boss*, Jack thought. "Do you know who has access to or custody of her files? I'm looking for a particular file on a case she worked on ten years ago — Rudy Kelly?"

The woman just shrugged. "It was probably destroyed. We destroyed all the old files after three years. When she died all her cases were assigned out. I remember that case, but I'm not sure why I remember it. I wasn't with Ms. James ten years ago. You may want to check with her chief investigator, Dick Radek."

"Do you know where I can locate him?"

"No, I'm sorry. Wait, I think he mentioned once that he lived in Stuart — by the water. Yeah, he was saying how he got in just before the property values went skyrocketing."

It wasn't much but it was a start. Jack thanked the woman and started to leave when he remembered something else — private investigators were usually ex-cops.

"Do you know if Mr. Radek was an ex-cop?"

"Yeah, I think he was," she replied. "He mentioned one time he was retired from the Miami police department."

*Bingo*, Jack said to himself. "Thank you very much," he said as he headed out the door.

~

"You got a call here from a guy named Jack Tobin," the sergeant told Detective Sam Ellis when he picked up the telephone. "You wanna take it or you want me to give him a song and dance?"

"No, no I'll take it," Ellis told him. "He's a friend of mine."

They'd met on a case years ago. Jack was defending the insurance company in a hit-and-run accident where the victim died. Sam was assigned the homicide investigation. Sam, like Jack, was divorced and they'd enjoyed each other's company. They met once in a while and shared a few war stories over a couple of beers. Sam's stories were always better than Jack's because he was a homicide detective.

"Hey, old buddy, I thought I'd never hear from you again. Retired in the lap of luxury, huh?"

"Yeah right," Jack replied. "You haven't seen Bass Creek yet. There's no luxury to be found. By the way, you've got my phone number and an open invitation to visit, so don't hesitate."

"Yeah, yeah. I'll get over there one of these days. You know this job, Jack. No rest for the weary."

"You need to take time for yourself."

"Yeah, yeah, okay. What's up? It's not like you to call me just to update your invitation."

"Well, I do need a favor."

"Sure. What is it?" It was just like Sam to agree to the favor even before he knew what it was.

"I'm trying to get the address of a fellow named Dick Radek. He's retired from your department. I'm not exactly sure what he did."

"I remember Dick. He was in homicide when I first came on the force. Good cop, good guy. Sure, I'll get his address and phone number for you. Where can I call you?"

"You can't. I'm calling from a phone booth on the side of the road. I'll call you back. How much time do you need?"

"Thirty minutes. And Jack... "

"What?"

"You need to get yourself one of those car phones. A rich man like you shouldn't be without a luxury like that."

"Yeah, right. I don't believe in those things. Guys like you can listen in too easily."

Sam laughed. "I didn't know you were so paranoid."

"I'll talk to you later."

Thirty minutes later Sam had Dick Radek's address and phone number when Jack called him back from a phone booth in Stuart.

∽

Dick Radek lived in a typical middle-class three-bedroom, two-bath, ranch-type house in Stuart. His just happened to be on the Intercoastal Waterway, where it stuck out like a sore thumb. His neighbors' homes were all mansions, each one with its own yacht in the backyard.

"I bought at a good time," Dick told Jack when he saw him noticing the contrast. "They've been trying to get me out of here for years. They buy these places and come in and knock down the old homes. I can't tell you what I've been offered for this house."

They were sitting on old green deck chairs on the screened-in back porch looking out on the water. Dick couldn't have been more hospitable when Jack knocked on his door a half hour before, ushering him into the house and right through to the porch before the introductions were completed. As soon as Jack was comfortably seated, Dick handed him a beer without asking. He had opened one for himself as well. He'd been fully retired for a year, and although his large frame was still muscular and powerful, it was quite apparent he'd spent a lot of his spare time out here doing just this. His gut told that story.

"Why don't you sell?" Jack asked.

"I like it here. Besides, I know it pisses all of them off that I'm still around. You know, the white trash in the neighborhood. I kinda like that too."

Jack smiled. "I guess you expected me, huh?"

"Yeah, Sam Ellis gave me a heads up."

"I figured he would." Jack knew cops stuck together. If Sam Ellis was going to give Dick's address out, he was going to call first and run it by Dick.

"Sam didn't say what you wanted, though. He just told me you were a good guy, whatever that means."

"I'm representing Rudy Kelly." Jack just threw the words out there and waited for a response. Dick didn't say anything.

"Do you remember the case?" he asked after a couple of seconds.

"Sure do." A draft of cold air had entered the room. The friendly guy who had invited him into his house was starting to clam up. Jack knew instinctively there was something Dick Radek did not want to talk about.

"Do you mind if I ask you a few questions about it?"

"Depends on what you ask."

"Look, it seems like I've hit a nerve here for some reason. I'm trying to save a young man's life and I'm running out of time. I'm just doing an investigation, trying to find information that might help my client, nothing more. There's no agenda here, okay?"

Dick seemed to loosen up. "I hear ya. Go ahead, ask your questions. I'll answer them if I can."

"Why did Tracey James get out of the case?"

"Money. Tracey never did anything unless there was money in it. Frankly, I was surprised when she took the case. The woman, Rudy's mother, had no money. I thought Tracey might be bleeding her for whatever she could get out of her."

"She would do that?"

"Oh, she could be a bloodsucker — but not this time, at least not as much as usual. There was something about this case. It haunted her until the day she died."

"I'm not sure I understand. She didn't take the case for money but she got out because of money?"

"That's about right. Tracey was definitely conflicted when it came to this one. I'd never seen her like that before or since. She really wanted to help that woman and her son. And I'll tell you something else, she did a damn good job while she was on the case."

"I know, I've read the file. She ripped the chief detective a new asshole during that suppression hearing."

"Yeah, that's what I heard. I wasn't there. You know, she planned on getting back on the case before she was killed."

"What?"

"Yeah. I didn't know Tracey had a conscience until Rudy Kelly came along. When he got convicted, she was sick about it. She knew the public defender fucked everything up and she just couldn't let go."

"Wait a minute. I'm not following you here. She got out of the case almost ten years ago — and you're telling me she planned on getting back into it?"

"That's about the size of it."

"Why after all these years?" Jack felt like he was pulling teeth again.

"Somebody contacted her, I don't know who it was. She wouldn't tell me. But whoever it was gave her some information that she felt would free Rudy. She tried to contact Rudy's mother but found out she had died. That's when she really got motivated — she felt she let that woman down. So she called that detective, Wes Brume."

"Why'd she call him?" Jack asked, surprised at what he'd just heard. His surprise was about to turn to shock.

"I think part of it was just to let the little peckerhead know she was coming back. She always thought that Brume set Rudy up. She knew she got to him in that suppression hearing and she wanted to plant a seed in his brain, hopefully, to give him a few sleepless nights."

"You said part of it was just to let him know she was coming back — what was the other part?"

"I'm not sure — maybe she wanted to squeeze him to come clean. Maybe she thought what she had was good enough to do that. It was a stupid move on her part."

"Sounds like you advised against it?"

"Oh yeah. There was no purpose to the call. It's pretty hard to squeeze a bad cop. They'll kill you first, which is exactly what I think Brume did. I should have been more forceful in my advice but I wasn't paying attention, wasn't piecing everything together like I should have. I was working on something else at the time. A week after she called Brume, she was dead. Hey, how about another beer?"

Radek had just dropped a bombshell, and Jack was desperate to learn more — he couldn't have cared less about another beer. But he could tell this was hard on Radek; Jack sensed that the old cop was probably trying to hide his emotions. He probably blamed himself for Tracey's death.

"Sure," he said to Radek's back — he was already halfway to the kitchen.

"I usually have a cooler out here," he told Jack when he returned from the kitchen with two more beers. "It keeps the beer colder. But I ran out of ice yesterday and I haven't gotten out yet today."

"It tastes plenty cold to me," Jack replied after taking his first sip.

"That's because when I take two out, I put two in the freezer." *It's going to be a long night,* Jack thought to himself. "By the way, what's your interest here?" Dick asked, once he was comfortably seated again in his favorite deck chair. "From what Sam told me about you, it certainly isn't money."

Jack smiled and took another sip. "Rudy's father was my best friend. He's dead now. Let's just say I'm repaying a debt."

"I hear ya."

"I'm trying to locate Tracey's file," Jack said after a few more minutes of silence. Dick didn't answer. "It must still exist if Tracey was getting back into the case," Jack persisted. Still there was no response from Radek. Jack tried to stay cool although he was boiling inside.

"All right, let's assume a certain person has it but they don't want to give it up. Maybe I could get a copy? It might just save a young man's life."

Still he just sat there, looking out at the water in total silence.

Finally, after several agonizing minutes, Dick spoke.

"As I told you a few minutes ago, I think that fuckin' fleabag cop killed Tracey over this case."

"I thought she died in a car accident."

"She did, but it was a mighty suspicious car accident. Two o'clock in the morning — what was she doing out at two o'clock in the morning on a weeknight? I knew this woman's personal habits — she *never* went out during the week. There was no other car involved and no brake fluid in the brake line. Although the investigator said that it probably leaked out because of the accident, I went over that accident scene thoroughly and I couldn't find any traces of brake fluid."

"So you really think Brume killed her to shut her up?"

"I don't know. No — yeah, that *is* what I think. She was probably shaking him down and he's a cop. If he's dirty, he'd kill her first."

It didn't make sense to Jack. From what he knew of the case the cops had definitely fucked up and had overreached with Rudy, but it wasn't something to kill someone over — especially a high-profile attorney like Tracey James, unless she had information that would nail him to the wall. But if she had that kind of information, why make the call at all?

"I've been gnawing on this like a bone," Dick told him. "I wasn't crazy about Tracey. She was a good boss — she paid well." Jack knew that line. "But like I said, most of the time it was about the money, and she could be a real hardass. But still, I'm a homicide detective. You can't kill my boss and expect me to go quietly into the night. I've got to find out."

"You think there's something in the file to help you?"

"I don't know. I've been over it a hundred times. I can't find anything. But that doesn't mean it's not there."

"What about the person who contacted her? Have you tried to find out who that is?"

"Have I? I checked the calendar — checked out everybody who came to see her the month before her death. I talked to all our employees. I checked the telephone records to her home and the office. I couldn't check them all. We had twenty adjusters and five lawyers at the time, ads all over the state, receptionists, telephone solicitors — I'm talking about thousands and thousands of telephone calls in a month. I checked out every call from and to Bass Creek, every call in Cobb County, all the long distance calls; and I did a random sampling of the rest. I came up empty. Nada. Zilch. The only thing I have left is that file and I'm not letting it go."

It was Jack's turn not to answer right away. He knew he needed to offer Dick something to get that file — or even a copy of it.

"Maybe we can help each other. Look, you think this cop killed your boss. I want to get Rudy free. We're not in conflict. If I discover something, I'll give it to you. You do the same. But let me copy the file."

Dick thought about it for a moment. "All right, there's a copy place down the road. I'll go with you in the morning and we'll copy it."

He stood up and headed for the kitchen, returning moments later with two more beers.

"There's another person you might want to talk to," he told Jack after he handed him a beer and sat down.

"Who?"

"Joaquin Sanchez."

[ **T W E N T Y - N I N E** ]

While Jack was traveling around the state "investigating," Nancy and Pat had been busy shopping for the latest computer technology and setting it up in the office. Then they began the long process of scanning all the documents they had received from the state and loading them into the new computers. Pat was clearly the most knowledgeable. Nancy had spent her time at Tobin, Gleason and Gardner mostly as a word processor. She didn't mind taking direction from Pat, however. Unlike her superiors at the law firm, Pat was a pleasure to work with.

Every morning they came to work in jeans or shorts. The first order of business was breakfast at the local diner, the Pelican. They'd started eating there the week before, which made them *almost* regulars. It wasn't a very large place — an old railroad-car diner complete with a once-shiny aluminum façade that had lost its luster considerably over the years. Dolores was their waitress — the only waitress in the place.

"Just call me Dolly," she'd told them the first morning they came in. "We ain't got no specials. We don't do waffles. It's pancakes; eggs any way, with ham, bacon or sausage; or cereal, cold or hot. We got oatmeal, Cream of Wheat, corn flakes and Special K. What'll it be?" Dolly just stood there staring at her pad, pen in hand, her black reading glasses resting below the bridge of her nose — ready for action. Pat and Nancy looked at each other and almost burst out laughing. They'd been coming back every day since, always sitting in the same booth.

Dolly was more familiar now. "Hiya, girls. Ya gonna have the usual?" she'd ask as soon as they were seated. Dolly didn't seem to remember that, although Pat ordered the same meal every day, Nancy didn't.

"How long did you work for Jack in Miami?" Pat asked Nancy one morning as she waited for Dolly to deliver her daily bowl of oatmeal and bananas.

"About a year."

"How'd you like the big firm atmosphere?"

"I hated it."

"How about Jack?"

"Him too."

"Really?" Pat laughed. She enjoyed finding out about the "other" Jack. "Tell me about it."

"He was nothing like he is now. It's almost like he was a completely different person. He never smiled. He never talked to me until the day he saw in the paper that your friend Mike had died. Since then he's been great — like a second father." Just then Dolly arrived with Pat's oatmeal and Nancy's bacon and eggs. *Youth*, Pat said to herself. *They can eat anything.*

"I hated my father," Dolly interjected. They both looked at her and smiled and politely waited until she was a safe distance away before they resumed their conversation.

"Jack's behavior sounds a little strange — almost like a Dr. Jekyll and Mr. Hyde thing," Pat remarked.

"Not that bad. Jack was never mean. It was just like he wasn't there — emotionally. You know what I mean?"

"I think so."

"Now he's as warm as a person can be. It's almost like your friend

Mike's death opened the floodgates to his emotions. Just look at the way he's working this case. His heart and soul are in it."

"Yeah, I see that. But I worry what will happen to him if he's not successful."

"You mean if Rudy dies?"

"If Rudy is executed."

"Oh, I don't even want to think about that."

"None of us does," Pat replied. "But it's a distinct possibility."

"I just don't think Jack's going to let that happen," Nancy said. "After all, he's personal friends with the governor. If worst comes to worst."

"I didn't think about that. Maybe you're right."

~

Back at the office, they jumped right into their work. Pat noticed that while she was setting the computer equipment up, Nancy was reading one of the files.

"That's a lot of information to digest," Pat said in a nice way.

"I know. But it's so interesting — the investigation, the hearings, the trial."

"You really like this legal stuff, don't you?"

"Yeah, I think I'm going to make it my life's work."

"Really?"

"Yeah. Jack said something to me about becoming a lawyer when he asked me to come with him. I never thought of myself in that category before, but just him saying it made me start thinking about it and once I get going, I don't stop."

"Do you have your degree?" Pat asked.

"I've got a two-year degree and about fifteen credit hours past that. There's a four-year school in Vero Beach, Madison College, where I can get my bachelor's degree in a year. There's a law school in Fort Lauderdale, two hours away. If I can schedule my classes two or three days a week, I can still work for Jack part-time. Dad's got a V.A. disability pension plus social security, so we can make ends meet."

"Wow! I guess you *don't* stop once you get going. But I don't hear anything about a social life in those plans."

"What social life? I don't have a social life now."

"I can't believe that," Pat told her. "A beautiful girl like you?"

"Thanks for that, Pat, but I never quite fit in in Miami. I wasn't fast or flashy enough, or something. And guys my age just seem like jerks to me. They've got one-track minds. There's no substance or soul."

"It doesn't change as they get older, honey. The guys with real substance are few and far between, no matter how old you are. But you'll meet someone."

"It can wait until I get out of law school."

"Love waits for no man or woman. When it happens, it happens," Pat said, staring out the window.

Nancy looked at Pat and was about to ask her about her own personal life. But she stopped herself. She could see Pat wasn't ready to go that far.

[ **T H I R T Y** ]

Jack spent Monday night at Dick Radek's house and woke up the next morning with a hangover. He and Dick had sat on the back porch until the wee hours of the morning drinking beer and solving the problems of the world. Now with his head pounding, he couldn't even remember what one of those problems was.

He showered quickly, put on the extra pair of slacks and shirt he'd brought with him and waited for Dick to wake up so they could go to the copy place.

It took a little over an hour to have the file copied. He and Dick went out for breakfast. Then he dropped the old detective off and headed for Indiantown, where Joaquin Sanchez now lived permanently. Dick had called the night before ostensibly to let Joaquin know Jack was coming. But Jack knew the real reason — the address. Dick had to get Joaquin's permission to give out his address. *They've still got each other's back.*

Joaquin also lived on the water, a small canal that meandered out to Lake Okeechobee. He was cleaning his boat when Jack arrived. Jack rang the bell and stood at the front door for ten minutes before he thought to look in the backyard. *So much for being an investigator,* he told himself as he walked around the house and discovered Joaquin hard at work.

Joaquin was very friendly. "I can't help you with much," he said.

"I wasn't on the case too long." But he had reread his report the night before and went over it in detail with Jack.

"There's no doubt in my mind this Geronimo guy killed Lucy Ochoa. Rudy was just in the wrong place at the wrong time. The problem is you've got no firsthand information. The guy I talked to — Pablo — he'll probably help you but everything he knows is hearsay."

"Did Dick tell you that Tracey talked to somebody about this case before she died? Somebody who gave her new information?"

"Oh yeah. He's been talking about nothing else for the last year. I try to get him to forget about it — to come fishing — but he just sits there on his back porch drinking beer all day and festering. You know, it's a hard thing for a cop to take when somebody is killed on his watch. He's convinced that's what happened to Tracey."

"How about you? Are you convinced?"

"No. But I wasn't close to the situation, Dick was. You learn in this business to trust your intuition. I trust Dick's intuition."

"Do you have any idea who would have called her?"

It was clear that Joaquin had already thought this through because he answered immediately. "Either Raymond Castro or José Guerrero — those were the two guys with Geronimo the night of the murder. It's been ten years; they might have come back to town, heard about Rudy's situation and decided to do something. That's the only possibility I can come up with."

Jack thanked Joaquin for his time and was about to leave when Joaquin remembered one more, small piece of information.

"Just before she dropped out of the case, Tracey sent a letter to the state attorney about this Geronimo fellow and attached my report. She sent me a copy of the letter, I guess because it was my report. I've got an extra copy if you'd like it."

Jack didn't know how much good it would do but he took the copy and thanked Joaquin again before heading back to Bass Creek.

~

That night, on their evening run, he told Pat all about his

trip. They took a special route, one Pat had discovered just the day before when Jack was out of town. It was a secluded path through the woods.

"Covers about ten miles but we can get off anywhere we want."

Jack loved the new run. They were hidden among tall pines and ancient oaks. The arms and elbows of the oak trees were brimming with Spanish moss, which created an eerie atmosphere that made them feel even more secluded and alone.

Jack started in on his story right away, and by mile three he was summarizing what he'd learned. "So Tracey James is dead, and her chief investigator thinks she was murdered by Wesley Brume, the investigating detective in Rudy's case, a theory that I don't buy at all. Yet, Tracey *was* getting back into the case. And she found out something — something that she believed would free Rudy and possibly incriminate Brume. Radek thinks that's why Brume killed her. Radek doesn't know who Tracey talked to but he thinks the information is somewhere in her file, which he is guarding with his life. Joaquin's pretty sure it was one of the two guys who saw Rudy go into Lucy's trailer, but he's got no proof.

"I'm certain now after talking with Radek and Joaquin that this Geronimo guy killed Lucy Ochoa. Unfortunately, the guy Joaquin talked to — this Pablo person — is dead. I checked on him as soon as I got back into town today."

"What does it all mean in terms of stopping Rudy's execution?" Pat was getting lost in this barrage of facts. She understood the part about Rudy being innocent. She just didn't understand how they were going to prove it.

"So far it means nothing. Everything I found out is inadmissible. I have absolutely no basis to file an appeal right now. I need to find some evidence to put this Geronimo — or anyone other than Rudy, really — in Lucy's trailer that night, and I need it fast. I agree with Dick Radek about one thing — the evidence is in the files. I haven't read Tracey's file yet, but there's got to be something in the files I've looked at already that I'm missing."

"Why don't you read the files again?"

"I don't have time. I'll read Tracey's file tomorrow. The next day we're going to see Rudy. Then I've got to start writing a brief even though I have nothing to write about."

"You'll find something, I'm certain of it. Listen, about me going with you to see Rudy — I think you should take Nancy instead."

"You don't want to go?" Jack looked disappointed.

"Of course I do, but Nancy is really tuned into this case. I think she can help you more because she knows the details so much better. She's poring over those files."

"Both of you could come." They had already passed the five-mile cutoff, running comfortably, unaware of the distance they had traveled.

"No," Pat said firmly. "I'd just be a distraction. You need to lay out for Nancy as you have for me all the information that you've got — and all the dots that need connecting."

"Nancy's just interested in being a secretary."

"Not anymore, Jack. You changed that — you made her believe she has what it takes to be a lawyer. She's done all the legwork to make that happen — checked out the schools and everything. And she's on this case. Nancy will find that needle in the haystack you're looking for. Take her along."

Jack didn't want to give up so easily and it had nothing to do with Nancy.

"Well, she can stay at the office and go over the files while you and I visit Rudy."

"We can go another time — I'm not going anywhere. I think she needs to meet Rudy."

"Why do you say that?"

"I don't know. Woman's intuition, I guess. Once she meets Rudy she'll find what you need." Jack knew the discussion was over. He chuckled to himself.

"What?" she asked.

"I was just thinking about Nancy. You know, I didn't speak to her at all for the first year she worked for me."

"She told me that. She said you were an uptight lawyer type until she found you crying in your office the day you heard Mike had died." Jack thought about that for a moment.

"She's right. The day I found out Mikey died changed a lot of things for me. I hadn't cried in about ten years. Since then I've been like a busted dam. I broke down after I saw Rudy for the first time. I cried on the way home after you arrived — I was so happy to see you here. Hell, last night I was watching a movie in my bedroom and I started crying. I'm becoming a blubbering idiot." They both laughed.

"You're just living again, Jack. Warm blood is flowing through those veins."

"Maybe so." He suddenly took hold of her arm and they both stopped running. He looked at her, his hands now resting on her hips. "I was serious about crying on the way home the first day you arrived. Having you here has just meant so much to me. I mean, now I feel comfortable — confident that I can get this thing done."

Pat rested her sweaty arms loosely around his neck. "You weren't exactly a shrinking violet before I arrived on the scene."

"Maybe not, but this is different — this is a labor of love. And I needed you to be part of it." Pat didn't say anything. She just hugged him. And he hugged her. There among the tall pines, the wide oaks, and the Spanish moss, they silently rested on each other.

Later, after finishing his swim, donning his shorts, tee shirt and flip-flops and making a quick run to the grocery store for some steaks, Jack passed Pat's open bedroom door on his way to his own room. He turned to look inside but didn't see her.

"Jack, could you come here for a second?" Her voice came from the private bathroom adjacent to her room. That door was also open, but he couldn't see inside from where he was standing.

"Sure, what is it?" he answered, walking into the bathroom. Pat was standing by the already running shower in her birthday suit. Jack immediately had all his questions about her body answered. Her stomach was flat, her breasts firm — she looked fabulous. He didn't know what to say. Pat did the talking.

"I'm awful sweaty. When I step in this shower, could you just wash my back? I can't get to it myself."

"Sure," he replied, taking a step forward.

She looked at him. "Jack!" she exclaimed.

"What?" *Oh, no — did I do something wrong at this crucial moment?*

"If you're going to wash my back in the shower, you need to take your clothes off!"

"Oh. Yeah right. Give me just a second."

For some strange reason, he retreated to the bedroom as he started pulling off his shirt, as if modesty prevented him from removing his clothes in front of her. He still had his shorts on when he realized how ridiculous he was being and started to move back towards the bathroom. Now he was in a hurry — experience told him that time was of the essence in these matters. He was taking a couple of jogging steps trying to hop out of his shorts, which were now down around his ankles, when he fell face forward on the bedroom floor with a loud thud. Pat came running into the room to see what had happened. When she saw Jack on the floor, his shorts still around his ankles, she burst out laughing.

Jack felt so ridiculous, he started laughing himself. There they were — Pat, buck-naked, standing at the bathroom door, and Jack lying on the floor in a kind of fetal position, shaking with laughter as he tried to slip his shorts all the way off.

"This is a very unusual style of foreplay, Jack. But it certainly is amusing."

Jack was laughing so hard now he couldn't speak. He almost lost the ability to breathe as well when Pat stretched her right arm out and leaned against the bathroom door. The bedroom was dark but the light was on in the bathroom, silhouetting her figure in the doorway like the sculpture of an ancient Greek goddess. Jack's mouth went dry.

He washed her back and her front. He kissed every inch of her body and when he was done, she took him to bed. They made slow, sweet, passionate love. Later, Jack just lay there in her arms. He'd never felt like this before — in the arms of someone who knew him better than he knew himself, who had told him in no uncertain terms *by her actions* that she loved him. These were arms he knew would never let him go.

[ T H I R T Y - O N E ]

Jack picked Nancy up at her home in his pickup truck early on
Thursday morning for their trip to Raiford. It was a long drive and
they were scheduled to be there that afternoon. She looked very
lawyerly dressed in a navy blue pantsuit.

"Where's the Cadillac?" she asked. "I thought we were traveling
in style."

"The Cadillac stayed in Miami," Jack said. "Along with the style."

He'd had to do some maneuvering to get Nancy a pass to see
Rudy. When he'd called the prison the afternoon before, his request
had been forwarded directly to the warden himself.

"We're already doing you a favor, Mr. Tobin, by giving you a
private room. We can't make it a party," the warden told him.

Jack had a real distaste for government bureaucrats who reveled
in throwing their weight around, but he also knew how to press the
right buttons to deflate them.

"I was talking to Bob Richards the other day about my appointment to the state attorney's position in Cobb County — that's
coming up in a couple of months — and we discussed mutual
cooperation among agencies. That's becoming a problem and Bob
wants me to head up a task force to identify the issues...." It was
typical government double-speak but something the warden
caught onto right away.

"You say there's only two of you?"

"That's right."

"I think we can accommodate your needs just fine."

"Thank you, warden."

"My pleasure."

Nancy was overwhelmed that Jack had invited her on the trip, but she didn't want him to know. She wanted to impress upon him that she was qualified to be his assistant. She had stayed up half the night reading Tracey James's files. She now knew parts of the case as well as or better than Jack.

"I have a list of questions to ask Rudy," she told him when they were on the highway heading north to the prison.

"I'll look at them when we get there," Jack told her. "But I'm really not concerned about the facts of the case when I visit Rudy. I've got a few things I need to ask him — such as, what did he and Tracey James discuss when she came to visit him. Other than that, it's just a visit."

"Why am I here, then?"

"You're working on Rudy's case so you need to meet him. When you're representing people, Nancy, there has to be an emotional connection. This is your opportunity. Give your notes to me. Let me worry about the substance. You just concentrate on getting to know Rudy."

Four hours later, they arrived at Raiford prison. As promised, the warden had made all the necessary arrangements so that their journey from building to building, and guard to guard, was even easier than Jack's last visit. Still, Jack could tell from the expression on Nancy's face that she was freaked out when the first set of steel bars clanged open and then shut behind her. She was now in prison. The sounds, the smells were not something she had anticipated. Jack put his arm around her shoulder as they walked along, just to assure her that she was safe — or, at least, as safe as he was.

They were escorted to the same room where Jack had met Rudy the last time. They sat in two of the bolted chairs and waited for him to arrive.

They heard him long before he walked through the door — steel clanging, chains rattling, his shuffling feet contrasting with the heavy steps of the guards. Two guards entered the room first, followed by Rudy, then two more guards. *They must increase security as the execution gets closer,* Jack surmised. He stole a glance at Nancy, who was rigid in her chair. He patted her on the arm.

She just looked straight ahead like a seasick angler while Rudy was maneuvered into one of the chairs across from them. Jack knew she would have instantly felt better if she'd seen the smile lighting up Rudy's face.

"Hey Jack, how are you?" he said with the ease of a man who didn't have a care in the world. "And who is this nice lady?" He looked right at Nancy and she finally brought her eyes to meet his. And, in that moment, she felt the fear lift from her. He was a beautiful man, there was no doubt about that — and that smile, and those eyes that danced. She was smitten, but it was something deeper than that, something she had never felt before.

"I'm Nancy," she heard herself say.

"Pleased to meet you, Nancy. I'm Rudy." He held out his cuffed hands and she shook them. "Did Jack rope you into this?"

"No. Well, yes and no. He brought me over from Miami." She felt like an idiot, not knowing what to say.

"So you came from the big firm? How do you like Bass Creek?"

"Oh, I've been to Bass Creek before, fishing with my dad. I really like it."

"You like to fish? I love the water, that's — that was my favorite thing. I used to go out in this little boat I had, but I usually didn't fish. I just liked being out there, floating around, watching all the birds and the animals along the shore — I even liked the gators. That was my world, a world that Jack's trying to keep me from getting back to." He smiled and looked at Jack. "Isn't that right, Jack?"

Jack smiled back. "I guess so, Rudy."

Nancy was mystified. "I don't understand. I thought we were trying to get you back there?"

"Yeah, I'm sorry, you are, in one sort of way. But I've got my heart set on going back in a different way. I'd like to go back there as a bird — like an osprey, soaring over my kingdom."

"You mean you don't want to get off death row," she said, almost in a whisper.

He leaned in, like it was just the two of them there. "I can't say that — Jack's here. And now you're here, and I know there's a reason for that. I'm just not sure it's about saving me. Maybe, somehow, there's another purpose. Something we don't see yet. But if it is to save me," he said, and she could almost feel his eyes seeing right into her heart, "then I want to live. And find out what I'm supposed to do with the rest of my life. But if it's my time to go, I know where I'm going and who I'm going to see when I get there."

He'd been smiling the whole time. Nancy didn't know what to say. It was as if this was the first conversation she'd ever had with anyone.

"Who are you going to see when you get there?" she asked, her voice still quiet.

"My mom and dad. They're waiting for me," he said, a twinkle in his eye, his smile even bigger. She had a sudden urge to reach across the table and hug him. Here in this cold, dreary prison, she was talking to a convicted murderer she had just met — and she *knew* this was the man she had been waiting for all her life.

"How do you know? How can you be so sure?" she asked, not out of any disbelief in what he was saying, but with a genuine curiosity.

"When you're by yourself all day and you know what's probably going to happen to you soon," and Nancy dropped her eyes for just a moment before looking up again into his face, "if you let yourself, you can feel and see things you wouldn't normally see. What I feel and what I see in my mind makes me sure."

"I never thought about it like that," she replied. She wasn't afraid at all now to be honest and say what she was thinking. "But I guess if I was about to die, I'd like to know that somebody was waiting for me on the other side."

"I'll be on the other side. I'll be one of your special people."

She didn't know what to say. It was almost too much, and she slipped back into the role she had prepared for. "But we're here to save you, Rudy."

"I know, I know — but there's a reason you're here whether you save me or not, I just know it. There's a reason we're meeting. However it goes for me, you are now one of my special people."

"And you're one of mine," she said, softening again, and reaching again for his manacled hands.

~

Later, on the drive home, she and Jack talked about the visit.

"I'm sorry Jack. I'm sorry I talked so much."

"Don't be sorry. That's why I brought you with me."

"But you had things to talk about and I took up your time. And I was saying the stupidest things — I don't know where they were coming from."

"You were just responding to Rudy, and Rudy comes from a different place — a place where few people ever go."

"Do you really think so?"

"Absolutely."

"Because that's what I was thinking. It's like he sees things nobody else sees."

"Yeah," Jack replied. "And they say he's slow. Maybe we should all be so slow. We might see things a little clearer. Besides, I had enough time with Rudy to get any questions I had answered. Unfortunately, I didn't learn anything new. We still have no issues to appeal."

"I'll find what you're looking for, Jack. I'll go through our files tonight with a fine-tooth comb. If there's something we're missing, I'll find it."

Jack just nodded. He knew now why Pat had insisted on Nancy coming. Pat had known instinctively that the visit would inspire Nancy. And she also knew that he needed the help — an extra set of eyes.

They drove in silence for a while. Jack could tell that Nancy was still going over in her mind the events of that afternoon, trying to make sense of it.

"He just spent the last ten years of his life in jail and he seems happy as a clam."

Jack just nodded in agreement. He knew there was more to come.

"Do you think he really doesn't want to live?"

"I've thought about that myself a lot. And I've come to the conclusion that Rudy is the true definition of the eternal optimist. That's the way his father was when he was a kid. Rudy is facing death so he's putting a positive spin on it. That's not to say he doesn't see things that we don't or that he doesn't believe what he says, because he does. But if we save him, he'll be just as positive about that."

"What do you think he meant when he said we might be involved for another reason we don't yet know about?"

"I have no idea. It's hard enough to try and understand a human being facing death with a smile. I can't comprehend any more than that."

They stopped at a greasy spoon for a burger and ate in silence. When they finally got back on the road it was dark.

"I felt something between me and Rudy," Nancy said as Jack exited off the highway a few miles from Bass Creek.

"I saw that," Jack said, looking over at her. "There was definitely something going on between you two."

"I'd love to go out on the river to some of his favorite spots. The way he described it, it sounds like heaven."

"I'm pretty sure that's the way he sees it too."

Nancy sighed. "We definitely have things in common. It's just my luck to meet the man of my dreams on death row." Jack just smiled.

[ **T H I R T Y - T W O** ]

Nancy called him at seven the next morning. He had just finished his sit-ups and was going through his daily stretching routine when the phone rang.

"Jack, it's me, Nancy." As if he didn't recognize her voice. She sounded awfully excited. "Jack, I'm at the office and I think I found what you're looking for."

"Don't tell me over the phone. I'll be there in twenty minutes."

"Who was that?" Pat asked. She was still in bed, lying next to the spot Jack had so recently vacated.

"It was Nancy. She found something." He was already moving toward the bathroom as he was talking. He brushed his teeth in the shower, didn't bother to shave, dressed in a flash, kissed Pat goodbye, and headed for the office.

Nancy looked like something the cat dragged in. She was still dressed in the same pantsuit from the day before, although the jacket was off and slung haphazardly on a chair in Jack's office and her white blouse was wrinkled and stained with office-brewed coffee. There were dark circles under her eyes. He could tell she was bone-weary but very excited.

"What did you find?"

"Take a look at this." She handed him a thin manila file. He opened it and saw several pages that appeared to be the results of chemical lab analyses. There were blood and urine test results and toxicology reports. It took him a moment to realize what he was reading. Then it came to him in a flash.

"That's it! That's what I knew in the back of my head was missing — the lab analyses in the coroner's report. Where was it?"

"It was one of those little files in the back of one of the boxes that apparently none of us ever got to when we went through the stuff the first time." Jack remembered. He had read the investigative reports thoroughly but had ignored the thin files at the bottom of the second box. He was just too tired to read them and assumed they were unimportant.

"Now take a look at this." She handed him a second thin manila file. He opened it and started to read a two-page police report dated on the same day as the murder about a suspected rape *of Lucy Ochoa!* His heart started to race. He could feel the blood coursing through his veins at breakneck speed as he tried to slow his eyes down and read the report — and then the lab results again. A picture started to emerge — a very sinister picture.

"Do you know what this means?" he said.

"I think so," she said, watching his eyes dart across the pages. "Although it's taken me most of the night to figure out what you figured out in a couple of minutes."

"Take me through it," Jack said, hoping to calm himself while he listened to her explanation.

"Apparently, they found semen inside Lucy Ochoa the night she was murdered. The blood type from the semen was AB. That was different from the blood type on the carpet, Rudy's blood. So they started a separate rape file. I'm not exactly sure why. I think they were up to no good but I'm not exactly sure how it worked."

"Your analysis is very good, and your research was excellent," Jack told her. "You may very well have saved Rudy's life with your tenacity. Let me put the pieces together for you.

"The blood and the semen created a big problem. It put two people in the house. So they — the prosecutor and the police —

decided to eliminate the problem by creating two crimes. By having a separate rape investigation, they didn't have to produce that file for the defense in the murder case. And also, since it was a criminal investigation, the documents weren't public records, so nobody — including the press — could get at them.

"The press usually gets at least some of their information through a public records request. The state attorney knew that."

"Why did we get the rape file?"

"We made a public records request for all documents relating to Lucy Ochoa or Rudy Kelly. The criminal investigation of the rape case — an investigation that, in fact, never existed — ended years ago. Once the investigation was over, those documents became available. Apparently, nobody has made a public records request since the original murder investigation ended."

"I think I get it," Nancy said. She was following but it was tricky, and this was all new to her. There was one other thought she had to get out before she lost it. "What about the coroner's toxicology report? Wouldn't the defense have seen that? And wouldn't that show the semen and the different blood type?"

"It would if the defense had seen it. Note that the toxicology report is titled: 'Addendum to Coroner's Report.' I'll bet the coroner was in on this little scam. He didn't issue his toxicology report with his initial report. It wasn't forwarded to the defense and the idiot who was representing Rudy never thought to request it later. And nobody picked up on the discrepancy in the appeals."

"What about Rudy's blood analysis? Wouldn't that have been part of the coroner's report?" Nancy asked. She felt a little stupid but she was still putting it all together.

"No. The coroner is only concerned with the body of the deceased. The semen was in Lucy's body. Rudy's blood that was found on the carpet was analyzed by the police — they used a crime lab in Miami."

"Wow! So the two blood types were never described in the same report! So where do we go from here?"

"Well," Jack said, "I finally have an issue that I can appeal. I'm confident that when the Florida Supreme Court finds out what the state attorney and the police did, we'll get a new trial and, if Rudy gets a new trial, he will not be convicted again."

"You really think we can get him out of prison?"

"I really do. It's a long process but the worm definitely turned today and you, Nancy, made it turn."

Nancy didn't know what to say. She was definitely excited but the prospect of Rudy's freedom down the road wasn't enough for her. She wanted Rudy to walk out of prison right away.

"What do we do next?" she asked.

"Next, I have to write this brief. I can probably do it in a week. As I said before, I anticipate the court will give the attorney general's office maybe a week to respond and oral arguments will be set a few days after that. We'll get a couple of days before the execution is scheduled in case we need to go to the next step, the Supreme Court of the United States. I don't think we will, though. Nancy, this was great work."

"What do we do between now and then?" she asked urgently, ignoring the compliment.

"I'm going to be tied up doing this brief, mostly."

"Well, I'm going to continue to run down leads. Maybe we can find out whose semen that was. If that's all right with you?"

"Sure. Just be careful."

"I will. I just want to do whatever I can for Rudy."

[ **T H I R T Y - T H R E E** ]

"All right, ladies, stretch. Reach a little more. Stretch. That's it. Let's run in place — knees up high. Come on, Nancy, you can get those knees up." Nancy smiled and raised her knees a little higher. Their instructor always seemed to be able to tell when someone could give it just a little bit more. She was so demanding!

She appeared to be in her mid-thirties and fit the stereotypical model for an aerobics instructor — on the small side but every muscle perfectly toned. Nancy thought she looked Mexican, or perhaps Puerto Rican or even Indian. She had creamy, shiny smooth skin and long, silky black hair that she tied in a bun for class. And she was a boundless font of energy.

Nancy had been in the class for two weeks and it was killing her. But she was already starting to see a difference. She'd never exercised before — didn't need to, or so she'd thought. Now that her abs were tightening and her biceps and legs were showing some tone and definition, she realized this might be something that was good for her.

It was a little storefront studio on Main Street — Bass Creek was too small for a health club. They were a small group, only eight of them, and they were starting to get to know each other. They met three times a week and usually went out for coffee afterwards. This Friday night the five of them who were single were going to go out for drinks.

Nancy had not joined the class to tone up, however. She had read about Maria Lopez in the transcript of the suppression hearing. Maria had been the receptionist at the police department at the time of Rudy's interrogation and still worked there ten years later, although she was now an administrative assistant to the chief of police. Nancy had been impressed by the forthrightness of Maria's testimony at the hearing. She suspected Maria had been pressured to "forget" some of the specifics about what happened at the police station when Rudy's mother tried to stop the interrogation. But Maria apparently hadn't forgotten anything and didn't hesitate to give the details.

Nancy thought Maria might still have a sour taste in her mouth about what occurred ten years ago to a young Puerto Rican boy. If she could tap into that distaste, maybe she could learn something about the case — something that didn't show up in the police reports or the transcripts. So Nancy started going to the police department for innocuous reasons — once to pick up a form, two days later to pay a parking ticket she'd gotten deliberately. On the second visit, she managed to spot Maria sitting at her workstation, identifying her by the nameplate on her desk. At five o'clock that evening, Nancy waited near the police station in hopes of seeing Maria leave and orchestrating some way to strike up a conversation. As luck would have it, Maria headed straight over to the aerobics studio. Nancy didn't find out she was actually the instructor until she joined the class herself the next day.

The first night out for coffee at the Pelican — Dolly wasn't working, thank God — Maria asked Nancy what she did, and she told her that she was a legal secretary.

"Who for?" Maria asked.

"Jack Tobin. He's new in town."

Maria recognized the name immediately. "He's going to be the new state attorney but he's working on the Rudy Kelly case now."

"That's him," Nancy replied, trying to appear reluctant to talk about Jack or her work.

"That case is such a tragedy." Nancy didn't follow up — she just nodded. But her heart was pounding. *Maybe she knows something.* But she calmed herself. *Don't be too eager. If it's in there, let her bring it out.*

On their second coffee night, Maria was even more forthcoming.

"If you only knew the real story about that murder, you wouldn't be able to sleep." Nancy suspected that Maria was the one who wasn't able to sleep. Again, however, she decided not to seem too curious. *Wait until Friday night, when she's had a couple of drinks.*

It took Jack the whole week to write his brief and edit it to where it was moderately acceptable. He faxed it to the court and the attorney general's office. The appellate division of the AG's office handled all appeals in the state, and Jack had contacted their office when he started the brief so that it could be assigned to a particular individual who would be prepared to respond quickly. He had contacted the court as well with the date of execution so the appellate process could be expedited. Normally, appellate cases in the Supreme Court could take three to six months or longer. This appeal had to be decided in a matter of days after the briefs were filed.

Jack knew from experience that the initial brief was the most important part of the appellate process. It had to be clear and concise and had to make the case quickly. Good appellate lawyers spent weeks poring over the initial brief, editing and re-editing, until it was a finely honed dagger, stabbing directly and mortally at the legal deficiencies in the lower court. Jack didn't have the luxury of time, so he concentrated on the short, sweet and to the point part of brief writing.

The point was prosecutorial misconduct. The state attorney, the police, and the coroner had conspired, in his opinion, to keep the semen evidence from the defense, depriving Rudy Kelly of the best evidence to exonerate him — that somebody else was in Lucy's trailer that night. Even if it wasn't a conspiracy, Jack argued, creating a separate rape file deprived the defense of evidence that would support reasonable doubt.

Jack knew the court would probably not find prosecutorial misconduct — they rarely did. Appellate judges were an arm of government just like the police and the state attorney. There was an institutional bias there, at least when it came to the issue of intentional wrongdoing. But by raising the *possibility*, he gave the appellate court an opportunity to "split-the-baby," a term used in legal circles to describe judicial decisions that benefit both sides in some way. By ruling against Jack on the prosecutorial misconduct issue and for him on the more neutral deprivation of evidence argument, the court could give each side something while still reaching the result Jack was really after — the right result. It was a tactic he had used many times in the past.

As he expected, the Supreme Court immediately issued a schedule for the parties to follow. The attorney general had seven days to respond on behalf of the State of Florida, and oral arguments would be five days later. Rudy's execution was scheduled for nine days after the oral argument date. Whether it was in the Florida Supreme Court or the United States Supreme Court, it was going to be a last-minute decision that would decide Rudy's fate.

Like Nancy, Jack couldn't just sit around and wait after he submitted the brief. He decided to learn everything he could about the chief investigating officer, Wesley Brume, and the former state attorney, Clay Evans IV, and to visit both men. He knew there was no real benefit in continuing the investigation. Neither man was going to admit to anything. But something compelled him to go forward. He wasn't quite sure what that something was.

⁓

Wesley Brume did not want to talk to Jack Tobin. He avoided the first three calls, but when Jack persisted, he knew he couldn't duck the conversation forever. This prick was going to be the new state attorney and Wes couldn't afford to make him an enemy before he even started. He didn't have that kind of power. *Why would* the governor appoint a lily-livered, scum-sucking, criminal-loving son-of-a-bitch like this Tobin guy to be the state attorney? It just didn't make sense. It was like being in bed with one of the bad guys.

He took the fourth call.

"Brume here."

"Mr. Brume, I'm Jack Tobin."

"I know who you are. I know you're going to be the new state attorney. I also know you're now representing Rudy Kelly. So what do you want with me?"

"I'd like to have a conversation with you."

"About what?"

"About all of the above." Jack didn't want to tip his hand just yet, although he was sure Brume knew exactly what he was after.

"Well, I'd prefer that we delay a face-to-face meeting until you come on board as state attorney." The Grunt was still holding out hope that the governor would come to his senses and jettison this commy pinko.

"We can't always get what we want in this world, Mr. Brume. You and I are going to be working together. I think we should start to get to know each other. When the governor offered me this job, he and I talked about the necessity of forming partnerships."

There it was — the veiled threat. *"If you don't talk to me, I'll call my friend the governor, whose ass I've had my nose up for the last twenty years."* Wes wanted to vomit. These politicos were all alike. The only guy who had any real balls was Clay Evans, and he rode the Kelly case to an appointment on the federal bench. But he had to meet with this guy. He'd only been appointed police chief last year and he needed two more years on a chief's salary before he could retire with a chief's pension. *Besides, he ain't gonna get squat from me. I'll dance him around the room for a few hours, then show him the door.*

~

They met at Wesley Brume's office. Jack would have preferred more neutral ground, but the Grunt insisted on his office. He wanted the upper hand.

"Would you like some coffee, Mr. Tobin?" Chief Brume asked as he leaned back in his fake leather chair and propped his feet up on his cheap, particleboard desk. Jack wanted to laugh. If this was Wesley Brume's feeble attempt at intimidation, it was having the opposite effect. Wesley Brume would learn about real intimidation very soon.

"No thanks."

"Well then, what can I do for you?" the Grunt asked as he sat up in his chair and began to shuffle some papers, pretending to be a very busy man.

"Well, I know we *might* be working together in the future and I wanted to clear the air about some things."

The word "might" had its intended effect. *What the hell does he mean "might"? Is he trying to intimidate me?* He decided to ignore the remark.

"What air, exactly, needs to be cleared, Mr. Tobin?"

"Well, I'm representing Rudy Kelly and you were the chief investigating officer in his case, so in a way I'm investigating you and your actions."

"Have you found anything I did wrong?"

"Oh yeah, and I'm not finished yet." The blood rushed to the Grunt's face. He knew his feeble attempt at remaining calm wasn't working. His face was burning and his temples were throbbing. He decided to abandon the act, pointing his finger at Jack.

"I don't give a shit who you think you are coming in here and accusing me like this, but I'm not gonna stand for it. Get the fuck outta here."

Jack didn't move. In fact, he leaned back in his chair as the Grunt had done moments before. "Calm down, Mr. Brume. Nobody is accusing you of any criminal activity — at least, not yet. I'm just saying that a few mistakes were made."

The Grunt didn't hear the last part. He was too busy choking on the words "at least, not yet." Jack didn't keep him in suspense too long.

"We know about the separate rape file. It's part of my brief before the Supreme Court on prosecutorial misconduct. I just don't know whose idea it was — you or Mr. Evans. My guess is it was Mr. Evans's idea and he got the coroner to go along. Mr. Evans, or I should say Judge Evans, won't talk to me and I figure when the time comes to discuss these matters he might throw you under the bus — so I thought I'd come to you beforehand and give you the opportunity to tell me the real story."

There was a moment of silence. Brume was sweating now — boiling and sweating. Jack decided to turn up the heat full blast. He could now see that Wesley Brume was the pawn in this operation. If Tracey James had in fact been murdered, Brume hadn't made the decision.

"Oh by the way," Jack continued, "I know Tracey James called you before she was *killed* — and told you she had new information *and a witness.*"

"Who's the witness?" Brume blurted out. His reaction settled a fundamental issue in Jack's mind that had existed since Dick Radek made the accusation. *Tracey James definitely was murdered!* He remembered Joaquin Sanchez's words about Radek: *I trust his instincts.* He looked at Wesley Brume and just shrugged.

The Grunt's mind was racing. This prick was a cool customer, but he had to be bluffing. He wouldn't be here if he knew who the witness was. On the other hand, he had a point — Clay Evans would give him up in a heartbeat. He was tempted but only for a moment. This die had been cast a long time ago. He had to stick with Evans. It was time to end this charade. He stood up.

"Like I said a few minutes ago, Mr. Tobin. Get the fuck outta here. You ain't the state attorney yet. You go around accusing police chiefs and federal judges of crimes without any evidence and you never will be."

Jack stood up as well. "Thanks for the advice," he said and walked out of Brume's office.

Brume slammed the door behind him and sank back into his fake leather chair.

[ **T H I R T Y - F O U R** ]

The following Saturday Jack took Pat for a boat ride on the Okalatchee River. He didn't take the big boat, his twenty-eight-foot Hatteras — he took the dinghy. It looked very much like the dinghy Rudy had bargained for so many years before.

Pat was a somewhat reluctant passenger.

"Why do we have to go out at six o'clock in the morning?" she complained. She wasn't an early morning person. Besides, it was cold. She had to wear a parka and sweatpants over her bikini.

"You want to be on the water when the sun comes up so you can feel nature's changing of the guard."

"I'd rather be under my down comforter."

Jack laughed. "If you feel the same way about this trip when it's over, I'll owe you one. We'll go to the opposite extreme: I'll take you to the finest restaurant in the city of your choosing and wine and dine you. Afterwards we'll stay at a five-star hotel." Pat had her eyes closed, dreaming as Jack spoke, a smile spreading across her lips. Money had never meant much to her, but it was nice to be with a man who had the means to make fantasies come true.

"Okay, it's a deal. And if I do like the trip, I'll make one of *your* fantasies come true." Jack looked at her and smiled. He wasn't going to touch that line. He'd let her surprise him.

He started the little outboard and they puttered out into the darkness. Pat scrunched her hands and shoulders together trying to stay warm.

The Okalatchee was no more than a hundred yards across at its widest point and some very big boats traveled its waters. Six o'clock in the morning was the fisherman's rush hour and Jack had to be careful maneuvering the little dinghy without lights. They motored about twenty minutes in an eastward direction staying close to shore — Pat hugging herself and keeping a watchful eye out for the big boats. Suddenly Jack turned right and headed for some thick brush. Pat thought he was docking the boat on the shore for some reason, but he kept going through the thicket, motioning her to bend down as they went under the branches and came out into a narrow canal bordered on both sides by mangroves, cypress trees and tall pines. Jack continued a ways down the canal then cut the motor and let the dinghy drift.

The change was stark. They had gone from the sound of the motor and the slapping of the waves on the side of the boat in the busy river to the cacophonic drone of thousands of crickets interspersed now and then with the croaking of frogs in a dark, narrow, secluded canal. It was eerie and more than a little frightening.

They sat there quietly. Pat could hardly make out Jack's silhouette it was so dark. Then the sky began to gradually lighten. The surrounding vegetation was so thick they couldn't see the sunrise itself, only its effects. The transformation was seamless. The drone of the crickets and the croaking of the frogs faded away to nothing, and for about ten or maybe fifteen minutes, there wasn't a sound to be heard. A brief mist settled on the calm, glistening water. Everything was still, like a photograph, and Pat didn't dare move for fear of disturbing the picture. For the first time in her life she felt it, that she was a part of nature like the sky and the trees and the water — and the birds and the crickets and the frogs. *How many mornings have I had in my lifetime and I never experienced this, never knew this feeling existed.* She looked at Jack. He was motionless, too, taking it all in.

As quickly as it had stopped, the action started again. Now she could watch as well as hear. Herons and egrets waded at the water's edge or sat on branches looking out over the water. Smaller birds patrolled overhead. Pat made out the head of a gator just offshore, intently watching a heron. The heron gradually took a few side-steps away. High above, atop a tall pine, an osprey surveyed the world below. She watched as it took off from its perch, circled the perimeter of the canal not once but twice, then suddenly swooped down in a deadly dive into the water, arising instantaneously with a fish in its talons.

"Wow!" she exclaimed, the first noise either of them had made in about half an hour. "That was magnificent."

"Yeah," Jack replied. "You never get used to that."

"You win the bet," she said. "I wouldn't have missed this for the world. I've never experienced anything like this before. I actually feel like I'm a part of it. You know — nature."

"Yeah, I know. This is where Rudy thinks he's going to be when he dies."

"He might be right."

"Oh, I think he is."

"Nancy said Rudy told her to come out here."

"He did."

"Why haven't you brought her?"

"Because I wanted to bring you first. Alone. I plan on bringing Nancy but I'm going to wait. If the worst happens, if things go bad with Rudy, this may be a source of comfort for her."

"That's a good idea, but you don't really think things are going to go bad for Rudy, do you?"

"Not at all," Jack said, his voice full of quiet confidence.

The sun had burned off the morning mist and warmed the air. Pat took off her parka and her sweatpants. As she did so, she took one more glance around and decided not to stop there. Off came the bikini as she stood up in the boat.

"What are you doing?" Jack exclaimed with a chuckle.

"I'm becoming one with nature," she sang as she dove into

the water.

"There's a gator over there," Jack said when she came back to the surface, pointing towards the shore.

"I know," she said nonchalantly. "Wasn't it you who told me that gators won't hurt you? Now, are you coming in?"

Jack almost overturned the little dinghy in his haste to shed his mortal apparel.

~

The Supreme Court building had all the features of the classic Roman style, with broad marble steps leading to a vast entrance guarded by massive circular columns. Just inside the main door, however, was an immediate reminder of the modern age — a security-screening checkpoint.

Pat had flown up to Tallahassee with Jack the night before and she accompanied him that morning to the oral argument. She had never been to an appellate argument before. The courtroom itself was somewhat like a college classroom and somewhat like a concert hall. There were semicircular rows of dark mahogany benches for public seating that sloped down towards a podium in the middle. On each side of the podium were tables and chairs for the lawyers. The podium faced an elevated stage with a wide mahogany dais where the seven judges sat. The lawyers at the podium faced the dais and looked up at the judges as they made their arguments. It was an intimidating atmosphere, and to Pat it seemed deliberately designed that way.

She sat in the far back row trying to be as inconspicuous as possible. There were three separate cases set for oral argument that morning. The lawyers arguing those other cases sat in the public area right behind the podium. Besides Pat, there was nobody else in the courtroom.

*Rudy Kelly vs. the State of Florida* was the first case on the docket. Jack chose the table to the right of the podium. He removed his brief and some other reference documents from his attaché case, set them on the table and sat down to await the entrance of the distinguished jurists of the Florida Supreme Court. The attorney for the state followed the same procedure on the other side of the podium. At nine o'clock sharp there was a rap on the door behind the judges' dais. A black man in a blue uniform appeared. "Hear ye, hear ye, hear ye," he bellowed in a magnificent deep, melodic voice. All the lawyers immediately stood up, as did Pat. "The Supreme Court of the State of Florida is now in session. All those who have grievances before this court may now come forth and be heard." As he spoke, the seven Supreme Court justices, six men and one woman, entered the room and took their respective places at the dais. When they were all seated, Chief Justice Robert Walker turned to the lawyers.

"You may be seated," he told them. Everybody sat down. Chief Justice Walker got right down to business. "The first case this morning is *Rudy Kelly vs. the State of Florida*. Counsel, are you ready to proceed?"

Jack stood up first. "Jack Tobin, counsel for appellant Rudy Kelly — I'm ready to proceed, Your Honor." His counterpart followed suit: "Emory Ferguson from the Florida attorney general's office on behalf of the State of Florida. We are ready to proceed, Your Honor."

"Very well," the chief justice replied. "Mr. Tobin, you may proceed."

Jack approached the podium. "Thank you, Your Honor." He'd barely finished the sentence when the first question came his way. It was from Judge Thomas Flood, the most conservative juror on the bench and a strong advocate of the death penalty.

"Mr. Tobin, is it correct that this case has been before this court two times already?"

"That's correct, Your Honor."

"Isn't that enough? Doesn't there have to be an end to these appeals at some point?"

"With all due respect, Your Honor, the answer is no. There should never be a line drawn in the sand when somebody's life is at stake and the possibility exists that a mistake was made."

"What new evidence do you bring us?" The question came from Judge Escarrez, a new member of the court and a conservative Catholic. Jack did not know his views on the death penalty.

"Well, Your Honor, we have discovered that the deceased had semen in her vaginal cavity at the time of her death. The blood type of that semen did not match Mr. Kelly's — so it was not his. This was a material piece of evidence not revealed to defense counsel and it could have caused a jury to conclude that someone was in the deceased's home after Rudy Kelly left — and that that someone committed the murder."

"That's an awfully big leap of faith, Counsel," said Judge Arquist, the female judge, a moderate on the court. "The presence of semen in the vaginal cavity in and of itself does not suggest anything about time, does it?"

"Yes and no, Your Honor. For instance, if the deceased had sex that morning or even afternoon, she probably would have done something to remove that semen, either taken a shower or wiped herself clean in some other manner. And even if she didn't, the semen wouldn't have been there if she had been walking around all day, and the evidence was that she had worked that day and she had, at least, been to the convenience store. So the probabilities are that she had sex that night and probably sometime close to the time that she was murdered — maybe just before.

"Since the coroner was never asked and never testified about this semen at trial and since he is now deceased, there is no contemporaneous testimony about when the deceased had sex."

"Is it accurate that there is no evidence in the record of nonconsensual sex, such as bruises around the vagina or bruises on the body — the kind we might normally find in a rape situation?" The question came from John McClellan, another moderate, who was also a proponent of the death penalty. There were no liberals on this court, so Jack knew he wasn't going to get any softball questions.

"That is accurate, Your Honor, but it's not decisive as to whether this evidence was relevant to the issue of guilt or innocence. For instance, a jury could conclude that someone entered the house after Mr. Kelly left, had consensual sex with the deceased, and then killed her."

"Is there any evidence she had a boyfriend?" Judge McClellan pressed.

"No, Your Honor, but that doesn't mean anything. The evidence shows that she either had consensual sex with someone other than Mr. Kelly that night or that she had nonconsensual sex that left no telltale marks. In either case, she had sex with someone that night other than Mr. Kelly and a jury could have concluded that that person killed her. Because the defense never knew about that semen evidence, they could not present that theory to the jury."

"But Counsel, your client admitted he was in the house that night around the time of the murder. His blood was on the carpet, and as I understand his statement to the police officer, he said he might have killed her. That's pretty incriminating evidence, isn't it?" It was Chief Justice Walker.

"At first glance, Your Honor, but when you consider that Rudy Kelly was a nineteen-year-old, borderline retarded boy who lived with his mother; that his mother was excluded from the interrogation; that no recording devices were used in the interrogation even though the Bass Creek police department had both audio and video recording devices readily available; that the only evidence of what young Rudy said was written by the investigating officer; and that that same officer participated in the decision to keep this semen evidence from defense counsel — when you consider that without Rudy Kelly's so-called confession, there is no case, no evidence at all, then you begin to see that this is a very weak evidentiary case. One that certainly does not warrant the death penalty."

"This evidence that you've just discussed is not in the record, is it, Counsel?" asked Judge Scott, the only black jurist, also a moderate.

"Yes, it is, Your Honor. It's in the transcript of the suppression hearing. For some reason, the public defender never brought to the jury's attention the circumstances under which the so-called confession was given, even though the judge had ruled at the suppression hearing that it was admissible evidence. As you may recall, this failure on the part of the public defender was the issue in the second appeal. I hope this court can see how things are adding up in this case. If the jury knew how the "confession" was procured and also knew that the state hid semen evidence from the defense, they never would have convicted this young man."

"That's an opinion, Counsel." The voice was that of Judge Copell, the last member of the court. It was very rare in a thirty-minute oral argument for all the judges to ask questions. Jack was encouraged by their attentiveness.

"Yes sir, it is, but one based on experience." There were a few former trial lawyers on this panel, and they knew who he was.

"Are you seeking a new trial or are you appealing the sentence of death?" The question came from Chief Justice Walker again.

"Either, Your Honor. We'd prefer a new trial so that we can completely exonerate Rudy, but if you commute the death sentence because of the weak evidence, Rudy will still be around and we will have time to discover who the other person was and request a new trial on the basis of that evidence." It was another question Jack was encouraged by, because it indicated that at least one jurist was thinking of options.

"That's a pretty damaging charge you make in your brief, Counsel — that the state attorney, the coroner, and the police department conspired to keep this semen information from defense counsel — isn't it?"

"Yes, and it's one not lightly made, Your Honor. But there had to be discussions about this evidence and they must have realized the defense was entitled to this information. And they all had to agree to start this separate rape file, which, by the way, kept this information from being a public record, discoverable by the press. This was well thought out, Judge. That's why I made the charge."

When it was his opportunity, Emory Ferguson did exactly what Jack expected him to do. He harped on the fact that this was the third appeal and that there had to be finality to the process at some time. He went over the evidence that Rudy was in the house at the time of the murder and that *his blood* was found on the carpet. There was no doubt about that evidence. When asked by Justice Arquist what possible reason the state could have had for creating a separate rape file, he provided a well-rehearsed and at first glance plausible explanation:

"If they had wanted to suppress evidence to convict Mr. Kelly as counsel suggests, they would have destroyed the evidence. Nobody would have known. Instead, knowing that this semen did not connect to the murder, they started a separate file, preserving the evidence in case any additional exculpatory evidence came up."

In his brief rebuttal, Jack pointed out that Richard Nixon should have destroyed the White House tapes but he didn't. It was a stupid decision but it didn't mean that he wasn't guilty of obstruction of justice. He concluded with a reminder to the court of what was at stake:

"As I said before, this case involves a nineteen-year-old, borderline retarded young man, it is a circumstantial evidence case and we now know exculpatory evidence was kept from the defense. A case like this does not warrant the death penalty. As you all know, our system of justice is flawed. Since 1976 when the death penalty was reinstated in this state, fifty-eight people have been executed and twenty-five *have been released from death row.* We know at least one innocent person has been executed. That's not a very good record. It's a record that should make one pause when confronted with the facts and circumstances that we have here."

∽

Outside the courthouse, Pat threw her arms around him.

"You were magnificent — my knight in shining armor. Those judges were peppering you with questions and you didn't even hesitate. I couldn't think like that on my feet if *my* life depended on it. I think you clearly won. I think they're going to overturn the conviction — at the very least the death penalty portion."

"You really think so?"

"Don't you? They have to. I didn't know about those statistics. They've released half the number of people that they killed? That's abominable."

"Yeah, it is, and I do think they are going to at least overturn the death penalty portion of the conviction, but sometimes you need somebody else to validate your feelings."

"That's what I'm here for, honey — to validate your feelings." She kissed him hard on the lips. "I've never been so proud to know somebody in my whole life. Did I tell you that you were magnificent? Did I tell you I love you?" This time Jack kissed her.

On the plane ride home, he re-analyzed the entire oral argument.

"Normally, I always leave an oral argument knowing that there was something I forgot to say. When those judges start hitting you with questions, you can't remember everything. But I don't feel like I missed anything this time."

"You didn't," Pat told him. "You hit every point. Don't worry. Rudy could not have had a better advocate today."

Her words seemed to calm him once more — at least for a while. But when they were home and in bed she watched him toss and turn all night. Time was running out and the pressure was becoming overwhelming. At one point, she heard him mumbling in his sleep and leaned over to listen to the words:

*"Don't give up! Don't ever give up!"* she heard Jack telling himself.

[ **THIRTY-FIVE** ]

Pat told Nancy all about the oral argument at breakfast the next morning at the Pelican. Even when Jack was in town, Pat never brought him to the Pelican. This was her and Nancy's private sanctuary away from the office.

"Mornin', girls, ya havin' the usual this morning?" Dolly asked about ten minutes after they were seated. There were three other people in the joint at the time. If this wasn't their special place and Dolly wasn't their own very special incompetent waitress, they probably would have walked out. But they hardly noticed. It was business as usual and besides, they had a lot to talk about.

"I will," Pat said, as she always did.

"I'm going to have poached eggs on whole wheat toast," Nancy told Dolly. It was the first time she'd ever ordered poached eggs, but Dolly didn't flinch.

"Youse both having coffee?" Dolly asked, as she did every morning.

"Decaf," Pat replied, as she always did.

"Diet coke," said Nancy, which was the only "usual" she had.

Dolly wrote the drink orders down, never acknowledging that she had, once again, gotten them wrong. The woman was consistent.

"Do you really think they're going to give Rudy a new trial?" Nancy asked after Dolly had departed.

"Maybe not a new trial — at least, not yet. But I feel confident and so does Jack that they will change the death sentence to life imprisonment. That will give us time to get an even stronger defense organized."

"Good, because that's what I'm working on right now."

"You are?"

"I am. I've become friends with a woman at the police department and she's telling me things. I mean, nothing earth-shattering yet, but she's on the verge. It's weird. As Rudy's execution date gets closer and closer, I can feel that she's going to bare her soul. She's afraid, but something deeper inside of her is fighting to overcome her fear."

"What is it that she knows?"

"I don't know. She worked for the police department when Rudy was first brought in. She testified at his suppression hearing when Tracey James tried to suppress his confession."

"Did you tell Jack about all this?" Pat asked.

"Not yet. Not until I have something concrete."

"Time's running out, you know. The execution is next week. Jack could force her to talk."

"Pat, you know that won't work. The woman won't talk until she's ready."

As Nancy finished the sentence, Dolly arrived with Pat's oatmeal and bananas, and two fried eggs with sausage and white toast for Nancy.

Nancy waited until Dolly was out of earshot. "At least she got close. I mean, I did order *eggs*."

Pat started laughing. "You know, a good investigator has to start listening when a person is providing clues," she said between fits of laughter.

Nancy was puzzled. "I don't get it."

"Well, what does Dolly ask us every day when we come in?"

Nancy thought about it for a minute. "She asks us if we're having the usual."

"Right — and I always say yes and you always give your order. Correct?"

"Yeah."

"Has she ever gotten my order wrong?"

A smile of recognition spread across Nancy's face. "She wants me to eat oatmeal and bananas every day."

Pat almost spit out her food she was laughing so hard. "That was good — but you get it. She wants you to be consistent. If you're consistent she'll remember what your order is — at least food-wise. She'll probably never get the drinks right."

"What the hell is she writing on the pad, then?"

"Love letters to the cook," Pat said. "I don't know."

It was Nancy's turn to laugh. Pat was so good for her —for her and Jack. They were both so wound up, they probably would have killed each other by now — if Pat wasn't around. She kept it loose.

"What?" Pat asked when Nancy kept looking at her.

"Nothing."

"Come on. You've got to share."

"All right," Nancy said. "I was just thinking that I've gotta go into the kitchen to see what this cook looks like."

Dolly heard the two of them laughing out loud from behind the counter and glanced over. *What the hell are they always laughing about?*

[ **T H I R T Y - S I X** ]

They got the word from the Supreme Court by fax two days before the scheduled execution. It was a fourteen-page opinion, a four to three split decision, the majority opinion written by Justice Flood. "A jury's decision cannot be overturned except on the basis of clear error," the opinion read. The question of whether Rudy's confession should have been suppressed had been addressed by a previous appeal; there was no need to address it again. With the confession and the forensic evidence — Rudy's blood in the trailer — the evidence of guilt was overwhelming, the opinion concluded. Chief Justice Walker, Judge Arquist and Judge Scott disagreed. In a dissenting opinion written by Justice Walker, the minority adopted Jack's argument: "The presence of semen from an unidentified person places some doubt that Rudy Kelly killed Lucy Ochoa. Based on that additional circumstantial evidence, we would overturn the death sentence given by a jury that did not have this evidence."

Neither Pat nor Nancy had to read the opinion. They could tell what it said simply by watching Jack. He had grabbed the pages off the fax as they came in and arranged them in order before starting to read. They both saw the eagerness and the hope in his eyes fade soon after he began. His shoulders sagged. His face drained of color. He seemed to slump farther into his chair as he read each page. Nancy ran out of the office before a word was said. Pat walked behind Jack's chair and softly began to massage his shoulders.

"I thought we had them," he said after several minutes, his voice a monotone. Then he took the pages that he had so carefully arranged and slammed them down on the desk. "I thought we had them!" he yelled.

Pat just kept rubbing.

Jack put his head on the desk and stayed motionless for the longest time. Pat went back to her computer. She knew he still had other options. He had a brief already written for the Supreme Court of the United States. All he had to do was tweak it a little bit and fax it. He had already notified the court it might be coming and given the date of the scheduled execution. And then there was the governor. They had discussed both possibilities many times while jogging — there was no need for her to mention them now. Eventually, Jack would act.

"It's amazing," he finally said in a relatively normal tone, "that seven distinguished jurors can hear the same argument and four of them can come to a completely different conclusion from the other three." Pat could have commented but she didn't. This was a one-person conversation. "It's all about predisposition — mind-set," Jack continued. "You can argue about scholarly points and logic and all that legal mumbo jumbo until the cows come home, but in the end it all comes down to mind-set: the people in favor of the death penalty versus the ones who aren't sure — certainty versus uncertainty. And certainty wins every time. That's the problem with this fucking country: It's run by a bunch of idiots who are always certain they're right."

Pat still didn't say anything. She knew he had to get this anger out before putting his brain back in gear. She was almost surprised when he picked up the telephone and dialed.

"Is Governor Richards in?" he said, skipping hello altogether. "Well, would you tell him that Jack Tobin called? Tell him it's urgent. It's about Rudy Kelly. I'm faxing him the Supreme Court's decision as soon as I hang up. He has my office number and my home phone. Tell him I'm going to be here all day waiting for his call."

He spent several hours working on his brief to the United States Supreme Court. He faxed it in the early afternoon and called the clerk to make sure they'd received it, once again explaining the urgency and the scheduled execution date and time.

Four more times that day he called the governor's office but the governor never took his call. "I shouldn't have waited," he told Pat late in the afternoon. "I should have driven to Starke and told Rudy and then I should have headed straight for Tallahassee and confronted the bastard in person."

Pat wanted to tell him that he couldn't have finished his brief and made the drive at the same time. She also wanted to tell him to calm down. The governor might be his last chance. But this was not a time for giving advice.

"He'll call you," she assured him. "He'll call you tonight. We can head for Starke first thing in the morning."

~

They didn't go jogging that night. Jack made the five-minute car ride from the office to home in two minutes, and then they simply sat and waited for the phone to ring. At 7:45, it did.

Pat was shocked when Jack just kept sitting there. When she made a move to pick the phone up, he stopped her.

"Let it ring. The answering machine will click on in a second."

She couldn't believe it — waiting all day and now letting the answering machine take the call. *It must be some kind of macho thing*, she told herself.

The machine clicked on: "This is Jack Tobin. I'm not in right now. Please leave a message at the beep and I'll get back to you as soon as I can."

The machine beeped and the distinctive voice of Bob Richards came on.

"Jack, this is Bob. Sorry I couldn't get back to you earlier. I was tied up in meetings all day. I've read the opinion —" Jack picked up the receiver.

"Hi, Bob." He intentionally sounded a little winded. "Just got in the door. Thanks for calling back."

"You bet, Jack. Listen, I read the opinion. Man, you were so close. One more justice and you would have had it." He sounded so sympathetic.

"Thanks, Bob. Listen, this kid is innocent. I'd stake my life on it. I just need some more time to prove it. You can do that, Bob. You can call this execution off and give me the time I need." Jack had rehearsed what he was going to say all day. He knew he had to be short and direct.

"Jack, you have to understand something." Bob began a speech he had probably rehearsed all afternoon as well. "I was really pulling for Rudy. I hoped the decision was going to go the other way because I trust your judgment. I've read the police reports. There is a question there. But you have to understand my position. If I delay this execution even one day, I will be out of office so fast you'll think I disappeared before your very eyes. I'm up for reelection next year, Jack. I can't help you. I hope you understand."

It was the speech Jack had hoped against hope he wouldn't hear — but it was the speech he expected. Bob Richards, the consummate politician, would take all sides. He'd tell Jack he believed his client was innocent but he'd also tell him his hands were tied and ask for his understanding. Jack knew it was futile, but he couldn't give up just yet.

"Bob, we're talking about a man's life here. Doesn't that take precedence over politics?"

"It's not my decision, Jack. I'm just the public's representative."

"But the public doesn't know the facts, Bob. You do. The public doesn't know how flawed the criminal justice system is. You do — or at least you should."

"I'm sorry, Jack. I can't help you." Bob Richards hung up the telephone.

Ten minutes later, the roller coaster they'd been on took one more surge upwards out of the depths of despair. The phone rang again. This time Jack answered it instantly. It was Nancy.

"Jack, I've got something. It's big."

Jack cut her off before she could say anything more. "Don't say anything over the telephone. Come over here."

"I'll be there in half an hour."

Two hours later there was a knock on the door. Pat answered it. A Cobb County sheriff's deputy stood in the doorway. "Good evening, ma'am," he said. "Is Mr. Tobin in?"

As he was saying the words, Jack appeared in the entrance parlor. "I'm Jack Tobin. Can I help you?"

"Mr. Tobin, there's been an accident. I believe you know a Ms. Nancy Shea?"

"Yes, she's my secretary. What's wrong?"

"I'm sorry, sir, but she didn't make it."

It was as if Jack and Pat had been fighting skirmishes all day with the Supreme Court and the governor and just when they thought they might survive, the heavy artillery hit them. Pat doubled over and fell back against the steps leading to the upstairs. Jack just leaned against the wall and put his head in his hands. The sheriff's deputy, not knowing what else to do, kept providing information.

"She was about fifteen minutes out of town on a dirt road near State Road 710 when she must have lost control of the car. She hit a telephone pole and the car burst into flames."

"Okay, okay," Jack said, pulling himself together. "We'll follow you there." He looked at Pat, who just nodded, her face a blank.

"Has anyone contacted her father?" Jack asked.

"I did," the officer replied. "He's the one who told me to come here. Another officer is taking him to the scene. I can drive you folks if you want."

"We'll be all right," Jack said.

They both started crying in the car on the way, neither one of them saying a word. Jack almost missed the turnoff — it was indeed a secluded dirt road — but Pat saw the flashing lights through the trees and motioned silently to him. When they pulled up, police and firefighters and a couple of rescue personnel were standing around near the car, and a few people from a subdivision about half a mile down the road were gawking from farther away. The car was a charred wreck, still steaming, and there were hoses still lying about and puddles around the wreckage. Jack could see a stretcher with a body under a sheet being loaded into the back of an ambulance. A police officer standing next to the ambulance was writing notes on a little pad.

*How long was she stuck in that car before somebody arrived? Was she unconscious or — please God, no — trapped and struggling to get out?* Questions were shooting through Jack's brain like poison darts. He had to stop thinking about how she might have suffered or he was going to lose it again. Analyzing the facts and thinking them through, that's what he needed to do. *What was she doing out here? What did she so desperately want to tell me? and dammit, why didn't I let her?*

Pat saw Jim Shea off in the shadows leaning against a tree. She went over and put her arm around him and tried to offer what comfort she could. Two weeks earlier, Jim and Nancy had invited them over for dinner. They'd had such a nice evening, and Pat couldn't help but notice how close father and daughter were. There had only been the two of them since Nancy's mother died.

He raised his head and looked at Pat, a vacant stare in his eyes. "I put the gas can in the back of the car," he said hollowly. "I put the gas can in the back of the car," he repeated, looking back down at the ground. Pat understood what he was saying. There was nothing she could do to stop him from blaming himself, so she just kept her arm around his shoulders.

Jack went looking for the officer in charge. He was directed to a tall, lean state trooper named Anthony Burrows. He introduced himself and asked Trooper Burrows what happened.

"We're not really sure, Mr. Tobin. But Blaine Redford, an

accident reconstruction specialist from the sheriff's department, is already here and there's a homicide investigator as well. They may be able to help you more than I can."

Jack took off to find Blaine Redford. He was happy about one thing: Since they were outside the town limits, he didn't have to contend with the Bass Creek police department and Wesley Brume.

Redford was down the dirt road away from the crowd, a notebook in one hand and a flashlight in the other, which he was methodically sweeping back and forth across the road.

"Trying to find what caused her to lose control?" Jack asked.

"Partially," Deputy Redford said, not breaking his concentrated gaze at the flashlight's beam. "I'm also looking for — "

"Skid marks," Jack interrupted. Blaine Redford looked up, wanting to see who this person was who was so knowledgeable.

"Jack Tobin," Jack said, reaching out to shake hands before he realized Deputy Redford didn't have a free hand. "I'm an insurance defense lawyer. The victim, Nancy Shea, was my secretary. I don't want to bother you but I'm interested in finding out what happened to her. I'm sure you understand."

Deputy Redford stopped walking and looked at Jack. "I understand. I have a daughter myself. I saw her father earlier. I know you want some answers but I don't know what to tell you. This is my third time walking this road. I can't find any obstacles. I can't find any skid marks."

"That's pretty unusual — no skid marks?"

"Not necessarily. Not if she lost control of the car. I just can't find any reason why she would lose control — no slippery ground, no sharp turns. It might be mechanical, but I'm not likely to find out much from what's left of that car. Besides, according to her dad, she kept it really well maintained."

Jack had worked with enough accident reconstruction specialists over the years to be able to tell instinctively that Officer Redford was well suited to his job. He was ticking off the possibilities one by one. He could work with this guy.

"What about another car?"

"Yeah, I've thought about that," Redford said. "Another car could have bumped her off the road. I saw some tracks in the dirt a little farther back that were a little deeper than others. Two cars, side by side — if she went off the road there, at the speed she was going, she would have headed straight for the telephone pole. The thing is, I can't tell if they were made at the same time. Other cars have been over this road since then, so I don't think I can get a clear print of the other car's tire."

"So what you're telling me is that you think she was run off the road?"

"That's my best guess, but you'll never be able to prove it. Not unless there was an eyewitness. I've given this scenario to Detective Applegate from homicide. He's canvassing the neighborhood as we speak, but the only houses around here are pretty far away."

"I see," Jack said. "You *will* try and get a print of that second car, won't you?"

"We certainly will. Forensics is on their way. But like I said, I don't hold out much hope."

"What about the fire? Isn't it unusual for a car to burst into flames like that?"

"Absolutely. But I talked to the father and he says he put his boat's gas can full of gas in the car earlier in the day because he was going to go fishing in the morning. I still wouldn't expect the car to burst into flames like that, but it did — and the gas can explains why it did. It's unusual but explainable."

Jack liked the thoroughness of his thought process — no detail left out. "If the person who drove her off the road saw the gas can, he could have easily dropped a match in the car and watched it light up," Jack offered.

"That's a level of speculation I can't get to, Mr. Tobin."

"I hear ya. Listen, are you in the office tomorrow?"

"Yup. No rest for the weary."

"You may get a call from the governor. Tell him what you told me, will you?"

"Sure thing," he said, looking a little quizzical. As Jack walked away, Redford wondered what the hell the governor would be doing calling him about a traffic homicide in Cobb County.

Jack and Pat drove Jim Shea home. The man was inconsolable, convinced that he had caused his daughter's death. Pat kept telling him it was an accident. Jack didn't say anything. He was sure that telling him he thought his daughter was murdered was not going to make the man feel any better. Pat made sure he took a sleeping pill when they arrived at his house, and they hung around until he started to nod off.

They left for Starke the next morning at six o'clock. Both of them were now in a stupor, and it wasn't just from lack of sleep. Events were propelling them along and they couldn't stop to think about anything for fear that the reality would immobilize them. They barely spoke on the trip. As they got closer to their destination, Jack told Pat he wanted her to come with him into the prison to meet Rudy.

"You worked so hard on his case with me and he is Mikey's son. Besides, Rudy is so special." She started to shake her head, but Jack kept going, making every argument he could think of. The truth was that he was overwhelmed, as was Pat. They had been leaning on each other for the last twenty-four hours. Jack was afraid that without Pat next to him he might fall flat on his face. It was a disconcerting feeling to a man who had spent his whole life in the center of a courtroom.

Pat kept looking straight ahead through the windshield. "I can't, Jack," she said a long silent minute after he stopped talking. "It's not about me or you, it's about Rudy. He's going to need you today to talk about the options you have left and to help him deal with what may be coming. But he doesn't need to be meeting people for the first time and making small talk."

Jack knew she was right. And he knew he'd been thinking about his own needs more than Rudy's. He didn't say another word about it.

"Let's find a hotel and I'll register us," she said. "You go stay with Rudy."

~

Jack met Rudy in their usual spot. Rudy still gave him that smile, but his hands were shaking somewhat and Jack could see a glimmer of fear in his usual jovial eyes. *He is human, after all*, Jack thought.

"They told me about the appeal," he said when he was finally seated. This time all but one of his army of bodyguards left. "I know you feel bad but you did the best job you could, Jack."

"It's not over, Rudy." Jack didn't want to give him false hope, but he wanted him to know there *was* still some hope, however tenuous. "There's still the United States Supreme Court. One justice will read my brief, and if he or she thinks there is something there, they will issue a stay of the execution until the full court can review the case. I'm also going to call the governor again this morning. There's some new information I need to give him. He can order a stay."

Jack had already made the decision that he was not going to tell Rudy about Nancy. He had enough on his plate already. If he asked what the new information for the governor was, Jack would make something up. But Rudy didn't ask.

"I now know how Jesus felt," he said after they'd sat silently for a moment or two. "He knew he was going to see his father but he didn't want to have to go through death to get there. That's kind of the way I feel right now. I want to get to the other side, to be with my mom and dad, but I don't want to have to die in the electric chair to get there."

Jack just nodded. This was a conversation he'd never had before, and he never wanted to have it again. He had no answers, no comforting words, but if Rudy wanted to talk, he was there to listen.

He stayed with him most of the morning and would have come back for the afternoon — he only had one call to make, to Governor Richards — but Rudy sent him on his way.

"Jack, I want you to go. I appreciate everything you've done for me. I appreciate your friendship, but I kinda just want to be alone now. It would make it too tough for me to see you out there when they're strapping me in. I just want to close my eyes and think about where I'm going."

Jack wanted to argue but he knew Rudy was right — about everything. Both he and Rudy stood up and Jack came around the table and hugged him. The guard let them alone. There were tears in Jack's eyes as he looked at Rudy for what might be the last time.

"If I had a son," he whispered in Rudy's ear, "I'd want him to be just like you."

"I'm lucky enough to have had a dad who was just like you, Jack."

"I love you, Rudy."

"I love you too, Jack."

Jack started for the door but Rudy stopped him one last time. "Jack," he said, awkwardly reaching for his pocket with his manacled hands and pulling out an envelope. "Take this."

Jack took the envelope and read the words written on the outside: "To be opened on my death." He looked at Rudy and nodded. Then he was gone.

≈

He called the governor as soon as he reached the hotel. As usual, Bob Richards was busy. Jack left the number of the hotel and made his secretary promise to have him call as soon as possible. "This is literally life and death," he told her. He lay down on the bed next to Pat to wait for the governor's call and instantly fell asleep. Three hours later, Pat nudged him. "The governor's on the line." He was immediately awake and took the phone.

"Bob, thanks for calling back." He wanted to shoot the son-of-a-bitch, but not yet. While there was still an ounce of hope, he was going to play nice.

"What's up?" Bob asked curtly.

"Last night about ten minutes after I talked to you, my secretary called me and said she had something big. I told her to come to the house. Two hours later there's a knock on the door and a sheriff's deputy is telling us she's dead."

"Geez, I'm sorry, Jack. You don't need this on top of everything else."

"I'm not finished, Bob. The accident reconstruction specialist from the Cobb County sheriff's department, a fellow named Blaine Redford — you need to write that name down — told me he thought it was murder."

"What do you want me to do, Jack?"

"I want you to call Blaine Redford and talk to him. And if he tells you that he thinks Nancy was murdered, I want you to call off this execution. Nancy was killed because she knew something, which means we're getting close."

"Close to what, Jack? Do you think somebody was waiting in the woods for your secretary and killed her?"

"Yes. Just like they killed Tracey James."

"Who? Look, Jack, I consider you a friend. That's why I call you back every time you call. But I've got a state to run. I can't run down every lead you come up with. Frankly, I think you're out there on this one. You need some rest."

"Just call him, will you? Maybe I appear to be way out there, but a man's life is at stake and you're the only chance I — we — have."

"Okay, okay, I'll call him. But if he doesn't have any proof, I'm not going to stop this execution. And I'm not calling you back." Bob Richards hung up the phone.

~

At 4:30 that afternoon, the office temp Jack had hired to babysit the office while he and Pat were away called. She told him that he had just received a fax from the United States Supreme Court. The Petition for Stay of Execution had been denied.

That evening, Jack and Pat joined the all-night vigil at the gates of Raiford, singing and praying with anti-death penalty advocates, none of whom had ever met Rudy.

## [ T H I R T Y - S E V E N ]

"Old Sparky" was the affectionate name given to the electric chair at Raiford. The three-legged oak chair was constructed by inmates in 1923 when the State of Florida decided that hanging was too brutal a procedure for executions.

At 6:00 on the morning of October 22, 1996, while Jack and Pat were singing "Amazing Grace" outside the prison gates, the prison barber started shaving Rudy's head, his right calf and a small patch on his chest where a stethoscope would eventually be placed to determine if he was dead. When the barber's work was done, Rudy showered and returned to an empty holding cell, where he was met by the warden, the chaplain and several of the guards. The warden read the death warrant to Rudy. One of the prison guards then applied an electrolytic gel to his bald head and right calf.

Outside, the protesters were singing "Come By Here, Lord."

Rudy was led into the death chamber. The curtain was pulled open and two reporters and two government officials, one from the legislative and one from the executive branch, watched the proceedings from the small viewing room. The rules allowed for the victim's family members to attend, as well as representatives for the inmate, but nobody showed up for either Lucy or Rudy.

Rudy looked out at those behind the glass and smiled shyly, as if he was embarrassed at what was about to happen.

Rudy's chin, chest, arms, wrists, waist and legs were strapped to the chair. A black hood was placed over his head and pulled down over his face. A metal cap attached to an electric cable was then placed on his head and an electrode was attached to his right calf.

Outside, the protesters were reciting the Lord's Prayer and had come to the line: "Forgive us our trespasses. as we forgive those who trespass against us …."

At 6:59, the executioner was fixated on the phone outside the death chamber where the warden stood. That phone was going to have to ring if a reprieve was going to come. It never made a sound. At 7:00, the executioner pulled the lever and 2,000 volts of electricity surged into Rudy. His entire body lurched, straining against Old Sparky's numerous straps. Then he was still. Two minutes later the prison physician entered the death chamber, stethoscope in hand.

Outside, somebody with a radio shouted, "It's over!" People started crying. Jack held Pat and the two of them cried in each other's arms.

PART

# [ T H R E E ]

[ T H I R T Y - E I G H T ]

It took Jack several weeks to open the letter Rudy had given him at their last meeting. It was a short letter, and Jack could tell it had been written slowly, maybe over a period of days. The penmanship was very good.

*Dear Jack,*

*If you are reading this letter then I am with my special people —
happy and content. Thank you again for all you did for me.
Jack, you know I'm a simple person, but I think about things. I
think God put us here for a purpose and the purpose wasn't
saving me. I think it's bigger than that. I think we are here to
change how things work for people like me. It's not right, Jack. I
think my mother and father, you, me and Nancy — this was our
reason for being here — or maybe just one of the reasons. I've
thought about this a lot. It gives somebody like me a headache to
try and write it down. You're the only one left, Jack. Don't let
this go. Don't give up because I'm gone, Jack. Remember.*

*Love,*
*Rudy*

After the new flood of emotions had subsided, Jack started to deconstruct the letter in his own mind. He'd had similar thoughts, but none so clear and focused. *And they say he was slow! He was slow enough to see things that the rest of us miss. How did he know Nancy was dead? Why did he tell me to remember? That's exactly what his father told me so many years ago.*

He made the decision right then that he was going to heed Rudy's advice no matter where it took him.

His first step was to call Blaine Redford, the accident reconstruction deputy, to see if he'd found out anything more. He hadn't. Jack asked him what he'd said to the governor, and Redford told him the governor had never called. Then Jack phoned the homicide detective, Lawrence Applegate, to see if he'd been able to determine where Nancy had been just before she was killed. Detective Applegate said she'd been at Maria Lopez's house. He'd questioned Maria, and she'd said it had just been a social call, that they were friends from aerobics class.

Jack knew different. He knew that Maria had given Nancy a piece of evidence that Nancy had believed would free Rudy. So, a few days later, on a Saturday, Jack paid a visit to Maria Lopez. He brought Pat along with him. He knew he needed her, but he wasn't sure why.

Maria lived alone in a subdivision just outside Bass Creek called "Foxtrot." It was a nice place, and Jack knew it had probably taken just about every penny she'd saved as administrative assistant to the chief of police. But he also couldn't help remembering that this was the home Nancy had visited the night she was murdered.

They exchanged a few pleasantries, although Maria was clearly uncomfortable. Pat commented on the pictures of a boy and a girl hanging on the living room wall, and Maria told her the kids were grown now and living in Miami. *She must be older than she looks*, Jack thought. She also told Pat — she was pretty much ignoring Jack — that her ex-husband had run out on her not long after the children were born, and she'd raised them alone.

Then Jack started to explain exactly why they were there. For the first few minutes Maria gave him the same polite, deferential "I don't know anything" routine she'd given the police, but Jack was not going to be turned away. He'd lost too many people for that.

"Maria, I know you're afraid." They were sitting in the living room, Maria and Pat on the couch and Jack in a chair facing Maria. "I know that you're thinking: If they killed Tracey James and Nancy, they can kill me." Maria's eyes shot a darting glance at him. Jack read her look.

"Yes, Maria — I know. I know Nancy was murdered and I know Tracey James was murdered. And I know they were murdered because of the information you gave them." Maria wanted to disagree with him — at least as far as Tracey James was concerned. But she didn't dare. She was playing the silent game for as long as she could. Jack continued. "And I know you're thinking that you're next. After all, you work for one of the murderers."

Maria couldn't believe her ears. Jack Tobin had just accused her boss, Chief Wesley Brume, of murder — a fact that she knew to be absolutely true.

"And you probably *are* next," Jack said quietly, leaning forward. "You can't just stay silent, Maria, and hope this will go away. The cat is out of the bag and these guys will not rest until all evidence against them has been eliminated. And that means you, Maria. You need help because they're going to kill you. Not right away — maybe a few months from now when all this has died down. They'll arrange for an accident and you'll be killed — just like Tracey and Nancy. There is no way around that fact."

Jack watched her intently as he spoke, looking for some sign that she understood the gravity of his message. Hell, he couldn't make it any clearer. But Maria never changed her expression. She either looked straight ahead or at the floor. He had tried to create in her all the fear that he could. Now it was time to make his pitch.

"If you tell me what you know, I'll protect you, Maria. I won't breathe a word of it until I have a plan to put these people away. One way or the other, I'm going to do something — I don't know what it is yet. But when I start, you will be protected, I assure you. And I have the resources to do it. Maria, I'm your only hope. Help me to help you."

Maria still sat on her living room couch expressionless. Jack stood up and started rubbing his temples and pacing. When he reached the far end of the room and was out of earshot, Pat put her right hand on Maria's shoulder and spoke softly.

"Maria, you have to trust somebody. Trust him. He needs to help you as much as you need him. He feels that he failed Nancy and Rudy."

Maria looked straight into Pat's eyes. Pat held her gaze. She knew what the woman was looking for. She nodded encouragingly to her. "Speak to him. Tell him what he needs to know."

Jack was still pacing, and Pat motioned for him to come back and sit down. When he did, Maria started to speak, but she didn't look at him. She kept her gaze down at a spot on the floor near his feet.

"Two years after Rudy was convicted of Lucy Ochoa's murder, we — I mean the police department — received a letter from the police department of the City of Del Rio, Texas. I was a receptionist/secretary at the time, and it was my job to open the mail. The letter said they had just arrested a man named Geronimo Cruz for rape and murder. It just so happened that he had a Florida driver's license that listed an address in Bass Creek. It was a typical inquiry letter. They wanted to know if we were looking for him for any reason or if we could supply them with any information that would assist them in their investigation or prosecution."

Maria looked up into Jack's face for the first time. "I should tell you that it was common knowledge among the Latinos of Bass Creek that a man named Geronimo killed Lucy Ochoa. When I read this letter, I immediately told Wesley — he was a sergeant then — about it. I knew he had investigated Lucy's murder. He called the state attorney, Clay Evans, right there and then from the phone at my desk, and I heard him telling him about the letter. He listened to whatever Clay Evans was saying, and then I heard him say, 'I'll be right over,' and as soon as he put down the phone, he set out for Mr. Evans's office with the letter in hand."

She dropped her eyes to the floor again. "I never heard anything after that. It was never mentioned again. I never saw the letter again."

At first, Jack couldn't believe what he was hearing, but after a few moments it all made sense to him. Everything fell into place. Rudy's case had been very high profile. All the local affiliates covered it, as did the national news media, probably because of the gruesome nature of the crime and the "boy-next-door" qualities of the young man who supposedly did it. At the time this letter surfaced, Clay Evans was being considered for a federal judgeship solely because of the attention he received for the successful prosecution of the Kelly case. If that case had gone south, his prospects would have as well. *He probably promised Brume something, maybe the chief of police job, in return for shit-canning the letter.*

"Why didn't you tell somebody about this when it happened?" Jack almost shouted. Pat gave him a look like daggers.

"Who was I going to tell? Who was going to believe me — a poor Latino woman with two kids and no husband? If I had the letter I would have said something. Without it I couldn't risk it. I had two kids to protect. I finally told Nancy. I had to. I couldn't let Rudy die without telling someone. But look what they did to her *and* Tracey James."

Maria was sobbing now. Pat put her arms around her and comforted her.

"Jack, you've got to stop!" she said. "It's not this poor woman's fault. She didn't do anything."

But Jack was still thinking about Nancy, and about Rudy. And in his frustration he wasn't able to stir much sympathy for Maria. *She was rewarded for her silence! She's the administrative assistant to the chief of police! Doesn't she know how she got that job!* But the more rational part of his brain knew Pat was right. Maria hadn't spoken up because she was afraid and she had probably correctly assessed the situation: Nobody would have believed her. And the danger to her and her children was very real — Tracey James and Nancy could have attested to that *if they were still around!*

"I'm sorry, Maria. I didn't mean that. I guess I'm still on edge.

Listen, for now until we figure out what we're going to do, let's just pretend we never had this conversation."

Maria didn't say anything. Her sobs had stopped, but the tears were still running down her face.

~

Jack came up with a plan two weeks later. Bob Richards had called to mend fences.

"How are you doing, Jack?" Bob asked in his most sympathetic voice. Jack was about to tell him to go fuck himself when the idea struck him.

"I'm okay Bob, thanks for asking." The governor started to say something else equally insincere —apparently he couldn't help himself — when Jack sprang the question. "Is the job still mine, Bob? Or did I go too far?"

"I'm not sure, Jack. I didn't know you still wanted it."

"Well, I do — that is, if you still want me."

"Let me think about it. I'll get back to you in a few days."

It was a good performance, probably because he'd had no time to rehearse. After that, it had been easy to seal the deal. He called David Williams, a state senator from Miami and an old acquaintance he'd supported and campaigned for in the past. David was now the senate president. Jack asked him to put in a good word for him with Bob Richards. Next, he called a few very wealthy contributors to the governor's campaign that he knew and asked them to do the same thing. It was totally out of character for him and it made him feel a little slimy, but he kept telling himself it was for a higher purpose. By the end of the week, the state attorney's job was his again.

~

He and Pat paid another visit to Maria Lopez after Jack's new position had been secured.

"I start work as the new state attorney in a couple of weeks, and I want you to come work for me." This time Jack was sitting on the couch so he wasn't directly confronting Maria. Pat took the chair. It was a subtle move that he never even would have considered if Pat hadn't suggested it. *I need to keep this woman around,* he smiled to himself.

"I can't," Maria said, with an edge of desperation in her voice. "If I go to work for you they'll know I talked to you. They'll kill me."

"Maria, I'm going to move against these guys soon. I don't know the exact time frame because certain things have to happen over which I don't have any control. I can't explain it any better than that right now. But if they get wind that I'm planning something against them, you'll be in danger no matter who you're working for." Jack was failing miserably at the reassurance game.

Pat took over at that point. "Maria, our plan is not only to have you work for Jack, but to have you come live with us as well. Not forever — we don't want you to have to give up your house — but until this is done. We have a big place and we're going to have two retired Miami police officers, homicide detectives, living with us and guarding us twenty-four hours a day. One of them will drive you and Jack to work and pick you up every day. We're going to make you as safe as you can possibly be."

"I don't know. What about my kids?" Pat had known she would be overwhelmed and her first thought would be about her children.

"We've discussed that," Jack jumped in, "that maybe they would go after your children. " Pat looked warningly at him, but he knew where he was going this time. "We've looked into their circumstances, and as you know, neither Carlos nor Maria is attached. Neither has started on a career path yet. We can relocate them and give them new identities temporarily. We have the resources to do that." He chose not to mention that this part of the project would be completely under the table.

Maria just looked at him, as if to ask by her expression, *Isn't that illegal? Won't you be the state attorney?*

Jack returned her look with a smile. He shrugged his shoulders. "I don't plan on being in this job very long. Just long enough, if you know what I mean. So what do you say, Maria? It's not a foolproof plan but it will make you and your children as secure as you can possibly be — because whether you agree to work for me and live with us or not, all hell is going to break loose in this town soon, and you're going to be in the middle of it." Pat gave an exasperated sigh, but Jack felt strongly that he had to be honest with the woman.

"I could refuse to talk," Maria said quietly.

"They'll kill you anyway," Jack told her. "They won't take that chance. Especially since they've been so successful with their other murders."

Maria was silent for a while. Finally, she took a deep breath and sighed. "I guess I have no choice. What happens to me when this is over and you leave?"

"I'm not leaving town and you'll always have a job with me."

Somehow that did the trick, and her face visibly relaxed. Jack looked over at Pat with satisfaction, and she gave him a knowing look that told him just how close she thought he'd come to blowing it.

~

Two weeks later on a Monday morning, Jack's first day as the new Cobb County state attorney, Wesley Brume came to work and found a plain white envelope planted squarely in the middle of his desk. He opened it and read the letter inside:

*Dear Chief Brume:*
*I am resigning my position in your office effective immediately.*
*I've enjoyed working for you.*

*Sincerely,*
*Maria Lopez*

Wesley Brume was livid. When he found out the next day that Maria Lopez had gone to work for Jack Tobin, he hit the roof.

## [ T H I R T Y - N I N E ]

A few weeks after taking over as state attorney in late January, when the staff had settled in and were fairly comfortable with their new boss, Jack took the opportunity to slip out of town for a few days alone. He had meticulously planned the trip, calling the warden of the Ellis unit of the Texas Department of Criminal Justice himself and setting up an appointment to interview Geronimo Cruz. He told the warden that he was investigating whether Geronimo had anything to do with Lucy Ochoa's murder. He neglected to tell him that Rudy had already been executed for the crime and that he planned on indicting Bass Creek's chief of police and a federal judge for his murder. Those details certainly would have affected the level of cooperation he received. As it was, the warden was delighted to help a fellow member of law enforcement solve another crime. When Jack told him he was going to bring a court reporter and a videographer to the prison in the event Cruz decided to talk, the warden almost laughed into the phone. Cruz was a tough nut. He wasn't going to tell anybody anything. But the warden didn't tell Jack that. Why discourage a man who was passionately pursuing justice?

"Sure, bring 'em along," he drawled. "Anything we can do to help."

The Ellis unit of the Texas penal system was located just outside Huntsville. It was a maximum-security facility, holding close to two thousand prisoners. All executions in the state took place at Ellis and Geronimo Cruz, who had been convicted of rape and murder in 1994, occupied one of the death row cells.

Jack left the court reporter and the videographer at the front desk, telling the guard there that he might need them at a moment's notice and to process them now. The guard had to call the warden to get clearance, which took a few minutes and made Jack wildly impatient. *Fucking bureaucracy! You set everything up beforehand and you have to do it all over once you get there.* Eventually, everyone received the necessary clearance and Jack asked the guard how he could get in touch with him.

"There's a phone in the room you're going to. It's on the wall," the guard told him. "Just pick it up and it will ring here. I'll send them back."

"If you go on break, please explain everything to your relief man. If this guy decides to talk, I'm going to need these people right away. You understand, don't you?"

"Yes sir."

Before Jack left them, he had the court reporter and the videographer set up their equipment in the waiting room. "When I call you, you need to be there and you need to be ready, understand?" Both of them nodded without looking up from what they were doing. It wasn't the crisp military response he'd gotten from the guard, but these people were in business for themselves: If things didn't go right, they wouldn't get paid. Jack was confident they would be ready when — and if — the time came.

The procedure to enter the inner sanctum was almost the same as at Starke. Jack went through one set of bars and then a second set. He was led down a narrow hallway to a room, a little larger than the one at Starke, that contained a metal table and four chairs all bolted to the floor.

*They must send all the prison architects to the same design school,* Jack mused. He was in a rare mood now and was actually looking forward to meeting Geronimo Cruz. Somehow he knew they were going to find common ground.

A few minutes after he entered the room, he could hear the guards ushering Cruz down the hall, the chains rattling familiarly as Cruz walked along. While the guards maneuvered him into one of the chairs, Jack was a world away, arranging in his mind how he was going to persuade Cruz to testify for him.

Geronimo Cruz looked taller than his six-foot height because he was so thin and wiry. He had lightly tanned skin and a neatly trimmed moustache and goatee. His eyes were large and glassy, like he had just smoked a few joints before breakfast, and he had a smile on his face. But it wasn't anywhere close to Rudy's open, generous smile. It was a malevolent sneer. Jack had heard cops say that when you were in the presence of a killer you could feel it. He felt it as soon as Geronimo Cruz walked in the door. He felt a shot of adrenaline rush through his veins, and his heart started racing. It was as if his body knew danger was close by.

But he remembered his purpose and could feel a Rudy-like calmness come over him. He had a plan for Geronimo Cruz and he was going to follow it come hell or high water.

"Mr. Cruz, my name is Jack Tobin. I'm the state attorney for Cobb County, Florida, and I'm here investigating the murder of a woman named Lucy Ochoa in the town of Bass Creek in 1986." It was a mouthful but Jack just put it out there and then shut up. Cruz didn't say anything right away. He just looked at Jack and then chuckled through his sneer a few times. "So, investigate," he said, leaning back in his chair.

"Your name was given to us after the murder by two men, Raymond Castro and José Guerrero. They said you dated Lucy and went to her trailer the night of the murder." Cruz chuckled through his sneer again, this time louder than before. He knew it was a lie. Ray and José hadn't known his last name, and he had talked to them after they talked to the police. He was certain they'd never told the police that he went to Lucy's trailer. He was also certain that after that first interview they'd never spoken to the police again. He actually hadn't left town until after they did.

"So are you here to arrest me, or what? What took you so long?"

"Not exactly. Someone else was arrested and convicted for that murder."

"So why are you talking to me?"

"Because I think the person who was convicted was wrongfully convicted."

"And you want me to confess to get this other person out of jail? What is it, your son or something?"

Jack ignored the remark. "I want you to confess but not to get anybody out of jail. The person who was charged with this murder has already been executed."

Cruz paused for a second, thinking his hearing must have been off. Then he started laughing. "You're kidding me, right? You want me to confess to a murder that somebody else was convicted and executed for?" Jack nodded. "Man, if you could just get me some of that shit you're smoking, I'd sure appreciate it. The stuff they've got in here is garbage."

Jack again ignored the remark. Up to this point, Cruz was acting just as he'd expected.

"Look pal, you're on death row here in Texas for rape and murder. Your appeals are over and your execution date has been set for three months from now. I'm sure you know that they kill their people here in Texas."

"So what? Just because I'm scheduled to die you want me to cop to another murder? For what? So you can feel good?"

Jack leaned over the table towards Geronimo and lowered his voice. The guards didn't seem to notice, or maybe they didn't care so long as the prisoner was behaving himself.

"Look," Jack began, "I represented the kid they executed. His name was Rudy Kelly. He was half Puerto Rican and he worked at the convenience store near Lucy's. Now I'm the state attorney for Cobb County. I have reason to believe that the investigating officer and the state attorney at the time knew about you — or at least learned about you later and did nothing to stop Rudy's execution. They let Rudy die so they could put a feather in their own caps. Because of this case, one of them became chief of police, and the other became a federal judge. I plan on prosecuting both of them for murder, but the first thing I need to establish is that you killed Lucy. I can do that without you: I can take a blood sample and match the DNA to the semen that was found the night of the murder. You slit the throat of that woman in Del Rio with the same type of serrated knife that killed Lucy. I think a jury can put those facts together rather nicely, but it would be more forceful if I had a videotaped confession from you as to how the murder occurred. I think the jury would be more likely to convict these two men with your testimony."

Cruz's glassy eyes widened as he listened.

"Hot damn!" he exclaimed when Jack was through. "You're a wolf in sheep's clothing, Mr. State Attorney. I don't think they like you folks fucking with each other, you know that? Especially over a couple of spics like me and this Rudy kid. They might fry *your* ass."

Jack could see he was getting to him. "I'll worry about my ass. How about it? Are you in or out?"

Geronimo Cruz had never confessed to anything in his life, not even to himself. But this was enticing. He needed something, though. He always had to get something. There had to be an angle to play. He couldn't just do this for nothing.

"I'll tell you what," he said, leaning in. "If you can assure me that I'll be around for the end of this trial, that I'll be able to know these fuckers were convicted, I'll do it."

"Can't do it, Geronimo. I can tell you I'll try like hell to have this trial in the next three months, and if I can't do that, I'll file a motion to have your execution delayed. I don't think it will do any good seeing as how they like to kill their people here on time and nobody in law enforcement, including judges, is going to want to help me. But I'll try, if necessary."

"I like it that those bastards don't like what you're doing and won't help you. You give me your word you'll file a motion to have my execution delayed?"

"I will."

"Here in Texas?"

"Yes."

"Will you come here and argue it yourself?"

"If you give me a videotaped sworn statement here today, I sure will."

Cruz thought about it for a moment. He knew Jack might be bullshitting him, but he knew every kind of bullshitter there was, and Jack wasn't any of them.

"What the fuck, let's do it."

Jack picked up the phone on the wall, hoping there weren't going to be any bureaucratic wrinkles suddenly cropping up to slow things down. Cruz was ready to talk now. Any delay, even a delay of fifteen minutes, could sour the whole deal.

The same guard was there. "They're on their way," he told Jack. Five minutes later, the court reporter and the videographer were in the room with Jack, Geronimo, and the two guards, all set up to record the confession.

This was Geronimo Cruz's finest moment. The court reporter swore him in. He looked directly into the camera and began speaking clearly and precisely. He even dropped the sneer for a more solemn, regretful look. He told the camera that he was sorry that someone else had died for a crime he had committed. At Jack's prompting, he stated that he would have confessed earlier had he known Rudy was on death row. He mentioned that he was scheduled to die in Texas and that he had not been promised anything for his testimony. And then he told them how it happened, from the moment he saw Rudy staggering along the street from the direction of Lucy's trailer up to and including how he pulled the knife out of his pants and slit Lucy's throat just as they both were about to climax.

## [ FORTY ]

Jack had a big house but he only had four bedrooms. So when Maria Lopez, Dick Radek and Joaquin Sanchez moved in, he and Pat decided that she should move all her things from one of the guest rooms into Jack's master bedroom.

"We're not actually living together; we're just sharing the same bedroom," he said with a matter-of-fact look on his face.

"I agree. It's just out of necessity and it's only temporary. It's not a commitment."

"Right," he agreed. "And it's not like we haven't been sleeping together every night anyway."

"And taking showers together to save water."

"Right again," he said, beginning to lose it. "We're just doing this for the team." And then they both burst out laughing.

Joaquin brought his boat over from the other side of the lake and kept it in the extra slip at Jack's dock so he could go fishing. He and Dick worked out a schedule that allowed Joaquin to fish from six to nine in the morning. One of them would then escort Jack and Maria to work while the other stayed home with Pat. Joaquin slept during the day while Dick watched the house. Joaquin was a runner, so he ran with Jack and Pat at night, a small .22 pistol tucked inside his running shorts.

The arrangement worked out well for the first three weeks until

Pat tried to start a mutiny.

"Is this around-the-clock security all that necessary?" she asked one morning at breakfast when they all happened to be present. "I mean, Dick, I love you and you too, Joaquin, but do I need you guys shopping with me for underwear? The only time I feel alone anymore is when I take a shower in the morning after Jack and Maria have gone to work."

Dick and Joaquin stared straight down at their breakfast. They both were experienced enough to recognize a domestic dispute when they saw it. These questions were for Jack to answer.

"I don't know what to tell you, honey," Jack began. He knew it was hardest on her because she didn't have the luxury of escaping into the normal routine of the office like Maria and he could. "The only way we can ensure that nobody else gets killed is to account for all of our whereabouts day and night. You're in danger because you're close to me. If you go out of town — say if you went to New York for a couple of weeks — you'd be fine. I don't think anybody would follow you there. So if you're feeling a little penned in, just take a trip. Anybody else have any other thoughts?"

Dick and Joaquin didn't look up from their plates.

"Sounds good to me," Dick said, shrugging his shoulders.

"Me too," mumbled Joaquin from behind his coffee cup.

Jack made the mistake of trying to add a little levity.

"Poor Maria has to ride with me to work every morning *and* have lunch with me every day." The "Poor Maria" line did not go over too well with Pat. Maria knew it right away and knew how to save the situation better than Jack.

"The people in the office are starting to talk," she said. "And you don't help the situation, Jack, when you have your arm around me every time we walk in and out the front door." They all knew that was part of the plan — to make it common knowledge that Jack and Maria were together at all times. The people who were watching needed to get that message. "But don't worry, Pat, I don't like *gringos*."

Pat smiled and came back with a zinger of her own. "We've all noticed," she said with a waggle of her eyebrows, which made everyone laugh except Joaquin, who turned a little red. Sometime during the first two weeks, he and Maria had bonded. During the third week, he abruptly stopped his morning fishing routine. Everyone assumed he had simply decided to sleep in, until he emerged from Maria's bedroom one morning. Nobody said anything until a few days later at breakfast. Jack and Pat had their heads together, and Maria and Joaquin were sneaking glances across the table when Dick suddenly blurted out, "I feel like a fifth wheel around here."

Jack almost spit his oatmeal out he started laughing so hard.

"I can set you up with Dolly at the Pelican," Pat offered. "I hear she's available." She had taken to dragging Dick to breakfast at the Pelican whenever the others left early for the office.

"I don't know if I could take her asking me if I wanted the usual every night," Dick shot back, bringing them all almost to tears.

They were laughing again now, but the problem had not been resolved.

"Do you want to take a vacation? Get out of here for a few weeks?" Jack suggested again.

Pat hesitated. "I don't think so. You're all dealing with the circumstances, so I guess I can too. But Jack, when is it going to end? What I really mean is, when is it going to start?"

"As soon as I have an opportunity, Pat, I promise you. As soon as I have an opportunity." Pat nodded. She knew he was doing his best, although she didn't quite understand what he meant by an opportunity. There were certain things Jack kept to himself.

"All right," she sighed. "But when this is over, you're going to take me to Europe."

"Hell, when this is over, I'll take us all to Europe."

## [ FORTY-ONE ]

Jack's "opportunity" finally arrived two months later.

He had inherited an aggressive young lawyer named Todd Hamilton, who had been with the office for two years before Jack took over. Hamilton had all the makings of a potential superstar in the business. He was smart, articulate, handsome — and had one gigantic pair of *cojones*. Although he'd grown tired of prosecuting the usual small-town felonies, instead of packing his bags and heading for the big city, he'd stayed put and dug deep to find the corrupt underbelly of Cobb County. He was already in the thick of a major investigation when Jack was appointed.

As Miami, Fort Lauderdale and the Palm Beaches grew and grew and grew, real estate developers began to run out of the necessary dirt to churn their profits. They couldn't go south or east: It was hard to build condominiums and single-family homes in the Atlantic Ocean. They couldn't go north: Everything up to Fort Pierce and Vero was pretty much built out. So they did what Horace Greeley had suggested to a much different crowd about a hundred years before — go west! Even west created some problems, however, because of a rather large freak of nature called the Everglades. But just north of the Everglades was Lake Okeechobee, and it wasn't long before the land around the lake started popping up on radar screens as prime property for future development. Developers began to gobble up acreage at bargain-basement prices. Few people noticed. Unfortunately for the buyers, Todd Hamilton was one of the people who did.

There are always a few minor start-up problems when converting a basically rural area into a sub-sub-sub-suburb of the metropolis — minor irritants such as land-use, zoning and environmental regulations that must be removed. Politicians need to be paid off at the state and local level, and environmental regulators need to be taken care of. Zoning officials and city and county code enforcement officers have to get their cut as well, although theirs is usually quite a bit smaller because of their position in the food chain. The big dogs eat first.

While everybody was feeding at the public trough, Todd Hamilton was taking notes and following the money trail. By the time he approached Jack about convening a grand jury to start handing out indictments, Hamilton could trace money flowing from four separate companies that had purchased land in Cobb County to the personal bank accounts of state senators and representatives, state environmental commission employees, and assorted other parasites — to the tune of millions of dollars. He could also show where zoning restrictions had been removed and permits had been granted in protected wetland areas and estuaries without any valid basis.

Jack was ecstatic when Todd presented his evidence to him, but not for the obvious reasons. Jack had known all along that the biggest impediment to bringing Wesley Brume and Clay Evans to justice was getting an indictment from a grand jury. In Florida, a state attorney can prosecute most crimes by *information*, which basically means that the state attorney has the discretion to determine whether there is probable cause to charge someone with a crime. The only time a state attorney is required to get an *indictment*, a finding of probable cause from a grand jury, is when the potential punishment is death. Since Jack intended to charge both Evans and Brume with first-degree murder, he would have to have a grand jury convened to get an indictment — and there was the rub. The chief judge of the circuit court would have to convene the grand jury, and the chief judge of Cobb County — the *only* circuit judge in Cobb County — was Bill Sampson, Jack's predecessor as state attorney. Bill Sampson would *never* convene a grand jury to consider the indictment of Clay Evans, a sitting federal judge, and Wesley Brume, a chief of police.

While grand juries *must* be the source of indictments in first-degree murder cases, they can be convened for any type of felony and often are asked to issue indictments for high-profile crimes like the corruption case Todd Hamilton was investigating. A grand jury indictment in such a case shields the state attorney from charges of unfairness or playing politics or things of that nature. Bill Sampson would have no problem convening a grand jury to investigate corruption. Once the grand jury was in place, however, Jack could ask them to issue an indictment in any case he wanted. This was the "opportunity" he had told Pat he was waiting for.

Still, he waited until the grand jury had been in session for a month before he told Todd Hamilton that they were going to take a break from his case for a few days to present another case.

The proverbial shit was about to hit the fan.

## [ FORTY - TWO ]

Jack first addressed the eighteen grand jurors on a Monday morning, when they were fresh and, hopefully, attentive. He didn't pull any punches. He told them that he wanted them to indict the former state attorney and the investigating detective in the Rudy Kelly case for murder because the two of them knew Rudy Kelly was probably innocent, but they coerced testimony and hid evidence to get a conviction, then later refused to talk to the real killer because they didn't want to spoil the verdict they had already obtained. They let Rudy Kelly die in the electric chair without checking out the facts that would have made him a free man. He meticulously laid out the evidence he planned to present at trial: that three men were a few hundred yards from the murder scene on the night of the murder; how two of them were questioned that night and then disappeared; how the third, a man named Geronimo, was never questioned and was never found.

He told them about Rudy — how Rudy was a very affable, almost retarded young man who had been to visit Lucy Ochoa on the night of her murder. He told them about Wesley Brume's interrogation of Rudy and the so-called confession written in long hand by Wesley Brume without the aid of readily available video and audio recorders.

When he had given them an overall view of the case, he focused on the specific details that incriminated Evans and Brume. The first was the rape file.

"They found semen in Lucy Ochoa's vaginal cavity," he told them. "And the blood type — they didn't have DNA testing back then — was different from the blood type of the blood on the carpet, which was Rudy's blood when he fell and cut his hand. They put that information in a separate rape file and didn't tell Rudy's attorneys about it." He spoke the next two sentences with special emphasis, punching every word home: *"It was evidence that someone else was in Lucy's house on the night of the murder and they hid it from defense counsel. That rape file was only uncovered last year."*

Next, Jack informed them of the letter Tracey James sent to Clay Evans just before she left the case, telling him that one of the three men who was on the street that night — the one called Geronimo, who disappeared before anyone could talk to him — was undoubtedly the killer. And he told them how she had attached Joaquin Sanchez's report of his interview with Pablo Gonzalez. He repeated two sentences from Tracey's letter verbatim:

*"Release the boy or at least delay the trial until we can jointly investigate who and where this Geronimo person is. Let us work together to see that justice is accomplished."*

The third important piece of evidence was the anticipated testimony of Maria Lopez, that two years after Rudy's conviction, the City of Del Rio police department sent a letter to the Bass Creek police department informing them that they had just arrested an individual named Geronimo Cruz for rape and murder.

"According to Ms. Lopez, Wesley Brume called Clay Evans immediately and told him about the letter and went directly to his office. There is no evidence that the Del Rio police department was ever contacted, and the letter disappeared."

The final elements in Jack's case were the confession and the blood testing of Geronimo Cruz.

"You will see a video recording of a sworn confession by Geronimo Cruz in which he describes in detail how he murdered Lucy Ochoa. We blood-tested Mr. Cruz, who is on death row in

Texas for the rape and murder of another woman. His DNA matched the semen found in Lucy Ochoa. There is no doubt he is the killer.

"There is also no doubt that an innocent young man was executed by the State of Florida," Jack concluded. "Evidence was intentionally hidden; other evidence was intentionally not followed up on. The people who did that — whether they are part of law enforcement or not — should be prosecuted for their actions and should receive the punishment they deserve."

His presentation had the earmarks of a closing statement, which was exactly what Jack intended. He trusted juries — a lot more than he trusted judges — to go out on a limb and make the right decision, but he had to convince them at the outset that they were doing the right thing. Like Judge Bill Sampson, they would initially be reluctant to indict a state attorney and a police officer. But unlike Bill, they wouldn't be worried about their own jobs if they did so.

He started to present his case that very afternoon. He read them Wesley Brume's testimony from the suppression hearing, then the testimonies of Rudy's principal, Bill Yates, and Benny Dragone, his employer at the convenience store. The combination pretty much painted a picture of Wesley Brume as a snake. Next, he introduced his documentary evidence — a certified copy of the rape investigation and Tracey James's letter to Clay Evans with Joaquin's report attached. He followed up with something he hadn't mentioned that morning, live testimony from Charley Peterson, the public defender who had represented Rudy at trial.

Jack had had a hard time finding Charley Peterson but he eventually located him through a relative in town. Charley had retired unwillingly from the practice of law. His drinking had gotten so bad that he was eventually disbarred, a fact Jack did not know about when he'd filed Rudy's appeal. A disbarred Charley Peterson would have been another factor in Rudy's favor. Charley was now clean and sober and teaching at a small college in western North Carolina. When Jack phoned him and told him about the rape file, he was so angry he offered to come and testify at any time without a subpoena.

Charley Peterson knew that he bore some responsibility for Rudy's death because of his drinking, and he intended to make up for it by testifying honestly and forcefully. He told the grand jurors that he was never told about the rape file and that if he had known about it, he would have introduced the semen evidence at trial. It was significant because it put somebody else in Lucy's trailer besides Rudy. He was convinced that the jury in Rudy's case would never have convicted him had they known of the semen evidence.

Jack ended the day on Charley Peterson's testimony. He was going to call Maria first thing in the morning and finish with Geronimo Cruz's video confession.

Jack had a master plan to help ensure a successful outcome. He knew the grand jurors would want to give both Clay Evans and Wesley Brume the opportunity to appear before them and tell their story. He also knew that once they were subpoenaed, Evans would call the governor, and there was always the chance that Bob Richards would fire Jack on the spot. Although he had some evidence to persuade the governor not to take such a drastic course of action, he had to allow for that possibility. Part of his plan was simply to finish his case before either Evans or Brume received their subpoena. Then, even if he was fired, the grand jury would already have the evidence they needed to issue an indictment.

The other part of his plan was to deal with the governor directly. He had Maria call and make an appointment for him to see Bob Richards on Wednesday morning at ten o'clock. He then made arrangements with the sheriff's office to have Clay Evans served with his subpoena before Wesley Brume, on Wednesday morning at 9:30.

Clay Evans called the best criminal lawyer he knew when he received his subpoena. Then he picked up the phone and called Bob Richards. He knew the governor a little from social functions and such, but the two men were not close and Evans wasted no time letting Bob Richards know this was not a social call.

"Do you know what that crazy son-of-a-bitch you appointed state attorney is trying to do?"

"You mean Jack Tobin?"

"Who else? He's convened a grand jury down there in Cobb County and he's trying to indict me for the murder of that Kelly kid who was executed."

Bob Richards couldn't believe what he was hearing. "You're kidding me."

"Do I sound like I'm kidding? This guy has gone off the reservation, Bob, and he's your problem."

"I can't believe this."

"Well, you better believe it. And you better do something fast. You know that grand juries are putty in the hands of prosecutors. You'd better fire that son-of-a-bitch before they bring back an indictment or all hell's gonna break loose."

"Calm down, Clay. I'll take care of this. As we speak, he's sitting in my waiting room. I'll fire him right now and call you back. Don't worry, I'll take care of it."

"You better."

Bob Richards was in a rage when he hung up the phone. He didn't need a federal judge breathing down his neck. He also knew something like this was going to be a major, major news event. He had to try and squelch it before it took on a life of its own. He picked up the phone and yelled at his secretary to bring Jack Tobin into his office immediately.

Jack walked into Bob Richards's office with a smile on his face. He could tell by the governor's expression that he had received the bad news. His casual smile caused the usually well-controlled politician to explode.

"You son-of-a-bitch! You set me up! You've been planning this thing all along, haven't you?" He didn't wait for an answer. "And now you stroll in here with that shit-eating grin on your face. What the fuck are you here for? You know I'm going to fire you, don't you?

Did you really believe in your wildest dreams that I would let you prosecute this case? You're fucking crazy."

Jack just stood there listening. He'd expected this — the outrage, the indignation. It was going to make what he was about to do that much sweeter.

"Let's take a walk, Bob."

"What for?"

"It's a little stuffy in here."

"I don't want to walk anywhere with you."

"I think you do. I think you want to hear what I have to say before you do anything rash."

Jack's statement made Bob Richards pause. He was angry, *almost* out of control, but Jack was right. He *never* wanted to do anything to hurt his political career. He didn't know what Jack was up to, but he had to listen.

"Let's go to the garden," he snapped, walking past Jack and out of the office at a clip.

When they were safely in the garden, Richards turned to Jack. "So what do you have to say for yourself before I fire you?" Again, he didn't wait for an answer. "Do you have any idea what the fuck you've done? You're trying to indict a sitting federal judge for murder. Are you out of your mind?"

"Maybe, but you're not going to do anything about it."

"Is that some kind of a threat, Jack?"

"That's exactly what it is, Governor. I'm glad you can see that."

"And what do you have to threaten me with?" Richards had obviously played this game before. He wanted to see Jack's cards.

Jack took a small tape recorder out of his pocket and turned it on. Bob Richards heard his own voice on a telephone tape recorder telling Jack at one point that he thought Rudy was innocent and, in the next moment, that he couldn't do anything about it for political reasons. Richards already knew about Geronimo Cruz's confession because Jack had sent him and every judge on the Florida Supreme Court a videotape of it, along with the DNA test results. He immediately put two and two together. If the public found out that the State of Florida had killed an innocent man and that he, the governor, had believed that man to be innocent but had refused to act for political reasons, he was finished.

Richards came out swinging.

"That's an illegal tape recording of a telephone conversation and you're trying to blackmail me."

Jack just smiled. "Well, you're wrong and you're right, Bob. You're wrong about our telephone conversation being illegal. My tape machine came on before I picked the telephone up. As a matter of fact, you were speaking to the recorder when I cut in. You're not going to be able to claim that the telephone conversation was surreptitiously recorded. You're right, however, that this is blackmail, because if you attempt to fire me, I'm going to send copies of this tape to every news station in America. This will be national news, Bob. Everyone will be shocked that a governor used a death sentence for political purposes, and you will be a pariah."

The governor's demeanor turned on a dime. His anger faded like a light on a dimmer switch.

"Why are you doing this, Jack? I thought we were friends. I went out of my way to put you in this job."

"You went out of shit, Bob. You gave me this job because I know some people who can help you get to the next level. This job was all about politics and we both know it, so spare me the bullshit. And don't you dare call me your friend. Rudy Kelly was my friend. His father, Mike, was the best friend I ever had. I pleaded with you. I begged you to spare this young man's life and you blew me off. Don't you ever call me your friend."

"I don't know what to do. I just got off the phone with Clay Evans. He wants me to fire you and I told him I would."

"Well, call him back and tell him you're going to let the judicial process work. Tell him you're sure he will be vindicated. Then do what you did to me — hang up."

"What about the press? This is going to be a huge story."

"It certainly is. You tell the press the same thing. Stick that strong jaw of yours out and tell them that you're not going to interfere with the judicial process. Tell them that this nation is based on laws, not men — that it's a matter of principle. Personally you might be appalled at what has transpired, but you cannot interfere. You're good at that bullshit, Bob."

Richards missed the sarcasm in Jack's voice. "You think it will work?"

"Absolutely. Look, if they get off, you can say the system worked. And if they get convicted, you can say the same thing. This is a win-win situation for you, Bob."

Richards walked along the garden path for a moment with his right hand rubbing at his chin. He suddenly stopped and turned to Jack. "What about the tape?"

"I'll give it to you when the case is over — completely, appeals and everything."

"Even if you lose?"

"Even if I lose."

"What assurances do I have?"

"That's the rub, Bob. You have to trust me and I know it's hard for people like you to trust anybody."

"What choice do I have?"

"None if you want to stay in politics."

The governor's shoulders slumped as he turned and walked away from Jack. He was beaten and they both knew it. "All right, Jack, it's a deal. But don't fuck me."

"Don't worry, Bob. It's not you I'm after."

[ **F O R T Y - T H R E E** ]

The rumor in Miami was that Jimmy DiCarlo was a made man, and Jimmy did nothing to dispel that rumor. He was a criminal defense lawyer who specialized in drug trafficking cases, and his clientele included a number of big-name mobsters. Truth be told, Jimmy was Jewish. His mother divorced his father, Jacob Bernstein, when Jimmy was four. Two years later, she married Giovanni DiCarlo, or Joe as everybody called him, a Brooklyn carpenter, who adopted Jimmy when the boy was ten.

In Jimmy's world, truth was a combination of perception, manipulation, intimidation and whatever else was needed to get the story told the right way. If people wanted to think he was a made man, that was fine. It helped in his work. Prosecutors who weren't crusaders, who just wanted to put in their time until private practice beckoned, did not want to play games with a man as connected as Jimmy. They accepted his version of the truth whenever possible, and consequently Jimmy's clients spent very little time in jail. If necessary, Jimmy wasn't above delivering a satchel full of cash to an undisclosed location to get the deal done. After all, there was truth, and then there was truth with money sprinkled on top.

Jimmy came to Miami on a football scholarship, although he never played a minute in an actual game. He was a big man, standing six foot four in his bare feet. In his "playing" days, he weighed in at two fifty-five, a defensive tackle who didn't have the speed — or the heart, for that matter — to break into the starting lineup. Still, his office was littered with football paraphernalia from his "playing" days. Anyone walking in off the street would have thought Jimmy had been the star of the team. It was all a matter of perception.

These days, Jimmy was a high-rolling bachelor who hit the clubs a few nights a week and feasted regularly on filet mignon and other assorted delicacies. Although he still appeared muscular, Jimmy's weight had ballooned well past the three hundred mark. In order to maintain a youthful, virile appearance, he wore a corset to shift his belly more towards his chest, dyed his thick hair jet-black and kept it gelled and combed straight back. When he was decked out in one of his many black Armani suits, adorned with gold tie clip, gold cuff links and gold Rolex, his head protruding from a stiff white collar, Jimmy commanded attention. He looked tough; he looked successful. He also looked like he was about to explode at any minute.

Jimmy had appeared in Clay Evans's courtroom many times, and Judge Evans had been impressed at how he handled himself. Jimmy had a thick, strong voice — one you could not turn away from. When he was standing in front of a jury, or over a witness, *he* was always the center of attention. It was hard not to believe him because he was so forceful in his delivery.

There were whispers around the federal courthouse in Miami that some of Jimmy DiCarlo's satchels of cash eventually made their way into Clay Evans's pockets. But those whispers were usually made at a late hour after many drinks, when false courage helped a man say what he wouldn't otherwise. Nobody in his right mind would utter those words in the light of day for fear that Jimmy might find out.

Although he'd handled a few murder trials, they weren't Jimmy's strong suit. That didn't matter to Clay Evans. Jimmy was strong, smart, and sharp on his feet, and he would do anything necessary to win a case. He was the man Clay Evans wanted to represent him *and* Wesley Brume.

Late Wednesday night after he returned from his visit to Tallahassee, Jack received a phone call.

"Hello?"

"You're about to make me a rich man and I just wanted to call and thank you."

Jack had an unlisted phone number and he knew just about everybody who called him at home. But he didn't recognize the voice on the other end.

"Who is this?"

"Oh, I'm sorry," the voice oozed, sarcastically. "I forgot to identify myself. This is Jimmy DiCarlo."

Jack knew who he was but decided to play along.

"Jimmy DiCarlo, Jimmy DiCarlo.... I knew a lawyer in Miami by that name."

"One and the same."

"And what can I do for you this evening, Jimmy?"

"Like I said, I'm just calling to thank you because you're about to make me a rich man."

"I am?"

"You most certainly are. Once you indict my clients for murder and we get the case dismissed, I'm going to own you. Is it true you're worth upwards of twenty million dollars?"

Jack ignored the question. "A grand jury is about to indict your clients, Jimmy, not me. Congrats on getting the job, though. It's certainly a step up from those drug dealers."

Jack could tell he'd hit a nerve. "Whatever," Jimmy said dismissively before continuing his taunting. "Indicting a sitting federal judge for murder — this is my wet dream. I'm going to sue your ass for millions."

"Aren't you getting a little ahead of yourself, Jimmy? There's the little matter of a criminal trial in the way of your quest for gold. It's a good move, though, trying to instill some doubt and fear here at the outset. But you can save your breath. I didn't earn my money picking daisies. Now, is there another reason you called?" Jack already knew the answer to his question.

"Actually, there is. My clients are not interested in attending that charade you're putting on before the grand jury. Is there any way we could bypass the formalities of showing up just to take the Fifth?"

Jack knew he could make them show up — just to piss them off — but he wanted to get his indictment as quickly as possible now that everybody knew what he was doing. Jimmy DiCarlo certainly didn't deserve any favors, calling him late in the evening and threatening him, but this wasn't about Jimmy. He still wasn't going to let him off the hook that easy, though.

"*How to Win Friends and Influence People* — did you write that book, Jimmy? You call me up at home in the middle of the night, insult me, and then ask for a favor. That's real smooth. I hope you bring this routine to the courtroom."

"Are you going to make us show up, or what?" Jimmy snarled. He was tiring of the game he had started.

"Nah," Jack replied. "Just send me a letter stating that your clients intend to take the Fifth and they won't have to show up." Jack wasn't through. "There's another reason you should be thanking me, Jimmy."

"Oh yeah, what's that?"

"I'm going to make you famous. When this indictment comes down, it's going to be national, maybe international, news. You'll be a household name before it's over."

"You're probably right," Jimmy replied, realizing for the first time that this might be his big chance to hit the national scene.

"There's only one downside to that," Jack teased.

"Oh yeah, what's that?"

"You better not fuck up. Goodnight, Jimmy." Jack hung up the phone.

~

The grand jury brought back an indictment for first-degree murder against Clay Evans and Wesley Brume on that Friday afternoon.

It didn't hit the national press until Monday, but it hit with a bang. CNN led the evening news with it. It made the broadcasts on NBC, CBS, and ABC as well. By Tuesday, Bass Creek was crawling with news trucks, reporters and television crews. Jack knew the case was going to generate publicity — he just didn't realize how much.

He wanted Rudy's murder to be a public issue and he knew he had to be a part of that, so on Tuesday afternoon he gave his first interview to the Associated Press.

"I can't talk about the specifics of the case," he told the reporter, a blonde who looked young enough to be his daughter. "But I can tell you that these men will be prosecuted to the full extent of the law. This is a nation of laws, not of men. The message everyone should take from this indictment is that nobody is above the law."

"Have you spoken with the governor? Isn't there a possibility he could remove you from office for indicting a sitting federal judge?" Jack knew somebody had planted those questions. He only answered the second one.

"I think the governor will let the judicial process take its course. He's a man of integrity. He's not going to interfere with the pursuit of justice."

At that moment, in Tallahassee, Bob Richards was reciting the same script Jack had given him just a few days earlier.

"Jack Tobin is a capable lawyer and I'm sure the men who have been charged have capable lawyers. If they are innocent, the judicial process will vindicate them."

Jimmy DiCarlo was the last to weigh in, but his statement was the most quotable of the day and was the one that led the news reports that evening.

"Jack Tobin once represented Rudy Kelly. He argued his appeal before the Supreme Court and lost. Rudy Kelly's execution was a mistake but it was a mistake at many levels. Jack Tobin cannot accept that. He's looking for someone to blame. He shouldn't be on this case."

Dressed in his black Armani, white shirt, and silver silk tie, his jet-black hair slicked back, Jimmy looked like a very fleshy movie star.

～

The day didn't end at the office for Jack and Maria. Dick was at the wheel when they pulled into the driveway at home and encountered a whole new circus — a crowd of reporters, TV trucks and gawkers spilling over the front lawn.

"I guess our nice, comfortable lifestyle is over," Dick mused.

"This will blow over soon," Jack told him.

A week later they were still there, however, and everybody in the house started feeling a little claustrophobic. Jack, Pat and Joaquin couldn't go jogging, and Dick, who had stopped drinking and started exercising when the job began, couldn't go swimming. Nobody could go out of the house to do anything. Even shopping was a major project. There didn't seem to be any end in sight, either. After the indictment, arrests still had to be made, pleas had to be entered, and motions had to be filed. There was plenty to keep the press buzzing.

"I've got to do something," Jack told Pat one night when they were lying in bed. "I can't put everybody through this for months."

"Do you have any ideas?"

"Yeah, there's a fellow I used to fish with a while back, Steve Preston. He owns a big ranch — thousands of acres — about twenty miles outside of town. His son was his foreman and when he got married, Steve built him a big house right on the ranch, a couple of miles down from his own place. Well, the son's wife didn't want him to be a rancher anymore and they moved to Atlanta and the son took a job with Coca-Cola. Steve was crushed.

"As far as I know the house is still vacant. Steve showed me the place when it was still under construction. It's a huge house — bigger than this. I think I'll call him tomorrow and see if he wants to rent it."

"That'll be a change," Pat said noncommittally. "Have you discussed this with any of the others?"

"Not yet. I wanted to talk with you first. What do you think?"

"I guess it will be all right if you think it's necessary."

"I've *got* to do something. We can't continue like this. Pat, why don't you get out of here for a while. Take a vacation."

Pat sat up in the bed and looked at him. She didn't say anything for a few minutes, and he couldn't tell if he'd said something to make her angry.

"Jack, how do you feel right now?"

"What do you mean?"

"I mean you're in the middle of this case. You've been through a hell of a lot. How do you feel?"

It was Jack's turn to hesitate. He propped himself up and looked into her eyes.

"Losing Nancy and then Rudy has been devastating for me, and I know it's been the same for you. But in spite of that, I've never felt more alive. I can actually feel the blood flowing through my veins. I know we're doing the right thing." His eyes were suddenly on fire. He was talking with his hands. "And it's not just the fact that Rudy was innocent and that our criminal justice system is broken. It's bigger than that for me now. I see the innocent and the guilty. It's like I was just born and I'm looking at the world for the first time. I know this kind of thinking is nothing new. People have been saying it for years. But it's new to me. We never ask ourselves why people commit murder. We don't even see them as people. We don't care if they grew up as animals, living in filth, squalor and hopelessness. We don't question whether mom was a drug addict or a prostitute or whether her johns beat the shit out of her son every night — I'm not kidding you, this is the *normal* background for a lot of these people. We don't ask because we don't want to know — because we might have some responsibility there. It's easier to just kill them.

"No, it's not just about Rudy anymore, and it's not about winning or losing because, frankly, I'm probably going to lose. This is what I'm going to be doing for the rest of my life. That's what Rudy was trying to tell me in his letter."

He took a deep breath and Pat thought he was finished, but he wasn't. Not yet. "This new vision I have affects my whole life. I see people I never saw before. I care about them like I have never cared before. I see you. I love you so much it hurts. I've never felt like this about anyone. Do you have any idea what I'm talking about?"

Pat stroked his cheek softly. "Yes, Jack, I know. I've known for a long time. That's why I'm not going anywhere. I think the others feel the same way, but maybe you should bring it up with them — just to get a feel for where everybody is on this."

"I think you're right."

"But not tonight," she said as she kissed him gently on the lips. "Tonight you're mine."

Jack put his arms around her as they slid back towards the pillows.

Before he could talk to the group, another problem arose that caused him to rethink everything he had said to Pat the night before. Dick and Joaquin brought it to his attention at breakfast the next morning.

They were sitting around the dining room table, each reading his own newspaper and eating scrambled eggs and hash that Joaquin had prepared. (Pat had suggested the separate newspapers. "If everybody has their own newspaper in the morning," she'd said, "they'll feel more comfortable, more at home.")

"Have you read this article about you?" Joaquin asked.

"I glanced at it," Jack said. "It's a pack of lies."

"Jack, this article says that you screwed so many people out of money when you were a defense attorney that some of them want to kill you."

"I've had death threats during my career but nothing like they're talking about here. This is just sensationalism."

Dick and Joaquin just looked at each other. "He doesn't get it," Dick said to Joaquin.

"Get what?" Jack asked.

"Jack, this story was planted," Dick said.

"So?"

"So, there was a reason it was planted."

"Yeah, to smear me. So what? I'm a big boy, I can take it."

Dick looked at Joaquin again and threw up his hands. Joaquin knew it was his turn to try and explain.

"Jack, why do you think somebody would want to plant a story that there are tons of people out there who want to kill you?"

"I don't know. It's part of their defense strategy, I guess."

"Think about it, Jack. Your opposing counsel is Jimmy DiCarlo. Jimmy DiCarlo is a gangster. I know, technically he only represents gangsters, but we all know he's either a gangster himself or he's very close to those who kill people for a living." Joaquin paused for a breath and Dick jumped in. It was like the old days when they'd teamed on so many homicide cases.

"If you were hit — murdered, that is — the obvious suspect before this article would have been either Evans or Brume. That kept the risk you and Maria and Pat are facing at a more manageable level."

Jack was starting to get it. "Oh, so you think they planted this article to provide a little cover. Create a few more suspects. Come on, guys, isn't that a little far-fetched?"

"Not really, Jack." It was Joaquin again.

Jack just looked at them. "You guys are serious, aren't you?"

"Dead serious," they said, almost in unison.

"All right, all right, let's just suppose you're right. What are we going to do about it?"

"If they're going to take you out," Dick explained, "it will probably be on the ride to or from work." Jack could tell now that the two of them had already discussed this. "Catch you on a side street or something," Dick continued. "We've always felt that's been the most vulnerable part of your day."

"And Maria's too, and whoever was driving!" Jack exclaimed. Both Dick and Joaquin nodded. "Oh no! This is getting way too dangerous. I've got to call this off." Just then Maria came out of her room and joined them.

"What's all this commotion about?" she asked. Pat was walking down the stairs from her bedroom.

"Yeah, what's going on?" she added.

"These guys think Jimmy DiCarlo is going to have me whacked," Jack said as nonchalantly as if he were asking somebody to pass the toast.

"What!" Pat cried out.

"You're kidding!" Maria exclaimed.

"No we're not," Dick said. "We think it's a real possibility." Maria and Pat looked at each other in shock.

"I'm going to call this whole thing off," Jack said. "I'm going to dismiss the case today."

"Don't we have a say about that?" Maria asked. They all looked at her, more than a little surprised. "Look, I didn't want to be a part of this thing originally, but now I'm in it and I can't explain it but I feel good about it. I think it's the right thing to do." Pat stole a glance at Jack as if to say *I told you so*. "Besides, as you told me once before, Jack, they're not going to stop just because this case is dismissed. They're still going to come after me at some point."

Jack looked at Joaquin, who nodded in agreement. Dick nodded his assent too. "So what do we do?" he asked.

"One of my many jobs after retirement was being a bodyguard to the rich and famous," Joaquin told them. "Many of them had these special cars that were bulletproof head to toe. You can order them in New York. They'll deliver them in a week, even sooner if you pay extra. They're expensive, though, and I'd want to include some extra modifications."

Jack didn't ask about the modifications — that was Dick and Joaquin's specialty. Overall safety was his responsibility. "Never mind about the money," he said. "Will this modified car solve the problem?"

"Partially," Dick replied. "You're safe at the office but this house has always been a bit of a problem. We're sitting ducks here, although I can't see us being attacked with that crowd outside. It'll happen in the middle of the night if it happens here. We need extra guns, too. I can take care of that."

"I'm already working on the house problem, though it was supposed to be for a different reason," Jack said, looking over at Pat. "I have a friend who might have a vacant ranch house. It's big enough for us and it's fenced and gated."

"That'll work," Joaquin nodded. "How soon can we move in?"

"I'll call him today."

"And I'll call the car place," Joaquin said.

Before he left the table, Jack looked at each one of them.

"Are you all sure this is what you want to do?"

Everyone nodded their assent.

## [ F O R T Y - F O U R ]

Clay Evans and Wesley Brume were never arrested the way people like Rudy were. They were afforded the special courtesies reserved for celebrities and people from the upper crust of society. At a predetermined time, they appeared in court, whereupon they were formally arrested, a plea of not guilty was entered and bail was set at two hundred fifty thousand dollars each, a sum that the bail bondsman, who was also present, immediately paid. They never even came downwind of a jail cell. They simply had to face a gaggle of reporters and television cameras outside the courthouse, as well as a gathering of ordinary citizens, many of whom were actually cheering for them.

At this initial hearing, Jimmy DiCarlo took the opportunity to file a Motion to Dismiss the entire indictment, a motion that Jack had expected. Outside the courthouse, basking in his newfound fame, Jimmy told the press that he had filed the motion, which sent them into a feeding frenzy. They had no idea what the motion was about; they just knew there was action, and action caused a reaction, and they could report on all of it — Jimmy on the steps of the courthouse talking about the motion, Jack at his office commenting on it. It was kind of like a tennis match or some other sporting event, only the stakes were just a little higher.

From the outset, Jack knew he had some legal hurdles to

overcome to get his case before a jury. The biggest problem was the question of immunity. A prosecutor enjoys absolute immunity for any actions he takes in prosecuting a case, regardless of his or her motive. A police officer is a little farther down on the totem pole and has only limited immunity. The long and the short of it was that Jack could probably prosecute the Grunt with the evidence he had but not Clay Evans *unless* he could convince the judge there was an exception to the rule. He had a basis for making the argument. It just depended on whether the judge would buy it or not. *The judge* — that was another part of the problem. He had no idea who the judge was going to be. Bill Sampson had handled the preliminary hearing, but he was not going to hear the case, Jack was sure of that. Bill had been the former state attorney of Cobb County. He had replaced Clay Evans in the job and he had worked very closely with Wesley Brume, which normally might not have been such a bad thing: To know Wesley was to despise him. But Bill was too fresh in the job and this case was a political hot potato. He was definitely going to hand it off. *But to who?*

That question was uppermost in Jack's mind as he read Jimmy DiCarlo's Motion to Dismiss. It was based totally on the immunity question. Something else was bothering Jack as well, something Jimmy had said to the press — that Jack himself should be removed from the case. His prior representation of Rudy was a sticky issue. The court could rule that having been Rudy's lawyer at one time, he couldn't now prosecute Rudy's prosecutor: He was on too many sides of the case. The judge probably wouldn't address that issue unless Jimmy objected in court, and his statements to the media gave every indication that he was heading in that direction.

Jack decided to try and handle the representation issue outside the courtroom. When a reporter asked him about Jimmy's comments, Jack replied by taunting Jimmy.

"It sounds like he doesn't want to face me in the courtroom. If he gets rid of me, he'll probably get somebody with less experience. That's an understandable approach."

Jack figured that by appealing to Jimmy's manhood and calling him a coward, albeit in a very nice way, he could cause Jimmy to backtrack on that issue. The strategy worked.

When the young female reporter raced to Jimmy's office to tell him Jack had called him a coward in so many words, Jimmy fell right into the trap.

"There's no way I want Jack Tobin off this case," he told her. "I'm going to enjoy taking him apart — er, I mean taking his case apart in the courtroom."

Jack smiled when he saw the interview on the eleven o'clock news. He was glad that Clay Evans had picked Jimmy to represent him, not that Jimmy was stupid or anything. He was a very capable attorney. But Jimmy was the proverbial bull in the china shop. He usually succeeded through aggressiveness and intimidation. Jack hoped to win by using Jimmy's aggressiveness to trap and outmaneuver him. He was off to a good start.

Of course, there was another guy he had to worry about and that was Clay Evans. Evans was admittedly lazy. He'd used his political connections to get every job he'd ever had, but he was no idiot. Evans had a brain and he knew how to strategize behind the scenes. Jack could see his hand already in this case. It was obviously Evans's decision to have Jimmy DiCarlo represent both himself and Wesley Brume. The Grunt could never afford DiCarlo's fees. Evans undoubtedly figured out that the Grunt was his biggest problem in the case. If the Grunt agreed to testify against him in return for a deal, Evans could be in serious trouble. Since Chief Brume had some real exposure, that scenario was not out of the question. By having Jimmy represent both of them, Evans prevented that sort of deal from ever being made. It was a shrewd move — one that deserved respect. When Jack set the bait, he had to set it for Evans as well as big Jimmy.

Jack called Steve Preston not long after his meeting with the other members of the household. Steve was delighted to hear from him. Yes, his son's house was still empty. Jack could rent it if he wanted. He understood the circumstances and assured Jack that nobody who worked at the ranch would mention that he or his people were there.

"It's partially furnished, Jack — the living room, one bedroom, and there's a workout room. My son was kind of a physical fitness nut. You may want to come over and look at it and see what else you need. It's ready right away. The front gate is electronically operated and I'll give you some electronic keys when you get here."

Jack drove over with Pat and Dick. Steve's house was a quarter of a mile from the front gate, and they had to buzz him from there.

"God, this is quite a spread," Dick exclaimed after they had exchanged pleasantries with Steve and were driving across the open plains to their new home, which was some two miles southwest of the front gate.

"Most people don't know there are ranches like this in Florida," Jack told him. "I certainly didn't until I met Steve."

"What's that smell?" Pat asked, scrunching up her nose.

"That's the cows, city girl," Jack teased her. "You're going to have to get used to them. They won't get close to the house, though. You'll only really get hit with the smell on the drive in and out."

"This is just about perfect, Jack," Dick raved. "Only one road in and out. We can see someone coming for miles."

"Steve says he'll show us the back roads to Bass Creek so nobody will be able to follow us from town."

"That's great," Dick said, but he knew the professionals they were dealing with would find out where they were living and how they traveled back and forth. He didn't mention it, though. The most important thing was to be able to see them coming.

The house was indeed enormous, and they spent about an hour figuring out where everybody was going to stay. Pat had brought along a pad and was ferociously writing down everything they'd need to fully furnish the place.

She left the next morning at four for Miami and spent the day ordering linens, furniture, kitchen supplies, and the like. Two days later, an eighteen-wheeler pulled up and, under Pat's direction, moving men began unloading everything.

The car didn't arrive for two weeks. Apparently, Joaquin's special modifications took longer than expected. It was a black Mercedes limousine and it cost two hundred thousand dollars.

"This will stick out like a sore thumb in Bass Creek," Jack remarked.

"It won't matter," Joaquin said. "It's a fortress. Nothing can penetrate it."

"I still think we're taking this way too far. I've thought a lot about it since our initial conversation. Jimmy DiCarlo thinks he has a great case. Hell, he's looking forward to suing me when it's over. He's filed a Motion to Dismiss that he thinks he's going to win. Why in God's name would he or his clients risk all that to try and kill me? It doesn't make sense."

Joaquin answered for himself and Dick. "Our job isn't to make sense of all the nuances in your case, Jack. Our job is to react to the facts presented, and that newspaper article told us that you were being set up for a possible hit. And you may be right. As a matter of fact, you probably *are* right — they're probably not going to hit you now. But I've been involved in enough criminal cases to know they can go south in a heartbeat, and if this case goes bad on them, they're going to try to kill you and they're going to try to kill my Maria. I'm not going to let that happen."

Jack still wasn't convinced. "I don't know. It just seems so unreal."

"Trust us, Jack," Dick chimed in. "We've lived in that unreal world."

Jack discovered Joaquin's special modifications on his first ride from the ranch into town.

"What are those holes for?" he asked, noticing that there was a hole in the middle of the windshield and the rear window, in the front passenger side window, and in the rear driver's side window. The holes were covered by small glass disks that could be moved from side to side like a peephole cover, only these holes were much bigger.

Dick was driving that day. "Think about it, Jack. We're on the road. We get ambushed. We have these guns but how are we going to fire them? Roll the windows down?"

"What guns?"

"Look under the backwards-facing seat behind the front seats."

Jack pulled up the seat and saw what appeared to be four submachine guns and boxes of ammunition.

"What are those, AK-47s?"

"Yup."

"What are those other contraptions?"

"Night-vision goggles."

"Why are there four sets?"

"Because there may be as many as four of us in the car at one time. While we're lounging out here on the range in the middle of nowhere, Joaquin and I are going to teach you, Pat and Maria how to use an AK-47," Dick said with a big smile.

Jack just closed his eyes and slowly shook his head a couple of times. He'd left security up to these guys because he wanted to make sure everyone was safe. Now he felt like a star performer in the theater of the absurd.

〰

While Jack and the others were rearranging their home life, the case against Wesley Brume and Clay Evans was moving right along. As Jack had suspected, Bill Sampson punted and asked the state's Supreme Court to appoint a retired judge to hear the case. There were hundreds of retired judges in Florida, most of whom had stepped down at the mandatory age of seventy but were still willing to work. They filled in where there were shortages caused by illness, death, vacation, or in special circumstances like this one. It was up to the Supreme Court to appoint a judge to hear the case. They chose Judge Harold Stanton from Miami.

Jack obviously knew who Judge Stanton was, but he'd only tried two cases before him and they were both many years ago. Judge Stanton had made his name on the criminal bench, and it was quite a name. He was known as Hang 'Em High Harry. It was said of him — behind his back, of course — that he never gave less than the maximum sentence and that he never met a defendant who was innocent. Both statements were exaggerations of Harry Stanton's very conservative record.

At first glance, Jack thought Hang 'Em High Harry might be perfect for this case, but he decided to check him out. He called his old friend Harley Booker.

Harley Booker was eighty years old and had practiced criminal and civil law in Miami for over fifty years. In his heyday, Harley had often been referred to as a lawyer's lawyer because he was the first person any experienced trial lawyer in trouble would call. Harley had simply been the best.

He was almost retired now, still puttering around his office for a couple of hours a day.

"Haalo," Harley's deep Southern accent resonated on the other end of the line. His secretary had retired years ago.

"Hi, Harley, this is Jack Tobin."

"Jackson, my boy, how the hell are ya?" Harley's vocabulary — outside the courtroom — was as colorful as his personality. Inside the bar, he was a polished, homespun philosopher.

"Fine, Harley, just fine, but I need some help."

"I don't believe that for a second. I never met anybody as competent as you in the courtroom — except for myself, of course."

"As I well know from experience. You've taken my pants down a few times."

"That's when you were a young 'un, Jackson. You needed a little learning, and not the book kind. So what's the problem?"

"Well, I don't know if you know this, Harley, but I'm the state attorney in Cobb County now."

"I didn't know it until I started seeing you and Jimmy DiCarlo trading blows on the news every night. Don't know much about the case, but I can tell you're already inside his head."

"It's a murder case."

"Only kiddin', pardner, I know all about it. I've always thought Clay Evans was a crook. Got to be honest, though, I didn't know he was a murderer. Serves him right to have Jimmy DiCarlo as his lawyer — Jimmy's been payin' that sum-bitch for years. The money's goin' to be flowin' the other way now. I'm sorry, what was your question?"

"We just got Hang 'Em High Harry appointed as our judge. I just wanted to know if that was good news or bad news."

Harley thought about it for a minute. "Well, it might look good for you, pardner, off the top, but I think you've just got your ass stuck in a bucket of cowshit."

Nobody could spell it out like Harley.

"Why do you say that?"

"Well, pardner, he's a law and order guy, but he's a guy who likes to stay in the box, if you know what I mean."

"I'm not sure."

"He's so straight he starches his undershorts. He's always been on the right side of things. Middle of the road — God, the law, and apple pie. He hated me because I played outside the lines. He once asked me, 'Harley, why do you represent all them criminals?'"

"What did you say?"

"I just walked away from the sum-bitch."

It was hard getting a straight answer from Harley, he enjoyed the art of conversation so much. Jack knew he would eventually get the right answer. He just had to keep at it. "I still don't understand why he's bad for me in this case."

"Because you're upsettin' the applecart, boy. You don't prosecute a prosecutor, especially when he's now a federal judge. A cop you might get away with, but you just aimed your guns a little too high. Son, I believe Hang 'Em High Harry is gonna hang your ass out to dry."

It wasn't what Jack wanted to hear, but he needed to know more. "You said he didn't like you, Harley. How did you maneuver around him?"

"Good question, Jackson. I knew you'd get it all out of me. I let the sum-bitch know right away that I was gonna appeal his ass if he ever stepped outta line with one of his rulings. He prides himself on never having one of his convictions overturned on appeal. He thinks he's some kind of intellectual, but the real reason is he never goes out on a limb. He's in the box! Always in the box! Now I'm not sayin' he's dumber than a stump or anything. He's probably smarter than a jackass, but not by much."

"So the way to approach him is to let him know he's on shaky legal ground?"

"That's a start, Jackson, that's a start. But give the man somethin'. Give him a little fear so he's listenin' to ya — he wants to keep his record intact — but give him a solution too. You know, create a need, then solve it."

"Gotcha. Thanks, Harley!"

"One other thing," Harley continued. "Don't blow smoke up his skirt. He hates that. Give it to him straight. Tell him what you got. Let Jimmy toss the cowshit, because you know he will."

"Is Jimmy really a gangster like everybody says?"

"Nah, he's worse. He's a gangster wannabe. But he's dangerous, son. There's nothin' he won't do for a client if the money's right. You keep that in mind."

"I will. Thanks again, Harley."

"Hell, call me anytime, son. I'm lookin' forward to seein' you gut old Jimmy there."

Jack just sat by the phone chuckling for a few minutes. That Harley was a character — and a fountain of knowledge.

[ **FORTY-FIVE** ]

Jack didn't have an opportunity to see Judge Stanton until the hearing on the Motion to Dismiss. It was strange: This was one of the most important moments in the entire case and he wasn't nervous at all. He had prepared his legal memorandum even before he called the grand jury into session. All he had to do now was review his research and strategize. His strategy leaned heavily on incorporating Harley's tips into his overall approach.

As for Jimmy DiCarlo, he had a new love, besides himself: television. In the week leading up to the hearing on his motion, he managed to get himself on a major station every night and at least one cable channel. The press was enjoying itself as well. A good story like this was fodder for the cable talk shows and made easy headlines for the newspapers. On the morning of the motion hearing, the area around the courthouse was teeming with news trucks, talking heads, television cameras, reporters and throngs of ordinary people.

Jack understood the media presence, but he didn't understand the people. What was their stake in this? Did they really want to see justice done? The most surprising thing was that when he and Jimmy DiCarlo walked up the courthouse steps, they cheered Jimmy as if he were a movie star, while all he heard were catcalls and boos. Jack couldn't miss the opportunity to take advantage of the situation, however. He sidled close to Jimmy as they reached the top of the steps.

"They love you, Jimmy. But if you win today, it all goes away. This crowd is nothing compared to what it will be at trial." He didn't wait for a response. He headed straight for Judge Stanton's chambers.

So far, Jimmy was telegraphing all his punches nicely. Jack hoped it stayed that way. Jimmy had filed a second motion the week before asking to have the hearing in open court, but Judge Stanton denied the request the next day. He wasn't going to allow the press to make a circus of his courtroom, at least not yet. He allowed one reporter in his hearing room after instructing her in so many words to sit down and shut up and if she did anything to disrupt the hearing in any way, she would be removed by the bailiff.

As a normal practice, clients did not attend motion hearings held in chambers. Although Clay Evans wanted to attend and offer his legal expertise during the argument, he decided against it. Even though he was one of the accused, he was still a sitting federal judge and the possibility existed that Judge Stanton might resent his being in chambers and offering his legal opinions. It was an unnecessary risk. Jimmy could handle the proceedings himself.

Once inside the hearing room the lawyers sat on opposite sides of a long table that jutted out from the middle of the judge's desk. The clerk was seated to the judge's left and the court reporter was at the far end of the table in a position where she could watch all the lawyers and the judge as he spoke. The only other person in the room was the news reporter, and she was seated in a chair in the corner clearly trying to be very quiet. At 9 a.m. sharp, Judge Stanton entered the room from a side door and sat at his desk.

"Are we ready to proceed?" he asked without acknowledging anyone in the room.

"The defense is ready, Your Honor," Jimmy said.

"The state is ready, Your Honor."

"Very well. Mr. DiCarlo, it is your motion, you may proceed."

Jimmy spent the next half hour outlining the facts, referring to the transcript of the grand jury testimony as necessary and then discussing points of law. Jack noticed that Jimmy's fiery rhetoric was completely absent. He was going through the motions! Apparently he didn't want his day in the sun to end just yet, even though it exposed his clients to a murder trial. The seed Jack planted had sprouted. And Clay Evans had made a tactical mistake letting his lawyer appear alone at this hearing. Jack chuckled to himself. There was a certain delicious irony in the thought of a crooked judge being sold out by a crooked lawyer.

"I agree with most of what Mr. DiCarlo says, Your Honor," Jack told the judge when it came his turn to speak. "The prosecutor does enjoy absolute immunity in the prosecution of his case regardless of his motives. But this case is about what these men did two years *after* the prosecution of Rudy Kelly was over. They were presented with evidence of someone else's guilt and they hid that evidence. As a result, Rudy Kelly, an innocent man, died in the electric chair. That fact alone takes this case outside the zone of immunity that a prosecutor normally enjoys."

"But is there enough evidence that their actions were criminal?" the judge asked. Jack jumped on the question.

"The court is absolutely right to focus on that issue. This court already knows from the facts admitted in the motion that Lucy Ochoa had sex with someone other than Rudy Kelly the night of her murder *and* that on the night of her murder a man named Geronimo was down the street having a beer when Rudy left Lucy's trailer. The police never talked to this Geronimo fellow *because he disappeared right after the murder*. Two years after Rudy's conviction, the Bass Creek police department receives a letter from the Del Rio, Texas, police department stating they have just arrested a man named Geronimo Cruz for rape and murder and he has a Florida driver's license listing an address in Bass Creek. They want to know if the Bass Creek police department has any information on this individual that might help them in their prosecution. I have a witness who says Wesley Brume called Clay Evans as soon as he received this letter and immediately went to his office with the letter in hand.

After that, the Del Rio police department was never called back and the letter disappeared. Is that enough to convict? I'm not going to make that argument now. Is that enough to send the case to the jury? I'm not even going to make that argument now. Is it enough to let the case go to trial? Well, the law favors a trial on the merits whenever possible. Only in the rarest of circumstances should a case be dismissed before trial. If you allow this case to go to trial, Your Honor, the public's interest will be served, the law will be followed — and you can still give counsel the same relief he is asking for by granting a Motion for Acquittal during the trial itself. Besides, we may hear some new information. Something always happens at trial that you don't expect. Perhaps somebody in the Del Rio police department can shed some light on this mysterious letter. I don't know."

It was a very brief argument but it gave the judge options, which is what Harley had suggested.

"Do you have any rebuttal, Mr. DiCarlo?" Jimmy was ecstatic over Jack's argument. He could have a trial and have that national exposure for another month or so and still have the case decided by a Motion for Acquittal. It was perfect — but of course he couldn't tell the judge that.

He could have argued very forcefully that it was unfair to put his clients through the trauma of a trial when there wasn't enough evidence to convict them. He could have — but he didn't.

"Not at this time, Your Honor."

Judge Stanton put his head down and started rubbing the sides of his temples pretending he was thinking hard. The truth was that Jack's argument made sense. You never decide a case before trial unless it is a total sham. And he could still dismiss the case after the trial began on a Motion for Acquittal, which is exactly what he planned to do.

"All right, I'm not going to dismiss this case at this time. I agree that the same relief can be provided through an acquittal motion. In making this decision, I am by no means indicating that there is

enough evidence to send this case to a jury. Do I make myself clear?"
Both attorneys stated that they understood. "While we're here, why
don't you gentlemen take out your calendars and let's talk about
setting this case for trial. How long do you think it will take?"

"A week," Jack said.

"Two weeks," Jimmy countered.

"Two weeks?" the judge scoffed. "What do you need two weeks
for, Mr. DiCarlo? There's no forensics. We know how the death
happened. Hell, we know who did it. Do you want to bring the
state's executioner in to testify *how* he did it?"

"No, sir," Jimmy replied rather sheepishly. He really didn't have
an answer for the judge. He just wanted to keep the trial going for
two weeks.

"The way I see it, it's real simple," the judge continued. "The
question is, did your clients intentionally let Rudy Kelly die in the
electric chair. Now Mr. Tobin here, he's got to put on a circumstantial evidence case, so he might take a few days. The only
decision you've got to make is whether to put your clients on the
stand or not — that is, if I don't dismiss the case after Mr. Tobin
rests. Now is my analysis accurate?"

"Sounds about right to me, Judge," Jack replied.

"Yes sir," Jimmy answered meekly. He was starting to wonder if
maybe he rolled over on the motion a little too quickly.

"All right then, let's say a week. It will probably take a day to
pick a jury. I don't see a big problem there. If we need to we'll go into
the next week, but let's not plan on it. The sooner we get this circus
over with the better. Now, how much time do you need to get ready
for trial?"

"We're ready, Judge," Jack offered. "I'll need a week to get my
subpoenas out but that's it."

"How about you, Mr. DiCarlo? Do you need a few more months
to hit every show on television?" The judge clearly meant it as a
joke, and everybody took it as one. Even Jimmy laughed.

"I can be ready in two or three weeks, Your Honor. I need to check some things out." Jack knew exactly what he was talking about. He'd stuck in that little teaser about the Del Rio police department to send Jimmy on a wild goose chase. If he kept him occupied, Jimmy wouldn't see the real surprises he had in store for him.

"Fine. We'll set it for three weeks from today. And let me say this, you two gentlemen are fine lawyers. I'm not going to put a gag order on you. But see if you can control the personal barbs and let's not try our case in the press, okay?" He looked right at Jimmy as he spoke.

"Yes sir," Jack replied.

"Sure, Judge," Jimmy chimed in, hardly paying attention. There were cameras out there waiting for him.

[ **F O R T Y - S I X** ]

An amazing thing happened shortly after the motion hearing, much to Jimmy's disappointment. The press went home and the crowds dispersed around Jack's office and the courthouse.

"Where did those people come from?" Jack asked the group at dinner one night. "They weren't from Bass Creek."

"Maybe there's a group of sensation seekers out there that go from event to event," Pat offered.

"Yeah, or maybe the press pays them to show up," Dick added. "There's no hype if there's no crowd."

"You're getting awful cynical in your old age, honey," Joaquin said, punctuating it with a tsk-tsk and a wagging finger. Dick whacked him on the shoulder.

"Don't 'honey' me. I'm not your sweetheart."

"Thank God," Jack said. "I don't know if Maria's ready for that yet." They all had a good laugh, really enjoying themselves for the first time in a long time. "I think we can actually relax for a while," Jack added. "With the crowds gone and Jimmy getting his trial, I think the heat's off."

Dick and Joaquin suddenly turned serious and looked at each other. No words passed between them but each knew what the other was thinking. Joaquin answered Jack for both of them. "The heat's not off, Jack, just because the crowds are gone and Jimmy DiCarlo has his trial."

"I don't understand," Jack felt he was saying for about the hundredth time. He prided himself on being a canny strategist, but these two operated in a world with which he was totally unfamiliar.

Dick coached him along. "Think about it, Jack. Jimmy DiCarlo wasn't involved in Tracey or Nancy's murders. Just because he's happy he has a trial doesn't mean the heat's off."

Jack thought about it for a second. "You mean Evans or Brume might not be happy with what happened at the motion hearing, and either of them or both might take action on their own?"

"Precisely!" Joaquin exclaimed. "We have to stay prepared for that possibility." The brief euphoria was gone, replaced by the familiar tightness-in-the-chest feeling they'd been living with for weeks.

"I've thought about that," Jack said. "I wonder if the two of them acted in concert or if one of them committed those murders on his own." Nobody had an answer.

In spite of Dick and Joaquin's foreboding, the next few days were sunny and relaxing, and everybody started to feel better again. Jack and Maria continued their same old routine but left work early — Jack to go home and take long runs with Pat, and Maria to join Joaquin in the sanctuary of his fishing boat. Dick found solace in the exercise room, which had a weight bench, a stationary bike and a treadmill. Dick had been a weightlifter in his active days, and he enjoyed reacquainting himself with the bench. He liked the bike too, but he avoided the treadmill like the plague.

Three days into their semi-vacation, Joaquin made an announcement at dinner. "Maria and I are going to take a vacation if that's okay with you, Jack. I'm going to take her home with me."

Jack was a little surprised but realized it was a good idea. Why should they all suffer while they were waiting for the trial to begin? "That's a great idea. Just make sure you get back here three or four days before the trial so I can prep Maria." He looked at Maria, who couldn't hide the smile on her face. It wasn't hard to figure that she was looking forward to some extended time alone with Joaquin.

Later, as they were getting ready for bed, Jack once again urged Pat to take a vacation as well. "There is absolutely no sense in all of us hanging around here," he said as emphatically as he could.

"Where would I go?" she protested mildly.

"Anywhere you want, Pat. Go to Europe for a couple of weeks. Relax on the Riviera."

"I couldn't relax without you, Jack. I told you before, we're in this together. I'm not going anywhere." She slammed the pillow she was fluffing down on the bed, pulled the sheets back and started to get in. "Wait a minute!" she stopped, her left knee resting on her side of the bed. "Why don't you come with me? You've got nothing to do and you need the rest."

"No way, Pat. I've got a trial to prepare for."

"Jack, you've been preparing for this trial for months. You could do it in your sleep! The only way you could be better prepared is if you were relaxed and rested."

He was about to renew his protest but he knew she had a point. The only item on his calendar for the next three weeks had been the motion in Texas to delay Geronimo's execution. But Texas had decided to delay the execution for six months on its own for administrative reasons — apparently there were a few other people that had to be killed before Geronimo's number came up. So his plate was clean. Besides, if he and Pat took a break, Dick could also get some needed R and R.

"Okay, let's say we took a break for ten days or so — where would we go?"

"I don't know. Anywhere."

He thought about it for a few minutes as he hopped into bed and pulled the covers up. He turned to face her in the bed, a smile on his face.

"You look like the cat that swallowed the canary," she said suspiciously. "Let's hear it."

"Well," he began, stretching the word out. "We're both Irish and neither one of us has ever been to the Old Country."

"Ireland," she mused. "That's a great idea."

Jack was into it now. "We could fly Aer Lingus first class from Miami."

"Wouldn't that be too expensive on such short notice?"

"What are you talking about? I'm rich! Besides, nothing is too expensive for the woman I love." She leaned her head back and gave him a strange look as if to ask, *Who are you?* They both started to laugh at the same time. Jack touched her playfully under the covers.

"Save it," she snarled, "for the Old Country."

He laughed. "We'll tell the others in the morning."

The next morning the two of them emerged from the room as frisky as newborn colts. Joaquin and Dick noticed it right away. Over oatmeal, Jack laid out their plans.

"We're only going for ten days and we all need a break. You too, Dick."

"I think I'll stay here."

"There's no reason to do that, Dick," Jack protested. He noticed Joaquin was silent on the matter.

"The truth is," Dick said, pausing for a moment, "I like it here. There's something about the open range. And don't get me wrong, I like all you folks, but I think I'm going to enjoy the solitude. Maybe I'll get Steve to loan me a horse and I can play cowboy for a few days. I was a pretty good rider when I was a kid. I think I'd like to try it again."

"All right," Jack said, "then it's settled. I've got to go into the office for a few hours and get things set up for our departure. Pat's going to make the reservations today."

"We're going to leave this morning," Joaquin informed them. Jack could tell the two of them were anxious to go.

"That's fine. We'll see you the Wednesday or Thursday before the trial starts."

"We'll be here," Joaquin said as he and Maria almost bolted from their seats.

Jack and Pat said goodbye to Dick the next morning and headed for Miami, leaving Dick to guard the house, the black Mercedes and the AK-47s.

"We're flying into Shannon," Pat told Jack on the ride. "It's on the west coast of Ireland."

"I know where it is," Jack snapped playfully. "I'm Irish too, you know."

The first-class trip across the ocean was magnificent. Aer Lingus was a great airline, much better than the domestic flights they were both used to. Their plane left at night and they arrived the next morning. Jack noticed as he looked out from his window seat that they seemed to be flying towards the light. He could already feel himself starting to unwind. Pat was fast asleep, resting her head against his shoulder. *I think I landed on my feet this time*, he thought as he touched her smooth, soft skin.

They rented a car at the airport and headed straight for Galway, a small city northwest of the airport where they promptly took a room at a bed and breakfast and went to sleep.

That night they walked the town and eventually settled at a little pub that was packed with local students and tourists. A band was playing the tunes that they had listened to all their lives. Everybody seemed happy. They were all singing along, dancing and laughing. Later, Jack and Pat walked back to their room under the moonlight.

"This was a good decision," Pat said as she nestled under his strong right arm.

"I'm glad I talked you into it," he chuckled softly.

They spent two days in Galway, sightseeing during the day and drinking a few Guinnesses at night.

"It tastes so good here," he said, his upper lip frosted with the foam. "Like a malted or something."

"A malted with a wallop."

On the second day, he bought her a Claddach ring. Two hands

clasping together around a heart, the Claddach was a symbol of love and friendship.

"You know, the Claddach ring originated right here in Galway," the jeweler told them. He was very friendly. He also gave them a few suggestions of where else to go. "You shouldn't miss the Aran Islands," he continued. "They're brilliant. You can catch the ferry just up the road a wee bit. And when you come back there's a lovely town just north of here called Clifden. The pubs are lively there and you'll have a great time." Jack felt like paying him for his information as well as the ring.

They caught the ferry to Inishmore, the largest of the three islands, the next morning. It was a chilly day and the seas were rough, and Pat got a little seasick on the ride over. She recovered over some hot tea and shopping at the local wool store. The Aran Islands were famous for their wool sweaters. After that, they rented bikes and rode the entire length of the island, stopping only to hike up to Dun Aengus, one of the prehistoric ring forts on the island.

Dun Aengus was perched on a rocky cliff high above the sea, and the view of the breakers below, the endless blue of the Atlantic stretching away to the west, and Galway Bay nestled among the green slopes to the east, was breathtaking. Jack's heart almost stopped as he saw Pat walk to the edge of the cliff and peer over. He wanted to shout but was afraid he'd startle her, so he just stood and watched with a combination of dread and awe. He was not about to go to the edge of that cliff.

On the ride back to the ferry he paid close attention to the farmland. This was a rocky, rocky island and the farm fields were divided into very small squares, maybe thirty or forty feet across. The plots were separated by low walls fashioned from carefully stacked flattish stones, all holding together without the benefit of mortar. Jack had never seen anything like it before. He couldn't begin to comprehend the amount of labor it must have taken to fit the stones together so perfectly.

"No wonder the Irish drink," he shouted back over his shoulder as he kept pedaling. "Can you imagine making those stone fences all day?"

"Or tilling that rocky soil? Just looking at it is making me thirsty."

They spent that night at a B & B in Clifden, as their jeweler/tour guide had suggested. After dinner and a few beers, Jack was exhausted and crashed on the bed.

"I can't even take my clothes off," he moaned.

"Don't you worry, honey," Pat said, creeping over towards him. "I'm going to take your clothes off for you. And then I'm going to help you relax like you've never relaxed before."

That night she took him to new places — caressing and kissing him all the while. When she finally brought him to a climax, he felt so satisfied, so perfect, so *loved,* that he wanted to cry for joy. *This woman, this absolutely wonderful woman, is a gift from God — and the devil!*

They headed south the next morning. "My senses have been overwhelmed these last two days," Jack told her on the drive. *Especially last night,* he wanted to add but didn't. Irish Catholics didn't make a habit of talking about sex the next day. That much he'd definitely inherited from the Old Country.

"Inishmore was just incredible! Where are we going now?"

"I have to stop in Galway for a minute, then I think we should head for Killarney and the Ring of Kerry." She could tell he'd been reading his tour book.

"What are we stopping in Galway for?"

"I'm going to give our jeweler a little tip to thank him. Why don't you do a little shopping while I do that."

"I can do that. Shopping is one of those things I do very well."

After a brief respite in Galway, they were off again in the direction of Killarney.

It was a little jewel of a town, essentially unchanged for hundreds of years except that its quaint old buildings now housed shops and pubs. It was a very popular tourist spot because it served as the gateway to the Ring of Kerry, the name given to the road that followed the coastline around the Kerry Peninsula, wending its way past some of the most spectacular views in all of Ireland and, some said, the whole world. On a clear day — and Jack and Pat had a clear day — the lush countryside in its many shades of green and the sparkling hues of the embracing sea could melt the hardest heart, which said nothing about the effect on a couple of lovebirds like Pat and Jack.

The drive itself conjured up other emotions. It took a brave soul to drive just about anywhere in Ireland, and the Ring of Kerry was especially daunting. Many stretches of the road didn't seem wide enough for two cars, and driving over a hill without being able to see what was coming stirred more than a few moments of sheer terror in Jack. There was so much he'd never encountered before: Irish drivers who always seemed to think there was plenty of room to get by even though the road seemed to Jack to be little more than one lane wide; sheep wandering here, there and everywhere with apparently no regard for the difference between field and pavement; and most disconcerting of all, having to drive on the wrong side of the road, for God's sake. And they called vacations relaxing?

Jack needed a break and pulled off the main road at a country store next to a bridge that led to a small offshore island. The store was called Tobin's, and he took that as a sign that they should cross the bridge. "Maybe I have family in this area," he said, and Pat looked at him like he was nuts.

There was only one road on the entire island, but mercifully it was devoid of traffic. They drove for about fifteen minutes until they came upon a quaint little village, where they stopped for lunch and a leisurely stroll. The church, named after St. Ambrose, was the centerpiece of the village, as was the case in many Irish towns. Pat started walking towards the open doors, as if she was being magically drawn to the place, and Jack followed behind. It was an old church, probably several hundred years old, but it had been recently painted. The wooden floor was uneven and creaked as they walked over it towards the altar, a plain mahogany table covered by a thick white cloth with a white candle at either end. The midday light filtering through the stained-glass windows made the air dance with colors and added to the simple beauty of the interior.

"I love it!" Pat said in a reverential whisper as she leaned on the communion rail. And just like that, Jack knew this was the time and the place.

Pat thought he was kneeling to say a prayer, but when she glanced down at him, he was looking up at her and he had something in his hand. He didn't know what he was going to say until he said it.

"Patricia Eileen Morgan, my lifelong friend, the love of my life — here in this simple church, in the home of our ancestors, I pledge my lifelong love and devotion to you and I beseech you to grace me with your hand in marriage."

She could see clearly now that he held a diamond ring in his hand — the reason for the second visit to the jeweler in Galway. He stood up and looked into her eyes, hesitant for a moment.

Pat had thought this day had passed her by long ago. Now, as it was happening, she realized it had been worth the wait. This was perfect. Here in this place, in this country, with this man.

"Yes, Jack. Yes, I will share the rest of your life with you. I love you as I never have loved anyone in my life, more than I ever thought I could love. I love you as a friend, a lover and a man, and I will love you forever."

He hugged her so hard she thought he was going to break something, but she didn't care. They were both crying and laughing and hugging and kissing. And then he pushed back from her slightly, and she looked into his eyes and caught her breath. He took her hand, and looking at her with an expression she would never forget, he slipped the shimmering ring onto her outstretched finger.

They arrived home on a Wednesday afternoon and were met

by Joaquin, Maria and Dick. It was like a family reunion, with hugs all around. Pat had taken the ring off to save the surprise for later, as the two of them had discussed. They wanted to make a special moment of it.

"Let's go to the Taqueria tonight," Jack suggested. "We can celebrate the end of our vacations and the beginning of a lot of hard work." Joaquin checked with Dick in that silent way the two men had. Dick shrugged his shoulders as if to say, *Why not?* It was all Joaquin needed.

"Okay, sounds great." There was something he and Maria wanted to tell the group anyway.

Over dinner and a few beers, they laughed and told stories of their various adventures.

"I guess my cowboy days are over," Dick confessed. "I was out helping round up some steers when my horse got spooked and threw me. I drove around the rest of the time in a pickup." Everybody laughed. Dick was a master of the self-deprecating story.

"I caught a bass," Maria piped in to everybody's surprise. "A big one, too."

"It's true," Joaquin added. "It's a Mexican bass and it drinks beer and smokes cigars on occasion." As he spoke, Joaquin handed out cigars to the men. "And tonight I ask my friends to have a drink and a smoke with Maria and me in celebration of our engagement."

Amid the joyful exclamations, tears welled in Dick's eyes. He was so happy for his friend. Pat leaned over and kissed Maria, who had already produced her engagement ring and was showing it to everybody. Pat caught Jack's eye, and he just nodded and smiled. They had been upstaged. Jack's look told Pat that he too agreed that they could hold off their announcement for another day. Joaquin and Maria were entitled to their own moment.

"A bottle of your finest champagne," Jack told the waitress, and that one was followed by others as they toasted Maria and Joaquin for several hours.

Afterwards, when they were the only ones left in the place,

Joaquin left to bring the car around, and Dick moved towards the front door. The two men could have fun, but they never forgot their duties. At the restaurant entrance, Dick quickly ushered the ladies and Jack into the back seat while Joaquin stood at the driver's side door shielded by the door itself and looked out across the road into the thick brush on the other side, searching intently for any sign of trouble.

*These guys can get carried away with this stuff sometimes,* Jack thought, but he had too much respect for the two of them to dwell on it.

And then, in an instant, everything changed. Shots rang out, and as if in slow motion Jack watched Joaquin slump to the ground at the side of the car. Dick went into automatic, surveying the situation in a heartbeat and then moving to where Joaquin was lying. He picked him up and started packing him into the car, oblivious of any danger to himself.

"Jack, pull him across to the passenger side," he yelled. Jack reached over into the front seat and began pulling Joaquin across as best he could. Dick was already behind the wheel and they were speeding away.

"The emergency room is only five minutes away," he said, turning briefly to look at Maria, who was clearly in shock. "I don't think he's hurt that bad," Dick said, turning his attention back to the road. "He was shielded by the door."

They arrived moments later at the emergency room and Dick carried Joaquin in — right past the front desk and through the double doors shouting at the top of his lungs, "Gunshot wounds! We need a doctor. This man is dying." He obviously knew how to get people's attention. Two doctors came running from different directions.

"What happened?" the first one asked.

"He was just shot by a sniper outside a restaurant. He's losing blood."

"Put him on the table," the second doctor directed. He looked older and more experienced, and he cut Joaquin's shirt open while they loaded him on the table. Then he started probing, moving his hands expertly over Joaquin's chest.

"His lung is collapsed and he's bleeding internally. We've got to get him to surgery. Nurse, nurse!" he shouted. A nurse appeared from nowhere. "Get an IV started and get this man up to OR. Page Dr. Cutler and tell him to meet me there." He then turned to Dick, Jack, Pat and Maria, who were all crowded into the ER hallway. "I've got to move. We're going into emergency surgery. I'll let you know something as soon as I can." He disappeared through doors leading to the stairway, taking the steps three at a time.

Another member of the ER staff led them to a waiting room in the main hospital where they began their vigil — a vigil that was to last almost the entire night. They sat there in silence, nobody wanting to verbalize the fear that gripped them all.

Pat could see all the emotions on Jack's face. The man simply couldn't take another death in the pursuit of justice.

At about five in the morning, the doctor finally came in to see them.

"We've stopped the bleeding and fixed the lung," he said tiredly. "But he's lost a lot of blood. We think he's going to be okay, though. It's going to take a while. By the way, there are some policemen downstairs who want to talk to you." He shook hands with Pat and Maria and left. Dick grabbed Jack and pulled him into a corner of the room.

"I'm not going to talk to the police. You have to, but don't say anything."

"I'm not going to. I think Brume did it."

"So do I," Dick said. "But why do you think so?"

"Well, I don't want to get into it too much because of the trial, but I think Brume killed Tracey and Nancy and shot Joaquin on his own — not literally on his own, but he had it done without Clay Evans."

"It was a sniper, I'm sure of it," Dick said. "You don't make a shot like that from that far away unless you're a sniper. I was one myself.

I'll check to see if anybody on Brume's little police force was a sniper in the service." He turned to leave, but Jack grabbed his arm.

"Don't do anything foolish, Dick."

Dick Radek sneered at him. "I signed on to help you finish this job, and I'll help protect the people I promised to protect. But however your little trial ends, Counselor, when it's over those boys are going to be dead."

[ F O R T Y - S E V E N ]

The press and the crowds reappeared for day one of the trial. Jack could not believe all the television trucks that were camped on the little square outside the Cobb County Courthouse. Jimmy DiCarlo was already there, standing on the courthouse steps surrounded by a bevy of reporters and cameras. Jack walked by him within hearing distance, his own gaggle chasing after him for an interview.

"This injustice will be over this week," Jimmy was telling them. "My clients will be exonerated and this fiasco will be exposed for what it is — one man's personal vendetta." His timing was perfect, as he looked directly at Jack just at that moment.

The press immediately shifted attention to Jack, hoping he might respond. They flew at him.

"Jimmy says this is a personal vendetta on your part," one reporter shouted at him while thrusting a microphone in his face.

Jack never stopped walking. "That's Mr. DiCarlo's opinion. Unfortunately for Mr. DiCarlo, this case is going to be tried in the courtroom and not out here on the courthouse steps." He kept walking up into the courthouse, having to force his way through.

Judge Stanton had entered an order barring the public from the courtroom for jury selection, so once Jack managed to get himself inside, he was safe. There were only two courtrooms in the entire courthouse, and the trial was in the main one. It was a cavernous old place with high ceilings, noisy ceiling fans, creaky floors, creaky old mahogany pews where the "congregation" normally sat, and a massive mahogany dais where the judge presided. The acoustics were miserable, but both lawyers were blessed with great, booming voices and would have no trouble making themselves heard.

Wesley Brume and Clay Evans were already in the courtroom waiting anxiously for Jimmy DiCarlo to finish his closing argument on the courthouse steps. He sauntered in a few minutes after Jack, looking like a man about to go on a Sunday picnic.

Judge Stanton arrived promptly at nine, waiting just offstage for his presence to be announced by the bailiff.

"All rise! The Circuit Court in and for Cobb County, State of Florida, is now in session. All those having business before this court, come forward and be heard."

There was no need for such ceremony since nobody was in the courtroom but the lawyers and the accused, but Jack liked the formality of it all. Old Hang 'Em High Harry shuffled out before the bailiff had finished his little spiel.

"Is everybody ready?" he asked after he motioned them to be seated.

"The prosecution is ready, Your Honor," Jack said, standing briefly.

"The defense is ready," Jimmy DiCarlo replied, somewhat more casually.

"Any motions before we bring the jury panel in?"

Both lawyers answered in the negative.

"What's your pleasure, gentlemen? We can do individual questioning or we can bring the entire panel into the courtroom and let them listen to all the questions. That would certainly speed the process up. I don't see a problem with that method in this case because I don't think anybody is predisposed one way or the other. I think jury selection should be pretty quick and pretty smooth."

Both lawyers agreed.

"That's a pretty good start, gentlemen. You keep agreeing with me and we'll get this trial over in no time." He turned to the bailiff. "Bring in the panel."

The original panel consisted of about fifty of Cobb County's finest citizens selected randomly from the voter registration list. They were seated in order in the pews that were normally reserved for the spectators. Jack began the questioning. He asked each juror some individual questions about their personal life, their spouses, their children, their jobs — then he started to bore into the area of real concern.

Jack believed that jury selection was not *selection* at all but *elimination*. He hadn't selected the panel, and he only had a certain number of peremptory challenges. He had to ask questions that would identify the jurors he didn't want. He concentrated on questions about law enforcement and the judicial system. Questions like: *Do you believe that some police officers violate individuals' rights by, say, beating them up while arresting them or forcing a confession?* Members of the panel who had a hard time believing such things happened were stricken immediately. Or: *Do you believe that some state attorneys hide evidence in order to get convictions?* With questions like that he was already starting to try his case without putting any evidence on. Or: *Would you have any problem convicting a police officer who forced a confession or who hid evidence? Would you have any problem convicting a judge if the evidence showed that he was guilty?* Most people had a problem with the second question. Judges were held in high esteem and federal judges were on an even higher pedestal. Jack knew he would have to live with panelists who admitted they would have a problem convicting a judge but would do it if the evidence supported the conviction.

Judge Stanton's prediction proved correct. It wasn't that hard finding a jury of twelve citizens for this case. By five o'clock that afternoon, a jury had been empaneled.

"We'll start opening statements first thing in the morning," Judge Stanton told counsel after the jury had been dismissed. "Be here at 8:30 just in case you have some motions for me to entertain."

Once again, Judge Stanton appeared to be an accurate prognosticator when Jimmy DiCarlo filed a rather lengthy motion to exclude evidence the next morning promptly at 8:30. It was a tactic. Jimmy was trying to unnerve Jack before the trial even started.

They were in chambers. "Is there a particular reason we have to take these issues up now, Mr. DiCarlo?" the judge asked. "I've got a jury in the other room waiting to get started." It was a phrase both Jack and Jimmy had heard many times in their careers. Judges always tried to move lawyers along by using the jury in the other room as a lever. Jimmy was not about to be intimidated.

"Yes, Judge, there is. I don't want Mr. Tobin to be bringing up inadmissible evidence in his opening statement. That's why I need a ruling now."

"Can you be more specific, Mr. DiCarlo?"

"Yes, I can, Your Honor. I believe from the witness list that Mr. Tobin is going to attempt to elicit testimony about how Rudy Kelly's confession was obtained by Chief Brume. While that evidence may have been relevant in the trial of Mr. Kelly, it has no relevance in this case at all."

The judge looked at Jack. "Is that true, Mr. Tobin? Do you intend to elicit testimony about how Rudy Kelly's confession was obtained?"

"Yes I do, Your Honor, and I'll tell you why it is relevant. We intend to show that Mr. Brume, and later Mr. Evans, tried to wrong-fully incriminate Rudy Kelly from the outset. It's a pattern that started before Rudy Kelly was arrested. It's relevant to show their intent. I'm not trying to suppress the confession as Tracey James attempted to do in the original murder trial. I'm trying to show the state of mind of these men from the very beginning."

"It's too remote, Judge. You're going back over ten years. That's just not fair."

"Why is it not fair?" Jack asked. "The witnesses are here. We have a transcript of their testimony. You can cross-examine them. You can even use the passage of time as an argument. It's relevant, Judge."

Judge Stanton thought about it for a moment. "I tend to agree with Mr. Tobin on this one. Intent is relevant and the passage of time does not make it irrelevant. This is a circumstantial evidence case, and I believe I'm required to allow circumstantial evidence of intent to be admitted. Motion denied. Is there anything else before we bring the jury in?"

"No, Your Honor," Jimmy DiCarlo replied.

"Okay, gentlemen, let us go out there and meet our adoring public."

The attorneys and the accused were ushered into the courtroom by the judge's bailiff while the judge stayed behind. The courtroom was packed. The pews that had held potential jurors the day before were now filled with excited spectators eager to see the show. When the lawyers were in place, the bailiff notified the judge and stood by the door. Moments later, the judge rapped on the door three times, giving the bailiff his cue.

"Hear ye, hear ye, hear ye, the Circuit Court for Cobb County, State of Florida, is now in session — the case of the State of Florida versus Wesley Brume and Clay Evans, the Honorable Harold Stanton presiding. All rise." As he said those last words, the old man entered the courtroom in all his majesty, his black robes flowing. It was theater at its finest.

"Be seated," the judge said, taking his own place on the dais. He waited while the spectators settled into their pews, and then he proceeded to read them the riot act. "If you moan, if you groan, if you say anything, express any emotion, I will have you forcibly removed from this courtroom, do you understand?" There were a few mumbled assents and nods, but for the most part the audience sat silently, frozen in place. Judge Stanton had this power thing down. He then addressed the press, which occupied the front two rows. "There will be no running out of here to share a tidbit with your colleagues across the street, do you understand? You will come in and leave with everybody else, got it?" They all nodded, but old Harry wasn't through. "And if I even *see* a camera, the person holding it will be arrested immediately." He didn't ask them if they understood that statement; he just looked at the bailiff, satisfied that he had made his points, and said, "Bring in the jury."

The bailiff disappeared and returned minutes later with fourteen jurors, the twelve who were chosen to decide the case and two alternates — nine men and five women, the two alternates being a man and a woman. Jack liked those odds. Men were more likely to convict. In Jimmy DiCarlo's mind, they were more likely to support law enforcement. Only time would tell who was right.

Jack normally liked to keep his opening statement short. Give the jurors enough to get them interested but leave them hanging a little so they'll pay attention. In this case, however, it was more important to poison the well at the earliest possible moment. He decided to give them *almost* everything he had.

Jack walked to the podium empty-handed. He spent a moment pretending to situate himself. He was actually waiting for the jurors to become a little impatient and focus their attention on him. It was a tactic he'd learned many years ago as a young lawyer. When the time was right, he moved his eyes from the tips of his shoes and looked at each one of them individually.

He started by telling them about Rudy.

"Rudy Kelly was nineteen years old, liked by everybody. Never did a thing wrong. Rudy worked at the convenience store for a man named Benny Dragone. You'll meet Benny. He's going to testify." Already he was having a conversation with them, as if nobody else was in the courtroom. "Now Rudy was, what you might say, 'a little slow.' His principal, Bill Yates, will tell you that young Rudy did not have the intellectual capacity to finish high school because he was so slow. He received an attendance certificate instead of a diploma. That is why he was working at the convenience store. It was the only job he could get. Mr. Yates will also tell you that Rudy was so friendly he would talk to anyone. That's why Mr. Yates told Officer Brume, one of the defendants here —" Jack paused to point directly at Wesley Brume, who started squirming in his seat as if on cue. "He told Officer Brume that he should not talk to Rudy without his mother being present — something that Benny Dragone also emphasized to Officer Brume.

"Now I should tell you at this point that Rudy did visit Lucy Ochoa, the young lady who was murdered, on the night she was murdered. According to Rudy, Lucy invited him over to her trailer that evening. He slipped and fell while he was there and cut his hand. On that same evening, three men were down the street drinking beer. Their names were Raymond Castro, José Guerrero and Geronimo Cruz. The police interviewed two of those men, Raymond Castro and José Guerrero, soon after the murder. They *never* interviewed Geronimo Cruz. This is an important fact because within a couple of weeks of the murder, all three men disappeared, and Mr. Castro and Mr. Guerrero were never to be seen or heard from again.

"Based on a description given by a woman named Pilar Rodriguez and the two men I just mentioned who disappeared, Officer Brume decided to pick up Rudy for questioning. He went to the convenience store where Rudy worked and spoke to Benny Dragone. Benny did not want to let Rudy go with Officer Brume because he didn't trust him. But Officer Brume threatened Mr. Dragone with the health department and he relented, a fact that still haunts him to this day. Brume took Rudy to the police department and, before he started to interrogate him, Rudy's mother, Elena, arrived and demanded to see her son. She was kept in the waiting room while the interrogation proceeded. Elena died several years ago from breast cancer. You will hear her testimony about this event from an earlier proceeding.

"The Bass Creek police department at the time had very sophisticated audio and video recording devices they had purchased with taxpayer money specifically to record witness statements and confessions. The murder of Lucy Ochoa was and is the most gruesome and most famous murder that ever occurred in Cobb County. Yet, when Officer Brume sat down to interview Rudy, he neglected to sound-record or videotape the interview. Officer Brume wrote

Rudy's confession out in longhand on a yellow pad and had him sign it. And the confession was not really a confession at all. Rudy admitted that he was at the house that night and admitted that he cut his hand, but he told Officer Brume that when he left, Lucy Ochoa was still very much alive. Apparently there was some further prompting by Officer Brume because he wrote on his yellow pad that Rudy said he could kill Lucy if she made him mad enough and he may not have remembered it. '*He could kill Lucy if she made him mad enough.*'" Jack repeated the words for emphasis. "That was the so-called confession of Rudy Kelly. They took a blood sample at that time and matched it with some blood at Lucy's trailer, and eventually they arrested and charged Rudy with Lucy Ochoa's murder.

"Now the police had some other very important evidence that they did not disclose. In fact, nobody knew about it until recently — ten years after the murder. There was semen in Lucy Ochoa's vaginal cavity, which meant that she had had sex that night, and the blood type of the semen was different from the blood type of the blood on the carpet — Rudy's blood. DNA testing was not available back then, so they could not even attempt to do a DNA match, but they knew someone else had been in the house! What did they do with that evidence? Well, they created a separate rape file and the semen evidence was never produced to Rudy's attorneys. The fact that someone else had been in Lucy's house and had sex with her that night was kept from the defense!" Jack felt that fact needed repeating as well. "And by creating this separate rape file, they kept this evidence hidden from everyone.

"The case that the prosecution — that Mr. Clay Evans — " Jack took the time to walk over and point Clay Evans out to the jury, "presented against Rudy Kelly was a lie because the basic premise was that Rudy Kelly was the only person in Lucy Ochoa's trailer that night."

Jimmy DiCarlo had had enough. He jumped to his feet. "Your Honor, I object. Counsel is now testifying. He is providing his own opinion to the jury when he knows that this conviction, with all these facts presented, was upheld by the Supreme Court of the State of Florida. That is improper."

"Approach," the judge said, motioning to the lawyers. When they arrived at sidebar, he proceeded to bite Jimmy DiCarlo's head off. "Counsel, if you make a speaking objection in open court again, I will hold you in contempt. You stand up, you make your legal objection, and you ask to approach. Grandstanding in here will land you in jail. Do you understand?"

"Yes, Your Honor," Jimmy replied. "But I had to do something. You can't unring a bell." The judge understood Jimmy's point. Jack was testifying and Jimmy couldn't let that statement stand without challenging it immediately.

"He's got a point, Mr. Tobin. You know better than to pull a cheap stunt like that."

"I apologize, Your Honor," Jack replied. "I should have said that there will be testimony that the case they put on was a lie, because Charley Peterson, Rudy's public defender, is going to testify to that fact."

"Not in this court. That's opinion testimony about an ultimate fact and I will not allow it. If you attempt to elicit that testimony, I'll hold you in contempt! Do you understand me?"

"Yes, Your Honor."

"Good. Now let's proceed. I'll give the jury a curative instruction. And Mr. Tobin, let's wrap this up. This is opening statement, not closing argument."

"Yes, Your Honor."

The lawyers walked back to their respective positions, and Judge Stanton addressed the jury. "Ladies and gentlemen, I have sustained Mr. DiCarlo's objection. You are not to consider Mr. Tobin's last statement that the case presented by the prosecution in the Rudy Kelly case was a lie. The Supreme Court of the State of Florida has ruled on that issue."

Jack was pissed. He didn't think the judge's curative instruction needed to go that far. But he had more pressing matters at hand. He was still standing in front of the jury.

"As I was saying, the prosecution's case did not mention the semen found in Lucy Ochoa's vagina and the public defender representing Rudy knew nothing about it." He paused to see if Jimmy DiCarlo was going to shoot out of his seat again, but Jimmy was a little too smart to take the bait. "So Rudy was convicted of first-degree murder and sentenced to death.

"That was 1986. In 1988, the Bass Creek police department received a letter from the Del Rio, Texas, police department. They had just arrested a suspect in a rape and murder case and he had a Florida driver's license that listed an address in Bass Creek. It was just a general inquiry letter to see if the suspect was wanted in Bass Creek for anything or if the Bass Creek police department had any information that might be helpful to them. The suspect's name was Geronimo Cruz.

"Maria Lopez was a secretary in the police department at the time, and she opened the letter from the Del Rio police. She brought it to the immediate attention of Wesley Brume, who in turn immediately called Clay Evans." Jack pointed to each defendant as he said his name. "Ms. Lopez heard Mr. Brume tell Mr. Evans that he would be right over and she saw him leave for Mr. Evans's office with the letter in hand. According to Ms. Lopez, the letter was never seen again — it certainly was never placed in Rudy's file — and the Del Rio police department was never contacted.

"You will hear from Geronimo Cruz. You will see his videotape confession to the murder of Lucy Ochoa. In addition, you will learn that the DNA from the semen found in Lucy Ochoa matched that of Geronimo Cruz. There is no doubt that he murdered Lucy Ochoa.

"This case is about a police officer and a prosecutor who were so zealous to convict Rudy Kelly of murder that they wrote out their own confession, hid evidence from the defense and refused to contact the Del Rio police department for fear that their conviction would go south. As a result of their actions and intentional inactions, Rudy Kelly was executed in the Florida electric chair on October 22, 1996."

As soon as Jack sat down, Jimmy DiCarlo was on his feet walking around the courtroom feigning outrage at the remarks Jack had made about his clients.

"Ladies and gentlemen, both my clients are lifelong public servants. Wesley Brume is now the chief of police of the Bass Creek community he has served so well over the years. Clay Evans was appointed to the federal bench after many years as a prosecutor in Cobb County. Rudy Kelly's case is only one of thousands of cases these men have investigated and prosecuted successfully over the years.

"Were mistakes made in Rudy Kelly's case? Yes. Did a tragedy occur? Yes. But that does not mean these honest public servants should be accused of a crime — and certainly not the crime of murder. There are some things Mr. Tobin did not tell you in his very lengthy opening statement. He did not tell you, for instance, that he was Rudy Kelly's attorney before he became the state attorney, so he can hardly claim to be acting here as a disinterested prosecutor. He did not tell you that Rudy Kelly had no fewer than three appeals to the Florida Supreme Court, where all the facts he told you about were brought to the attention of the highest court in this state — and all three appeals were denied. He did not tell you that he personally argued the last appeal and made virtually the same argument he presented to you this morning — the separate rape file, all of it. And his appeal was denied. He did not tell you that he made a personal appeal to the governor of this great state and brought all these facts to the governor's attention in a bid for clemency. And his request was denied.

"The fact is that Rudy Kelly was at Lucy Ochoa's trailer on the night of the murder around the time of the murder. His blood was found there. She was killed with a serrated knife. A serrated knife was found in Rudy's bedroom. And Rudy admitted that he could have killed her and not remembered it. That's pretty incriminating evidence.

"This was a tragedy. And mistakes were made at every level of state government. But convicting these men of a crime would be another tragedy. Don't make that mistake."

It was a short, sweet counter to Jack's very lengthy discussion of the facts, but it was very effective. Jimmy DiCarlo practically strutted back to his seat next to his two clients.

The judge dismissed the court for the lunch break as soon as Jimmy finished his opening statement.

They say that good trial lawyers can win a case with their opening statement, convincing the jurors of the merits of their case *without presenting a scintilla of evidence.* Jack had hoped to do just that, but he could tell by the gloomy faces on Pat and Dick, who were waiting for him outside the courthouse, that Jimmy DiCarlo might have turned the tables on him.

"He was pretty convincing, wasn't he?" Jack said.

"It's still early," Pat said, reaching out to stroke his shoulder.

"It doesn't matter," Dick said.

"Your witnesses will convince them," Pat reassured him, but he could tell that she didn't believe her own words.

After lunch, Jack tried to start his case with none other than Wesley Brume. He approached the judge before the bailiff brought the jury in.

"I'd like to put Mr. Brume on the stand, Your Honor."

"Mr. Tobin, I know you didn't make your reputation as a criminal lawyer, but there are basic rules that you should know. The defendant doesn't have to testify, and you can't put him on the stand to prove your case." Jimmy DiCarlo, who was standing beside Jack for this sidebar conference, chuckled out loud at the judge's comments, which were made in jest.

Jack paused to let them have their fun. Then he proceeded to make his point.

"Your Honor, Mr. Brume already testified ten years ago at the suppression hearing. I believe I can read his testimony into the record as an admission. All I'm asking the court is for permission to put Mr. Brume on the stand and ask him to read his answers from ten years ago." Jimmy wasn't laughing anymore.

"Judge, I object. My client has the right not to take the stand." Jack could tell by his expression that Harry Stanton appreciated the strategy. Jimmy was already starting to lose it.

"Well, Mr. DiCarlo, you don't disagree that Mr. Brume's prior sworn testimony is admissible, do you?"

"I do, Your Honor."

"And what is the basis for your objection?"

"Relevancy, Your Honor. What Mr. Brume testified to in a suppression hearing ten years ago has no relevance to this proceeding where he is a criminal defendant and it may be prejudicial."

"Prejudicial?" the judge said in a disbelieving tone. "His sworn testimony under oath as a police officer may be prejudicial, is that your argument, Counsel?"

Jimmy was a good trial lawyer because of his presence and his speaking voice and his aggressiveness. Logical analysis was not his strong suit.

"Maybe it's not prejudicial, Judge, but it's certainly irrelevant to any issues in this case."

"How do you respond to that argument, Mr. Tobin?"

"Well, Judge, I think his testimony will take about ten minutes. We could do a dry run outside of the jury's presence, and then you can make a decision on whether the testimony is relevant."

"That sounds logical. Why don't we do that? Mr. Brume, take the stand here. Mr. Tobin, do you have a copy of Mr. Brume's testimony for him to read?"

"Yes I do, Your Honor, and I have a copy for you and for his counsel as well. As you can see, sometimes a question was asked and it took three or four more follow-ups to get the answer. I've tried to avoid that for purposes of time and clarity and have highlighted the relevant questions and answers. With your permission, Your Honor, I will read those questions, which were originally asked by Rudy's lawyer, Ms. Tracey James, and then Mr. Brume will read his responses. I also anticipate that the court will instruct the jury beforehand that this testimony was given ten years ago in a separate proceeding and that Mr. Brume was a detective then investigating the murder of Lucy Ochoa and that he is simply reading his previous testimony."

"I see," the judge said as he studied the document. "Very good. Then let's proceed." Judge Stanton was starting to enjoy himself. It was obvious that Jack had anticipated this entire scene before the trial began. This was going to be a real battle.

Jack then positioned himself in front of Wesley in the witness box and read the first question from the record.

"Officer Brume, why did you pick up my client for questioning?"

"He was identified by three people as a suspect," Wesley Brume answered, reading from his copy of the transcript.

"Would those three people be Pilar Rodriguez, Ray Castro and José Guerrero?"

"Yes."

Jack skipped down to the next highlighted section.

"Before you picked my client up, you talked to his high school principal, Mr. Bill Yates, is that correct?"

"Yes."

"And Mr. Yates told you that Rudy had an intellectual deficit, that he couldn't keep up with the other students academically, correct?"

"Yes."

"They passed him academically to the tenth grade, although they shouldn't have, but after that he just received an attendance certificate, correct?"

"Yes."

"Did Mr. Yates tell you anything else about Rudy?"

"No."

"You're sure?"

"Yes."

"He didn't tell you that Rudy was very affable, that he'd agree to everything you'd say; that in all fairness you shouldn't question him without either his mother or a lawyer present — the principal didn't say those things to you?"

"No. I don't remember him saying anything like that."

"You don't remember him saying anything like that or he didn't say anything like that: Which is it, Officer Brume?"

"He didn't say anything like that."

"You picked Rudy up at the convenience store where he worked, correct?"

"Yes."

"Did you speak to his boss?"

"Yes."

"Was he reluctant to let Rudy go with you?"

"Somewhat."

"What does 'Somewhat' mean, Mr. Brume? Does it mean he was reluctant or he was not reluctant?"

"It means he didn't want me to take Rudy at first but after we talked and I told him the importance of the investigation, he agreed that Rudy should go with me."

"You mean he agreed after you threatened him with the health department?"

"That's not true. I would never do that."

"So you took Rudy to the police department?"

"Yes."

"And you began questioning him, correct?"

"Yes."

"And according to your report, you began questioning him at 3:18 p.m., correct?"

"Yes, that's correct."

"And isn't it true, Officer Brume, that before you started your interrogation of Rudy, his mother arrived at the station and demanded to see her son and that you not question her son without her being present?"

"To my knowledge the mother didn't arrive at the station until I was almost finished with the interview."

"When she did arrive, did she request that you stop the interview?"

"Yes."

"But you didn't?"

"No."

"Why?"

"He'd agreed to talk to me. He's an adult and she's not a lawyer."

"Did you tell him his mother was outside and she wanted to see him before he answered any more questions?"

"No."

"Is that because you knew that he wouldn't talk to you anymore if he knew his mother was outside?"

"No. I was almost finished anyway. At that point it wouldn't have made a difference."

"Where did this interrogation take place?"

"In the interrogation room at the police department."

"I've heard about that room. It's equipped with a television camera, is that correct?"

"Yes."

"And you have audio recording equipment in there as well, correct?"

"Yes."

"But you didn't use either?"

"No, I didn't."

"Was there a reason why you didn't, Officer Brume?"

At this point, Wesley paused and looked up at Judge Stanton.

"Your Honor, this is ridiculous. Do I really have to keep reading this? This all happened ten years ago, and it's got nothing to do —"

Judge Stanton interrupted him. "Mr. Brume, I made my decision. Now just continue as you were instructed. Mr. Tobin, what was the last question?"

"It was about whether there'd been a reason he didn't use the recording equipment."

"Ah yes. Okay, Mr. Brume, get on with it. Read your response."

Wesley sighed, picked up the transcript and began reading his "part" again.

"No. There was no reason in particular. We rarely use the video camera. And I didn't have a tape available."

"What would you have had to do to use the camera, just get a videotape?"

"Yes."

"Where was the videotape?"

"In the equipment room."

"And where is the equipment room?"

"Down the hall."

"And the recording equipment, would you have found a tape for that in the equipment room as well?"

"Yes."

"Can you be more specific, Officer Brume? How long would it have taken you to walk down the hall, fetch the video or recording equipment, or both, and install them before beginning your interview?"

"Three to five minutes."

"Is it accurate that this recording equipment was in the interrogation room to be used for interrogations?"

"Of course."

"Is it accurate that when you brought my client in for questioning he was already a suspect in this murder?"

"Yes."

"And he was your only suspect at the time?"

"Yes."

And is it accurate, Detective Brume, that in your twenty-plus years as a police officer in this department this is the most heinous crime you have ever investigated?"

"No question about that."

"Did you have Rudy make a written statement?"

"No, but I had him read my notes and sign them."

"Did you tell him to sign them?"

"Yes, of course."

"Was he allowed to make changes?"

"I don't understand."

"It's very simple, Officer Brume, did you let him edit your notes?"

"Of course not."

They had come to the end of the part of the transcript Jack had copied and highlighted, and he turned to the bench.

"That's it, Your Honor. I'm obviously using this testimony to show in Mr. Brume's own words the circumstances under which the initial investigation took place. It's exactly what I told the jury in my opening statement."

The judge didn't even look at Jimmy DiCarlo for a response. "Well I think it's relevant. Let's bring the jury in. Mr. Brume, you can stay where you are."

Clay Evans bolted from his chair. "Judge, you can't be serious. This is not relevant to the charges against us."

"Sit down, Mr. Evans," the judge shouted. "This is my courtroom and you are a defendant. If you have a point to make, whisper it to your lawyer. I don't want to have to hold you in contempt." The judge motioned to the bailiff to get the jury.

The jury filed in and the judge instructed them just as Jack had requested, telling them that this testimony had originally been given ten years ago in a separate proceeding and would be read by the prosecutor and defendant Brume. "But remember, ladies and gentlemen," Judge Stanton said looking at the jurors, "this was the sworn testimony of Officer Brume at the time."

They repeated their reading of the transcript word for word, with Jack enjoying every second. If Jimmy DiCarlo hadn't been so flustered by the outbursts of his own clients, he could have suggested that Jack alone read the transcript to the jury, keeping his client off the stand, and Judge Stanton would doubtless have agreed. But the whole thing would have been far less effective that way, and as they went through the little dramatic reading, Jack was secretly enjoying the fact that he'd gotten away with it, forcing Wesley to look just as duplicitous now as he must have looked ten years ago.

Jack followed Wesley Brume's performance with live testimony from Principal Bill Yates.

Yates told the jury he was now retired but that he remembered talking to Wesley Brume about Rudy ten years before. Rudy's death had obviously had an effect on him. There were tears in his eyes as he testified. He and Jack had spent some time preparing for this moment. As they'd discussed and, indeed, practiced, Jack asked almost exactly the same questions Tracey James had asked ten years before, and the principal gave almost exactly the same answers.

"Mr. Yates, you were Rudy's high school principal for all four years he was at Bass Creek high school, is that correct?"

"Yes."

"And did Officer Wesley Brume come to see you ten years ago to interview you about Rudy?"

"Yes."

"And could you tell the court the reason for the visit?"

"He wanted to find out about Rudy, how he had been as a student."

"And what did you tell him?"

"I told him that Rudy was a very nice, motivated young man but that he was slow. Not retarded but slow. If I recall correctly, I think his IQ was somewhere around seventy-five. Bass Creek was a small school. We didn't have special programs for children like Rudy, so we did the best we could. After two years we put Rudy in a vocational program. He never received a high school diploma, just an attendance certificate."

"Did Detective Brume tell you why he was inquiring about Rudy?"

"Yes. He said Rudy might be a suspect in the murder of Lucy Ochoa."

"And how did you respond?"

"I believe I told him he must have been mistaken. I knew Rudy very well back then, and I never believed he was capable of anything like that."

"Did Detective Brume tell you that he was going to bring Rudy in for questioning?"

"Yes."

"How did you respond to that?"

"I remember telling him that Rudy's mother should be with him for that, or that he should have a lawyer in there. I told him how friendly Rudy was, and how naive he could be. I told him Rudy wouldn't know how to protect himself. He would respond to every question he was asked even if it wasn't in his best interests."

"Did you have a reason why you told him that?"

"Yes, I did. I just naturally assumed he wanted to conduct a fair investigation and I thought it was something he needed to know."

"I have no further questions, Your Honor."

"All right," Judge Stanton said. "Mr. DiCarlo, do you wish to cross-examine the witness?"

Jimmy and Clay Evans had discussed the principal's appearance beforehand and had decided that they had nothing to gain from a cross.

"No questions, Your Honor."

Benny Dragone was next, and Jack had prepared him for a repeat performance just as he had Principal Yates.

"Do you remember the day Detective Brume took Rudy Kelly in for questioning?" Jack asked after a few preliminary questions were out of the way.

"Yes."

"Where were you at the time?"

"At my store. Rudy worked for me. He worked the counter. I gave him a job because I knew his mother, Elena. It was a favor to her."

"What do you recall about that day?"

"Detective Brume wanted to take Rudy over to the station for questioning. I told him that I wouldn't let him speak to Rudy until I talked with his mother."

"Why did you tell him that?"

"I knew he was looking at Rudy as a suspect in Lucy Ochoa's murder and I didn't trust him. I never trusted Brume, and I knew

Rudy wouldn't be able to deal with him by himself."

"And how did Mr. Brume respond?"

"Well, like I told Rudy's lawyer back then in that hearing, Brume threatened me. He said he'd get the health department over to my store for an inspection. And I knew exactly what he meant."

"And what did he mean?"

"He meant that he'd make trouble for me if I didn't cooperate."

"So you did?"

"Yeah. And I've regretted it ever since."

"No further questions, Your Honor," Jack said, returning to his table.

"Mr. DiCarlo, cross-examination?"

"No, Your Honor."

"Good. We're going to wrap up for the day. Ladies and gentlemen of the jury, I admonish you again not to talk to anyone about this case. Do not read the newspapers, watch television or listen to the radio. Do not discuss it with your spouses. Do you understand?" Everyone nodded. "Court is adjourned." The judge rapped his gavel. "I'll see you all at nine a.m. sharp. I want the lawyers to be here at 8:30 just in case you think of anything overnight that you wish to discuss with me before we get started." It was just how he'd wrapped up jury selection. Judge Stanton was nothing if not consistent, Jack thought as he gathered up his papers.

## [ FORTY-EIGHT ]

Jack was very pleased at how things had gone on the first day of trial, especially after the opening statements. He had succeeded in surprising Jimmy DiCarlo by putting Wesley Brume on the stand and had established through Bill Yates and Benny Dragone that Brume had manipulated Rudy into talking to him alone and had lied about the circumstances under oath. Maria would testify about further lies and manipulations tomorrow and then the trial would shift to the rape file and Clay Evans's involvement. It would heat up at that point, he was sure. After the first day, however, he became convinced that DiCarlo and Evans were content to feed Wesley Brume to the wolves. Poor Brume, he didn't even see it coming.

He hadn't seen Maria since Joaquin had been shot. She spent her days and nights at the hospital. They'd set up a cot for her in Joaquin's room. Dick had been up that afternoon to check on Joaquin's progress.

"How's he doing?" Jack asked on the ride home.

"Still the same. He hasn't woken up yet and that worries Maria, but I talked to the doctor and he said everything is fine. He said Joaquin's just resting. He'll wake up in his own good time."

"That's great," Jack said. "I don't mean to sound mercenary, Dick, but Maria is scheduled to testify first thing in the morning tomorrow. I don't know what to do. I haven't talked to her. I haven't prepped her."

"You don't need to prep her, Jack. She'll tell the truth. I'll get her there. I'll drop you off early and I'll go pick her up. She and I have talked about it already. When she's through testifying I'll take her right back."

"Thanks, Dick."

That night Pat rubbed his back in bed trying to loosen him up, but it was no use. Jack was as tight as a steel cable wire.

"It went pretty good today," she said, trying another approach.

"Yeah, it did, but tomorrow is the big day. In this business things can go south in a heartbeat."

"Well, we'll just have to say a prayer."

"Or two."

Dick dropped Jack off early the next morning and went to get Maria as planned. Jack was not sure he'd be seeing either one of them anytime soon. Maria had a mind of her own, and right now her mind was on one thing only — tending to Joaquin.

He'd called Charley Peterson the night before and told him to be there early, just in case. It was not uncommon to take witnesses out of order in a trial. He did it all the time, especially with expert witnesses like doctors. But this case was different. He felt strongly that in order to convince the jury, he needed a meticulously logical progression of witnesses.

Jack and Jimmy DiCarlo were ushered into the judge's chambers promptly at 8:30. Stanton was in a chipper mood. Jack could tell he was enjoying himself, but he didn't know if that was good or bad.

"Any motions this morning, gentlemen? Any new theories you've spun in the middle of the night?"

"No sir," Jimmy replied.

"No, Judge," Jack added.

"All righty then. Mr. Tobin, how many witnesses do you have left?"

"Three, Your Honor. The last is a video."

"Good, good. Then you should finish up today. Mr. DiCarlo, have you made any decisions about who you're going to put on?"

Jimmy had seen Geronimo Cruz's video deposition. It was powerful and he didn't want the jury to see it. Now was probably the time to make the objection.

"Not entirely, Judge. I know I'll have at least one witness, but Your Honor, I do have an objection to Mr. Tobin's video — the Geronimo Cruz confession. We can stipulate that Mr. Cruz killed Lucy Ochoa. We don't need the video."

Judge Stanton looked at Jack. It was heating up already. He loved it.

"What do you say about that, Mr. Tobin?"

"I'd like the jury to see it, Judge. It removes any doubt."

"I'm sure you would, Counsel, but if Mr. DiCarlo is stipulating to its contents, I don't see why it's necessary."

"It's the specifics, Your Honor. He tells exactly how he did it, and the jury will be able to evaluate that evidence in light of what evidence the police had not only before the trial but two years after when they learned Cruz was in a jail cell in Texas."

The judge turned to Jimmy DiCarlo.

"He's got a point, Mr. DiCarlo."

"We'll stipulate to the facts. He can read a factual summary to the jury. It will save a lot of time, Judge."

"It's not the same, Your Honor. A stipulation won't have the impact."

"I understand that, Mr. Tobin, but we're not looking for emotional impact here, we're looking for facts. If Mr. DiCarlo's clients are willing to stipulate to those facts we don't need the Cruz videotape."

"Judge, I think I have the right."

"I don't think so. I think it's within my discretion. I'm not going to rule right now. I'll give you some time to come up with a better reason than the one you just proposed, but I want it by the time you present Mr. Cruz's deposition and I want you two to work out a stipulation of the facts in the event I rule against you, Mr. Tobin. Is that understood?"

Jack felt like he had been dealt a body blow to the gut, one that he hadn't anticipated and should have. He had no case law to support his argument and no time to do any research. He needed that video for its emotional impact. The jury had to see Geronimo Cruz — to understand what he did and how he did it — in order to understand what happened to Rudy and just how malicious the defendants' actions had been. Reading a stipulated statement of facts would not suffice.

"Is that understood, Mr. Tobin?" Stanton repeated in a firmer tone.

"Yes, Your Honor."

"Okay, let's go into the courtroom."

The judge walked into the courtroom with them. There was no formality today. When everyone was seated he admonished the spectators as he had done the day before. Then he told the bailiff to bring in the jury.

Jack was out of sorts for another reason as well. He had checked with the bailiff and Maria had not arrived. He was going to have to start the day with Charley Peterson as his first witness.

Charley was wearing an olive green suit and he looked perfectly calm as he walked forward, stood in front of the clerk and took an oath to tell the truth.

"Would you state your name for the record?" Jack began.

"Charles Nickleby Peterson."

"And Mr. Peterson, where are you employed?'

"Carolina Christian Teacher's College."

"And what do you do there?"

"I'm a professor of political science."

"And do you hold any professional degrees?"

"Yes, I have a bachelor's degree and a law degree from Georgetown." Jack hoped those credentials impressed the jury because what was coming wouldn't.

"Now, Mr. Peterson, you at one time were the public defender here in Cobb County, is that accurate?"

"Yes, I was."

"And you, in fact, represented Rudy Kelly in his trial for first-degree murder, is that correct?"

"Yes, I did."

Jack picked up the rape file that had already been stipulated into evidence, approached the witness and handed him the file. "Mr. Peterson, I've just handed you the state's composite exhibit number two, and I ask you to take a look at it." Charley perused the file and looked up at Jack when he was finished.

"Have you seen that document before?"

"Yes, I saw it for the first time when I testified before the grand jury."

"Do you know what it is?"

"Yes. It's a rape file. Apparently, the police found semen inside Lucy Ochoa after she was murdered and for some reason created a murder file and a separate rape file."

"Did you know anything about this rape file when you were representing Rudy Kelly?"

"No, I did not."

"Did you file a request for the state to produce all evidence relating to the murder of Lucy Ochoa when you were representing Rudy Kelly?"

"Yes, I did."

Jack handed him another document. "Can you identify exhibit number three?"

"Yes, that's my demand for discovery or, to put it in layman's terms, my request for all the evidence."

"Did the state ever inform you that semen was found inside the victim, Lucy Ochoa?"

"No."

"Would that have been significant for you?"

Jimmy DiCarlo was on his feet in a heartbeat. "Objection, Your Honor. Calls for speculation."

"Overruled. You may answer the question, Mr. Peterson."

"Oh yes, especially because the blood type was different from Rudy's, which meant somebody else was in her trailer that night. It literally was the difference between a guilty and an innocent verdict." Jack couldn't believe the judge allowed that statement in, but he asked another question quickly before Jimmy could move to strike the answer. He handed Charley the state's exhibit number four.

"Have you seen this document before, Mr. Peterson?"

"Yes, this is the coroner's report that was introduced by the state at Rudy Kelly's trial."

"Who was the coroner at the time?"

"Harry Tuthill."

"And where is Mr. Tuthill now?"

"He's dead."

"Is there anything unusual about this coroner's report?"

"Yes."

"Can you tell the jury what that is?"

"For one, there's no lab analysis in there at all. There's no mention of the semen found in the body. No mention of the blood type."

"Had you ever seen a coroner's report from Mr. Tuthill before Lucy Ochoa's murder?"

"Plenty. I had been the public defender at the time for fifteen years. Harry had been the coroner for twenty-five. Murder was not a common occurrence in Cobb County but it did happen, and Harry always did the report."

"Well, when he did the reports in the past were the toxicology results always in there?"

"Always."

"Did you work as a public defender before you took over the job as the public defender in Cobb County?"

"Yes, I worked as an assistant public defender in Miami for ten years."

"So your total experience in this field is twenty-five years?"

"That's correct."

"Have you ever seen a coroner's report in a murder investigation that excluded a major piece of evidence such as semen in the vagina from its findings?"

"No."

"Was there any advantage to the state in creating this separate rape file other than what we've already discussed?"

Jimmy DiCarlo was up again. "Objection, Your Honor. Speculation."

"Overruled. The witness can answer the question."

"Well, by creating a separate case that nobody knew about, they kept the semen evidence from being discovered by, say, a public records request. It's a way of keeping everything secret."

Jimmy DiCarlo was livid. "Your Honor, I move to strike the question and the answer."

"Overruled, Mr. DiCarlo. Proceed, Mr. Tobin." Jack couldn't believe his string of good luck with the judge. *Maybe Hang 'Em High Harry has an inkling these boys are guilty. He certainly knows the game they're playing.*

Jack decided to wrap it up there. The jury had to have the picture by now.

"No further questions, Your Honor."

Jimmy DiCarlo was on his feet before Judge Stanton asked him if he wanted to cross-examine the witness. For a minute Jack thought he was going to walk up to Charley and strangle him. As it was, he stopped about two feet away from Charley's face.

"Mr. Peterson, are you presently licensed to practice law in the state of Florida?"

"No."

"Are you licensed anywhere?"

"No."

"And the reason you're not licensed is?"

"I was disbarred." A collective gasp rose from the spectators' pews, followed by scattered murmuring. Up until now the public had been largely silent. Jack looked at the jury and saw expressions of shock there as well. He'd thought about bringing the issue out on direct examination but had decided not to. It was an unforgivable mistake. Judge Stanton was rapping his gavel.

"Silence! Silence!" he shouted. "I'll have everyone removed from this courtroom if I have to!" The murmuring stopped. "Mr. DiCarlo, you may proceed."

"Thank you, Your Honor. And what were you disbarred for, Mr. Peterson?"

"Drunkenness." There was another gasp from the pews. The judge rapped his gavel.

"I'm warning you, people." But they were already silent again, some of them leaning forward expectantly, apparently eager for the next revelation.

"You were a drunk?" Jimmy DiCarlo proceeded. He was in Charley Peterson's face now. Charley's shoulders slumped.

"Yes," he said quietly.

"And were you a drunk when you represented Rudy Kelly?"

"Yes."

Jimmy DiCarlo walked back to his table and retrieved a document and handed it to Charley.

"Take a look at that document, Mr. Peterson. We've marked it as defense exhibit number one." Charley looked at the document and then looked back at Jimmy DiCarlo.

"Before you came into this courtroom today several witnesses testified about the method Mr. Brume used to question Rudy Kelly. That document you now have in your hand is an order by Judge Wentwell, the judge in the Rudy Kelly suppression hearing, saying that you could put on evidence at Rudy Kelly's trial about how his confession was obtained, is it not?"

"Yes, it is."

"Did you put on that evidence? Did you call his principal, Mr. Yates, or his employer, Mr. Dragone, as Mr. Tobin did in this case?"

"No, I did not."

"Wouldn't that have been helpful to Mr. Kelly's defense?" Jack had no idea where Jimmy DiCarlo was going with this line of questioning.

"Yes, it would have."

"Did you fail to do that because you were drunk at the time?"

"Probably."

Jimmy DiCarlo picked up the coroner's report. "And this coroner's report, which you just testified on direct examination was so flawed. So flawed that you had never seen anything like it in all your years of practice. Did you bring that to the attention of anybody at the time?"

"No."

"Did you ask the coroner when he was on the stand where the rest of the report was — specifically the toxicology results?"

"No."

"Did you ask the state attorney, Mr. Evans?"

"No."

"And you didn't do so because you were drunk at the time, is that accurate, Mr. Peterson?"

"Probably."

"Did you participate in any of the appeals of Rudy Kelly's conviction?"

"No."

"But you knew there would be at least one appeal?"

"Probably."

"Probably? Do you know of any first-degree murder case where there was not at least one appeal?"

"No."

"So you knew there would be an appeal?"

"Yes."

"Did you ever offer by affidavit or sworn testimony to anyone that you were incompetent at the time you represented Rudy Kelly?"

"No."

"Ever at any time before Rudy Kelly was executed?"

"No."

"You more than anyone were responsible for his conviction and execution, weren't you, Mr. Peterson?"

It was Jack's turn to jump up. "I object, Your Honor. Mr. Peterson is not on trial here."

And it was Jack's turn to feel Harry Stanton's wrath. "Overruled. The witness will answer the question."

"I guess I was," Charley replied. He was now slumped low in the witness chair, his chin almost touching his chest.

"Has anyone charged you with a crime?"

Jack was on his feet again. "Objection!"

"Sustained. The witness will not answer that question," Judge Stanton directed.

"I have no further questions for this *witness*, Your Honor," Jimmy said with a sneer, turning his back on Charley and walking back to his table.

"Redirect?" the judge asked. Jack hesitated but only for a moment.

"Mr. Peterson, did Clay Evans know you had a drinking problem before the Kelly trial?"

"Yes."

"How do you know that?"

"He said things to me over the years."

"Like?"

"One time he told me he heard I was a pretty good lawyer until I climbed inside the bottle. Another time he told me that a client having me for a lawyer could kiss his ass goodbye."

"And this was all before the Rudy Kelly case?"

"Yes."

"So they were banking on you being drunk?"

"Objection."

"Sustained. The witness will not answer the question." But Jack had gotten what he wanted: He had to put that issue in the jury's mind. *You can't unring a bell,* Jack thought, remembering Jimmy's own words from a couple of days before.

"No further questions, Your Honor."

"You may step down, Mr. Peterson. Counsel, call your next witness."

Jack looked at the bailiff, who let him know by shaking his head that Maria had not arrived yet.

"Your Honor, may we approach?"

"Come on," the judge said, waving his arm at them.

When they reached the bench, Jack lobbied once again for the video confession of Geronimo Cruz. "Judge, I only have one more witness besides Mr. Cruz and she's not here. We haven't had any time to work out a stipulation of facts. The video confession is thirty-four minutes. I daresay that working out a stipulation and typing it up to read to the jury will take twice that long. So, using Mr. DiCarlo's own concern for efficiency, it will be much faster to show the video deposition."

The judge wasn't in the mood for a long discussion. "All right, Mr. Tobin, put the tape in and let's get it done. Your last witness better be here when it's finished, though. If speed and convenience are the reason we're using this tape, then you are not going to be able to delay this trial for one second because of a witness problem. Do I make myself clear?"

"Yes, Your Honor."

After he had set the television in front of the jury and put the tape in, Jack motioned to Pat, who was sitting in the back of the courtroom.

"You've got to go to the hospital and find out what's keeping Maria. If she's not here in thirty minutes, this case is over."

"All right, I'll run over there," Pat said, turning to go. *Thank God she's a runner,* Jack said to himself. *And that the hospital's only three blocks away.* Dick had their only car and he was already at the hospital. All Jack could do now was wait.

He concentrated on watching the jury as they watched Geronimo Cruz's video confession. They were paying close attention, which was good. *Now if Maria can only get here, we might convict these bastards.*

~

Three blocks away another drama was taking place. Earlier that morning, Joaquin had taken a turn for the worse. His heart had stopped and a Code Blue was called. Dick arrived while it was in progress. Doctors and nurses were crowded around Joaquin's bed. Maria was standing in the corner and appeared to be praying. There was no way he was going to convince her to leave at that moment. He couldn't even ask.

They put the paddles to Joaquin's chest several times before his heart started again. Minutes later all the doctors and nurses vanished as if they had been ghosts. Dick had seen many Code Blues in his day but he never got used to them. Still, this one was different — that was his best friend in the world lying on the bed being jolted around like a rag doll.

When Pat arrived, they were both standing over the bed saying the Hail Mary. She was out of breath from running and stood to the side until they were finished.

"What happened?" she asked.

"His heart stopped," Dick said.

"Is he okay now?"

"He seems to be. The nurse says his vital signs are stabilized."

Pat knew it was going to be next to impossible to get Maria to leave his bedside, but she had to try.

"Maria, we have fifteen minutes to get to the courthouse or the case is over. Everything Joaquin, you, Dick and Jack have worked for will be for nothing if you don't testify." She left herself out of the equation even though she was as much a part of it as they were.

"I can't leave him," Maria said desperately.

"You have to. Joaquin would want you to." She hated using Joaquin like that, but there was no other way.

Maria looked at Dick.

"Go," he told her. "I'll stay here. Pat's right, he'd want you to go."

He pulled his keys from his pocket and started to hand them to Pat.

"We don't have time to get the car. We'll have to run to the courthouse and hope we arrive in time."

~

The bailiff was moving the television from in front of the jury when they jogged into the back of the courtroom breathing hard. Pat could see the relief come over Jack's face.

"Call your next witness," the judge told Jack.

"The state calls Maria Lopez," Jack announced.

Maria walked to the front of the courtroom and took the oath from the clerk.

"Please state your name for the record," Jack said. Maria did not answer. She had a distant look on her face.

"Ma'am," the judge leaned toward her, "you must answer the question."

"Maria Lopez," she said, still looking dazed.

"And Ms. Lopez, where are you presently employed?"

"I'm a secretary at the state attorney's office."

Jack decided to lead her a bit. "You are presently my secretary, is that accurate?"

"Yes."

"And before you worked for me you worked at the Bass Creek police department, is that accurate?"

"Yes." She was still in a fog.

"And you worked specifically for the defendant, Wesley Brume, is that correct?"

"Yes."

"As his secretary?"

"Yes." The leading questions were over. She had to focus now.

"How long did you work at the police department, Ms. Lopez?"

No answer. Jack repeated the question. "How long did you work at the police department, Maria?"

"Objection, Your Honor." Jimmy DiCarlo was out of his chair

again. "Counsel is becoming too familiar with the witness." Maria looked at Jimmy DiCarlo and then at Clay Evans beside him and then at Wesley Brume, the son-of-a-bitch she knew had shot her Joaquin.

"Fifteen years," she said before the judge could rule on the objection.

"Counsel, you will refrain from calling the witness by her first name," the judge told Jack. "And ma'am, you will wait to answer the question once an objection is made. Do you understand?"

Maria turned and looked at the judge. "Yes sir." In that moment, Jack could tell that she was back.

"Could you tell the jury, Ms. Lopez, what positions you held at the Bass Creek police department?"

"For the first seven years, I was a receptionist. Then I became a secretary. Eventually, I became Mr. Brume's secretary."

"Ms. Lopez, I want to take you back to January 24, 1986. What was your position on that date?"

"I was the receptionist."

"And what were your job duties at that time?"

"I answered the phones, opened the mail, filed, did some light typing — that sort of thing."

"Do you recall what happened on that date?"

"Yes."

"And why do you recall that?"

"I testified about it in a hearing in March of that year, I think, and you showed me a transcript of my testimony just recently."

"What happened on that date?"

"Mr. Brume brought Rudy Kelly in for questioning, and later his mother, Elena, came to the police station and demanded to see her son."

"Do you remember what time she arrived?"

"Yes. It was 3:16 p.m."

"And why do you remember the specific time?"

"Elena made me write it down. It's in my notes, which are part of the investigative file, I believe. I also recently read it in my testimony."

"Did you let Elena in to see her son at that time?"

"No."

"Why not?"

"I was told not to by Detective Brume. Eventually another detective, Del Shorter, came out to talk to her, but she was never allowed to go back and talk to her son. Detective Brume was questioning him in the interrogation room."

Now Jack switched gears. He had a letter marked as exhibit number six, which he handed to Maria. It was Joaquin's copy of the May 2, 1986, letter from Tracey James to Clay Evans. Joaquin had mentioned it to Maria one day at the house and she told him she had seen it in Wesley Brume's office. They then told Jack about it. Up to that point, Jack did not know how he was going to get the letter into evidence. Tracey was dead; Clay probably was not going to take the stand. Joaquin had received his copy, but Joaquin couldn't verify that Tracey had sent it to Clay or that Clay had received it. Maria seeing the letter in Brume's office made that connection. Still, Jack knew admissibility was going to be a major hurdle.

"Have you ever seen this, exhibit number six, before?"

"Yes. I have."

"What is it?"

"It's a letter dated May 2, 1986, from Tracey James to Clay Evans."

"And who is Tracey James?"

"She was a private attorney who represented Rudy Kelly before the public defender took over the case."

"And when did you see this letter?"

"Right around the time it was written, probably a few days later. Clay Evans came to the police department to see Mr. Brume, something he had never done before. They were talking in his office and I came in because Detective Brume had to sign something that needed to go out right away. The letter was on the desk. While Mr.

Brume read through the document he was about to sign, I read the letter. I was standing over his left shoulder. As I was walking out of the room I heard Mr. Brume comment, 'She can't be serious.' Mr. Evans didn't reply, or if he did, I didn't hear his reply."

Jack addressed the judge. "Your Honor, I'd like to offer exhibit number six into evidence."

"I have several objections, Your Honor," Jimmy DiCarlo interjected.

"Approach," the judge said.

When they were at sidebar, Jimmy began his litany of reasons why the letter should not be admitted into evidence.

"I've never seen this letter before, Judge."

"I sent it to you," Jack said, "when I responded to your Request for Production. It's on my pretrial list of exhibits."

"Any other reasons?" the judge asked.

"It's hearsay, and besides, the only way he can introduce this letter is through either my client or Ms. James, and my client is not testifying."

The judge looked at Jack. "Response?"

"Your Honor, Tracey James is dead and there is an exception to the hearsay rule when a person is dead. In any case, this letter is not hearsay because it's not being offered for the truth of its contents. It's only being offered to show that it was sent and received."

The judge looked at Jimmy, who clearly didn't have a clue how to respond. If he had asked the right questions, Jimmy would have learned that Clay Evans left the police department that day with the letter in hand and that the letter Jack had showed Maria was Joaquin's copy, but Jimmy was too confused to think that fast.

Still, to Jack's surprise, the judge sustained the objection.

"I'm not going to let it in, Mr. Tobin. This letter is based exclusively on a memo written by Joaquin Sanchez, Ms. James's investigator, about a conversation he had with a man named Pablo. The memo is clearly hearsay. The conversation these two men had is clearly hearsay. A letter in which Ms. James says this Geronimo person was the killer because it is based on this *incompetent* testimony is also hearsay."

"But Your Honor," Jack replied, "I'm not offering it for the truth of the matter."

The judge smiled at Jack. It was a "gotcha" smile. "Mr. Tobin, I've been practicing for almost fifty years. I can't tell you how many times I've heard that exception raised and I still don't fully understand it. So let's be a little more concrete in our analysis. You want the letter in so the jury knows that Clay Evans was notified by Tracey James back in May of 1986 that Geronimo Cruz was the killer, but you're not offering it to show he was the killer, just that Evans was notified, is that accurate?"

"Exactly, Your Honor."

"Here's my problem, Mr. Tobin. You want to taint these men with this knowledge even though the knowledge is inadmissible and therefore *incompetent*, but you want to argue that it's okay because you're not offering it for the truth of the matter asserted. That's legal gymnastics, Counselor."

Jack knew the judge was right. As far as Jimmy DiCarlo was concerned, the two men might as well have been speaking Greek. He had absolutely no idea what they were talking about.

The judge addressed the jury: "Ladies and gentleman, I have ruled that exhibit number six is inadmissible and I instruct you not to consider any testimony that has previously been given about that letter. It should not be a part of your deliberations in any way."

He then turned to Jack. "Counsel, you may proceed."

"Thank you, Your Honor. Ms. Lopez, I'd like to go to the year 1988. What was your position in the police department at that time?"

"I was still a receptionist."

"Were your job duties the same?"

"Pretty much, yes."

"Did the police department receive a letter from the Del Rio, Texas, police department in the year 1988?"

"Yes. I don't remember the exact date, but there was this letter from the police department in Del Rio, and since it was my job to open mail, I saw what it was about. They had a Geronimo Cruz under arrest for raping and murdering a woman, and his driver's license, which was a Florida license, showed a Bass Creek address. The reason they were writing to our police department was to see if he had any record here, or if he was wanted for any crimes in our area. We got inquiry letters like that all the time — it was pretty typical."

"If it was a typical inquiry letter, why is it that you remember it?"

"Well, it related to the Kelly case and that was the biggest case we'd ever had."

"How did you know it related to the Kelly case?"

"Well, Geronimo was one of the witnesses who had disappeared after Lucy's murder. Most people in the barrio felt that Geronimo was the real murderer and that's why it was significant to me." Maria had gone too far with the last statement and Jack knew it. If he'd had a chance to prep her she never would have made such a mistake.

Jimmy DiCarlo didn't miss it. "Objection, Your Honor. I move to strike the answer as nonresponsive and hearsay. Judge, may we approach?" Jimmy was livid.

"Come on," Judge Stanton said tiredly.

Jimmy practically ran to the sidebar. "This is outrageous, Judge. She just testified for the whole neighborhood. I'm moving for a mistrial."

The judge looked at Jack, who jumped right in. "I agree that her last statement was improper, Judge. I think you can instruct the jury to disregard it, however. I don't think a mistrial is appropriate."

"I don't either, but Mr. Tobin, be very careful. You don't want your whole case to go down the tubes."

"Yes sir."

Jimmy wasn't done. "But Judge, they heard it. You can't erase it from their memory."

"I've ruled, Mr. DiCarlo. Now let's proceed. I'll instruct the jury."

Jimmy still wouldn't let it go. "But Judge —"

"The next word, Mr. DiCarlo, and you'll be held in contempt. Is that understood?"

"Yes sir."

The lawyers went back to their respective positions and the judge instructed the jury not to consider the last statement. He also admonished Maria. "Ms. Lopez, you are to testify only about what you know, not some scuttlebutt from the neighborhood or anywhere else, do you understand?"

"Yes, Your Honor."

"Proceed, Counsel."

"What did you do with the letter?"

"I told Detective Brume about it right away."

"And what did he do?"

"He told me to call the state attorney's office. I heard him tell the state attorney, Mr. Evans, about the letter. And then he said that he'd be right over and he rushed out of the office to go, I assume, to the state attorney's office."

"What happened to the letter?"

"He took it with him."

"Is that the type of letter that you would normally file somewhere?"

"Yes. Probably in the Kelly file."

"And did you file that letter?"

"No. I never saw it again."

The murmurs began anew in the courtroom. Judge Stanton pounded his gavel once more. "Silence!" he yelled again, looking threateningly at the spectators.

Jack sensed the moment. "No further questions, Your Honor."

"Cross-examination?" He barely had the words out before Jimmy was up and on his way over to Maria.

"Yes, Your Honor," he said as he moved in on her, getting as close as he could without too obviously crowding her.

"Now Ms. Lopez, I want to go back to your new employment with Mr. Tobin. Is it accurate to say you went to work for Mr. Tobin on the first day he started as the state attorney for Cobb County?"

"Yes, that's accurate."

"And it was the same day you resigned from the police department, correct?"

"Yes."

"And how long did you work for the police department — fifteen years?"

"Yes, that's correct."

"And you left without giving any notice — that's pretty harsh, isn't it?"

"I don't know what you mean," she said, looking straight into Jimmy's face.

"Is it fair to say you didn't like Mr. Brume?"

"Yes, that's fair," she said, looking past Jimmy and glaring at the fat little toad sitting at the defense table.

"And you didn't like the way he handled the Kelly case, did you?"

"No, I didn't like it."

"Specifically, you didn't like the way Rudy Kelly's mother, Elena, was treated when she came to the police department back in late January of 1986?"

"No, I didn't like it."

"They wouldn't have treated a white woman with such disrespect, would they?" Jack could have objected but he let the question go. The jury was entitled to the truth.

"No, they would not have," Maria answered, looking over at Wesley again.

"And you didn't like the way Mr. Evans prosecuted the Rudy Kelly case either, did you?"

"No."

"And you told this to Mr. Tobin?"

"Yes, I did."

"And you told it to him before he became state attorney?"

"Yes."

"And you and he planned your resignation from the police department *before* he became state attorney, correct?"

"Yes."

"Because he told you before he became state attorney and before he empaneled a grand jury that he was going to prosecute these two men, correct?"

"Yes."

"Because he already knew they were guilty?"

"Yes."

Like most attorneys when they get on a roll in cross-examination, Jimmy DiCarlo didn't know when to stop. He had hit a double and his runner was on the way to third with a stand-up triple, but Jimmy wanted that home run — so he kept going.

"Where are you living now?"

"On a ranch outside of town."

"And are you living with Mr. Tobin?" Jack couldn't believe the question. Maria hesitated.

"It's not like —"

Jimmy cut her off. "Just yes or no, Ms. Lopez. Are you living with Mr. Tobin?"

"Yes."

"And are you also living with a Mr. Joaquin Sanchez, who was an associate of Ms. Tracey James?"

"Yes," she said, her voice catching on the word.

"And is it true that you have been living with Mr. Tobin and Mr. Sanchez since the day you left the police department and went to work for Mr. Tobin?"

"Yes."

"Now I listened very carefully when you testified about this 1988 letter from the Del Rio police. Did you say Mr. Brume had you call the state attorney's office after he read the letter?"

"Yes."

"Did he tell you to get the state attorney's office on the line?"

"Ye-es," she said, with a questioning hesitation in her voice.

"Not Mr. Evans?"

"No, I don't think he said Mr. Evans's name specifically but I knew —"

Again Jimmy cut her off. "Did you hear Mr. Evans get on the line?"

"No. I had already handed the phone to Mr. Brume."

"And did you just assume Mr. Brume talked to Mr. Evans, or did you hear Mr. Brume actually say Mr. Evans's name?"

"I assumed he talked to Mr. Evans because Mr. Evans was the only state attorney who worked on the Kelly case."

"So you didn't hear him say Mr. Evans's name?"

"No."

"And when Mr. Brume had you get the state attorney's office on the line, he didn't tell you the reason, did he?"

"Specifically, no."

"You just assumed it was because of the letter he had just read, is that correct?"

"Yes."

"You didn't hear the content of their conversation, correct?"

"Well, I heard Mr. Brume say he'd be right over, but of course I couldn't hear —"

"You just heard Mr. Brume say 'I'll be right over'?"

"That's correct."

"How many state attorneys were there in the Cobb County office in 1988 besides Mr. Evans?"

"Four."

"And is it accurate that the police department spoke with all these attorneys on a regular basis?"

"Yes."

"And that would include Mr. Brume? He spoke to all these attorneys on a regular basis, correct?"

"Yes."

"And he went over to the state attorney's office to speak to these attorneys as well, didn't he?"

"From time to time."

"So he could have been calling one of these other attorneys for a completely separate reason, couldn't he?"

"I don't believe so."

"But you don't know for sure, do you?"

"Not for sure, no."

"And you have no specific evidence other than your assumptions, either that Mr. Evans was on the telephone or that Mr. Brume went to see Mr. Evans — and by specific evidence I mean you never heard Mr. Brume specifically tell you to get Mr. Evans on the phone; you never heard Mr. Evans's voice on the phone; and you never heard Mr. Brume refer to Mr. Evans while he was talking on the phone, is that correct?" Jimmy rattled it all off like a machine gun.

"Yes, it's correct. I didn't hear any of those things, but he read the letter and immediately told me to get the state attorney's office on the line."

"No further questions, Your Honor." Jimmy gave an arrogant look across at Jack as he walked back to his chair, as if to say, *That's the way you cross-examine someone.* But the look didn't phase Jack one bit. He was already rising when Judge Stanton said, "Redirect?"

"Yes, Your Honor. Thank you." Jack was by Maria but he was looking towards the defense table, right at Jimmy DiCarlo. "Ms. Lopez, counsel for the defendants just asked you if you have been living with me since you came to work for me, and you replied affirmatively. Is there a reason why you moved in with me?"

Jimmy was up in an instant. "Objection, Your Honor. May we approach?"

"Come on, come on." Judge Stanton put on his exasperated look but he was clearly eager to hear what was coming. The whole room seemed to be leaning forward, straining to eavesdrop.

"Judge, this is irrelevant," Jimmy said as he was still on his way to the bench. "I don't know what she's going to say, but I think it could be prejudicial."

"'I think it could be prejudicial' — that's an objection I haven't heard before. What's your response, Mr. Tobin?"

"Well, Judge, this is a door that Mr. DiCarlo opened. I did not ask a single question about where Ms. Lopez lives. Mr. DiCarlo wants to leave the jury with the impression that Ms. Lopez, Mr. Sanchez and I are living in some bizarre illicit relationship without allowing her to explain why she has been at my house — because it might be prejudicial to his clients. He should have thought of that before he asked the question and tried to smear all of us."

"I agree,"the judge remarked. "Mr. DiCarlo, you opened this door. We are now obligated to see where it leads. Objection overruled."

Jack walked back to the podium. Jimmy returned to the defense table and Clay Evans's angry glare.

Jack repeated his question. "Ms. Lopez, is there a reason you moved in with me?"

"Yes. I was afraid. Your investigator, Nancy Shea, had been to visit me, and I'd told her what I testified to here in court. She was killed right after she left my house."

The courtroom erupted, and the jury looked stunned. Several reporters jumped to their feet and started to clamber over their colleagues for the aisle; within seconds it was a stampede, and Judge Stanton could do nothing to stop them. After hammering the gavel several times and shouting "Silence!" at the top of his lungs to no avail, he ordered the bailiffs to clear the courtroom.

It took several minutes to get everyone out. Gradually the hubbub faded away as the room emptied, and those remaining — the judge, the lawyers, the accused, the witness, the jury, and the court personnel — were left in total silence.

Jimmy DiCarlo stood up. "Judge, may we approach?"

"Come up," the judge said, no expression or sign of impatience on his face. There was no audience to play to.

"Judge, I renew my objection to this line of questioning. I move to strike the answer, and I'm moving for a mistrial. We're not here to try the alleged murder of this Nancy person, whoever she is. The witness has just accused my clients of a murder unrelated to the charge actually before this court, and if that's not prejudicial, I don't know what is." Jimmy was almost shouting by the time he was done.

"Be careful there, Counsel. Remember who you're talking to. Mr. Tobin, do you have a response?"

"Yes I do, Your Honor. The witness, in her response to a perfectly justifiable redirect question, did precisely what a witness is supposed to do: She described facts. No personal opinions, no personal conclusions, just facts as she knew them. 'I was afraid' — fact. 'Nancy Shea visited me and I told her what I just told the court' — fact. 'Nancy Shea was killed right after she left my house' — fact, Your Honor," Jack said, barely able to contain his anger as he spat out the last three words.

"Mr. DiCarlo, I agree that this evidence does not put your clients in the best light, but that's your problem. You ventured down this slippery slope — not me and not Mr. Tobin. Your objection is overruled, your motion is denied, and your request for a mistrial is denied. Is there anything else?"

"No, Your Honor." Jimmy had the distinctly recognizable look of an outclassed litigator.

"Then let's proceed."

Jack returned to the podium. "Ms. Lopez, why was Mr. Sanchez living in the house?"

"He and Dick Radek are both living there. They are retired Miami police officers and they are serving as bodyguards."

"No further questions, Your Honor."

Jimmy had managed to compose himself — he was nothing if not relentless — and was already on his feet approaching the witness, so the judge didn't even ask him if he wanted to recross.

"This Nancy Shea — Mr. Tobin's investigator—she was killed in a car accident, wasn't she?"

"Yes."

"An accident?"

"That's what they say."

"And the 'they' you are referring to is the county sheriff's department and that's a totally separate department from the Bass

Creek police department?"

"Yes."

"But you don't believe that, do you?"

"No."

"No further questions."

Jack wanted the last word. "Your Honor, may I follow up? I only have one or two questions."

"Make it quick."

"Where is Joaquin Sanchez?" Jack asked Maria. She took the cue.

"He's in the hospital. He was shot the other night when we were all out to dinner."

"That wasn't an accident, was it?"

"Objection, Your Honor."

"Approach."

"Was this man actually shot?" Judge Stanton asked, looking at Jack.

"Yes sir," Jack replied. "It was no accident."

"Your Honor —" Jimmy started to speak but the judge stopped him. "Mr. DiCarlo, I'm inclined to agree with you that we can only try one murder at a time, but you keep opening these doors. I'll tell you what, I'm going to sustain your objection and I'm going to instruct the jury not to consider these last questions about Joaquin Sanchez and I'm not going to let anybody ask any more questions. This has gotten way out of hand. Mr. Tobin, are you done?"

"Yes sir. I'm resting."

"Mr. DiCarlo, are you ready to start your case? Do you have any witnesses to put on?"

"I have at least two, Judge — and possibly two more. I'd like to start tomorrow morning, if possible. And I do have a Motion for Acquittal."

"Okay. I'll call it a day right after Mr. Tobin officially rests. Be here at nine o'clock tomorrow morning. Oh, and Mr. DiCarlo, your motion is denied. I'll consider it only after all the evidence has been presented, including rebuttal evidence."

"Yes sir," both men replied at the same time.

~

That afternoon, Jimmy DiCarlo and Clay Evans had a late lunch in Jimmy's hotel room.

"I can't believe you did that!" Clay Evans shouted as soon as the room service waiter had left.

"Did what?" Jimmy asked, knowing full well what Clay meant. "I had to beat her up on the stand."

"You didn't have to beat me up in the process. You had her — you just went too far. Now the judge is thinking I'm a killer. He's going to send this case to the jury and I'm going to fry — I can see it in their eyes."

"We've still got a chance."

"What chance?"

"You could testify. You and Brume could say you never received that letter. You don't know what Maria Lopez is talking about."

"You still don't get it, you stupid fuck."

"Get what?"

"Tobin wants us to testify. He's waiting. He's holding something back. You can put Brume on if you want, but I'm not going anywhere near that stand. I'll take my chances."

Jimmy didn't say a thing for a moment. He took an enormous bite from his corned beef sandwich, chewed it down, then looked across the table at Clay.

"There's another way."

"What's that?"

"It involves *you* delivering one of those satchels of money to *me*."

"How much?"

"$250,000."

For a moment the thought crossed Clay's mind that Jimmy might have set everything up to get to this point. He'd already paid the son-of-a-bitch $200,000 for the worst fucking defense he'd ever seen. *Nah, he's not that smart. He just got out-lawyered.*

"And what do I get for my money?"

"Well, in this case if you eliminate the prosecutor you eliminate the prosecution. Nobody else would have brought this case in the first place."

"That's certainly something Brume doesn't understand. He's tried to kill everybody but Tobin."

"Are you sure it's been Brume?" Jimmy asked.

"Who else could it be? Which makes me wonder why the fat little fuck is killing everybody. He knows something is coming. Where are all the fuckin' honest people in this world?" Jimmy almost choked on his sandwich.

"If you're interested, I could set something up for tomorrow morning," Jimmy said, ignoring the tirade. "These guys are pros — they won't miss. And you and I will be giving a press conference on the courthouse steps."

"I've got nothing to lose. I'm a dead man anyway. All right, let's do it."

"You know the drill. It's the same as usual. This time, however, *you* put a bag with $250,000 on your back porch at midnight."

"Can't you give me a couple of days? The banks close in two hours and it will take me over an hour to get to Miami."

"No can do, Your Honor. These fellas aren't exactly bankers. They deal on a cash basis." Jimmy didn't feel the need to tell Clay that his cut was a cool $100,000. That amount, combined with the $200,000 he was paid to handle the case, and things were starting to look up for old Jimmy regardless of the outcome.

Later that day Jimmy stopped by to see his other client, Wesley Brume. Although he'd given Clay a guarantee, it was always wise to have a fallback plan. In the unlikely event Jack Tobin showed up at court the next day, he needed Wesley Brume to testify.

Wes was much kinder than Clay Evans had been in his assessment of the day's events.

"Things didn't go too well there at the end, did they?"

"Nah, but it's all part of the give-and-take of a trial. Tomorrow's another day and we've got some surprises in store for Jack Tobin."

"That son-of-a-bitch needs to be put in his place."

"You're right, Wesley, and you're the man to do it," Jimmy told him.

"Me?"

"Yes, you. You're the chief of police here in Bass Creek. The people need to hear from you. They need to know the truth. They need to know that Maria Lopez is a liar."

"What about Clay? He's a federal judge."

"He's a pussy. You know that — you worked with him for years. He doesn't have the balls to walk up there, take the oath and speak up for justice. You do."

The Grunt started scratching his head. Jimmy DiCarlo was sure right about him, but how the hell did Jimmy know him so well? He'd only talked to the guy one other time and that was a five-minute phone conversation. Clay had handled all the lawyer stuff, told him not to worry about it. Whatever. Wes had no qualms about testifying. He figured he'd eliminated all the problems already. He could just call Maria Lopez a liar, say the letter was a figment of her imagination and be done with it. There was one thing he wanted to make sure of, though.

"You did check with the Del Rio police department, didn't you?"

"Yeah, they have no record of a letter. The man who would have sent the letter is coming tomorrow. He's going to say he doesn't remember sending the letter and it's not in his files anywhere."

"All right then, I'll testify. I don't have anything to lose, do I?"

*Except your life, you idiot*, but Jimmy simply said, "Not at this point."

## [ FORTY-NINE ]

Dick saw the setup long before it started to unfold. They had already left the ranch and were on the back roads heading towards town. It was almost eight and the sun was up. Jack and Pat were in the back seat, Jack going over his notes, hoping that this was the day he had been waiting for — the day he got to cross-examine both Wesley Brume and Clay Evans.

Dick and Joaquin had planned out three separate routes to town that they alternated taking. Along those routes, they knew every turn in the road, every side road, every leaf that was out of place — every place where an ambush could be possible. When Dick rounded a turn and saw a car protruding from a side road up ahead, he instantly knew something was going down.

"Jack, get the guns."

"What?"

"Get the guns!" Dick shouted. "They're going to hit us up here." Pat had moved and Jack was scrambling to get the AK-47s from under the back seat. "A car is going to pull out in front of me," Dick told them very calmly but quickly. "As soon as I stop, a car is going to pull in behind us. Jack, stick your gun out that porthole like I showed you and start shooting as soon as they get out of their car. Wait until they get out. You want to hit somebody. I'll take the front car. I'm going to try and kill a few people and then I'm taking off. So be ready. Pat, you stay down."

Jack handed Dick a gun and put the nozzle of his gun through the back hole. He waited.

Everything happened in slow motion, and everything happened exactly the way Dick described it. The car he'd seen ahead pulled out, blocking the road. Dick put on the brakes, and another car pulled out from another side road behind them, blocking the rear. Three men got out of the front car, Uzis at the ready, and started shooting. The bullets ricocheted off the Mercedes. Dick returned fire through his front porthole, killing all three men. Meanwhile, two men had gotten out of the back car, firing as they emerged. Jack fired back, hitting one of them. Suddenly, the Mercedes lurched forward as Dick rammed the Cadillac in front of them, moving it just enough so he could maneuver around it. Then he sped away.

"Do you think they'll follow?" Jack asked, keeping a sharp eye out the back window. Pat was still on the floor.

"No," Dick replied calmly. "They don't know what hit 'em. They'll stay and lick their wounds."

Jack helped Pat up and they looked at each other with expressions that said, *What the hell just happened?* It felt like a dream. And here they were, almost as if nothing had happened, continuing their ride to the courthouse.

At around the same time, on the courthouse steps, Jimmy DiCarlo, flanked by his two clients, was wrapping up a half hour impromptu press conference, during which he once again predicted that his clients would be vindicated.

~

Jimmy had a habit, every morning before the proceedings started, of going to the courthouse men's room to primp. This morning was no different. Jack had not arrived yet, so he was sure everything had gone as planned. He was combing his hair in front of the mirror when, seemingly out of nowhere, Dick Radek was standing beside him. They were alone.

Dick spoke to the mirror. "If someone even bumps into one of my people from now on, I'm going to kill you."

Jimmy kept his cool and looked at Dick like he was a piece of dirt in his path.

"Get out of my way," he said as he started forward, attempting to brush the smaller man out of the way. In an instant he was against the wall, with Dick Radek's left hand covering his mouth and his right hand holding a pistol to Jimmy's left temple. It had a silencer attachment. Jimmy had the sudden urge to pee even though he had relieved himself moments before.

"I'm going to kill you, tough guy. Not your clients," Dick snarled through clenched teeth. "Do you want to be able to spend the money you've been making off these assholes?" Jimmy's eyes were bulging out of his head as he tried to nod his head up and down ever so slowly. "Here's what you're going to do. You're going to take your cell phone and call whoever you need to call and tell them it's off." Dick took his hand off Jimmy's mouth and moved away, now pointing the gun at Jimmy's chest.

"Now?" Jimmy asked, almost whining.

"Right now." Jimmy dialed a number. A few seconds later, he said. "It's over. Call everybody off." And hung up the phone.

"I am one of many," Dick said calmly. "You know how the game works. If something happens to me or to any of my people from this date forward, you are a dead man. You will not be able to run. You will not be able to hide. And you will not be able to spend your money. If you think I'm bullshitting, tough guy, try me." Dick turned and walked out of the bathroom.

Inside the courtroom, Jack was setting up his table for the day. He noticed that Clay Evans was eyeing him with a surprised look.

"Why Mr. Evans, you look like you've seen a ghost," Jack said. Clay Evans looked away.

Just then Jimmy DiCarlo walked in the courtroom. It wasn't

Jimmy's typical entrance. His face was pale and he looked a little disheveled.

"What the hell's going on here?" Clay whispered when Jimmy sat down next to him.

"I don't know. It looks like we've had some complications."

"What about my money?" Clay asked. Jimmy just shrugged.

"Don't worry. It's not over," Jimmy lied. It was over for him. He had his money.

Just then the judge walked into the courtroom. He had wanted to talk to the lawyers alone in open court but he hadn't gotten the word to the bailiff in time, and the courtroom was now full.

"Counsel, will you approach?" Jimmy and Jack came forward. Jack had to keep himself calm. He didn't dare look at the man standing next to him, the man he knew had tried to have him murdered that very morning. Instead Jack concentrated on Judge Stanton and listened as he delivered another near-fatal blow to his case. "I've been thinking about this all night and I've decided to reconsider and grant the defense's motion for a mistrial."

Jack immediately concluded that they had somehow gotten to the judge. He wanted to scream but he said nothing. "This record is too much of a mess," the judge continued. "We're only three days into this trial. I've ordered another panel of potential jurors up this morning and we can start over again in an hour. That should give you time to notify your witnesses. Jack, I know you have Charley Peterson in from out of town — has he left yet?"

"No, Judge."

"Good. We can go on Saturday if you want. By Saturday evening we should be where we are today. As I said, it's only a three-day delay. Jack, you don't call the prosecution's case a lie in your opening and you make sure Ms. Lopez doesn't talk about what everybody in the neighborhood knew about Geronimo Cruz. Mr. DiCarlo, you don't ask Ms. Lopez where she lives and who she lives with — understand?"

"Yes sir." Jimmy couldn't control his enthusiasm. He didn't

notice the judge was calling Jack by his first name.

"Good. I hate to do this, but we need to have a fair trial and we need to have a good record for appellate purposes." He looked right at Jack as he spoke the words. "And a three-day setback isn't all that bad when you take everything into consideration."

Clay Evans was somewhat happy about the new trial but he couldn't get it out of his mind that he had just spent $250,000 for nothing.

⁓

They picked a jury on that Thursday, and on Friday and Saturday Jack put on the same case all over again. It wasn't as spontaneous as before. No gasps from the peanut gallery — everybody knew what was coming. Jack called Maria in order this time, and he took away the force and effect of Jimmy's cross of Charley Peterson by establishing on direct examination that Charley had been disbarred. It made Charley seem a whole lot more credible. But Jack lost all the evidence about Nancy's murder and Joaquin being shot — evidence that had only come out because of Jimmy DiCarlo's incompetence. He still liked his chances, though, when he finished up on Saturday.

"We'll see you all on Monday morning," Judge Stanton said when Jack rested. The old man was becoming more relaxed and familiar with the lawyers, at least with Jack, and Jack became convinced that the mistrial was truly to clear up the record. Was the judge going to let this case go to the jury? He didn't know that yet. But the judge had given him the opportunity to try his case.

Jack spent Sunday out at the ranch with Pat. They went for a long run in the morning, something they hadn't been able to do. When they returned they had the house to themselves. Maria was still staying at the hospital with Joaquin, and Dick was off playing cowboy with Steve Preston.

Dick had really taken to the ranch life. Every opportunity he had lately he was on a horse or over working the cows with Steve's ranch hands. There was a rumor floating around that Steve had a sister who had lost her husband a few months ago and was staying out at the ranch, but it was just a rumor. Jack couldn't even remember where he heard it.

"Joaquin told you," Pat reminded him. "Just before he was shot." They were lying in bed relaxing after a long lovemaking session. Something they both had been missing.

"So you think he likes going over there because he likes being a cowboy, or is it the sister?" Jack asked the expert. It was nice talking about the mundane.

"Oh, I think he likes being a cowboy, but the sister's definitely in the mix."

"How do you know?"

"It's just the way he prepares to go over there. He always takes a shower. His jeans are always clean. I saw him plucking his nose hairs the other day."

"Ouch!" Jack exclaimed. "That's too much."

"You wouldn't do that for me?"

"I've got one of those battery-operated things that does the job," he said matter-of-factly. "But if plucking was the only way, I'd absolutely do it for you." He grabbed her up in his arms and squeezed her and they both had a good laugh. And then he kissed her because she was so close. And then he touched her because she was so close. And then he kissed her again and again....

～

"What's going to happen tomorrow?" Pat asked later, when they had made it as far as the kitchen for some sustenance. It was two o'clock in the afternoon and Jack was eating oatmeal.

"I don't know. Nothing may happen. He may not put on a case at all."

"What do you hope happens?"

"I hope both Brume and Evans take the stand. I've set this case up that way all along. I think Jimmy wants to put them on. The shootout the other day is a pretty good indication that they're nervous. Monday should be an interesting day."

~

The press must have sensed something dramatic was about to happen, or maybe they were there just because the trial was winding down, but there were reporters from all the major networks and CNN outside the courthouse. Everybody wanted an interview, and Jimmy DiCarlo tried to accommodate them all. Jack slipped into the courthouse through the side entrance.

"Fireworks are going to fly today," Jimmy told one and all but he wouldn't elaborate. "You're just going to have to wait and see."

Jimmy was becoming very comfortable in front of the cameras. So comfortable that he began to envision himself as one of those talking legal heads.

The judge entered the courtroom promptly at nine. Everybody was seated and waiting for him.

"Anything before we call in the jury?" Nobody said anything. The judge for some reason had a queasy feeling. "All right," he said to the bailiff. "Bring in the jury." The fourteen jurors filed in. When they were seated, the judge faced Jimmy DiCarlo.

"Counsel, you may proceed. Call your first witness."

Jimmy stood up. "Thank you, Your Honor," he said, sounding like he was about to make a speech. "The defense calls Jack Tobin to the stand." Pandemonium broke out in the courtroom. Everybody was talking. Jack checked the jury out. They were watching the peanut gallery. They had become what they were supposed to be — observers of everything.

Jack was probably the only one in the courtroom besides the defense who wasn't surprised. He'd anticipated it as a possibility.

The judge was desperately trying to restore order. He had taken some heat in the press for kicking everybody out the other day and he was determined not to do that again.

"Silence! Silence! Do you want to leave this courthouse?" All the time he was banging the gavel. It took a full five minutes and four bailiffs to restore order.

"Counsel, approach the bench." Judge Stanton immediately launched into Jimmy.

"We could have met in chambers and you could have told us what you wanted to do and we could have hashed it out in there. But you have to grandstand, Mr. DiCarlo. You have to send everybody into a frenzy. And just what is your basis for calling the lawyer who is trying this case to the stand?"

"He's a witness, Judge. His motivation for bringing this case is fair game. He never should have been the prosecutor on this case."

"Then you should have moved to recuse him, Mr. DiCarlo. That's the proper procedure. You don't call him as a witness in the middle of your trial. Jack, what do you say about this?"

"He's already established through other witnesses that I repre-sented Rudy and that, for instance, I talked to Maria about coming to work for me before I actually started as the state attorney. I don't know what else he needs."

The judge looked back at Jimmy. "Well?"

"I think the jury needs to hear it from Mr. Tobin."

All of a sudden a smile broke across Judge Stanton's face. "Sometimes you ought to be careful what you wish for, Mr. DiCarlo. You might get it." He sat back, the smile still on his face. "I'm going to allow it. Jack, take the stand."

"Yes, Your Honor."

"I'm going to address the jury before you begin, Mr. DiCarlo."

"Yes, Your Honor."

The judge told the jurors that they were to treat Jack's testimony like that of any other witness. "You can see that there's no other lawyer sitting with Mr. Tobin and it will be awfully hard for him to cross-examine himself. So I'm going to give Mr. Tobin some leeway in answering the questions. You may proceed, Counsel."

"Thank you, Your Honor," Jimmy nodded to the judge. He then proceeded to have Jack tell the jury how long he had been practicing and how he became state attorney of Cobb County. Jack told only the essential details.

"You represented Rudy Kelly, is that correct?"

"Yes."

"And you represented him in his appeal to the Supreme Court? His third appeal, correct?"

"Yes."

"And did you not raise all the arguments that you have raised in this courtroom — the separate rape file, the confession, Geronimo Cruz?"

"No, I did not. Your Honor, if I could explain?"

"Proceed, Mr. Tobin."

"The issue before the Supreme Court was whether Rudy was innocent or guilty. The actions of these two men, the defendants in this trial, were only an issue to the extent they affected Rudy's innocence or guilt. I did not have Geronimo Cruz's confession at the time. I did not know of the 1988 letter when I went before the Supreme Court — and I did not know it had been hidden. That was everything, you see. Once we had Cruz, we had his DNA and we got a confession and the case against Rudy fell apart. Once we got Cruz, we could see clearly what these men had done."

At that moment Clay Evans wanted to strangle Jimmy. He had argued until he was blue in the face against putting Jack Tobin on the stand.

"This guy will eat you for breakfast, Jimmy."

"No he won't. I can handle him." In the end, Jimmy had been too forceful. Clay had relented. Now, as he sat in the courtroom listening to Jack, he knew what a serious mistake he had made. One question and Jack had summarized the case against him and Brume.

Jimmy ignored Jack's answer.

"Isn't it true that you took the state attorney's job for the sole purpose of prosecuting these two public servants?" Jimmy motioned to the two rather hunched figures glowering at him from the defense table.

"No, and if I could explain, Your Honor?"

The judge practically chuckled. "Go ahead, Mr. Tobin."

"I had spoken to Maria Lopez before I took the job and she had told me about the 1988 letter from the Del Rio police so I knew they had hidden something and I planned to investigate that when I took office. I hadn't spoken to Cruz before I became the state attorney and I did not have his DNA sample, so I did not know that he was the killer until after I became the state attorney. Would I have taken the job if Rudy had been released? Probably not. I will admit I was obsessed with finding out all the facts about why an innocent young man was killed by the state and prosecuting those who were responsible. I planned to do that."

"And you didn't tell the governor about those plans, did you?"

"No."

"And that was the primary reason you took the state attorney's job?"

"Yes."

"Was it the sole reason?"

"I'd say so. I'd already agreed to take the position before I even knew about Rudy, but after Rudy's death I only took this job to investigate what happened to him and, if it was criminal, to prosecute those responsible."

"No further questions." Jimmy shot Clay a look of vindication. He'd told him his goal was to show that Jack had taken the state attorney's position under false pretenses, and Jack had said pretty much what Jimmy had predicted he would, *among other things*. It was the effect of those *other things* — the fact that Jack was searching for justice for an innocent man — that Jimmy didn't quite understand and that Clay saw written all over the jurors' faces. He glared back at Jimmy, who at this point he wanted to kill.

"Call your next witness," the judge told Jimmy.

"The defense calls Wesley Brume."

Jimmy steered away from any questions about how Rudy's confession was obtained. He had Wesley tell the jury how many years he had been a faithful servant for the Bass Creek police department and the many positions he'd held, then he went right to the point.

"Do you recall ever receiving a letter from the Del Rio police department?"

"No sir. I didn't know there was a Del Rio until I heard the name in this courtroom."

"If you had received a letter from the Del Rio police department mentioning a person named Geronimo in 1988, would you remember it?"

"Yes, I would."

"So what you're saying is — the 'facts' that Maria Lopez testified to never happened?"

"That's what I'm saying."

"No further questions."

"Your witness," the judge said, looking like he was ready to grab a bag of popcorn and enjoy the show.

Jack had been waiting for this moment for quite some time. For some reason, as he walked up to the podium, a memory from his younger years popped into his head. He had been the victim then and his friends had confronted the slime that had tried to violate his life. He remembered Mikey's older brother Danny leaning over assistant scoutmaster Daly, a hunting knife at his throat, and telling him, "And now you're going to disappear." He looked at the pudgy detective sitting in the witness box and he remembered what this man alone had done to Rudy. It was time to make Wesley Brume disappear.

He started by reminding the jury of the Grunt's past credibility problems.

"Mr. Brume, you were present when Bill Yates testified that he told you not to talk to Rudy without his mother being present?"

"Yes, I recall that."

"Do you still maintain that he didn't tell you that?"

"Yes."

"And you heard Mr. Dragone testify that you threatened him

with the health department?"

"Yes."

"Do you still maintain that you didn't do that?"

"Yes."

"And you heard Ms. Lopez testify that Rudy's mother, Elena, came to the police station to stop your interrogation of her son at 3:16 p.m. on January 24, 1986. It's in her notes, she wrote the time down. Do you remember her testimony?"

"Yes, I heard her testify to that."

"And your notes from your own records reveal that you began your interrogation at 3:18 p.m., is that accurate?"

"Yes."

"Do you still maintain that when Elena arrived at the station, you were almost done with your interrogation of Rudy?"

"When I knew she was there — yes."

"I'm not sure I understand your answer."

"She may have been there and I didn't know about it."

"So you dispute Ms. Lopez's testimony that she called back immediately to let you know Elena was there?"

"I dispute everything Ms. Lopez says."

"Now, you said something on direct which I found very interesting — you said you would have remembered a letter in 1988 if it had mentioned a person named Geronimo, is that correct?"

"Yes."

"Is that because a person named Geronimo was a witness in the Rudy Kelly case and had disappeared?"

"Yes."

"And what would you have done if you *had* seen a letter from Del Rio identifying a Geronimo from Bass Creek as a rapist and a murderer? Would you have contacted the Del Rio police department?"

"Absolutely."

"Would you have contacted Mr. Evans?"

"Either him or somebody in his office. I can't say I positively would have contacted him."

"But you never received this 1988 letter?"

"No."

"No further questions."

Jimmy DiCarlo finished his sterling defense with Philip Sheridan, a police sergeant with the Del Rio police department.

"What was your position in the police department in 1988, Sergeant?"

"I was in charge of records."

"If an inquiry letter to another department was sent by your department in 1988 inquiring about a suspect, who would have sent that letter?"

"I would have."

"Do you have any record of an inquiry letter being sent to the Bass Creek police department in 1988?"

"No. And I searched our records thoroughly."

"And do you have any personal recollection of sending a letter to the Bass Creek police department?"

"No, I don't."

"No further questions."

"Cross, Mr. Tobin?"

"No, Judge, but I would request that this witness stick around. I may want to call him on rebuttal."

"Very well. Mr. Sheridan, if you could wait in the witness room, we may be calling you momentarily. It won't be long. Any more witnesses, Mr. DiCarlo?"

Jimmy checked with Clay Evans one last time, hoping Clay would relent and take the stand. But Clay shook him off. There was no way he was subjecting himself to cross-examination by Jack Tobin.

"No more witnesses, Your Honor. The defense rests."

"Any rebuttal, Mr. Tobin?"

"Yes, Your Honor."

"Call your first rebuttal witness."

"The state calls Del Shorter."

~

Clay Evans could feel the Grunt squirming next to him. He at least felt somewhat vindicated because he knew the Grunt had lied to him. Somewhere along the way, Brume had learned that Del Shorter was working against them but he had kept that from Clay. Jack Tobin had been waiting for both of them to testify so he could bring Del Shorter out to crucify them. Clay had saved himself from the humiliation of being torn apart by Jack on the stand, but from little else. This trial had been a nightmare. Jimmy DiCarlo's defense had been the worst he had ever seen and now Jack was bringing Del Shorter out as the coup de grace. Clay thought of his decision to hire Jimmy DiCarlo and pay him $200,000 and his second decision to pay $250,000 to assassinate Jack. *Never has anybody paid so much for so little....*

"I'm retired and I've been living in Utah for the last ten years," Del told the jury.

Jack skipped over the story of how he'd found Del. It wasn't of interest to the jury. He had hired two people to go through all of Tracey's telephone messages for the month before she died. Through a painstaking process, they'd discovered one of the calls was made from the home of Del Shorter's sister in Stuart. Jack made the visit himself. It was not unlike the visit he had made to Maria Lopez the first time. The sister admitted that Del had visited and, in a fit of conscience, he had contacted Tracey James, but when she was killed he got scared and went back to Utah — which is where the Grunt had expected him to remain forever.

"In 1986, I was Wesley Brume's partner."

He proceeded to pound Wesley and, where he could, Clay into the ground as he responded to Jack's questions.

"Officer Brume sent me out on January 24, 1986, to meet with Elena Kelly and to keep her occupied while he interrogated her son. When she caught on to what I was doing, she demanded to see her son. I told her she wasn't a lawyer."

In response to questions about the rape file, Del admitted his own complicity.

"We knew we were hiding the semen evidence. That's why we created the rape file. There was no evidence of rape. Wes wasn't smart enough to come up with the idea himself. He told me about it immediately after a meeting with Clay Evans…. The coroner was in on it. He had to be."

The final blow was the 1988 letter, but even at this stage — even though he had made Jimmy look like a fool so many times — Jack held a little back so Jimmy could step right into it on cross.

"I knew about the letter. I saw it when Maria showed it to Mr. Brume. They knew it would blow their case. Evans was up for a federal judgeship at the time, and Brume was hoping when that happened something good would happen for him, which it did."

Jimmy DiCarlo had nothing to lose on cross. He went after Del Shorter with a vengeance.

"So you were part of this — this criminal activity — is that what you're telling this jury?"

"Yes."

"And I presume you told Mr. Tobin all about your participation before today?"

"Yes."

"And you have not been prosecuted for any crimes, have you?"

"No."

"Even though, if you had come forward at any time about what you knew, you could have stopped Rudy Kelly's execution?"

"Yes."

"You are as much responsible for his death as anybody, aren't you?"

"Yes, I am."

"Maybe even more so."

"I don't understand your question?"

"You took the call from Maria Lopez on January 24, 1986. You made the decision not to tell Wesley Brume that Rudy's mother was out there demanding to see her son. You made the decision to stall her!"

"I did not! I did not!"

"And you were the one who came up with the idea of a separate rape file!"

"I did not!"

"Oh no? Why is the rape investigative file signed by you? Why does it state, and I quote: 'It is the opinion of this investigator that this rape investigation should be separate from the murder investigation.'"

"I don't know. Probably because Brume wanted it that way."

"Or you wanted it that way."

Jimmy was actually making some headway. Jack was enjoying it because he knew what was coming. Clay Evans was enjoying it all in a way as well. He knew the ballgame was over and that Jimmy was simply no match for Jack. He had made a bad choice and he had paid dearly for it. At least now, at the end, he could sit back and watch Jimmy's evisceration.

"You knew Jack Tobin was getting close, so you got with your friend Maria Lopez and you made up this 1988 letter from the Del Rio police department and you fed it to Mr. Tobin so you wouldn't be prosecuted."

"That's not true!"

"There was never any letter, Mr. Shorter, and you know it."

"That's not true, Mr. DiCarlo, I have a copy right here. I made a copy of it and kept it. I'm not sure why. Maybe just because I thought I might need it someday."

Jimmy DiCarlo wasn't sure he'd heard the answer right. Clay Evans was practically giddy. He wanted to laugh out loud at this incompetent oaf with whom he had absurdly entrusted his life.

Del Shorter produced a document from his jacket pocket and held it out to Jimmy, who didn't even want to go near it.

"Take the letter, Mr. DiCarlo," Judge Stanton said softly. Jimmy finally took the letter.

"You could have typed this letter yesterday. The signature is unreadable," Jimmy said after a quick glance. Questions had long ago gone by the wayside.

"I didn't," Del countered.

"And you don't know if Wesley Brume ever talked to Clay Evans about this letter, do you?"

"No."

"No further questions." Jimmy tossed the letter onto the podium dismissively and walked back to his table acting as if he had decimated Del Shorter on cross. He didn't even hear Jack call Philip Sheridan back to the stand.

"Mr. Sheridan, I have a letter here purported to be from your police department dated June 16, 1988. The signature is kind of hard to read. Could you take a look at it and see if you could identify the signature?" Jack handed the letter to Philip Sheridan.

"That's my signature," Sheridan replied after examining the letter.

"And did your department normally send out letters like this when you believed a suspect came from another state?"

"All the time."

"How long do you keep those letters?"

"It all depends. We have what we call a 'pending file.' If the letter isn't answered, it stays in the pending file and is purged after three years. If it is answered, it becomes part of the criminal investigative file and is not purged."

"So, now that you have identified your signature on that copy, can you re-create for us what happened with this letter?"

"Sure. We probably sent it out and never received an answer and after three years purged it from our files. That's why I testified that I had no record of such a letter."

"Thank you, Officer Sheridan. No further questions, Your Honor."

Jack had the letter marked and admitted into evidence over Jimmy's strenuous objection.

"Redirect?" the judge asked, almost smiling. Jimmy had finally gotten the picture.

"No, Your Honor."

"Any more witnesses, Mr Tobin?"

"No, Your Honor. The prosecution rests."

Jimmy was up before Jack had finished. "We renew our Motion for Acquittal, Your Honor." There were actually some chuckles from the spectators and the press row.

"It's 11:30 right now," the judge said, looking at his watch. "I'm going to dismiss the jury for lunch and we'll discuss the Motion for Acquittal." The judge turned to the jury. "Ladies and gentlemen, I'm going to give you a long lunch. You don't have to be back until 1:30, at which time you'll hear closing arguments. I suspect that you will be deliberating by the end of the day. Remember all my admonitions to you. Do not talk about the case to anyone or among yourselves. Enjoy your lunch."

"Okay," the judge started after the jury had filed out, "I'm going to give it to you short and sweet so you have time to digest it over lunch and to modify your closing arguments if necessary. I'm dismissing the case against Clay Evans." A low murmur spread through the courtroom. Judge Stanton ignored it. "Mr. Evans was the prosecutor in the Kelly case. As such, he enjoyed absolute immunity. The only possible way he could be criminally responsible for Rudy Kelly's murder is if, *after* the prosecution was completed, he participated in some illegal scheme to have Rudy Kelly executed. I listened carefully to all the testimony and there is no evidence that Mr. Evans even knew about the 1988 letter from the Del Rio police department. Maria Lopez, the state's best witness on this issue, said she had no real proof that Wesley Brume even talked to Clay Evans about this letter. Mr. Shorter also admitted that he had no proof that Brume told Evans about the letter. Without this critical nexus, I must dismiss this case against Mr. Evans.

"As for Mr. Brume, he has limited immunity and there is ample evidence against him to send this case to the jury.

"That's it. That's my ruling. Mr. Evans, you are free to go. I'll see the rest of you at 1:30 sharp."

Jimmy was ecstatic. He went to shake Clay Evans's hand but thought better of it when Clay glared at him.

"We won this case in spite of you. If I had taken the stand, as you suggested, I'd be feeling like Brume over there — waiting for my death sentence. Goodbye, Jimmy. And don't ever show up in my courtroom again."

Jimmy knew Clay didn't mean it. Once he got back on the bench, he'd get a hankering for old Jimmy's satchels of cash and everything would be forgotten. For now, though, without even going near his remaining client, Jimmy headed for the courthouse steps and his afternoon press conference, where he explained to all who would listen how he had achieved Clay Evans's release. Nobody asked about Wesley Brume.

Late that afternoon, after closing arguments and less than an hour's deliberation, the jury came back with a guilty verdict against Wesley Brume. And the next day, in the sentencing phase of the trial, they recommended a life sentence without parole, which the judge approved. They would have given him the death penalty, but Jack had made something clear in his discussions with them.

"Rudy and I discussed this many times," he told them. "And we agreed that the death penalty has been arbitrarily applied in this country and we also agreed that the criminal justice system is too flawed to have a death penalty — just look what happened to Rudy. Therefore, I know Rudy would want me to ask you to give Wesley Brume the sentence of life in prison without the possibility of parole instead of death."

And they had agreed to his — to Rudy's — request.

When it was all over, Judge Stanton just looked at Jack and nodded. Jack read the message in that nod. By declaring a mistrial and cleaning up the record, he had ensured a solid case against Wesley Brume. Brume could appeal from now until Doomsday and he wouldn't get anywhere. As for Clay Evans, that case had always been a long shot. At least Stanton had let him put on his entire case, and he'd had a chance to show a fairly wide audience just what kind of man Clay Evans was. He'd wanted to finish the job, of course, to wring Evans's slimy neck with a well-fashioned legal rope, but the law hadn't let him. Jack had a real problem with the law that had let Evans wriggle away, but not with the judge. His friend Harley's assessment had been only partially correct: Harry Stanton was never reversed on appeal because he worked as hard as the lawyers to make things get done right.

Jack didn't leave the courtroom that day when everyone else did. He needed to be alone for a while longer. Mikey had told him so many years before that one day he was going to do a great thing and that it would be about the both of them. And now all he could think was how he'd failed to save Rudy and he'd failed to convict Clay Evans. But he'd given his heart and his soul — and he would have given his life.

What was it that Mikey had said so long ago? *"And when it's over — because you'll finish it, whatever it is, you finish everything you start — I want you to remember this day and what I told you."*

This case was over but *it* wasn't finished. In a way, *it* was just beginning.

He picked up his papers, pushed his chair in at the table, and turned to walk out of the courtroom. He knew he'd be back.

[ E p i l o g u e ]

# [ EPILOGUE ]

Jack and Pat finally told everyone that they were going to get married. It was two weeks after the trial. They were in Joaquin's room at the hospital. Joaquin had just received clearance from his doctor to go home, and he was awaiting his wheelchair escort. Dick was there with them and everybody was in a lighthearted mood.

"Why don't we get married together?" It was Maria who made the suggestion. "I mean, we all kind of fell in love together."

Pat liked the idea. "We could do it at the ranch and we could invite Steve and his family — including his sister." Everybody looked at Dick.

"Okay, okay, I've been seeing Steve's sister. But I won't be joining you at the altar," Dick told them. "I should tell you all that you will be getting married at my house. I made Steve an offer and he has verbally accepted it, which is good enough for me. I'll be a lot happier over here."

"Are you going to stand up for me?" Joaquin asked.

"Who else would?" Dick replied.

"I'd like you both to stand up for me," Jack said.

Pat looked at Maria. "Would you stand up for me, Maria?"

"Of course Pat, but I have to have my daughter as my maid of honor. Otherwise I'd ask you."

"I understand. Then it's all settled. When do you want to do it?"

"I'll need at least a month to recuperate," Joaquin said, a twinkle coming into his eyes. "With Maria's help, of course."

"Don't be fresh or I'll get a sixty-year-old nurse to take care of you," Maria said and they all burst out laughing. "I'll get with you, Pat, about timing."

Six weeks later, there was a small group in attendance, including Steve's sister — a pretty, pleasant woman in her mid-forties — when Jack and Pat, and then Joaquin and Maria, pledged their love to each other. Afterwards, they had a little reception at the house.

"I'm glad I rented this place to you," Steve said to Jack, clinking his champagne glass. "I thought I'd have to eat it. Now I've got a buyer and it still might stay in the family." They both laughed. *What a wonderful day*, Jack thought. *What wonderful people*.

~

Six months after that wonderful day, Clay Evans stopped at his favorite coffee shop near his home in a rural section of Homestead, a suburb of Miami, to get a cup to go as he did every morning. As he exited the building, someone said they heard what sounded like a firecracker going off. It came from the woods across the road. Clay Evans was killed instantly by the bullet, which pierced his skull and shattered his brain. The bullet came from an unregistered rifle and the police had absolutely no clues as to the perpetrator, although some were sure the shot had to have been fired by a sniper.

~

A few weeks after the trial was over, in the early morning before sunrise, Jack and Pat and Nancy's father, Jim, went out on the river in Jack's little outboard. They had two little urns containing the ashes of Nancy and Rudy. A few miles down the river, Jack made a right turn out of the busy traffic into a narrow canal bordered on both sides by thick mangroves and tall pines. He motored a ways down the canal and cut the motor. They sat in the dark for several minutes listening to the crickets drone and the frogs croak. As the sun started to rise, everything turned silent. Jack nodded to Jim and Pat, who placed the urns together, leaned them out over the water and slowly turned them so that the ashes intermingled as they fell. When they were finished, they all sat there silently, enjoying the tranquillity until the voices of the morning broke through. Birds appeared on shore and overhead, and Jack was about to start the outboard when something happened that none of them would ever forget. Two ospreys took off from atop the tall pines and circled the little canal twice, side by side. Then they hovered high above the little boat and flapped their wings before flying off.

After a few minutes, Jack started the boat and headed down the canal. Pat turned from the sights on the shoreline to look at him. He had a smile on his face and tears in his eyes, and he was mumbling something.

"What?" Pat asked gently.

Jack almost couldn't get the words out.

"I'm sure now," he told her.

"Sure about what?"

"That I can tell Mikey I'll remember. I'll always remember."

## ACKNOWLEDGMENTS

My greatest joy has always been my family and I have been blessed in that regard. My wife, Teresa, is my best friend. Her insight, suggestions and love have been invaluable to me during this process and, of course, in my everyday life.

My three children, John, Justin and Sarah, are my anchors. We have always been there for each other. I can not imagine what my life would be like without them. My daughters-in-law, Bethany and Becky, and my five grandchildren, Gabrielle, Hannah, Jack, Grace and Owen, make up the rest of my beloved inner circle. The next band of that circle is my brothers and sisters John, Mary, Mike, Kate and Patricia; and their spouses Marge, Tony, Linda, Bill and John. You form a unique bond when you grow up in a four-room flat in New York City with your mother and father and five brothers and sisters. My siblings have always kept me firmly planted on the ground. I also have an extended family of aunts and uncles, cousins, nieces and nephews, in-laws, close friends, and three godchildren, Ariel, Madison and Nathaniel, whom I love dearly. A note of special gratitude and love to my mother's twin sister, Aunt Anna.

A writer can never take total credit for the final product. The final product is a collaboration with the publisher and editor. Kate Hartson, the Publisher of Yorkville Press, has been a constant supporter and an invaluable resource. Robert Somerville, my editor, made sure sentences were sharp, punctuation was accurate and thoughts were clearly expressed. Thanks to Tina Taylor for creating a beautiful and striking book and cover design. I would also like to thank a special friend, Greg Tobin, who worked with me before this project began and gave me some insight into the finer points of the writing process.

Last, but certainly not least, are my friends who have read my work and provided me with their honest analysis and opinions. I am tempted not to name names because I'm concerned that I might forget someone. But, having filed that disclaimer, I'm going to give it a shot.

Dotti Willits, Kay Tyler, Robert "Pops" Bella, Peter and Linda Keciorius, Diane Whitehead, Dave Walsh, Lindy Walsh, Lynn and Anthony Dennehy, Caitlin Herrity, Gary and Dawn Conboy, Gray and Bobbie Gibbs, Linda Beth Carlton, Kerrie Beach, Cathy Curry, Dee Lawrence, Ron DeFillipo and Richard Wolfe.

Special thanks to my brother Mike, the original Mayor of Lexington Avenue.

— J.S.

James Sheehan is a trial attorney
who has practiced law for 28 years
in Tampa/St. Petersburg, Florida.
This is his first novel.